Private Lives

Tasmina Perry

Private Lives

headline
review

First published in 2011 by HEADLINE REVIEW
An imprint of HEADLINE PUBLISHING GROUP

1

Cataloguing in Publication Data is available from the British Library

ISBN 978 0 7553 5844 1 (Hardback)
ISBN 978 0 7553 5845 8 (Trade paperback)

Typeset in Sabon by Avon DataSet Ltd,
Bidford-on-Avon, Warwickshire

Printed and bound in Great Britain by
Clays Ltd, St Ives plc

Headline's policy is to use papers that are natural, renewable and
recyclable products and made from wood grown in sustainable forests.
The logging and manufacturing processes are expected to conform
to the environmental regulations of the country of origin.

HEADLINE PUBLISHING GROUP
An Hachette UK Company
338 Euston Road
London NW1 3BH

www.headline.co.uk
www.hachette.co.uk

To my brothers, Digs and Dan.

Prologue

She looked around the flat and smiled to herself. Silk drapes and tall windows looked out on to an iconic view: Tower Bridge and the slick black ribbon of the Thames glistening in the night. Sometimes she wanted to hug herself with excitement; just being here, in her own luxury flat, surrounded by all her nice things. Who'd have thought that someone like her would live in such a smart flat in the centre of one of the most exciting cities in the world?

Walking over to the kitchen, she poured herself another large glass of wine from the open bottle. Would he still come tonight? The thought of their last conversation jumped into her head, but she shook it away. No, of course he would come, he always did. She admired herself in the mirror: the long legs, the high breasts. Even in leggings and a T-shirt she looked fantastic. No, he'd come. She knew he'd come.

She sank back into the sofa then flicked through her favourite celebrity magazine. In her more honest, introspective moments she knew it was her obsession with magazines like this that had led her to choose this career path. Not that she could imagine Miss Davies, her careers adviser at school, calling what she did a career. But what was wrong with wanting to be rich and famous? She'd bet Miss Davies didn't have a flat like this one.

Tossing the magazine to one side, she knew she should get ready in case he did drop by. A bottle of nail polish was on the coffee table and she held it up to the light. Scarlet. He always said he loved it when she painted her toenails red. Slutty, that was what he meant. Well, she was happy to oblige in that department, especially when they'd be making up tonight.

One toenail had been painted when the doorbell rang. Flustered, she put down the polish and went to the door. She peered through the spyhole, expecting to see flowers or some small, tastefully wrapped box clutched in his hand. Instead she saw an unfamiliar man in a suit, his face stretched and bulbous in the fish-eye lens.

'Who is it?'

'It's Jack. Jack Devon. I'm a friend of Peter's.'

She frowned. Who was he? Had Peter sent him? Attaching the chain, she opened the door and looked through the gap. The man was about forty. Smartly but conservatively dressed, like an accountant. Pale watery eyes blinked behind small rimless glasses.

'What do you want?' She hadn't meant to sound rude, but it was past nine o'clock and she wasn't used to strange men turning up at her door, no matter what other people might say about her.

'It's about Peter.' He glanced behind him. 'Do you think we could talk inside?'

She felt a jolt of panic. Was he hurt? Was something wrong?

'Is he okay?' she asked.

'Under the circumstances,' replied the man.

'What circumstances?'

'I think it's best if we discuss this inside.'

She wavered for a moment, then slid back the chain and opened the door. He walked into the apartment, looking nervous, uncomfortable.

'I'm sorry to have to visit you so late,' he began. 'I don't enjoy this any more than you do.'

'Who are you?' she asked, folding her arms across her chest. 'What do you want?'

The man shrugged as they moved into the open-plan living space. 'It's not what I want. It's what Peter wants.'

She didn't like the direction this conversation was taking. 'And what's that exactly?'

2

He pushed up his glasses and rubbed his eyes. 'He wants you to start acting reasonably.'

Her heart was beginning to hammer in panic, but she was determined not to show it. 'So who are you? His lawyer?'

'No, not exactly,' he said. 'But that might be next. Blackmail is a criminal offence, after all.'

'Blackmail?' She almost laughed. 'Is that what this is about?'

Okay, so she had applied a bit of pressure, told him she wasn't prepared to wait any longer, maybe said a few things she shouldn't have. But that was hardly blackmail, was it?

'Does Peter know you're here?'

'Of course. He simply wants a solution that works for both sides. We really don't want to have to involve the police.'

She snorted nervously. 'You and I both know that Peter is not going to go to the police.'

The man blinked at her, then nodded. 'Indeed. Which is why I'm here.'

He moved over to the table and opened his leather briefcase. He pulled out a chequebook and held it up. 'How much?' he asked.

She glanced at the chequebook, then looked out of the window. 'I don't want his money,' she said.

The man allowed himself a small smile. 'Really. And who paid for all this?' He glanced pointedly around the apartment.

'I don't want *money*,' she snapped, trying her best to sound indignant. 'What I want is Peter.'

'Well, I'm afraid that's not an option any more,' he said flatly.

'We'll see about that.' She strode to the coffee table and snatched up her mobile. 'I'm phoning him.'

He shook his head, that half-smile again. The bastard was enjoying this.

'I don't think so.' He peered at his watch. 'It's two a.m. in Uzbekistan.'

'Uzbekistan? He's supposed to be here.'

'Just us here,' said Devon, gesturing with the chequebook again. This time her eyes followed the book, unable to look away.

'So give me a figure,' he said, sitting at the table.

She grabbed her glass of wine and took a fortifying sip. 'I've told you, this isn't about money. This is about Peter and me.'

'How much is it going to take?' he asked, taking a fountain pen from his inside pocket.

'How much would you suggest, Mr Devon? How much would you say a relationship is worth?'

'In this case, nothing, because your relationship is over.'

His words were simple and stinging, their impact cruel because she knew they were true. Perhaps she had pushed Peter too far, overplayed her hand. And now he had sent a lackey to mop up his mess. A thickness filled her throat and her vision blurred in a cloud of tears.

'I think you'd better leave.'

Devon remained seated. 'Believe it or not, I'm here to help you.'

She hated the note of sympathy, the pity she could hear in his voice.

'Take my advice,' he said slowly. 'Accept the money, move somewhere new, forget what's happened and just get on with your life. It's the smart thing to do.'

'It's never that easy though, is it?' she said, her voice cracking. 'Not when you love someone. Now please, just go.'

Devon hesitated, then put his chequebook back in his briefcase and stood up. 'Very well,' he said. 'Could I just use the bathroom?'

She nodded without looking at him. 'Upstairs.'

Her bedroom was on a mezzanine platform over the living space below. She watched him disappear towards her en suite, his sensible brown shoes clumping up the glass staircase.

His briefcase was still on the table. How much would he have paid? A decent amount, that was for sure. And Devon was right, it was the smart thing to do. Her own money wouldn't last long in this place. A person could quickly get used to expensive linens, parquet floors and stainless-steel kitchens. Nice things. Pretty things. Things that made her feel safe, secure, smart, successful. This was the life she'd always wanted. Still . . . for once, she had been telling the truth. It wasn't about the money this time. All she wanted was him – and she couldn't have him. No amount of lovely sheets would make up for that.

She rubbed her eyes with the palms of her hands to stop the flow of tears. Taking a few deep breaths, she tried to compose herself. Maybe she would call Peter herself, apologise for what she'd said, explain that he'd taken it all the wrong way. Yes, that would do it, she thought, feeling a little better. Maybe this was a test; when Mr Devon reported back that she had turned down the money, he would see that she truly loved him, not his credit cards.

She glanced up the stairs, frowning. He'd been a long time in the bathroom.

'Mr Devon?' she called. 'Is everything all right up there?'

There was no reply. Shrugging, she walked up the stairs towards the mezzanine platform. 'Mr Devon?'

At the top, she tapped on the bathroom door but couldn't hear a sound inside. 'Are you all right? Mr D—'

The door opened and Jack Devon stepped out. 'Yes. I'm fine.'

'Oh, good,' she stuttered, flushing with embarrassment as she turned to walk back downstairs. She felt a hard push from behind and her body jerked forward. Instinctively she reached for the banister, but she was moving too fast and momentum carried her on, her head slamming against the wall. Her body twisted as she fell, her shoulder cracking into the glass steps, her torso pinwheeling over, snapping her neck, her body landing splayed and broken like a puppet with the strings cut. It had been mercifully quick. Aside from one moment of air-sucking terror as her hand missed the rail, she had felt nothing.

She lay there staring up, her body motionless except for the faint flutter of her eyelids, barely aware as Jack Devon walked slowly down, and stood over her, watching the life ebb out of her body. He took a pair of latex gloves out of his pocket, put them on and moved methodically around the house, making sure everything was in place for whoever found her. Sometimes he had to create a story: the jilted lover who had taken their own life, the break-in gone wrong, but here she had done the job for him. The half-empty bottle of wine. A simple case of a tragic accident, slipping on the steps after too much alcohol.

Satisfied with his work, he pulled out his phone and made the call. 'It's done,' he said simply, then hung up. Removing his glasses and putting them in his pocket, he picked up his briefcase and let himself out. Out of her flat, on to the street, as if he'd never been there.

1

Six months later

As the man in the white leotard dangled from the trapeze and poured Krug into the top saucer of the champagne fountain, Anna Kennedy realised she had never seen a party quite like this. Not in the movies or in the pages of *Hello!* magazine. She had certainly never been to anything this grand, so spectacularly over the top she didn't know whether to get drunk and enjoy it or just stand there and watch it like she would a Tim Burton movie or the Cirque du Soleil.

She took a gold macaroon from a waiter on stilts and popped it in her mouth.

A little celebratory soirée, that was how her friend, the Russian businesswoman Ilina Miranova, had described the party to her. *Just a few close friends, nothing too extravagant.*

Ilina's definition of extravagant was certainly different from most people's – no surprise if her collection of 'close friends' was anything to go by. Her Holland Park home was packed with the great and the good: royals, billionaires, celebrities, at least one hundred of them milling around the house and the manicured gardens in couture and diamonds.

If I threw a party at three days' notice, I'd be lucky to get my best mate and a groceries delivery from Ocado, thought Anna, smiling to herself.

Not that any of this should have surprised her. Ilina, recently described by *Forbes* magazine as one of the world's wealthiest self-made women, had always been among her more colourful clients. As an associate in the media department at London law firm Davidson Owen, Anna had spent the last twelve months advising the Russian as she set about suing the British tabloid the *Globe* for a libellous story they had printed about her financial affairs. They had settled the case earlier in the week, when the Davidson Owen team had make it clear that they were prepared to take it all the way to the High Court. It wasn't as if Ilina couldn't afford to celebrate.

Across the pool someone waved at her. Anna waved hesitantly back, although she didn't recognise the handsome man in the navy suit. Was he a client? Or another lawyer perhaps? Maybe he was even calling her over for a drink. She was wearing her best black trouser suit after all, Italian, expensive, more expensive than she could afford.

The man turned as one of the butlers walked past, taking a glass of champagne from the tray.

Of course, she thought sheepishly. He thinks I'm a waitress.

She slipped off her jacket and let her dark hair down from her businesslike ponytail. Better, she thought, checking her reflection in a mirrored water feature, although she accepted that she was never going to compete with the exotic creatures drifting past her. At a party like this she was invisible. Not that that was a particularly bad thing; it meant she could have the mother of all people-watching sessions: the married celebrity necking with the model who was most certainly not his wife, and the high-profile lord who appeared to be preparing to snort a large amount of powder from a marble mantelpiece.

I assume that's snuff, she smiled, reminding herself that it was her job to be discreet.

Her mobile began ringing angrily in her bag. Reluctantly putting her flute of bubbly down, she scrabbled the phone out. Dammit, work, she thought, peering at the screen. Wasn't it always?

'Anna? Where the hell are you?'

It was Stuart Masters, the head of the media department at her firm.

'I'm at Ilina Miranova's celebration party,' said Anna, raising her voice to be heard over the banging music.

'What? At this time?'

She glanced at her watch. It was just ten o'clock. For a moment she imagined Stuart and his uptight wife Cynthia sitting in their perfectly ironed dressing gowns playing Scrabble.

'Well go and find Nick Kimble. We need to get an injunction. Right now.'

There was no point complaining. It was Friday night, the run-up to the weekend newspapers, and for an associate who specialised in short-notice injunction work, that meant being on red alert.

Stuart filled her in on the pertinent details. Hanging up, she looked urgently for Nick Kimble, her supervising partner at the firm. They'd arrived together straight from work, but Nick had abandoned her within five minutes saying he had to 'go mingle'. Had to go and see if he could sleaze up some poor model, more like, thought Anna. Sure enough, she spotted him at the bar, leaning over a girl young enough to be his daughter. He didn't look pleased to see his colleague.

'Sorry, Nick,' she said as she took his elbow. 'We need to talk. I've just had a phone call from Stuart.'

Nick rolled his eyes. 'Who's in trouble this time?'

'Shane Hardy again.'

'You mean happily married role-model-to-the-kids footballer Shane Hardy?' he said sarcastically. 'Let me guess, he's had another one of his moral slips?'

She nodded. 'His people want to meet tonight. The *News of the World* are going to run the story on Sunday if we don't injunct it.'

'I think you should deal with this,' he said, slugging back his whisky. 'Call counsel. Find a judge tomorrow morning.'

'Nick, a partner should handle this one. Shane's club is an important client.' It was typical of Nick to try and weasel out of it, especially now that he was at one of the primo parties of the season, surrounded by beautiful women.

He clapped her on the shoulder, a little too hard.

'Anna, my love, sometimes you need to step up to the plate. Think of this as your big break.'

'Nick, it's my dad's birthday this weekend. I have to be in Dorset.'

'Tell you what,' said Nick with a patronising smile. 'You speak to the client tonight. Get the injunction tomorrow. Let the media know they're gagged and I'll take it from there.'

Oh, right, you'll take over when all the hard work is done and you've slept off your hangover? she thought. Not for the first time, she bit her tongue and reminded herself that all she had to do was stick this out for another twelve months and she'd make partner. Then she wouldn't have to do Nick Kimble's dirty work ever again.

Her boss touched her on the forearm. 'Before you go, can you just pop to the bar and get me a drink? Champers, the good stuff, so I can mingle. Branson must be here somewhere. I wouldn't mind a slice of his corporate work.'

The crowd parted as Ilina approached them, shimmering across the floor like an exotic mermaid. 'Nick. Anna,' she purred, taking them both by the arm. 'So lovely to see you.'

'Ilina, your house is amazing,' said Anna truthfully. It was a perfect detached Georgian property, in a prime location, which had been extended and modernised with taste and elegance. Anna shuddered to think how much it would cost to buy.

'You are so sweet. Thank you.'

Nick shrugged dismissively. 'My wife and I looked at a property not dissimilar to this last year,' he said.

'Then I think I must be paying you too much,' said Ilina with mock-severity.

Anna couldn't resist a smile as Nick tried furiously to back-pedal.

'Of course, it would have been a stretch,' he spluttered. 'I wouldn't want to suggest that our fees are overly . . . that is to say, we try to price our services on a par with the—'

Ilina touched his arm, stopping him mid-flow.

'Did I hear you say you were going to the bar?' she said. 'I'd love a cocktail.'

'Of course, of course,' he said, backing away, almost bowing as he went.

Ilina laughed as she watched him scuttle off in the direction of the bar. '*ИДИОТ*,' she cursed in Russian.

'You're going to have to translate that,' smiled Anna.

' "Idiot". Or perhaps "wanker".'

'He does have his moments,' said Anna tactfully.

'Moments?' said Ilina. 'He has spent the whole night boasting about his brilliant victory with my case. The only time I hear from him is when he sends me bills.'

Anna had grown close to Ilina over the past few months, but even so, she knew it would be unprofessional of her to comment – even if it was true. Officially Nick was her supervising partner, but he seemed to spend all his time on the golf course, leaving her to handle her own caseload. In Ilina's case, she had been glad to be in sole charge. In the society columns, the Russian came across as frivolous and silly – an oligarchess who looked like Miss Ukraine and who could drop a million pounds on a shopping trip before lunchtime. Few people knew that under the jewels, she was a Harvard graduate who had used her father's Kremlin connections and her own sharp intellect to succeed in the ruthless, macho world of oil and gas. There was nothing silly about Ilina Miranova. Nothing silly at all.

'Ilina, I'm afraid I have to go,' said Anna. 'I have to meet a client, but thanks so much for inviting me.'

'Darling, just stay for a few minutes longer. I have prepared a little speech and we have a cake.'

Anna had seen the cake; a confectionery mountain would be a better description. With five tiers and a spun-sugar caricature of Ilina standing on top of a copy of the *Globe*, it put every wedding cake Anna had ever seen in the shade.

Ilina tossed her long blond hair over her shoulder and mounted a podium by the infinity pool.

'Darlings,' she began, 'thank you for joining me for my victory parade.'

She was an impressive public speaker, delivering her lines with confidence, wit and verve, and she had the assembled captains of industry in the palm of her hand. In fact, Anna was so busy watching the crowd that it took a moment before she realised that two hundred heads were turning to look at her.

'Anna Kennedy has been my rock in my time of need,' Ilina was saying. 'Her expert legal guidance has been second to none and I would recommend her services should any of you make the mistake of attracting the attentions of the gentlemen of the press.'

There was much laughter at this: there was barely a person in the room who wasn't regularly in the papers, whether in the gossip columns or the political pages.

'Please join me in toasting my saviour,' said Ilina, raising her glass towards Anna.

Anna willed the ground to swallow her whole, whilst trying her best to force a smile on to her face. Across the pool she could see Nick Kimble glaring at her, which was a small consolation, and she took it as her cue to leave, heading for the door via the cloakroom.

'I'm not surprised Ilina's pleased,' said a voice as she waited at the desk for her coat. 'Six-figure damages, a page-three retraction: pretty good work.'

Anna instantly recognised the woman behind her. Helen Pierce was a legend in the legal profession, a formidable partner at Donovan Pierce solicitors. She had often seen the cool blonde click-clacking imperiously into the High Court, but had never dared to speak to her. Donovan Pierce specialised in defamation and reputation management work and had one of the fiercest reputations in the industry – mainly due to Helen Pierce.

'Thank you,' said Anna, unsure of what to say next.

'Personally I always thought the claim was a little spurious,' said Helen, 'under the circumstances.'

'Really? Why would you say that?'

Helen gave a little tinkly laugh.

'Suing the *Globe* for suggesting she is a *shopaholic*?'

'It was hardly that,' said Anna, slightly annoyed by Helen's flippant tone. 'The *Globe* printed a sensationalist catalogue of Ilina's spending, blatantly designed to make her look obsessive, selfish and out of control, purely for the entertainment of their readers.'

'Miss Miranova's spending – out of control? I wonder whatever made them think that?' She raised her eyebrows, looking pointedly across the room to the caged leopards, the mountainous cake and the circus performers. No wonder she's such a bloody good lawyer, thought Anna. Even the tiniest of gestures could make you feel guilty or complicit.

'With respect,' said Anna, 'it is Ms Miranova's business how she spends her own money, and in actual fact, that story caused her a considerable amount of distress.'

Helen fixed her with a cool stare, but Anna merely returned the gaze, determined not to be bullied. The spell was broken when the cloakroom attendant brought their coats, but Helen didn't seem in any hurry to leave.

'So, how is life at Davidson Owen?'

'Busy,' said Anna, glancing at her watch again.

'I dare say you might make partner, if you can stick it out long enough,' said Helen.

'Within the year, hopefully.'

'Really?' laughed Helen. 'We both know Stuart Masters is a misogynist. You're to be congratulated for your loyalty, but you can't be under any illusions.'

Anna fought to keep her expression neutral, but her heart was hammering.

'Illusions?'

'I suppose you're aware of how many women partners have been appointed at Davidson's in the last ten years.'

'A few.'

'Two,' said Helen, fixing her with that gaze again. 'In their family division. It's not brilliant, is it: two new female partners compared to eighteen men?'

Where was all this leading? Was Helen just making conversation, or was there a subtext to her enquiries? It was starting to feel like a job interview – and really, wasn't that why Anna's heart was hammering?

'And how are things at DP?' asked Anna as casually as she could. 'I read in the *Lawyer* that Larry is finally retiring.'

Larry Donovan had set the firm up twenty-five years ago. He was loud, flamboyant, one of the few truly colourful characters in the industry. The rumour was that he and Helen maintained a respectful distance from each other, but there was no love lost between them.

'It's his leaving party in a couple of weeks,' said Helen. 'I thought the only way he'd leave the office would be in a coffin, but his new, much younger wife has apparently put him under considerable pressure to spend the money he's spent a lifetime acquiring.'

'So what's he going to do? A round-the-world cruise?'

Helen ignored the question. 'I'll cut to the chase, Anna. With Larry's retirement, we'll need to strengthen certain areas of the team.'

'You're offering me a job?'

Helen smiled.

'I'm offering you the chance of a lifetime.'

'Partner?'

'Not yet.'

Anna felt her excitement immediately abate, but offers like this were a game.

'In which case, I'm not sure there's any point in my leaving Davidson's,' she replied defiantly. 'Despite what you say, I've just pulled off a high-profile coup for the firm. You heard Ilina's endorsement. I think that puts me in a pretty good position for partner.'

Helen smiled. 'Nick Kimble has been telling anyone who will listen tonight that it's *his* high-profile coup.'

The sinking feeling in Anna's stomach told her it was true. Nick and Stuart Masters were tight; they played golf together, their wives were friends, there was no way Stuart would support her over Nick. But she couldn't let Helen see that she was right.

Her phone began to buzz angrily again. 'I really do have to go.'

'The Friday-night rush.' Helen nodded. 'Who's in trouble this time?'

Anna smiled coyly. There was no way she was giving up details about the case or her client.

'You remind me of myself, Anna. Tough, smart, ambitious. Let's talk again soon, okay?'

Anna nodded and dashed off, hoping to find a taxi sandwiched between the Bentleys.

Anna didn't think about the job offer at all the next day; there simply wasn't time. After a late-night meeting with the client, she'd worked far into the night. By ten a.m. she was instructing a barrister in a coffee shop in Pimlico; two hours later they had cornered a judge, and thirty minutes after that they were in possession of a gagging order preventing all major news outlets from running a juicy exposé about Anna's client, a Premiership footballer who had made the moral slip – as Nick Kimble had put it – of getting his mistress pregnant.

It was five o'clock by the time Anna was finally on the road, driving towards her parents' Dorset cottage, physically exhausted and emotionally drained from a heated verbal exchange she'd had with the *News of the World*'s legal manager. She wasn't yet thirty, but today she felt about twenty years older. She slid down the window and let the warm air ruffle her hair. It was actually a perfect time to be driving out of the city; traffic was quiet, and the late-afternoon sun cast long green shadows across the fields as she passed. But she still couldn't relax. Two days earlier, her mother Sue had called her to say they had something to discuss with her. She had refused to talk about it on the phone, and Anna had immediately imagined illness or financial problems with the business. Her parents Sue and Brian owned the Dorset Nurseries, a beautiful garden centre in the heart of Thomas Hardy country. It was a wonderful place, curated under her mother's tasteful, elegant eye. Wheelbarrows of plump dahlias and clematis surrounded luscious lawns, cabbage white butterflies fluttered around terracotta pots crammed with poppies and foxgloves. Five years ago, they'd added a quaint restaurant in a previously abandoned conservatory and had an immediate hit. On an evening like this, there was nowhere finer to sit and sip Darjeeling or sample some of Brian Kennedy's tarts and salads.

Anna's dad had learned to cook in the army and had always been exceptional in the kitchen; he had thrown himself into his new role with gusto. Which was why Anna was worried: they'd had money worries before – what business didn't these days? – and she knew it would kill him to have to give it up.

At last she turned her Mini into the driveway. The family home was a large thatched cottage that backed on to the perimeter wall of the nursery.

'Here she is . . .' cried her father, striding out to meet her, his arms open.

He was still wearing his chef's whites, complete with spots and smears from the dish of the day. 'Come on through to the kitchen,' he said, squeezing her. 'I bet you could do with a big glass of wine, eh?'

Her mother was sitting at the long oak table, writing in a ledger.

'You both look bushed,' Anna said as she walked over to kiss her mother.

'My elder daughter. She always says the sweetest things,' said Brian good-naturedly.

'I'm worried about you,' said Anna with a frown. 'You're working too hard. Both of you.'

Sue closed her book with a thump, looking less pleased than her husband.

'Actually, I couldn't be feeling better. You know we're taking three months' booking in advance for Saturday and Sunday now, so perhaps it's all paying off at last.'

'Fantastic,' Anna replied with a broad smile that belied her nerves. If the discussion wasn't about business, she wondered if it was something even more ominous. For a moment, her eyes met her mother's, but almost immediately Sue looked away.

'So how's work?' she said briskly.

'Busy. We settled our libel case on Wednesday. My client threw a big party, so my head's a little fuzzy.'

'Hair of the dog will sort that out,' said Brian, ushering her through the cottage.

The front room was cluttered and homely, with low beams, a wide brick fireplace and higgledy-piggledy pictures of her father's time in the army, her parents' wedding day, even a few framed squiggles from when she and her sister were kids. It was the sort of place where you could just curl up with a book and forget about the world, if it wasn't for the framed photograph, a new addition on the wall.

Anna flinched, then forced herself to look at it.

Her sister Sophie, clutching her National Television Award

16

for 'Best Factual Show: *A Dorset Kitchen*'. She was looking even more beautiful than usual, her pouty mouth painted scarlet, her long raven bob teased into Veronica Lake waves; her slim, curvy body poured into a form-fitting dress made her look more fifties starlet than celebrity chef.

Her mother was watching her.

'Did you see the Awards?'

Anna shook her head.

'You know me. No time for telly.'

'We went to the ceremony. It was wonderful.'

The atmosphere prickled. Her father softened it by handing Anna a large glass of wine. 'Lovely Sauvignon, this one.'

'And I have something for you,' she said. She bent to rifle through her bag and pulled out a gift-wrapped box, handing it to her father.

'For me?' said Brian, his eyes twinkling.

She grinned. 'Well I think yours is the only birthday we have in this house within the next twenty-four hours.'

'Open it tomorrow, Brian. At the party,' said Sue.

'Open it now, Dad. I'm not going to be here tomorrow,' said Anna quickly.

Sue looked at her husband, then back at Anna.

'When you said you were coming for your dad's birthday, I assumed you'd be here for the actual day.'

Anna glanced away. 'I have to get back.'

'So you can go to a client's party but not to your father's?'

Her mother's snipe hit its target. Anna shifted uncomfortably.

'I thought it was just a few friends coming round for drinks, not a proper party. You don't want me there anyway.'

'I'd love you to stay,' said Brian.

She desperately wanted to celebrate with her father. Family occasions used to be so important to the Kennedys, and whilst part of her knew she should be the bigger person, to rise above it as if what had happened had never even existed, she knew she couldn't bring herself to be in the same room as Sophie and her partner Andrew. Not yet.

'Is she definitely coming?' she said finally.

Her parents exchanged a look.

'Andrew's coming too,' said Sue briskly. '*He's* managed to get the day off work, and you know how busy he is.'

'Mum, leave it.'

'I'm just beginning to wonder if you are going to spend the rest of your life avoiding your sister?'

The high, taut cheekbones, the slender build that gave Sue her elegance were beginning to make her mother's face look hard. But Anna spent her entire working day standing her ground. She wasn't going to wilt under Sue's stern and uncompromising gaze.

'I'm not ready to see her,' she said, taking a swift swallow of wine.

'Well when are you going to be ready? You've not spoken to her for nearly two years. This is getting ridiculous.'

'She stole my boyfriend,' Anna reminded them.

'Yes, and she was wrong. But isn't it time you buried the hatchet? For us? For you?'

Anna looked away. They still didn't get it. She supposed to them it was just some romance gone wrong. Living in Dorset, far away from Anna's London life, they hadn't seen how badly hurt she'd been, how devastated by the betrayal. And if they had recognised it, then they hadn't wanted to take sides or get involved. She'd tried to block out the memory with work, with cigarettes and alcohol, with distance, but right now, it felt as raw and visceral as the moment she had first found her sister and her boyfriend together.

Sue's tone softened. 'Sophie is your sister, Anna. She's a good girl, a good daughter. Don't forget she saved our business.'

'Yes, it was all her.' Anna tried not to sound bitter.

Brian rubbed her arm. 'Let's talk about this later, hmm?'

Sue snorted.

'She's got to know at some point, Brian.'

Anna's instincts sharpened.

'Know what?'

'This is what your mum mentioned on the phone, love,' said Brian, his face full of sympathy. 'Sophie and Andrew are getting married.'

For a moment Anna couldn't breathe, her heart thudding, her

mind racing. She knew they were both staring at her, but she couldn't tear her eyes away from the floor. Deep down she had known what her mother had wanted to tell her. The newspapers had been on to the story, but she had wanted to ignore the whispers.

'He proposed last month and they want to do it quickly, first week in September, so not long,' said her dad. 'You know what Sophie is like once she gets an idea in her head. And she wants you to come, of course.'

Anna willed herself to inhale.

'Oh darling, it's going to be lovely,' said Sue. 'We offered to host it here, of course, but Sophie wanted to have it at Andrew's parents' place, that villa in Tuscany.'

The most beautiful house in the world. That was what Anna had thought when Andrew had taken her to Villa Sole on a romantic break. She'd even had a few thoughts about having her own wedding there, not that she and Andrew had ever talked about marriage in their three years together. They were too busy with their lives and their careers. *I thought we were happy.* Maybe they had been. Just not happy enough.

'Can't you come? Or at least think about it.'

Brian's sad, regretful expression was enough to make her resolve wobble.

She pictured her sister and her ex stepping out of some idyllic Tuscan church, ducking and laughing as they were showered with confetti. Andrew's witty, romantic after-dinner speech, telling everyone how much he was in love with his new bride. No, she couldn't put herself through it.

'I can't, Dad, it's work . . .' she said, searching for a reason.

'Oh, just leave her then, Brian,' said Sue impatiently. 'You know work always comes first with her. That's always been the problem, hasn't it?'

'And what's that supposed to mean?'

'Nothing,' said Sue. 'Just that Sophie has always been able to juggle her personal and professional life.'

'And that's why Andrew's marrying her, not me?'

'Come on, you two,' said Brian soothingly. 'Let's not make this bigger than it has to be. We're going out to Italy for the week, there's lots planned apparently. But I'm sure Davidson's won't mind you having a couple of days off, will they?'

The hangover buzzing lightly between her temples presented a solution.

'Actually, Dad, it's not Davidson's that's the problem. I've just got a new job, starting soon. I can't really take a holiday as soon as I've got there, can I?'

'A new job?' said Brian, looking at his wife uncertainly. 'That's fantastic.'

Anna felt buoyed, heady, steeled.

'Yes, I was only offered it yesterday. Donovan Pierce, they're the most prestigious media law firm in the country. It's a big step up for me, a trial for a partnership there.'

'Well done, love.'

Her mother pulled a sour face.

'I still don't see why you can't come to the wedding. There's more to life than work, you know.'

Anna drained her glass, her mind made up.

'Not for me, Mum,' she said. 'Not any more.'

2

At any other time, Sam Charles would have thought he had woken up in heaven. Lying on his back in a soft, warm bed, crisp cotton sheets against his skin, he could feel a gorgeous swelling, lapping sensation around his cock.

'Mmm . . .' he moaned, receiving a similar murmur from under the sheets. His mouth curled into a grin. God, a good-morning blowjob; how long had it been since he'd had one of those? Jessica must have . . .

'Shit . . .' he gasped, sitting up too suddenly, sending lights flashing across his vision. He pushed himself up against the headboard – a headboard, he suddenly realised, he had never seen before – and looked down into the green eyes of a very pretty redhead, her expression poised somewhere between amused and seductive.

'Did I do something wrong?' she asked.

'No. Yes,' he stuttered, looking around the room for clues, something, anything familiar to tell him where he was.

'Sorry,' she purred, disappearing back under the covers. 'I'll try harder.'

'Please, that's very nice, but . . .' He eased himself away from her and shuffled crab-like out of the bed. 'Just going to the bathroom. I'll only be a minute.'

He backed towards the en suite and shut the door behind him.

'Fuck,' he whispered to himself, sinking down on to the edge of the bath, his head in his hands. 'Fuckity fuckity fuck.' This couldn't be happening. He was engaged to Jessica Carr, the billion-dollar girl-next-door actress, America's sweetheart, the girl every woman wanted to be and every man wanted to sleep with. And that girl out there, the one with the luscious, lovely lips, she most certainly wasn't Jessica.

How the hell did I get here? His brain was like sludge and he had a world-class headache. He could remember how the night had begun: presenting the Rising Talent gong at the *Rive* magazine awards ceremony at the Royal Opera House. So far, so respectable. Then there had been the after-show party at Shoreditch House. He was pretty sure he'd behaved himself there too. But beyond that, he could remember very little.

He grabbed a cardboard notice from the sink, one of those unconvincing announcements about how the hotel was single-handedly saving the planet one towel at a time. The Thomas Hotel, he read. Not one he'd ever heard of before. Probably the nearest one they could find. Oh God, oh God. Why?

Actually, he knew the answer to that one only too well. His fiancée might be the most lusted-after woman in Hollywood, but like most things in Tinseltown, she was all smoke and mirrors. Jessica didn't get that amazing slim figure without endless lipo, Botox, spray-tan and boxercise. Sometimes she worked out for four hours a day, more if they were coming up to awards season. Sam could see her now, lying out on her side of the bed in her frumpy towelling robe, frozen in position as she did some ridiculous Pilates exercise, shooing him away as he tried to kiss her. 'My nails, Sam', 'My hair's just been done', 'I've got a six o'clock call': there was always some reason to push him away. Not that any of that gave him an excuse for cowering in the bathroom of some fleapit hotel in . . . he looked at the towel notice again. The Thomas, Fitzrovia. At least he wasn't too far from home.

'Sam?' called a lazy, sexy voice from the bedroom. 'You coming?'

He shook his head. *If only.*

'Just a minute.'

He splashed cold water on to his face and looked into the mirror. His expensively cut dark blond hair stuck up in tufts. His famous bright blue eyes were bloodshot. Well, you're looking fantastic, he thought sarcastically. No one would have known he was Britain's hottest actor, not to mention one half of one of Hollywood's premier power couples.

He stuck out his tongue. It looked grey and mottled, like a steak left in the fridge three days too long. How much had he drunk last night? He squinted, trying to remember, but all he could see was two still images, frozen in his mind: a tray of shot glasses filled with something sparkly, and some idiot sliding across the floor on his knees. He looked down at the grazes on his skin. That'll have been me, then.

Taking a deep breath, he wrapped a towel around his waist, mentally preparing a speech. *Terrible mistake, not your fault, must go, important meeting*, that sort of thing. But then he opened the door and there she was, lying stretched out on the bed. Long legs, firm, curvy. Not that horrible stringy LA version of femininity, all sinew and balloon tits. This was a real woman's body, ripe and fleshy. He could feel himself stirring back to life. *Down, boy.* He looked away and puffed out his cheeks.

'Listen, uh . . .'

'Katie,' she said with a half-smile.

'Yes, Katie. Look, I'm sorry, but I've really got to go. We overslept and I've got . . . a thing.'

She nodded and smiled.

'Last night was lovely, though, wasn't it?'

I bet, he thought, looking longingly at her body. He felt bad about hurting her feelings, but a maid could walk in at any moment. He knew how often staff in swish hotels tipped off the newspapers about what they saw.

For all he knew, there could be paparazzi waiting outside the room right now; maybe Katie had set the whole thing up.

'It was lovely,' he said honestly as he sat on the edge of the bed. 'But it shouldn't have happened. I have a girlfriend; a fiancée, actually.' He paused. 'So how indiscreet were we last night?'

'Quite discreet actually.' She smiled. 'Although when you tried to skateboard on your knees, some people might have said you were trying to draw attention to yourself.'

'Was that at Shoreditch House?' He wondered how many people might have witnessed it.

'Shoreditch House?'

'Wasn't that where we met?'

She looked confused. 'We met at Ed's house party. In Soho.'

Ed? Who's Ed?

'Don't worry, Sam. I'm not asking to marry you,' she said, planting feathery kisses on the curve of his neck.

He squeezed his eyes shut, struggling with the devil whispering in his ear: after all, he'd already cheated – well, probably, sort of – so why not go in for another round? He had plenty of friends who screwed around, especially in Hollywood. Not just with other women – wives of their directors, fans, the make-up girls on set – but with men too. At the all-male spas in West Hollywood, at networking parties. He'd listen to them boast about it and laugh along, but he'd think to himself, you poor saps. He wasn't like that. *Well you are now, aren't you?*

Katie ran her finger down his shoulder.

'Can't you just stay for half an hour?'

He was tempted. And not only because her hard nipples were rubbing against his arm. The truth was, he was lonely. Three hundred days of the year he was in bed alone. At any one time he and Jessica were in different parts of the world, shooting films or hopping from city to city on promo junkets, answering the same inane questions about their relationship. Yes, we've been together for four years; no, we haven't set a date just yet. And yes, we're still madly in love.

'Sorry. I wish I could,' he said truthfully. In another time, another life, he would have crawled back under the duvet, ordered room service, then maybe taken her out for dinner, cocktails. Had a normal conversation about music or art or just swapped a few jokes. She seemed like the sort of fun, feisty girl he used to go for before everything became about work, even his love life.

'I understand, don't worry,' she sighed, reaching for her dress, casually thrown over a chair. 'Listen, do you want me to pay the bill? I realise it might be a bit . . . sticky for you.'

Sam instantly felt a surge of guilt for wondering if she was some kiss-and-tell set-up, closely followed by relief and the glimmer of hope that he might actually get away with this indiscretion. He pulled out his wallet and handed her some crumpled bills.

'Thanks, Katie, that should cover the bill and a taxi to get you home. I feel awful about doing this to you.'

She smiled, slipping her knickers on under the folds of her dress. 'No worries.' Her eyes met his. 'You're lucky, you know.'

'Oh, I know that.' He couldn't resist smiling wolfishly.

'No, I mean to have the problem of getting out of a hotel without anyone seeing. Must be nice being that successful.'

'I wouldn't say that,' said Sam, pulling on his own clothes. 'It can be a complete pain in the arse sometimes, being constantly followed by the paparazzi, having them go through your bins. At least that's what it's like when I'm with Jess. Without her they seem a little less interested.'

'Sounds like a fair trade to me,' said Katie. 'The money, the fame, getting to do something you love.'

'I guess,' he said, knowing he sounded ungrateful.

'What's your secret?'

He shrugged. 'Right place, right time, I guess. As you say, I was lucky.'

'Well, do you think you could give me your rabbit's foot? The luck has eluded me so far.'

He frowned at her. He had the vague sense that he should understand what she was talking about, as if they'd already had this conversation.

Catching his blank expression, she rolled her eyes.

'You really don't remember much about last night at all, do you?'

He pulled a face.

'I can remember something about tequila.'

'Ah. Well, we spent a long time talking before you turned into Mr Disco. About how I'm trying to make it as an actress?'

Another flash of memory. The two of them singing Whitney Houston's 'I Will Always Love You' in the corridor of the hotel.

'Didn't you go on *X Factor*?'

'No!' she said, slapping him playfully on the arm. 'I went to Guildhall for three years.'

'Ah. Sorry.'

He looked at her with sympathy. Now he understood what she was talking about; it hadn't been so long since he was exactly where she was. Desperate for anyone to help him, take notice, give him a leg up.

Had she seduced him? No – he was pretty sure that after a bucketful of tequila, he'd have come back to this hotel very willingly. And anyway, he could hardly blame her. However talented you were, everyone needed a little luck. Sam had got his own break when he'd met Sir Andrew Kerr, an RSC actor, in a café just behind St Martin's Lane. He'd known Andrew was gay and almost certainly interested in him sexually – the decent thing to do would have been to let him down gently when he invited him out for dinner. But he didn't. Neither did he refuse to go on to a party and a club afterwards. The proposition from Sir Andrew, when it had finally come, several weeks and nights out later, had been rebuffed politely, and accepted with grace. But by this point Andrew had introduced his dazzlingly good-looking new protégé to a powerful inner circle of agents, producers and directors. And Sam had ruthlessly used the contacts to climb the ladder. A couple of years ago he'd bumped into Sir Andrew at the BAFTAs and the old man had been heartbreakingly decent about it. 'An actor must do what an actor must do,' he had said, offering Sam a brandy. 'It's all for our art, dear boy.'

He looked at Katie as she tied back her russet hair. She really was beautiful, and that body was sensational. If there were any justice in the world, she would be a huge star. But Sam knew he couldn't help her in the way Sir Andrew had helped him. Getting texts or phone calls from a gorgeous starlet really wouldn't help his already strained relationship with Jessica. Even so, he felt terrible leaving it like this.

'Why don't you give me your number?' he said finally. 'Maybe I can get my manager to sort something out.'

'Yes, thanks for phoning him. I appreciate it.'

'I've phoned him already?' He laughed nervously.

Katie pulled out an amateur-looking business card.

'And here's my number. In case you ever hear of a director wanting a hot, classically trained redhead.'

Without thinking, he reciprocated the gesture.

His phone began to buzz – a cue to move.

'Listen, I'd better be off,' he said. She moved in to kiss him, but he jumped up and made for the door. 'I'll definitely be in touch,' he added, holding up her card. 'And it was lovely.'

He slipped out of the room, cringing at the Do Not Disturb sign on the door, and walked quickly down the corridor. His mobile was still ringing, but the screen read 'Withheld number'. Jessica? Possible, but unlikely. She was filming in Boston, and it would be the middle of the night on the East Coast. Then again, it wouldn't be the first time she had called to check up on him.

'Ah sod it,' he whispered and pressed 'Accept'.

'I hope you've been behaving yourself!'

Sam's heart leapt into his mouth, before he realised that the voice was male.

'Eli?' he said, relief flooding in. His manager, Eli Cohen. No-nonsense, old-school, unshockable. Even so, Sam wasn't at all sure he wanted to be on the end of one of Eli's talking-tos.

'Of course it's me, ya schmuck,' growled Eli. 'Who the hell else d'ya think?'

'Where are you?'

'New York.'

'Why are you calling me at this time? It must be five a.m. where you are.'

'I'm an early riser. Especially when my favourite client is phoning me in the middle of the night to tell me he's found the new Rita Hayworth, giggling like some lovestruck college kid. Is there anything I should know about?'

Straight to the point, like a surrogate father. Sam winced.

'What do you mean?' he said, doing his best to sound innocent. He felt guilty lying to Eli, but he didn't want to make this situation any bigger than it had to be.

'What do I mean? When you call at three a.m. London time, raving about some hot chick, I gotta worry what I'm gonna read in the papers.'

'Don't be daft,' said Sam, as he reached the bottom of the stairs. 'I was presenting this Rising Talent award, remember? One particular girl stood out.'

Eli grunted. He didn't sound convinced.

'So you're sure you don't have anything to tell me?'

'No! I'm trying to help young actors!'

His voice echoed around the concrete stairwell.

'Whatever you say. Just keep your dick in your trousers, kid. It's not worth it.'

Sam felt himself flush.

'Stop worrying. Look, I've got to go. Talk later, all right?'

He eased open the door to the lobby and scuttled out through a side door, gasping as the sunlight hit him, scrabbling his sunglasses from his jacket. He forced himself to walk slowly, nonchalantly. Just a normal hotel guest out for a morning stroll, scanning the opposite pavement for paparazzi. Nothing: that was something at least. Even better, a black cab was approaching and he raised his arm to flag it.

'Chelsea Harbour, please.'

Sam had told the truth when Katie had asked about his fame. For a while it had been amazing, brilliant, the best job in the world, but lately it had begun to wear him down. Slumped in the back of a cab, however, he was glad that fame and money had bought him his discreet pied-à-terre by the river. In a few minutes he would be safe inside and he could put this horrible incident behind him.

'Hey,' said the cabby as they moved out into traffic. 'Aren't you that actor, wassissname?'

'I wish,' said Sam, pushing his sunglasses further up his nose. 'I get that all the time.' He could see the cabby looking thoughtful in his rear-view mirror.

'Sam Charles. That's his name,' he said finally. 'Done really well for himself that one, eh? That girlfriend of his, Jessica whatnot. She's a cracker, she is. Wouldn't mind being shacked up with her, eh. Eh?' he said, turning round for his passenger's approval.

'Yeah,' said Sam, looking out of the window to the world beyond his gilded cage. 'I bet that would be brilliant.'

3

Matt Donovan had never been more anxious, curious, angry or excited to take receipt of a birthday present in his entire life. He stood outside the smart Broadwick Street offices of London's most famous media law powerhouse, and exhaled deeply before he stepped inside.

You can do this, he told himself as he walked towards the glass and stainless-steel reception desk of Donovan Pierce solicitors. You have to do this, he reminded himself, recalling the last trying six months, which had seen his business collapse, his life savings depleted and his professional reputation as a lawyer sail perilously close to ruin.

'I'm here to see Helen Pierce,' he told the model-grade blonde behind the desk. She was as smart and chic as her surroundings – floor-to-ceiling windows and sculpted cutting-edge furniture all gave the impression of an ultra-modern global company that was connected in every sense.

'Can I take your name?' she asked without changing expression. Instantly he wished he'd splashed out on a new suit instead of the old faithful that had seen several years of service. Then again, until his father's remarkable offer a few weeks earlier, he'd been in no position to pay his mortgage, let alone invest in a wardrobe full of Paul Smith just to make a good impression.

'Donovan. Matthew Donovan,' he said as the blonde leapt up, tugging her tight pencil skirt into place.

'I'm so sorry, Mr Donovan. I'm to escort you straight to the boardroom. Everyone's very excited you're here,' she gushed, leading him down the corridor.

Matthew grimaced. He'd made it clear that a condition of coming here was that he should be treated just like any other employee, but he should have known: low-key was not the way his father operated.

Stay calm, he said to himself. It's only a job.

But as the door swung back, he was confronted by a roomful of people, all standing to clap. He gasped.

'Matthew!' boomed Larry Donovan, slapping his palm against the back of Matt's suit.

'So good to have you here at last.'

Matt stiffened in his father's alien embrace. Until six weeks ago, Larry Donovan had been a remote figure in his life. He had divorced his mother Katherine when Matthew was barely eight, and when he did swan in, it was always with a grand gesture or a theatrical flourish: the time he had turned up at Matthew's twelfth birthday party with a troupe of juggling clowns, or the day Matthew had passed his driving test and Larry had a Porsche Carrera delivered to his door, complete with a card reading 'There's a bottle of bubbly in the glovebox.' And now this, the biggest, most surprising gesture of all.

Keeping his arm around Matthew's shoulders, his father addressed the room.

'Everyone, this is Matthew, one of the best young lawyers in the country and a definite chip off the old block. Now that I'm being put out to pasture, I think he'll fill the hole nicely. Matthew's a family law specialist, which means that Donovan Pierce will now be able to provide a wrap-around service for our high-net-worth clients. Divorce work, pre-nups, post-nups and anything else he can think of.' His chuckle was as loud as a roar.

'Anyway, I know you'll join with me in welcoming him to the firm as my replacement as senior partner.'

Matthew smiled stiffly as the other partners and associates began to applaud again.

'Thanks, everyone, I'm very pleased to be here. Especially with that typically understated introduction.' There was a ripple of polite laughter. 'However, I'm keen to get straight to work. I'll certainly do what I can to live up to the hype.'

Larry nodded. 'Exactly right. I think we should crack straight on, let Matthew see what he's up against. What have we got on the slate this week?'

Having stepped down as senior partner, Larry was officially only a consultant for Donovan Pierce now, but the team still responded to his instructions as if he were a Roman emperor. As the department heads ran through their workload – a snooker player caught in a newspaper sting, an actress suing a magazine for printing a picture of her daughter, plus the big one, the libel case involving property billionaire Jonathon Balon – Matthew took a moment to weigh each of them up.

Sitting across from Larry was a blonde woman in her late forties, wearing a crisp white shirt and a bottle-green suit that matched her sharp eyes. The woman radiated authority and competence, not to mention a slightly frightening intensity. Helen Pierce was a legend in the legal world. Word had it she was more connected than the Cabinet, and she had a reputation as a vicious fighter in the courtroom. Matthew had met her before; there was no way someone of Helen Pierce's reputation would allow part of her firm to be handed over to just anyone, family or not, so he had been summoned to a 'casual lunch', which had quickly turned into an interrogation, with Helen grilling him on everything from his financial competence to obscure points of law. Matthew thought he had performed fairly well, particularly under such intense pressure, but then Helen had floored him by telling him she had asked a detective to look into his private life: his business, his divorce, his ex-wife, his son. 'Everything you have ever done, seen or thought can be used against you, Matthew,' she had said. 'I need to know how clean your dirty laundry is. I don't like surprises.'

The truth was, Matthew hadn't wanted to take the job – or 'birthday gift' as Larry had touted it when he had called him out of the blue two months earlier. His relationship with his father was difficult enough without the added problem of Helen Pierce. But really, he had no choice. When his father had offered him a large equity shareholding in Donovan Pierce, Matt had been a partner at a small three-man family practice in Hammersmith, but a combination of unpaid bills, rising rental and rates and an office manager on the take had left them financially torpedoed.

31

The meeting broke up quickly, leaving Matthew alone with Larry and Helen.

'So good to have you here at last, Matty,' said Larry, slapping his son on the back. 'How about we mark the occasion with a spot of early lunch?'

Matt glanced at his watch. It was barely ten thirty. 'How about tomorrow? I should probably get settled in. I'm keen to get my feet under my desk.'

'No can do,' said Larry. 'I'm not in tomorrow; semi-retired, remember? Come on, Helen, we need to wet the baby's head, eh?'

Helen Pierce looked unimpressed as she gathered her papers. 'I'm snowed under, Larry. The Balon case needs my attention.'

'Balls to Balon,' said Larry. 'This is an auspicious day! My boy has finally come home to his rightful place. We need to celebrate.'

He leaned out of the door.

'Denise!' he shouted down the corridor. 'Get us a table at Scott's, will you? The sooner the better. Matthew, Helen and I. Tell Mario I want a decent table this time.'

'How about we bring Anna Kennedy?' said Helen. 'She started today as well, remember?'

'Anna?' said Larry, frowning. 'Is she the good-looking brunette? Good. She can come as long as she doesn't drone on about work.'

Matthew was relieved to see that the restaurant was quiet. It was still early for lunch, and the chic dining room was only just beginning to fill. He knew how loud and embarrassing his father could be, especially when he got stuck into the claret. As they all sat down, he glanced over at Anna Kennedy, who looked as uncomfortable as he did. Then again, she could well be one of those ball-breakers who never cracked a smile. In the taxi to the restaurant she had been making calls, barking instructions at her secretary. She had only been at the firm one morning; surely she didn't already have a caseload? She caught him staring and he glanced away. She was undeniably a very attractive woman, who probably had men ogling her all the time. The last thing he wanted her to think was that he was a sleazeball, especially as he was her new boss.

'So where were you before?' he asked her as they sat down at the table.

'Davidson's. I did a lot of their short-notice injunction work. Privacy law and libel.'

Matthew nodded. Impressive.

'What brought you here?' he asked.

'Well, obviously DP has an international reputation for protecting the interests of . . .'

He placed a hand on her forearm. 'Don't worry, it's not an interview.'

She shot him a playful smile.

'Okay, it was the money,' she whispered.

Matthew laughed. Maybe she wouldn't break his balls after all.

'It's not too early for a Scotch, is it?' said Larry.

Helen flashed him a frosty glance that reminded Matthew of his mother.

'Just me, then?' said Larry, unfazed, waving the waiter back over.

'So what do you make of our little law firm, you two?' asked Helen.

'Well, I'm surprised nobody's growling and gnawing on bones,' replied Matthew.

'What?' said Larry, coming into the conversation late.

'I think Matthew is referring to Donovan Pierce's reputation.' She smiled. 'That we're the Dobermanns of the legal world.'

Matthew nodded.

'There's a certain truth to it, I do admit,' said Helen. 'But I prefer to see ourselves as protective rather than aggressive. Our client base is well known and wealthy and we do our best to shield them from the exploitation of the media.'

He couldn't help smiling. 'But who is exploiting whom here? Celebrities are happy to use the media when it suits them. The papers sell copies off the back of the stories, and firms like Donovan Pierce earn huge fees trying to keep the peace.'

Helen didn't react; instead she turned to Anna.

'What do you think?'

Clever move, thought Matthew. Deflect the question on to someone else.

'Well, an actress or a singer might have to push themselves to get noticed,' said Anna. 'That's just part of the job, but they should still be entitled to a private life. Everyone should.'

Matt looked at her, unsettled by her steely self-assurance.

'Come on, if some two-bit reality star happily sells their wedding or their divorce to *OK!* magazine, then they can't go "boo-hoo" if someone prints a photo of them coming out of AA.'

'Well the law might disagree with you, Matthew,' smiled Anna.

It was his first morning. He was senior partner. He couldn't let an associate get the better of him, and besides, he just didn't agree with her.

'Anna, the law is half cocked on this one,' he grunted. 'It's skewed in favour of the people who can afford expensive injunctions, libel trials and threatening letters from aggressive law firms. It's not justice, it's tyranny.'

'And it keeps the likes of us in hot dinners,' chuckled Larry, happily slicing up his starter.

Matt could feel the muscles in his neck beginning to tense. He knew he shouldn't get so worked up about it, but he'd spent twenty years struggling at the other end of the law, dealing with the fallout of broken families where money was often in short supply. And he'd learned that for people who couldn't afford to fight legal battles, justice was rarely served. He'd seen families crumble, decent working folk broken and children let down by an unbending system. In light of all that, it was hard to feel sympathy for a pampered soap star who didn't like photographers.

'Don't you ever feel guilty?' he asked finally.

'Guilty?' His father chuckled. 'We just provide a service, Matty. And we do it very well.'

'I read that *Poke* magazine is going to have to shut down because that awful MP you were acting for won six-figure damages.'

'The silly bastards shouldn't have claimed he was an enthusiastic cottager, then!' laughed Larry.

'But I thought they had photos of him hanging around Hampstead Heath.'

'Not illegal, son,' said Larry, giving a slow wink. 'He was walking his dog.'

Matthew bit his lip. He couldn't let his dad wind him up, not today. He turned to Helen instead.

'Isn't the truth that *Poke* got caught out because they couldn't prove the cottaging claims were true? They're a little indie magazine and didn't have the proper resources to fight the action.'

Larry swilled back his white Burgundy.

'A client came to us to sue the magazine and we sued them. Job done. And by the way, excuse me for earning a good living, which has kept you in nice houses, good schools, your mother in gin.'

'Don't speak about her,' said Matt in a low voice. Larry had always known which buttons to press to get a reaction from his son. Matthew was fiercely protective of his mother and had never forgiven his father for the way he had treated her and the way he had left them. Since her death a year earlier, those feelings had become even more complex.

'Why shouldn't I talk about her?' said Larry, looking more angered. 'You like to paint your mother as a saint, but you don't know everything about our relationship.'

'Some relationship,' said Matt. 'You were never there. Always out with clients, any excuse to stay away.'

'Maybe you should ask yourself why I chose to stay away.'

'All right, boys, play nicely,' said Helen firmly. 'If you can't leave your family issues behind, then there's no hope of us working together. I'm serious.'

'Don't . . .' began Larry, but whatever he was about to say froze in his throat, his cheeks turning pink. He tugged at his shirt collar.

'Are you okay?' Matt frowned, putting down his wine glass. He could see that there was sweat beading on his father's brow.

'I'm fine, don't fuss,' said Larry irritably, kneading his chest.

'Just indigestion, I should think.'

But Matthew could see something was badly wrong. He glanced at Helen and Anna, and the concerned looks on their faces told him his instinct was correct.

'Dad? What's the matter? Tell me!' he said.

Larry had now gone a pallid grey and was clutching at his stomach. Then, quite suddenly, he jerked and retched, spewing vomit over the starched white tablecloth. Someone at the next table let out a scream as he lurched forward in his chair, dropping his glass, which shattered on the floor.

'Someone call an ambulance,' shouted Matthew, catching his father under his arms and lowering him awkwardly to the floor. Larry was lifeless now, his eyes rolled up in his head.

'I think it's a heart attack,' said Anna.

'No shit,' snapped Matthew. He quickly undid his father's tie, trying desperately to remember what he'd learned about CPR in Scouts. He leaned down: no heartbeat, no breathing sounds. He had to do something, and do it quick.

I hope I've got this right, he panicked, clasping his hands together and raising them above his head.

'What are you doing?' gasped Anna.

'Get out of the way,' snapped Matthew. With every ounce of strength he punched down on to his father's chest, smashing his fists on to Larry's breastbone.

'He's killing him!' screamed a woman's voice.

But it had worked. Larry jerked on the floor, gasping out a strangled breath, his eyelids flickered and his eyes opened.

'What can I do?' said Anna urgently at Matthew's side.

Larry took Matthew's hand and gave it a small squeeze.

'This will do fine,' he whispered.

'Okay, the ambulance is two minutes away,' said Helen, calm and in control. She barked some instructions to the waiters and they moved a table out of the way.

As Helen began organising the restaurant, Matthew knelt, holding his father's hand which had gone worryingly cold.

Please God, he prayed silently, closing his eyes, I know he's been a sod, but I'd appreciate it if you didn't take this man just yet.

'Are you praying?' said Larry in a small but amused voice. 'I hope you're directing it downstairs. I think the big guy's given up on me.'

'I haven't,' said Matthew. 'Not quite yet, anyway.'

Although the ambulance was there within minutes, it seemed like an eternity. Finally, the drone of a siren swelled louder and the doors of the restaurant burst open, two paramedics rushing in. Matthew stepped back, trying to work out where the nearest A&E was. UCL in Euston. Ten minutes if the traffic was good, longer if there were the usual London snarl-ups, his mind scrabbling to think of anything except the horrific, horrible scene in front of him, his own father lying on his back, fighting for his life. There were times when Matthew had wished his father dead, but presented with the possibility, he realised how much he would give to prevent that happening.

A wave of loneliness engulfed him. He had lost his mother; he was about to lose his father too.

'Okay, old son,' said one of the paramedics, lifting Larry on to a stretcher. 'We'll have you out of here in a jiffy.'

How can they be so calm? thought Matt as he followed, feeling stupid and powerless as the stretcher was wheeled out on to the street. He could see Helen and Anna standing outside the restaurant looking grim, obviously expecting the worst.

Larry squeezed his hand again.

'Don't worry,' he whispered.

'I'm not worried,' Matthew said, trying to smile. 'You're as tough as old boots.'

'Less of the old,' said Larry.

As the crew pushed the stretcher into the ambulance, Matthew began to climb in beside it, but the paramedic stopped him.

'Family only, I'm afraid.'

'I'm his son,' said Matthew, looking down at this frail old man. 'I'm his son.' And he realised this was the first time he'd wanted to say that in years.

4

Helen Pierce twirled her favourite gold pencil between her fingers and looked out of her fifth-floor window, over the Soho skyline, hoping that today would be a better day than the day before. After Monday morning's conference meeting and the drama of Larry's heart attack, she'd only been able to bill four hours on her time sheet – her lowest daily total in two years. Even when she'd had a bout of swine flu, she'd managed to send out emails and draft letters to counsel from her sickbed.

Helen's work ethic was one of the reasons she was among the most successful lawyers in London. Although it was only nine thirty in the morning, she had already logged two billable hours to Jonathon Balon, the billionaire property developer she was representing in a high-profile libel case. After twelve months' work on it, fees were already in excess of one million pounds; when you factored in the rest of Helen's caseload, an assortment of reputation management, privacy and defamation disputes for footballers, oligarchs, movie stars and captains of industry, she could bank on clearing four million in annual fees in this financial year.

When the *Evening Standard* had listed her as one of London's most influential people, they had called her 'a wolf in chic clothing', a description that she secretly loved. She knew that some men found her image sexy: her sharp blond bob, hard green eyes and roman nose gave her the look of a striking Hollywood character actress, and she certainly made the best of her figure in tailored suits and her trademark patent heels. But what turned Helen Pierce on was the fact that she had the reputation of being the toughest media lawyer in London, and as London was the world's centre for libel action, that meant she was almost certainly the best at what she did in the world. Now that was sexy.

The shrill ring of her phone disturbed her from her thoughts.

'Miss Pierce?'

'Yes?'

'It's the clerk from Judge Lazner's office. Can I put him through?'

'Very well,' she said, frowning. What could he want?

Mr Justice Lazner, one of the High Court judges on the Queen's Bench, was due to sit over Jonathon Balon's libel case slated to trial in September. Balon had been the subject of a hatchet job in the prestigious American magazine *Stateside*, whose eight-page profile piece on the billionaire entrepreneur had claimed that he had got his start in business using money loaned to him by a North London gangster family as a way of laundering drug money. Balon had been understandably livid, especially as it did nothing to improve his reputation as a ruthless operator. Helen Pierce was his obvious first choice as legal representation: fight fire with fire, as he had put it. Helen had liked that.

'Good morning, Helen.'

Helen had spoken to Julian Neil, Judge Lazner's clerk, many times before.

'Isn't it?' she said, using her husky voice to full effect. She always flirted gently with any male of influence in the judicial system. 'Although I'm sure you heard about poor Larry?'

'How is he?' asked Julian.

'He's doing well, I hear. Soon be back at the bar at the Garrick, I dare say.'

The clerk gave a polite laugh.

'Send him our regards. Now, Judge Lazner has asked me to speak to you about Balon versus Steinhoff Publications.'

Helen nodded. How could she forget? Stacks of beige files wrapped in pink ribbons covered her desk, every one relating to her biggest case. She had been poring over them for hours over the weekend. Most libel cases didn't even make it to trial, often settling in the tense hours before court, but this was not a case

Helen particularly wanted to settle, partly because she thought she could win it and partly because of the hefty fees involved with a trial that would stretch well into the autumn.

'He wants to bring the trial forward,' said Neil.

Helen sat up straight, feeling an unusual flutter of anxiety.

'But we have a date. September the eighteenth.'

There was a grunt of disapproval down the phone.

'The courts are not here for your convenience, Miss Pierce. Another case has just settled that was pencilled in for four weeks in court. We propose your case takes its slot. Commencement three weeks Monday.'

Helen knew that 'we propose' was a polite way of issuing an order.

'You want us to begin in less than a month?' she said. 'But we're not ready.'

'Oh Helen. You're always ready. Besides, Judge Lazner spent half of last night looking though the case files and thinks three weeks for a pre-trial review should be more than ample. It's best to get these things sorted sooner than later, don't you think? Even you must want to get a holiday this summer.'

Helen cursed loudly as she put down the phone.

The judge had been correct when he had said that three weeks was long enough for the final preparations, but she didn't just want to be ready; she wanted to have anticipated every potential problem. Helen wanted to win every case – and most of the time she got her way. But this trial wasn't just about proving the allegations were wrong and being awarded damages. It was about restoring Balon's reputation. That was why people came to Donovan Pierce: the firm delivered. They weren't cheap, but their clients were happy to pay. The footballer who spent fifty thousand pounds on an injunction covering up his numerous infidelities could save himself hundreds of thousands if not millions in sponsorship deals. Expensive? They were cheap at twice the price.

Helen inhaled sharply and picked up her phone.

'Lucy, call the Balon team for a conference in the boardroom. Immediately.'

She sipped green tea as she collected her thoughts. She had to get this right. No loose ends, no variables. No prisoners. Slipping on her Armani jacket, she strode down the corridor into the boardroom, where her team were waiting for her, their expressions eager but anxious. They were all sharp graduates, the pick of the bunch, chosen not for their intimate knowledge of torts and case history, but for their commercial ruthlessness.

Anna Kennedy was in the seat beside her.

'How's Larry?' she asked as Helen sat down, voicing what everyone was thinking.

'He'll be fine,' said Helen briskly. She had no time for small talk right now. 'Change of plan. The Balon case is happening in three weeks' time, so you can all kiss goodbye to any holiday plans you might have had for the next few weeks.'

She watched their faces closely for signs of dissent. She knew for a fact that one of them had booked a trip to Jordan, and another was planning to attend his brother's wedding in California. They all knew the golden rule: Donovan Pierce came first. If any of them were perturbed by the news, they didn't show it. That was good; she had trained them well.

'Susie, I want you to go over all the witness statements, find the gaps.'

A trainee raised a nervous finger. 'Witnesses?'

'All of the people interviewed in the article,' said Susie, slightly impatiently. 'Plus Balon's *Stateside* staff, and friends, family, enemies and employees past, present and future.'

Helen gave a half-smile. She liked that 'future'; it showed her team were making sure everything was covered, even the unlikely scenarios. The unlikely was the one thing that was sure to screw you in court.

She turned to David Morrow, the handsome senior associate who had worked most closely with her on the case. 'David, by tomorrow I want a brief on my desk outlining all the weaknesses in the case. We don't want to be left exposed on any point.'

She gave each of them a rigorous task with a tight deadline, impressing on them her desire to leave no stone unturned, then stood and walked out. There was no time to waste for her either, as she closed the door on her office and took the first file from one of the stacks. The clerk's call had put the stop on her own

41

weekend trip to Ravello, but that didn't bother her. She led from the front and her priorities were always with the firm.

Flipping through the pages, she speed-read the file, scribbling notes as she went. The truth was, she trusted no one but herself to spot all the holes, to exploit any weakness in the other side's case.

She looked up with irritation as the phone chirped.

'Lucy, I said no calls.'

'It's Eli Cohen from Cohen Simons.'

'I see. Put him through.'

Cohen Simons was a small but influential management company with a roster of ageing Hollywood stars and a couple of exciting young ones; besides, any phone call from Tinseltown always piqued her interest. They were usually very high-profile, and high-profile was good for the firm.

'Eli,' she said. 'How's tricks?'

'Not good, Helen,' said the manager. 'This is a confidential matter. Can you talk?'

'Of course.'

She flipped her notebook to a new page.

'A client of mine is about to have a matter exposed in one of the nationals. Naturally we want to keep it under wraps.'

Helen allowed herself a small smile. She knew the pattern: this was going to be a juicy case.

'Okay, we'll start with the what, rather than the who. Tell me what's happened.'

'An actor client, a major star with a long-term partner, had a one-night stand a couple of weeks ago. Girl's blackmailing him. She wants a truckload of money or else she's going straight to the press.'

'Has she got any evidence?'

'Evidence? You talking man jam?'

'Man jam?' She winced.

'You know, a DNA sample from a sexual encounter. Although to be honest, he can barely even remember the sex, he was so wasted.'

Helen quickly scribbled 'Other parties?' If this actor had been drunk, there was always a chance other people could corroborate. A sloppy drunk on the pull didn't usually care too much about covering his tracks.

'I meant photos, video footage,' she said.

There was a pause. 'There's a photo on a mobile phone of them taken together in bed.'

'Have you seen it?'

'Not personally. But my client had it sent to him.'

'I'll need to see it asap.'

She paused for a moment, her sharp mind looking at the angles, assessing the risks.

'So you can get a gagging order, can't you?' Cohen asked. 'The British laws play to our side here, don't they?'

'Yes, but there are other sorts of deal we could set up.'

This was the stuff they didn't teach you at law school: how to broker watertight six-figure pay-offs, or to put it another way, how to bury the bodies so deep no one would ever find them. She couldn't count the number of secret confidentiality agreements she had drawn up to silence a mistress or a boyfriend. Of course there were other strategies too: arranging with an editor to kill off one story in return for a bigger one, an exclusive cover story about something else. Or you could even play hardball and hit the media where it hurt: in their budget. That was one of Larry's favourite tricks. Threaten to cut off their advertising, or permanently restrict access to a roster of stars. 'Play dirty,' that was what he used to say. 'It's all the bastards understand.'

She looked down at her notes. 'So how much does she want?'

'Five hundred thousand.'

'Pounds or dollars?'

'The chick is British, so I assume pounds. Although when she suggested it, my client panicked and told her to go fuck herself.'

Half a million sterling was big money, which meant a big name. A very big name.

'Who's the client? The President?' she said with a laugh.

Eli didn't laugh.

'Sam Charles.'

Helen smiled to herself. This was one of the perks of her job. She got to see beyond the curtain into the secret goings-on of

Hollywood, see how people really behaved when the cameras stopped rolling. After all this time, she really shouldn't have been surprised at anyone's behaviour, but she hadn't thought Sam Charles had that sort of ballsiness in him. But that was neither here nor there. The fact was that Sam Charles was one of the biggest stars in the world, especially as part of a Hollywood golden couple. Every newspaper and magazine in the world was going to want that story; no wonder this girl was asking so much.

'I can see why you want to keep it under wraps,' she said.

'This girl says she's going to go to the press if we don't give her an answer in twenty-four hours.'

'We'll see about that,' said Helen.

She paused to collect her thoughts.

'What's the girl called?'

'Katie.'

'And when did Sam last speak to her?'

'Maybe an hour ago.'

Helen jotted her strategy on her notepad.

'I want you to call Katie back. Stall her. Make out you need time to get the five hundred together.'

'Should Sam call her?'

'Definitely not. No more contact under any circumstances. Besides, she'll believe it more if it comes from his manager.'

'But we don't want to pay her off.'

'No, but it will buy us time. We don't want her going to one of the kiss-and-tell publicists or directly to the press if we can help it. Where is Sam now? I'll need to speak to him, get every detail of the encounter.'

'He's filming in Capri. It will be difficult to pull him out.'

Helen tapped her gold pencil on the pad and smiled.

'So we'll go to him.'

She put down the receiver and looked at the stack of Balon case files on her desk, wondering how many she could fit into her hand luggage, then shook her head. She really couldn't justify popping off to a glamorous Italian island on expenses, even if the Ravello jaunt was off. Balon was her priority, worth millions in fees and, if they won, priceless in publicity. Sam

Charles would pay handsomely too – and Helen rather fancied chatting about his indiscretions over a Bellini or two – but it was below-the-radar stuff and thus of less value to the firm. Reluctantly she picked up her phone and dialled Anna Kennedy's extension.

Within a minute the young associate was at her door, notebook in hand.

'Sit down,' said Helen.

'Is there a development in the Balon case?' asked Anna.

Helen shook her head.

'Sam Charles has been playing away,' she said, watching Anna's reaction. The girl simply raised her eyebrows. She was no star-struck groupie and had probably dealt with similarly successful clients at Davidson's. 'The young lady in question has threatened to go to the papers, and naturally Mr Charles wants to stop the media getting hold of the story.'

She paused for a moment.

'This is partner's work, Anna. The big time. I wanted to do this job myself, but with the Balon trial happening, it's just not possible.'

Anna nodded.

'I'm happy to take it,' she said, her expression neutral.

'This isn't some jolly to the Med, Anna.'

'I understand.'

'Then I'm sure you also understand that I need the Balon work on my desk before you go.'

'Of course,' said Anna, standing up and walking to the door.

'Oh, and Anna?' said Helen as she was leaving. 'Don't even think about making a single mistake.'

5

Matthew's heart sank the moment he saw Larry's new wife Loralee.

Wearing denim hot pants and jewelled flip-flops, the tall blonde ran up to the hospital ward's reception desk and immediately began shouting.

'Where is my husband? Take me to him at once.'

Call security, thought Matthew, taking a sip of the coffee he had just got from the drinks machine.

Although it had been over twenty-four hours since his father's heart attack, it was the first time that Loralee had visited the hospital. She had had to fly back from Mexico, where she had been on boot camp apparently trying to shift the excess weight she had gained on their month-long honeymoon.

Although the past day had been emotionally fraught, Matthew was glad that he had dealt with it alone. He had only met Loralee on two previous occasions, but he had quickly assessed that the fourth Mrs Larry Donovan was cut from the exact same cloth as the previous two. Selfish, grasping, young and above all, ambitious. She had been openly furious when Larry had announced his plans for passing the business to Matthew. 'Underhand, scheming little shit,' were the words she had used, if he remembered correctly. Obviously Loralee had had other plans for Larry's money.

Now he braced himself as the receptionist pointed in his direction.

'Hello, Loralee,' he said.

'What the hell's been going on?' she said, thumping her Chanel quilt bag on to the seat next to him.

Matthew tried to control himself. He hadn't slept in twenty-four hours and was tired, hungry and drained. The last thing he needed right now was a confrontation.

'Was he drinking?' she snapped. 'Did you let him drink? Did you upset him?'

'Lovely to see you too,' said Matthew.

'Cut the shit, Matthew,' she replied, narrowing her blue eyes. 'You knew he had high blood pressure.'

'I didn't, actually,' said Matthew tartly. 'We haven't even exchanged Christmas cards for about a decade, let alone medical histories.'

'So what happened?'

'Look, we were having lunch and he keeled over.'

'Just like that? I don't think so.'

'Well, yes, he had been drinking. You know what he's like.'

'Yes, I do,' said Loralee. 'I know my husband very well and I know he's promised to cut down on his drinking. He must have been agitated.'

Matthew looked away guiltily.

'I knew it!' said Loralee. 'You had a row, didn't you?'

He resented Loralee's implication that he had somehow deliberately brought on his father's heart attack, even if he had spent the last day accusing himself of the same thing. If only he hadn't given his dad such a hard time, if only he hadn't let him drink so much, if only he'd said no to going to lunch; every 'if only' possible had crossed his mind from the moment he had got into the ambulance to the time the doctors had finally told him that Larry was going to be all right. He inhaled deeply, the sterile hospital smell filling his throat.

'There was a heated conversation, yes,' he admitted. 'More of a legal debate really. But Loralee, from what the doctors were saying, he's had some heart problems before. Honestly, I had no idea about the high blood pressure.'

'And would that have made any difference?' she sneered. Matthew noticed with detachment just how white and even her teeth were.

'Of course it would have made a difference. I don't want anything to happen to him, he's my father.'

Loralee laughed mirthlessly.

'Is he? When it suits you, when there's something in it for you.'

The words stung. 'You mean the partnership? Don't be ridiculous. It was Larry who got in touch with me, not the other way around.'

'You expect me to believe that? Rather convenient, isn't it; just when your company is about to go belly up, along comes Daddy out of the blue to offer you the partnership.'

'I don't know what you're implying, but . . .'

'I'm not implying anything, *Matty*,' she said sarcastically. 'I'm stating it as fact. You jumped in and took advantage of a sick old man you don't give a shit about.'

'Loralee, listen . . .' he said, pulling himself up to his full six-foot-four-inch height. He had a rower's build, honed on the River Cam at university, and could look pretty intimidating when he wanted to be.

'No, *you* listen,' she hissed, lowering her voice so they couldn't be overheard. 'I love your father. I want what's best for us. You've had nothing to do with him for the past twenty-five years and he's been fine, absolutely fine. Then the second you come back into his life, he ends up almost dead.'

Her words had an unsettling ring of truth. He looked back into the private hospital room where his father lay, pale, weak, the irrepressible life force drained out of him. How could a man who had always been such a towering presence seem so small and meek in his hospital bed? He was glad Larry was sleeping. He would hate the feeling of being like that.

If only I hadn't accepted the partnership.

Matt wasn't a doctor. He had no idea if their argument had directly contributed to the heart attack. But it was inevitable that their working relationship was always going to be tense and destructive. There were clearly too many emotions – guilt, resentment – for it to be anything else. He knew he should have turned the offer down; for years he had wanted to punish his father, and rejecting Larry's offer would have been a lethal way to do it. But he had taken the partnership for other, selfish reasons, and look where it had got them.

'We've had a difficult relationship, that's true,' he said, feeling his cheeks turn red and angry. 'But don't dare say I don't give a shit about him. I've been by his bedside for twenty-four hours. I've had no sleep because he's my dad and of course I care what happens to him. Now can we stop this bickering, because it's not helping and in the scheme of things it doesn't matter.'

Loralee looked away and was silent for a few moments. When her eyes reconnected with his, they were glistening with tears.

'Look. I'm sorry if I flew off the handle, but this is very stressful for me.' Her voice wobbled. Her show of emotion caught him by surprise and he instantly softened.

'I know. I'm sorry too. Come on, why don't I take you down there?'

'No, it's fine. How is he?'

Matthew shook his head.

'He's sleeping. And I could do with some fresh air.'

She looked down the corridor nervously.

'How is he?'

'Don't worry, the doctors say he'll be fine.'

Loralee's eyes searched his.

'I feel awful not being there for him, but I got the first flight I could.'

Matthew nodded.

'He'll just be glad to see you now.'

She touched his arm, stroking it. Her hand lingered long enough for him to think there was something traitorous in her gesture.

'Thanks, Matthew,' she said. 'I think we need to be friends, don't we?'

He nodded, dismissing his paranoia. His father's heart attack had scared him, shocked him into realising there was something worth salvaging in their relationship. It was a time for being open and forgiving. Not cynical and suspicious.

'Sure. Friends,' he said slowly, turning and walking out into the warm summer air.

6

Sam sat back on the white leather seat of the Riva speedboat, his arm around a beautiful model, and sipped his eighth cocktail of the day. Okay, so it wasn't a real cocktail, but then this whole set-up was completely unreal: he was bobbing on the sparkling sea just off the coast of Capri, a former Pirelli girl named Adrianna was purring in his ear, and best of all, he was getting paid a small fortune to appear in an advert that no one he knew would even see. Still, he felt like a fraud. This Italian drinks commercial should have been like a holiday for him, a chance to lark about and recharge, but instead he felt edgy, distracted, as if he was watching someone else clink glasses and laugh and look relaxed and carefree for the crew.

'Cut!' shouted Dino the director. 'The light is no good. We stop until tomorrow.'

Sam breathed a sigh of relief. He wasn't sure for how much longer he could keep a cheesy smile pasted on his face, even with Adrianna running her fingers across his chest.

'You want to go out for supper, Sam?' she said, tipping her head seductively to one side. 'My grandfather is from Capri. I can show you around.'

He was tempted to say yes – Adrianna was drop-dead gorgeous and her cascade of coffee-coloured hair was tickling his shoulder – but it was that kind of thinking that had got him into this mess in the first place.

'I'm sorry, Adrianna,' he said, 'but I have a meeting this evening. Legal stuff, very boring.'

The model's smile faded – rejection was clearly something she was not used to.

'And I guess we don't want to make Jessica angry, do we?' she said bitchily.

Sam smarted at the jibe, but he had to agree with the sentiment. Actually, no, he thought. We really don't want to make her angry. That was why he had been desperately working with his manager and his new lawyer to contain this shit storm, and why he had been letting Jessica's calls ring through to message.

The speedboat circled back to a gleaming sixty-metre yacht moored off Capri's Marina Piccolo. He climbed on board and slipped into a towelling robe being held out for him by an attractive young stylist.

'Call for you,' said Josh, his PA, holding up his mobile. Unlike most high-profile Hollywood actors, Sam had held back from getting a PA until very recently. Now he had one, he admitted that it made his life considerably easier, although the thought that Josh might know about his indiscretion – probably did – made him feel sick. The fact that the whole world might soon know if he didn't cough up half a million quid – that made him feel worse.

'Who is it?'

'Wouldn't say,' shrugged Josh. 'Female caller, very insistent. Says it's urgent, personal business.'

Sam frowned, took the mobile and made his way to the stateroom on the mezzanine level of the yacht, hoping it was the lawyer – what was her name? Helen something? She was due any minute. Eli had reassured him the situation was under control, but he would feel much more secure hearing it from an expert.

'Hey, it's Sam,' he said when the door was closed.

'It's Katie.'

Immediately Sam could feel his pulse start to flutter. What the hell did she want now? If he was honest, he hadn't been all that surprised when Katie had called two days ago. Stupidly he'd given her his card, and to be frank, why wouldn't she call? *He* would have done. Any struggling thesp worth their salt would try to use whatever contacts they could to get a foot up on the ladder – and who better than a Hollywood star: correction, a *guilty* Hollywood star? He had been muttering something about getting her a meeting with Eli when Katie had dropped the bombshell.

'I want five hundred grand,' she had said, as if she was asking for a signed photograph. 'I have pictures. Very intimate pictures. I don't think Jessica will want to see them. Certainly not on the front page of the *New York Post*.'

He had hung up and called Eli, who had put it into the hands of this lawyer with the attack-dog reputation. Wasn't she supposed to put a stop to this? He stared at himself in a full-length mirror. In his oversized robe, he looked vulnerable. Scared. Which was exactly how he felt.

'What do you want now, Katie?' he said, trying to sound confident and in control.

'I thought I made that clear,' she said coldly. 'I want the money. Where is it?'

Sam frowned.

'I thought my manager was going to—'

'I said I wanted the money by five o'clock,' she snapped. 'Don't try and stall me.'

'Katie, these things take time,' said Sam soothingly. 'I can't just magic the sort of cash you're asking for out of thin air.'

'Oh sure. I bet you have that much in your wallet.'

Sam rubbed his eyes. How could he have been so wrong about this girl? That night at the party – the bits he could remember – and the morning in the hotel, Katie had seemed smart, sassy, decent. It was what had attracted him to her in the first place. He could understand her wanting to make the most of the situation, but this was insane. Wasn't it?

'Why are you doing this, Katie?' he said softly. 'I thought we got along that night. I said I'd help you out as much as I could.'

'Yeah, right,' she said sarcastically. 'Like you were ever going to call me.'

'But this is blackmail,' he said. 'I could go straight to the police. Do you want that?'

'Are you threatening me, Sam?' she hissed. 'Because I don't think you want to do that in your position.'

Sam winced. Clearly confrontation was not the way to go.

'Why not let me help you, then?' he said. 'You're an actress.

A pretty good one apparently. If you go to the papers, it's not going to look good for you either. You've got so much to lose.'

She snorted. 'Have I? From where I'm standing, I've got nothing to lose.'

She slurred the word 'nothing' and Sam realised she was drunk. No wonder she wasn't buying into the rational argument. Still he pressed on.

'Listen, I told you in London these things take time. I know it's hard. It's frustrating, and you just need that lucky break . . .'

'Like meeting a movie star at a party. Then having sex with him. That was pretty lucky, huh?'

Despite his anger, he felt a pang of sympathy for her.

'You're better than this, Katie. You're worth more than this.'

'Yeah, I know,' she said. 'Which is why my price has just gone up to six hundred thousand.'

'This is ridiculous,' he said, finally losing his cool. And where was his bloody lawyer when he needed her?

'What's ridiculous?' said Katie. 'Getting money for sex? It wouldn't be the first time.'

He felt his heart skip a beat. Had he heard her right?

'You're a . . . a *prostitute*?' he whispered. He felt sure the room was spinning.

'I prefer to call it escort work. How else am I supposed to live between auditions?'

'Oh Jesus . . .'

He sat down on the edge of the bed and rubbed his temples. He could see the headlines now. *Hollywood Star In Seedy Vice Girl Scandal. Lying Love Rat Shows True Colours. Slimy Brit Breaks Jess's Heart.* And all because he wanted a nice night out, free from all this fairy-tale bollocks, where he could drop the mask and be himself. There is no 'you' any more, he thought grimly. You're public property. A business. A machine to make money for other people.

'It's okay for you, isn't it?' said Katie. 'You've forgotten what it's like to have no idea where the next rent cheque is coming from. To have to walk five miles into the West End because you can't afford the bus fare. Don't tell me you haven't pulled a few tricks to get on.'

'You want a part, I can get you some auditions,' he said desperately.

'And I'm supposed to believe you?'

'Trust me, Katie.'

He heard her suck her teeth dismissively.

'I'll tell you who I trust. Blake Stanhope. I spoke to him this afternoon.'

'Stanhope?' The name of London's most notorious kiss-and-tell publicist sent Sam cold.

'He says the escort angle helps our cause. He thinks it makes the story worth over a million worldwide; he can maybe even get me on those American chat shows. So I'm thinking maybe it's actually a better move to spill the beans.'

'Please, Katie, Eli's getting you the money,' said Sam. 'Don't do anything rash.'

'You know what I want. I'm meeting Blake at nine o'clock tomorrow morning to take things further. I don't want to do it that way. But I will if I have to.'

'Katie, don't. Please,' he said, but the phone had gone dead.

Sam stared down at the handset for a moment, then with a curse, he threw it on the bed. He yanked the door open.

'Josh!' he shouted. 'Get me another phone. And where's that bloody lawyer?'

7

'*Ecco! Ecco! Taxi! Taxi!*'

Anna walked down the ramp as the hydrofoil clunked into dock in Capri's Marina Grande and pulled her sunglasses down from the top of her head.

Wow, she thought, taking in the pastel sugar-cube houses clinging to the towering cliff, watching the streams of chic day-trippers chattering excitedly as they disembarked from the boat. Thirty minutes earlier she had left Naples, one of Italy's poorest cities, with its crumbling tenements, and now she was here, the sparkling sea to her left and a branch of Roberto Cavalli to her right. She felt like Dorothy in *The Wizard of Oz*, swept up, whisked away and deposited in a fantasy land.

Where, though, she wondered, were Sam Charles's people? She picked up her overnight bag and wandered away from the dock. Thankfully she was travelling super-light – there had only been time to grab her pyjamas and her passport when she had stopped at her house on the way to the airport. But arrangements had been worryingly loose about how she was supposed to find her client.

'Don't worry, Sam's people will find you,' his manager Eli had told her breezily. All right for you to say, thought Anna, feeling the heat in her frankly impractical lawyer's suit. You're in an air-conditioned office in LA.

'Hey there!'

She turned to see a short, skinny guy running down the dock towards her. He was wearing shorts and one of those fancy Bluetooth headsets. He definitely looked like one of Sam's people.

'Anna, right?' he said, holding out his hand. 'I'm Josh, Sam's PA. I'm gonna take you to him.'

'Well, I hope we're going in one of those things,' she said, pointing to a line of open-topped taxis with bright striped awnings.

'Uh-uh,' said Josh. 'Even better.'

He took her bag and led her down some stone steps. At the bottom was a beautiful wooden motor launch, all polished wood and chrome.

Oh yes, very Sophia Loren, thought Anna as Josh helped her inside.

'So where's Sam?' she called over the roar of the engine as the boat zoomed out of the bay leaving a trail of foaming white wake behind it.

'Just around this headland,' replied Josh, pointing to a white yacht moored about two hundred metres from the shoreline.

'He's not staying in a hotel?' said Anna, surprised.

'He's working. Under the circumstances, it's best he's out there rather than on land.'

She wondered if Josh knew about 'the incident', and if he did, who else had been informed. She had no reason to doubt Josh's loyalty, but as she understood it, he was a new addition to Sam's team, and that posed a security risk. No doubt he was being well paid, but a story this explosive was worth hundreds of thousands.

'I hear you've just joined Sam,' said Anna casually.

'Yes, great way to start off, huh?' smiled Josh. 'And Sam's such a sweetheart too.'

Anna nodded non-committally. She hadn't made up her mind about Sam Charles quite yet. She always made a point of swotting up on her clients before she met them, so she had spent the entire flight to Naples reading a file of interviews, bios and news stories about the actor. Sifting through the gushing profile features, the overall impression she came away with was that Sam Charles was an operator. One minute he was just another member of some university revue show, the next he was making indie Brit movies and in the space of just a few years had graduated to Hollywood. That sort of meteoric rise didn't happen by accident. Even with the right contacts, management and partner, it took more than luck to get on in the most cut-throat town in the world. All the evidence says 'ruthless player', but I'm prepared to be proved wrong, she smiled to herself, thinking of Ilina Miranova, and the preconceived ideas of what she would be like before she met her.

The speedboat moored at the back of the yacht.

'No heels on board, I'm afraid,' said Josh, looking down at Anna's shoes.

She slipped them off and with Josh's help clambered awkwardly aboard.

'Sam's aft – that's the back of the boat to you and me.' Josh smiled.

Anna found Sam Charles leaning against the railings. His towelling robe hung open. His hair was damp, his tanned feet bare, and he was staring out to sea with a cigarette dangling between two fingers. She couldn't help but think he looked like a post-coital gigolo, but there was no mistaking that he was absolutely beautiful. It was a moment before he realised she was there.

'Hello,' he said uncertainly.

'Anna Kennedy,' she said, stepping forward with her hand out. When he still looked confused, she added, 'Solicitor from Donovan Pierce?'

'I thought Helen Pierce was coming?' he said.

'Helen's tied up in London, I'm afraid.' His look of worry was unmistakable. 'Don't worry. This is what I do. Injunctions. Privacy matters.'

She stopped herself from giving him a potted version of her CV. She knew he was assessing her, wondering if she was up to the job. She didn't take it personally. In all her years working in media law, she had learned that celebrities always wanted the best, and that meant the partner with their name above the door. Of course, the figurehead was not necessarily the person most suited to the task, but it was the perception of getting the very best that was important.

'Well I guess we'd better make a start,' said Anna quickly. She didn't want to give him time to start questioning her suitability. She was under strict instructions to get the job done as speedily as possible. 'Maybe we should go somewhere private?' she added.

'Sure,' he said, stubbing out his cigarette. 'Come over to my stateroom.'

Anna hadn't been on many yachts, so she was surprised and a little disappointed to find that Sam Charles's grandly titled stateroom was just a rather compact bedroom. She sat down at the small desk and opened her notebook as Sam paced about, distracted and anxious.

'She called me twenty minutes ago, you know,' he said, running his hand through his damp dirty-blond hair.

For a minute she couldn't stop looking at him. She'd met models before who looked other-worldly, but that was because of their long, skinny bodies and their exaggerated features. But Sam's handsomeness, his flawless skin, the intense, extraordinary blueness of his eyes made him look a breed apart.

'Who?'

'Katie. The girl. She said she'd been talking to Blake Stanhope.'

Anna nodded. She could well have done without Stanhope's involvement, but with a story this big, it was only to be expected.

'What else did she say?'

'She demanded more money, can you believe that?'

'You didn't tell her to eff off again, did you?'

Sam chuckled, the atmosphere between them thawing a little. 'Not this time.'

He sat down on the bed.

'Okay, coach,' he said. 'What do we do now?'

His gaze unsettled her. In the small room, surrounded by sea, it felt too intimate to be professional.

'Now you tell me everything. From the beginning.'

He smiled. 'I was worried you were going to say that.'

Despite his reluctance, Sam told her as much as he could remember about his encounter with Katie. Every now and then Anna would stop him to ask for more detail, scribbling down notes as she went. As she listened, she asked herself how someone so good-looking and successful could be so stupid. But then she had seen this kind of behaviour dozens of times. Whether it was an actor or a sportsman or a singer, celebrities thought they were bulletproof; they didn't think normal rules applied to them. She wondered how many other women Sam had slept with. Actresses, extras, models, wives. It didn't matter that he had Jessica Carr, one of the world's most desirable women, waiting at home for him. The bottom line was always the same: they did it because they could.

'So you had penetrative sex with her?' she asked. She felt her face flush; she was glad the light on board was peachy and low.

Sam pulled a face. 'Yes. We had sex. Well, very probably. But it's worse than that.'

'Kinky sex?'

'No!' said Sam defensively. 'She's a hooker.'

'You paid her?'

'No. Yes. Well sort of. I gave her some money to get a cab home and for the hotel. I was trying to be nice.'

Anna frowned.

'So if you didn't pay her for sex, why do you say she's a hooker?'

'She told me when she phoned just now. She said she's worked as an escort in the past. That's not going to look good, is it?'

Anna shook her head. 'It isn't ideal, no.'

'What can we do?'

For a second he didn't look like the cocksure, arrogant celebrity she had pegged him down as.

'We get an injunction to stop publication of the story.'

'For libel? But I slept with her.'

'She has to prove it.'

'She's got a photo on her mobile that shows us in bed. Who knows when she took it? Probably after the tenth tequila.'

'Can I see it?'

He passed the mobile across.

'Well, it shows you in bed, it doesn't show you having sex. Anyway, we won't get an injunction to prevent the libel, we'll get a gagging order on the grounds of privacy.'

'Privacy? How does that work?'

'Well, you were in a private place. If someone took a picture

59

of your sister in bed without her consent, you'd be outraged, wouldn't you? Just because you're famous, it doesn't mean someone can invade your private space willy-nilly. Plus the story will have repercussions on your family life – the courts take that into consideration. You're not the only one who could be harmed by it.'

Sam looked more hopeful.

'So you think we'll get the order?'

'The defence could argue that they have to publish the story in the public interest because you're a celebrity, a role model, but they're unlikely to be successful.'

Anna scribbled on her pad, sketching out her strategy. It was the thing she loved best about the law. Deciding on the best course, storyboarding the way she wanted it all to go. As she drew up the plan, she began to feel more and more confident. Helen's idea to stall Katie had been clever. It had bought them some breathing space and a strong chance to get a gag in before Blake Stanhope could go to the papers.

'Do you really think we'll be able to stop all the media from reporting the story? Papers and TV and everything?' asked Sam.

'Actually I think it's better to stop her before she can even approach the media,' said Anna thoughtfully. 'Once the press get hold of the story they can be mischievous with the information even if they've been injuncted – blind stories, juxtaposing pictures and headlines. Ideally we want to avoid the media ever knowing about this story.'

'So we gag Katie?'

She nodded. 'And Blake Stanhope. I'd want to check this with counsel – the barrister we instruct – but I think it's the best way forward.'

'So you don't think the newspapers will know about it yet?'

She shook her head.

'If she was telling you the truth, Katie hasn't even met Blake yet. He'll want to see her supporting evidence and make sure she's completely legit. He'll also want to make sure she's not going to pull out at the last moment. After all, it's a big thing telling the world that you're a hooker. So I doubt he'll start approaching the media for at least twenty-four hours, probably longer. And the papers won't just print it either. First they'll have to meet Katie, take sworn affidavits, et cetera, et cetera. And by that time, she'll be gagged.'

Sam still looked troubled.

'But can we move quickly enough? I won't be able to get to London until Thursday.'

'Don't worry.' She smiled. 'You don't have to be in court. It's usually swarming with court reporters, so if it's privacy you're after, it kind of defeats the purpose you being there.'

She watched him thinking it through. She could sympathise; it was a scary thing to have your whole life hanging in the balance, even if he had brought this on himself.

Finally he looked at her. 'Thank you,' he said simply.

His words made her feel confident and flattered.

'You're welcome.'

Josh was hovering at the door.

'Miss Kennedy?' he said. 'The tender is here to take you to shore.'

She stood up and closed her notebook.

'So what do we do now?' asked Sam.

She smiled at him.

'I leave you here in beautiful Capri, go back to London and instruct counsel.'

'What time is your flight?'

'First flight out of Naples tomorrow morning. I'm going to instruct Nigel Keyes, a very brilliant QC I've worked with before, and I'll give him your witness statement. I'm confident we'll get the temporary injunction by close of play. Then we go back next week, see the judge and get it extended. But that's usually just a formality.'

Sam hesitated for a moment, then turned to Josh.

'Can you get the boat to wait for a few minutes?' he said, then, turning to Anna, 'Do you mind if I cadge a lift over with you?'

'Not at all. It's your boat.'

'I think it's some Italian billionaire's borrowed for the shoot.'

'I thought all movie stars had their own yachts.'

'I spent the money on tequila.'

She waited for him on the deck, watching a flock of starlings wheel and dip over the headland as the sun sank towards the pink horizon. When he emerged, he was wearing chinos and a white shirt with the sleeves rolled up. One of those simple thrown-together outfits that somehow looked perfect on truly beautiful people.

He's a client, Anna, she scolded herself. You shouldn't be getting all gooey-eyed over him. And he's a cheater too.

'Where are you staying?' asked Sam as he helped her down into the launch.

'Studio Rosso, wherever that might be. The firm's travel agent booked it. As you can imagine, there wasn't an awful lot of choice at twenty-four hours' notice when it's peak season in Capri.'

'Tell you what, I'll give you a lift. Giovanni, that's my driver, he knows every house on the island. He'll know your hotel and has probably dated the owner's daughter.'

As they slid over to the marina, Anna could see a stretch of pebbly beach dotted with umbrellas; the sun-worshippers in their sarongs and tiny Speedos were rolling their towels and packing up for the day. Sam led her along the jetty and across the road, where a deeply tanned man in his sixties was leaning against a bottle-green Mercedes sedan.

'Anna, Giovanni,' said Sam. 'Giovanni, this *bella signorina* is Anna. Do you think you could drop her off at her hotel, Studio Rosso?'

Giovanni grinned, revealing a set of amazingly white teeth. 'It would be my pleasure. It is on the other side of the island.'

'That's good,' said Anna. 'At least I'll get to see some of Capri on my whistle-stop visit.'

'Have you never been here before, *signorina*?' asked Giovanni over his shoulder as they set off at breakneck speed.

'No, I wish.'

With the pressure of work, Anna hadn't had a proper holiday in over eighteen months. Her romance with Andrew had been sprinkled with mini-breaks to Prague, Dublin and Rome; they'd both worked as hard as each other, trying to scramble up the career ladder as fast as they could, but they had still found time for pleasure. As a single girl, there seemed less point taking two weeks off to spend it alone.

'In that case, I think we need Giovanni's pat-pending island tour,' said Sam.

'*Bellissimo*,' beamed Giovanni. 'I envy you, *signorina*, you get to see Capri for the first time.'

Anna laughed. 'That sounds good.'

The car pulled away up the hill towards Anacapri, the sprawling village at the top of the island. The windows were wound down, flooding the car with pine-scented air. Anna got a feel for the island immediately. It was lush but craggy – the sharp edges of the cliffs would suddenly jut up to the sky, then plummet down to the sea, their sides softened by green trees and bougainvillaea. Each villa they passed seemed more perfect than the last, each twist of the road revealed another ravishing view, and everything seemed old and crumbly and yet smart and elegant at the same time. Along the way Sam pointed out the sights of Capri – down the cliffs towards the Blue Grotto, the Faraglioni rocks, the San Giacomo monastery – with the confidence and affection of someone who had spent a lot of time on the island.

He leaned forward and tapped Giovanni on the shoulder.

'Can you stop here a moment?'

They pulled up in a dusty lay-by and Sam led Anna to a gap in the low boundary wall.

'Come on,' he said, offering her his hand. They shuffled carefully down a short, narrow path, brushing between bushes and emerging in a small clearing on the edge of a cliff.

Anna's eyes opened wide. They could see all the way down to the Marina Grande with its bustling pastel-coloured houses and smart schooners bumping against fishing boats. Beyond that, the jade and turquoise-marbled sea stretched across to the Bay of Naples, where she could see Mount Vesuvius rearing up on the mainland.

'Brilliant, isn't it?' Sam smiled, sitting next to Anna on a rock. 'It's hard not to feel like Cary Grant when you're up here.'

She looked at him in surprise. For some reason she hadn't expected Sam to feel the same rush of excitement about being here, that same love of old-school Hollywood glamour.

He pulled a pack of cigarettes out of his pocket and lit one.

'Can I bum a smoke?' she asked.

He grinned. 'Sorry for not offering. I thought I was the last of the smokers.'

They huddled like co-conspirators around his lighter's flame.

'I love the romance of this place,' said Anna, inhaling. The scent of tar tangled with the heady floral aroma from some honeysuckle. 'And I'm not leaving before I have a go in one of those convertible taxis, just so I can feel like Ava Gardner.'

'Well, you look the part,' he said, eyeing her navy pencil skirt and white shirt up and down.

She laughed nervously.

He blew a smoke ring. 'Jess likes bling,' he said quietly. 'The yachts, the private jets, all that conspicuous consumption, but I've never been able to get her to sit through *To Catch a Thief* and she probably thinks Fellini is a type of shoe.'

He gave her a sideways glance.

'You think I'm an arsehole, don't you?'

'I'm not here to judge you,' said Anna. 'I'm here to help you.'

He shrugged.

'I realise that most people think I should be doing cartwheels to be living with one of the most beautiful, successful women in America, but . . . well, I don't. I feel trapped. Being an actor is the only thing we have in common. Look, I'm not making excuses for having sex with that girl, but . . .' He gave Anna a look that indicated he wanted to say more. 'Sorry,' he laughed. 'I suppose I should be telling this to my shrink, not my lawyer.'

'Don't worry, I get it a lot,' said Anna. 'I've been thinking about having a couch put in my office.'

It was true: one thing celebrities, captains of industry and sports stars liked to do was offload their problems, to 'over-share', as they said on the American talk shows. Anna could sympathise – they were usually in trouble, after all – but she suspected it was usually less to do with introspection and more to do with a desire to talk about themselves. She looked at Sam, wondering if what he was saying was true. Maybe he was in a loveless relationship with Jessica. Or maybe it was something he had convinced himself into believing after he had slept with Katie, a way to justify an action he knew was wrong. One thing her line of work had taught her was that men didn't have to be unhappy with their partners to cheat on them.

Uncomfortably, her thoughts strayed to the night she had found her own boyfriend, the man she had trusted, in bed with her sister. She remembered Andrew's protestations that it wasn't how it looked, how it meant nothing, how it would never happen again. But that had been a lie too, hadn't it?

When Andrew had finally admitted that he was in love with Sophie, she had understood it. She understood that it was easy to fall in love with Sophie. Whether it was her beauty, her lusciousness, her slightly helpless charm, everyone who ever met her was pulled into her whirlpool.

What Anna could not understand, what had been so painful and made her feel completely stupid, was when Andrew had admitted that he was no longer in love with her, that the spark had gone from their relationship and she no longer made him happy.

Anna didn't know Jessica Carr and certainly had no idea how she felt about Sam. But she knew one thing: no one deserved to be in a one-sided relationship.

'If you really want to talk about it, can I give you some advice?' she said finally.

'What?'

She hesitated before she spoke.

'Think about why it happened in the first place. If you're miserable with Jessica, then maybe you should end it, not sleep with someone and then get an injunction to protect your relationship.'

'What? So now you don't want to get the gagging order?'

'I never said that,' she said, feeling a tremor of hostility. 'I just meant that if you're unhappy, you should change things to make yourself happy.'

Sam's cheeks flamed.

'It's not that easy, though, is it?'

Anna shrugged.

'It doesn't have to be this difficult.'

He turned and got back into the car without speaking. Anna silently cursed herself, knowing she had overstepped the mark. She knew she shouldn't let her personal experiences colour her professional actions.

They drove on through the island, each looking out of their own side of the car, the upbeat mood all but evaporated. Finally they entered Capri Town, where Giovanni stopped beside the bustling Piazzetta.

'Studio Rosso is down there,' he said, pointing towards a warren of back streets. 'Keeping going straight ahead and you'll see it. Tell Consuela I said *ciao*.'

'Thanks, Giovanni,' said Anna, climbing out. Just as she was about to close the door, Sam leaned forward.

'Hey, are you hungry?'

'Yes,' she said, a little too quickly.

'There's a fantastic restaurant just down there called La Capannina. All the greats have been there: Sinatra, Loren.' He smiled. 'You said you wanted your own Ava Gardner moment.'

She was glad they were back on civil terms, but she felt a pang of disappointment that he wasn't offering to accompany her. What did you expect, she thought to herself, a movie star wanting to go out for dinner with you?

'I'd come with you,' he said, as if reading her mind, 'but I think that being seen in one of Europe's busiest tourist spots with a pretty girl who is not my fiancée might get me in more trouble than I am already in.'

Anna laughed.

'See?' she said. 'You're learning.'

His expression became more serious, his blue eyes searching hers.

'Will you call me as soon as you're out of court? We can't let them publish this, Anna.'

She knew she was being played, knew her first assessment of Sam had been correct: he was an operator. Celebrities were good at making you feel as if you were the most important person in the world so you would go the extra mile to oblige them.

'I'll do my best,' she said and closed the door, waving as the car pulled away. She knew Sam Charles was probably a terrible

66

rogue with a string of girls in every port. She knew he had probably lied about what had happened with that girl Katie. She knew at the very least that he was a first-class actor.

Even so, as she turned to walk down the cobbled street, Anna couldn't help feeling that helping him was the most important thing in her life.

8

'Home sweet home,' called Larry, opening the door of his Cheyne Walk townhouse. He put his bag on the marble floor and breathed in the familiar smell – flowers, polish, coffee. Home. He'd never noticed how particular and comforting his house smelled until he'd spent five days in hospital. Five days? Had it only been five days? It had felt much longer. But then he couldn't remember a time when he'd actually stopped and thought about things for more than a few minutes. Sometimes, he'd discovered to his surprise, it was good to slow down and smell the roses every now and then.

Loralee bustled in behind him, taking his arm and leading him up the stairs to the master bedroom, handling him as if he was an infirm geriatric.

'Now you sit there on the bed and I'll get Irina to cook some lunch,' she said.

'Great idea, I couldn't stand all that tasteless muck in hospital. What about a nice steak?'

Loralee shook her head, her honey-blond hair swaying.

'No steak. The doctor said you've got to cut down on your cholesterol; we're switching to steamed vegetables and pulses until you're stronger.'

Larry groaned. 'How do they expect me to get stronger on that hippy swill? Well, what about a quick stiffener before lunch?'

'Oh no,' said Loralee, frowning. 'There will be no more booze either. One glass of red wine a day, that's good for the heart apparently. But strictly no spirits.'

'What is this, the bloody Gulag?' he spluttered.

She walked over and stroked his hair back.

'Come on now,' she said softly. 'We've got to look after you. We came so close to losing you, isn't it worth making a few little sacrifices?'

Sacrifices, he thought, it's all right for you to say, you're not the one making them. But instead he gave her a weak smile.

'Whatever you say, old girl.'

'Good.' She smiled, turning towards the dressing room. 'I've got to get out of these clothes, I smell of hospital.'

The dressing room was an indulgence Loralee had insisted on when she'd moved into the house eighteen months earlier. Larry had spent £100,000 knocking the master bedroom through into the second bedroom on this floor to create a giant climate-controlled space that his new wife soon spent an equivalent amount filling with shoes, dresses and bags.

'Oh, I forgot to mention,' she called from inside, 'Matt rang you this morning. He wanted to pop round once you were home.'

Larry felt a wave of happiness.

'Oh good,' he said, trying not to sound too pleased. He was well aware that Loralee wasn't overly fond of his son. 'When's he coming?'

'Well I told him today probably wasn't a good day.'

'Why not?'

'I said you'd be busy.'

'Busy?' he spat. 'I've retired, remember? The day is yawning ahead of me like a bloody unfilled tooth.'

Cheeky cow, he had a good mind to call Matthew up right now. He was sure he could feel his blood pressure rising again.

Okay, breathe, he told himself, massaging his chest as he stared out of the window towards the Thames and the tethered spikes of the Albert Bridge. He'd been bullish about the booze, but the truth was he really didn't want to go through anything like the last week again. After forty years in the fast lane, he'd managed to convince himself that he was pretty indestructible. Well, you got that wrong, didn't you, old son? Despite the balminess of the late afternoon he shivered. He knew that after such a close brush with death, people were often reinvigorated and liberated, grateful for a second chance. But instead he just felt hollow and lonely.

Loralee was humming to herself in the next room, just a little girl playing dressing up. Larry was under no illusions about his new wife, but he knew she cared about him. Was that enough to sustain him in his retirement? And the bigger question: what the hell was he going to do now?

The last few months had gone past in a blur of snap decisions: marriage, giving up the firm, reaching out to Matthew. They had all seemed like good ideas at the time, but they had left him with an aching hole to fill. The thought of there being no work to do, no meetings to go to, no phone calls to take, it all made his stomach churn.

What did people *do* when they were retired? Play golf? You might as well go down to the funeral parlour and pick out a headstone now.

In truth, it had been the death of his first wife Katherine that had made Larry reconsider his position. It had been more of a jolt than he'd liked to admit. In his mind, Katherine was still the young, vivacious girl he'd fallen in love with over forty years before. People as energetic and vital as Katherine Donovan didn't just keel over, did they? He looked down at the bruise on his arm where the nurses had attached his drip, and had to reflect that perhaps they did.

That was why he had given up work, that was why he had handed the firm over to Matty. He simply wanted to make amends for the way he had treated his first wife and his son. The two things had dovetailed together to make the perfect solution. Well, almost perfect. Loralee had been furious, despite the fact that they had more money than they could spend. But then how much would ever be enough for an ambitious young woman like Loralee? He looked up in surprise as he heard his wife's voice.

'*This* was why I said you'd be busy,' she purred. She was standing at the entrance to the dressing room, one arm draped on the door frame. She was naked except for stilettos, stockings and suspenders, plus a tiny white apron that skimmed her breasts and thighs and a nurse's hat perched at a jaunty angle, like a drunken sailor. 'I thought you might need some TLC.'

She walked slowly, seductively over to the bottom of the bed and crawled up towards him, as lithe as a panther.

'The consultant said you had to start taking regular exercise,' she growled, pushing him back on to the pillows and beginning to undo his shirt buttons. 'I think I've got just what the doctor ordered.'

He reached up, feeling the soft, smooth curve of her buttocks.

'Ooh, Mr Donovan, you mustn't,' she giggled.

Larry was grateful to feel his cock stiffen. Not bad for a sixty-five-year-old just out of hospital and on beta blockers, he smiled to himself. And all thoughts of calling his son drifted away.

9

'Excuse me? Could we just pull the sheet up a couple more inches?' said Matthew, feeling his cheeks redden. 'The, um, buttocks are in breach again, I'm afraid.'

The director made a sour face, but flapped his hand to an assistant, who scurried over to the bed and gently pulled the white sheet up Erica Sheldon's back. Matthew puffed his cheeks out and tried not to stare at the long expanse of tanned skin, the slim neck, the spray of deep red hair falling across the pillow. Christ, she was gorgeous.

In normal circumstances, of course, Matthew would have relished the opportunity to inspect the body of one of the world's most beautiful actresses at close quarters, but this was not normal. Surreal, bizarre, horribly embarrassing, yes. But normal? No. He was here on a sound stage at Shepperton Studios as Erica's lawyer to make sure the nudity clause of her contract was followed to the letter – and he couldn't get it wrong. It was his first real task as a partner at Donovan Pierce and he was determined not to screw it up, however far he was out of his comfort zone. He suspected, of course, that this was Helen Pierce's idea of a joke: the media law equivalent of sending the new apprentice to the store for a glass hammer or a bucket of steam. She was testing him, showing him she was in charge, so he wasn't going to give her the satisfaction of getting anything wrong. He had memorised the clause: which underwear Erica was allowed to appear in – 'tanga, brief or standard bikini, not G-string' – where the sex scenes were allowed to take place – bedroom, hallway, not bathroom unless obscured by shower curtain – and, in this case, exactly how many millimetres of 'gluteus maximus indentation' could be revealed.

Matthew had always been annoyed by legalese, the insistence on using impenetrable long-winded language when plain English would have been just as accurate. 'You may show the lower back but not the upper crease of the bottom', for example, would have been much clearer if they had simply put 'no arse crack'. He began to smile at the idea.

'Everything all right?'

Matthew looked up suddenly. Erica Sheldon was speaking to him. From a bed. Naked.

'Fine, yes,' he said quickly.

'Are we good to go here?' she asked, her expression serious.

'Yes,' said Matthew, clearing his throat. 'Good to go.'

'Just a hint of ass, right?' she added playfully.

Matthew gave her a thumbs-up, then realised what a dork he must look and turned away, cursing himself.

The scene was short, nailed on the second take, and as Erica and her leading man had writhed beneath the sheets, Matt was convinced that her modesty had been preserved throughout.

He watched as the actress climbed off the bed and allowed herself to be helped into a white robe. She caught him looking at her and Matthew made a show of putting the contract back into his briefcase and preparing to leave.

'Thanks for doing that.' She smiled, tying her hair back in a ponytail. 'I know it's a pain for you, but you wouldn't believe what some directors try to get away with.'

'Just watching your back,' he said.

She looked at him for a second and then laughed.

'Funny,' she said. 'I thought you lawyers were always serious.'

'Laugh a minute, that's us.'

'Really?'

'No, not really. You're right, most of us are actually deathly dull.'

'Gee, you're really selling yourself to me,' quipped the actress.

'Sorry,' said Matthew. 'It's just I'm not used to doing nude scenes.'

She giggled. 'Not *quite* a nude scene, thanks to your eagle eye.'

'Well, I think we got it just right. Enough coverage to protect your modesty. Just enough to get the audience going.'

'Get the audience going?' she chided.

'I didn't mean it like that. Not in any porno way.'

'*Porno?*'

'Not porno. Obviously not porno. Look, I'm sorry . . .'

She started to chuckle, her broad smile lighting up her face.

'Really, you English guys are funny.'

'Funny with bad teeth. All the clichés are true.'

'Your teeth look pretty good to me.'

Were they flirting? he wondered, snapping his briefcase hurriedly shut.

An officious-looking girl approached them. 'Ms Sheldon, the car's here to take you home.'

'Sure, just give me a minute,' she said, never taking her amused eyes from Matthew.

'Do you live around here?' he asked, hoping to deflect her probing gaze.

'Santa Barbara, actually, so no.'

'Actually I meant . . .'

'I know, I'm just teasing,' she said. 'I'm renting a house in Richmond. It's pretty handy for the studios, lovely garden.'

'Oh, whereabouts? I don't live far from Richmond myself,' he said, feeling himself slip into dinner-party mode.

'At the top of the hill, by the park. Say, are you going home now?'

Matt looked at his watch. There wasn't much point going back to the office. 'I suppose I will. I can do some work from there.'

'Workaholic, huh?'

'Actually I'm new at the firm, so I'm desperately trying to do extra homework, trying to keep up.'

'You need a ride, then? I'm going that way.'

Matthew opened his eyes wide.

'Me? In your car?'

She laughed and nodded slowly, like she was trying to explain something difficult to a child.

'Yes, in my car. I promise not to bite. Just wait while I change, okay?'

He willed himself to keep calm. After all, this was what he did now. Meeting celebrities was all in a day's work. If he melted at the first sign of someone he'd seen on the telly, there was no way he was going to be able to do the job.

Erica emerged from her trailer wearing skinny jeans, an open-necked navy polo shirt and ballet flats. She was carrying a crocodile-skin handbag in the crook of her arm and had sunglasses on top of her head. If possible, she looked even more sexy in casual clothes than when she was only wearing a sheet.

'Come on, funny guy,' she said with a wink, and led him across to a black Mercedes.

Matthew quickly jumped forward to open the door for her.

'We'll drop my friend off first, okay?' she told the driver. 'Where are we going?'

Matthew gave his address in Chiswick.

Sitting back in the leather seats, he watched as Erica rummaged around in her bag for her BlackBerry, then, finding it, switched it off.

'I hate that thing,' she said, dropping it back in the bag. 'It's like one of those horrible yappy dogs, always wanting your attention.'

She looked at him with those amused eyes again.

'So, Mr Lawyer . . .'

'Matthew, please. Matthew Donovan,' he said, offering an awkward hand to shake.

'I guess we should be introduced now you've seen my ass, huh?'

'I believe that is the proper etiquette, yes.' Matthew smiled.

They made small talk as the car zigzagged through the back streets from Shepperton to Chiswick.

'Okay, Matthew, so you're new to the firm, how come it's got your name above the door?'

'Long story. It was my father's firm.'

'So where were you before?'

Matthew shook his head.

'You won't have heard of the company.'

'Try me. I've sued a few of your tabloids before.'

'Actually it wasn't a media law firm, it was a family practice, so now I specialise in Donovan Pierce's contractual stuff plus divorce matters for high-profile clients.'

'Then you should actually speak to a friend of mine,' said Erica thoughtfully.

'Marital problems?'

She smiled sadly.

'Something like that. Have you got a card?'

'Yes, of course.' He pulled out one of his brand-new Donovan Pierce business cards and handed it to her. 'That's actually the first one I've given out.'

'Well then I shall treasure it,' she said, putting it into her bag. 'Must make you cynical, huh, dealing with love's great fallout every day.'

'Love sucks.'

'I don't know about that. My ex-husband was a jerk, but I live in hope.'

All too soon, the car pulled up outside his flat. Erica was looking up and down the deserted street.

'So what's Chiswick like for a night out?'

'Well, there're a few great places but nowhere that could compete with your social life.'

'You mean the red-carpet premieres, the gala dinners, the fashion shows, all those glittering events you see me attending?'

'Yes, those.'

'I go where I'm forced, contractually. Where you have to starve for weeks to be squashed into some sparkly gown, then make small talk all night with the most ruthless people on earth. You can keep it. Give me a burger and a beer any time.'

'Well, beer we can do in Old Blighty,' said Matthew.

'Here . . .' she said, reaching into her bag. 'My number. If you ever want to show an out-of-towner the giddy sights of Chiswick.'

He looked down at the card. It was like he was having an out-of-body experience. Erica Sheldon had just handed him her number.

'Are you serious?'

'Beats watching another movie on Blu-ray.'

Matthew stood outside his apartment block and watched the black Mercedes disappear down the street. For a moment he looked down at the card still clutched in his hand and a schoolboy grin spread across his face. Erica Sheldon. The biggest film star in the world wanted to go out with him. *Him*.

He glanced at himself in the reflection of a car. Matt was not vain in the slightest, but he had been teased so often about his good looks, by ex-girlfriends, by his old secretary, that he almost believed in them. But while his even features, thick dark hair and sporty physique had ensured a steady stream of gorgeous women at Cambridge, he was still no way a match for a movie star.

He shoved the business card into his pocket and let himself into the flat, a small two-bedroom apartment that overlooked the river. He chucked his keys on the kitchen counter and opened the fridge for a beer.

Sitting back on the sofa, he slugged back his lager and put his feet up on the coffee table.

Maybe it *was* time to start dating, he told himself, staring absently out on to the water. He was sure Erica's offer was just a friendly gesture, but what a place to start. At thirty-three, Matthew's social life had shrunk to almost nothing. After his divorce, the friends he'd made as a couple had been unwilling to pick sides, and had slowly vanished off the radar, while his good mates from university had started disappearing into family life just as he had done following his own marriage seven years earlier. Every few months he'd be invited to a barbeque or a dinner party, where almost inevitably there would be a couple of single girls dangled in front of him, complete with raised eyebrows and gentle shoves. And yes, he'd slept with a few of them, but the truth was, he'd been so battered by his ex-wife's betrayal that his heart wasn't in anything more serious than no-strings sex.

He touched Erica's card with one fingertip. Maybe he should call her. After all, she was nice. For a Hollywood star. He smiled to himself at how ridiculous that sounded. She was one of *People* magazine's Most Beautiful People. She earned upwards of fifteen million dollars per annum. Which meant that what she had earned for that minute-long arse-crack scene today was more than he took home in a year.

The growl of the intercom made him jump. He frowned. The only people who usually rang his doorbell were pizza delivery boys.

'Yes?' he said, pressing the button.

'It's Carla,' said the tinny voice.

He was completely thrown by the sound of his ex-wife's voice.

'Can I come up?' she pressed.

Carla never visited him. When their son Jonas came to stay, Matthew picked him up and dropped him off at the beautiful Notting Hill home that Carla shared with her second husband. They had a cordial but remote relationship, which was the way he liked it, because he wasn't sure if he could ever forgive her for what she had done.

There was a rap on the door and Matt slipped Erica's card back into his pocket before he opened it.

'Hi, Matt,' Carla said softly. 'How are you?'

She looked beautiful and more casual than usual, in a white summer dress, her honey-blond hair pulled back into a simple ponytail. From the moment he had first seen her in a crowded bar in Fulham, she'd always had the power to floor him with her beauty.

'You heard about Larry?'

He'd tried to contact her about Larry's heart attack the day it had happened. After all, Larry was Jonas's grandfather, and although the two of them had only met a handful of times, Matt had decided to let his ex-wife know. He had got through to Carla's voicemail and she had yet to call him back about it. Matt could only suppose it was the purpose of her visit.

'How is he?' she said briskly.

'He leaves hospital today, although he's got to watch out for another attack.'

'I was sorry to hear about it.'

Matthew looked at her carefully. Larry's illness was clearly not the reason she was here. As he scanned her face, he noticed that her eyes were rimmed pink. He had a stab of panic about his son.

'Carla, what's wrong? Where's Jonas?'

'Don't worry. Jonas is fine. Although I've been better.'

She wrapped her thin, sinewy arms around her body. She had slimmed down since they had lived together and she was groomed and styled immaculately. The perfect little millionaire's wife, he thought, immediately regretting the childishness. Then again, he knew he was still bitter. The night he had found out about Carla's affair still felt like yesterday. He remembered waving her off on a girls' night out. He remembered how she had forgotten her mobile and how he had seen it chirping on the breakfast bar, an insistent text message waiting to be answered. So he'd opened the message just to stop the noise. *My bed is still warm from you, when can you get away again? Dxx*

And just like that, his marriage, the stable family life he had always craved, was over.

'Can I get you anything?' he asked, walking over to the kitchen. 'Drink?'

'Coffee. One of your specials.'

He'd had so little contact with Carla's life in the last few years, but still there was this code between them. He guessed four years of marriage did that to you.

He brewed up a mug using the shiny chrome single-guy coffee machine and took it through to the living room. Carla was standing by his bookcase, looking at a framed photograph of her and Jonas lying in the sand cracking up with laughter. He knew it wasn't the done thing to keep photos of your ex-wife this long after the divorce, but well, it was a great picture, especially of Jonas. He'd been so excited to be on holiday.

She looked around at him and he could see that her eyes were full of tears. 'We look so happy there,' she managed, before her face crumpled and she was sobbing. He walked over and put an awkward arm around her shoulders.

'What's up?' he said gently. 'What is it?'

'David's left me.' Her words were almost inaudible among the sobs. 'He's left me.'

*My bed is still warm from you, when can you get away again?
Dxx*

David. A Notting Hill banker and a former client who'd invited Matt and Carla to his Christmas party after his divorce had been finalised. Six months later, Matt had found out that David and Carla had been having an affair from that very night. When he'd finally confronted her, Carla was defiant, telling Matthew that for all his desire to escape his father's influence, he had turned into him, devoting more time to his work than his family.

'Jonas barely knows you,' she had said with a brutality that was designed to wound.

She'd left him that night and moved straight into David's house, taking Jonas with her. The next day she'd delivered the *coup de grâce* by serving divorce papers on him, citing his 'unreasonable behaviour'.

For three years Matthew had hated David, funnelling all his anger and hurt on to the man who had taken his family away. He'd tried to step away from it, but it was always there in the back of his mind, colouring everything he did. Carla and Jonas were the real reason he had taken the job at Donovan Pierce. It was an opportunity to make some real money; money that would bring him back his pride, money that would pay for the best schools and holidays for Jonas. His son would want for nothing and he would pay for it. He'd hated David giving his family the security and comfort his ex-wife had always wanted. Donovan Pierce was the chance to level the playing field, make him David's equal.

Except David had gone. Matthew took a deep breath. How long he had wanted to hear those words. The banker with the smart house, the fast car, the fortune, the man who had turned Carla's head and taken his son. But somehow, now it had come, the victory felt hollow.

'Have you got a tissue?' sniffed Carla.

He gave her a piece of kitchen roll.

'Don't worry, Jonas is with a friend,' she said, blowing her nose and taking a seat on the sofa.

'And where's David?'

'Fucking his new girlfriend, probably,' she said with surprising venom.

Matthew resisted the urge to laugh. Carla had always been very against swearing, scolding him whenever he had uttered an expletive.

'He's having an affair?' he asked.

She snorted.

'Predictable, isn't it? And don't say "I told you so".'

'I wasn't going to.'

'I wouldn't blame you for doing cartwheels right now,' she said, more tears rolling down her face. 'I know I screwed up, but I didn't know where else to go.'

Matthew took the coffee cup and pressed it into Carla's unsteady hands.

'I need you, Matt,' she said, and he felt something deep inside him flutter.

'You need me?'

'You're a family lawyer.'

'You want me to advise you?' he asked, sitting down beside her.

'Why not? You're the best.'

He shrugged.

'I'm afraid that doesn't matter. I can't do it. It's a conflict of interests. Besides, are you sure this is what you want?'

It was a question he always asked his clients: 'Are you sure?'

She frowned.

'I know you're hurt at the moment, but you really need to be sure that divorce is the right way to go for you.'

He couldn't believe he was asking her to think about it, when all he had wanted for the last three years was for her to walk out on David. The truth was, he wanted to hear her say it.

'Yes, I want to divorce him,' said Carla, taking a small sip of her coffee. 'And I want to take him for every penny he's got.'

'Tell me what happened, from the start.'

'You really want to know?' She smiled weakly. 'If you can't represent me, what's this? Free advice?'

'Something like that.'

'Thank you,' she said, as she moved across the sofa and hugged him. 'Really, Matt, it's far more than I deserve.'

He froze for a moment, then hugged her back, smelling her hair, that same familiar scent of happier days.

'Right then,' he said, grabbing a notepad and a pen. 'From the beginning . . .'

He sat back down on the chair ready to hear her story, Erica Sheldon's phone number in his pocket well and truly forgotten.

10

'So is this injunction locked down or not? 'Cos from where I'm sitting, it looks like you're just sitting on your keisters over there.'

Sitting in the barrister's chambers, Anna looked at the computer screen wishing that Skype conference calling hadn't been invented. Not only could she hear Jim Parker calling from five thousand miles away in LA, but now she could see him. And Jim Parker really didn't look happy. She glanced over at Sam and Nigel Keyes, their QC. They didn't look over the moon either.

'As you know, Mr Parker, we arranged the temporary injunction last week, so we're here in court today to get everything finalised by close of play. We can't go any quicker than we are already going.'

'Sure, yeah,' snapped Parker. 'Meanwhile this hooker and her shyster PR guy are talking to the papers.'

Anna clenched her fists. Up until now she had been dealing with Sam's straight-talking manager Eli Cohen. Eli was old-school, he understood the process and trusted Donovan Pierce to deliver. Jim Parker, Sam's agent, on the other hand, seemed to think lawyers were slightly below criminals in terms of trustworthiness.

'The temporary injunction does gag them, Mr Parker,' said Anna. 'But obviously we'll all be happier when it's formalised.'

'And you can guarantee me this will kill the story dead?'

Anna exhaled, trying to keep her cool. She suspected that this was just Hollywood power play – Parker was flexing his muscle in front of his client, showing Sam that he was prepared to fight his corner, even if these Limeys weren't.

'There are no guarantees,' said Anna patiently. 'Last week's application was an *ex parte* injunction, which means Blake and Katie weren't in court. Today they'll be there with their lawyers. But still, today should be just a formality.'

'Don't give me a *formality*,' sneered Parker, his voice crackling through the speaker. 'There's always ways to fuck with people. It's what I do for a living.'

'With respect, Mr Parker, this is the British judicial system . . .'

'Cut the crap,' said Parker. 'I want a result. I want it by the end of the day. You call me as soon as you get that gagging order in your hands, okay? And Sam?'

'Yes, Jim?'

'You let me know if there's anything you need. I'm always at the end of the line for you, you hear?'

'Thanks, Jim.'

The screen went blank and Anna let out a silent sigh. Nigel Keyes QC raised a bushy grey eyebrow.

'Well, I think Mr Parker's position is clear,' he said, rising. 'Let's go and appease our American friends then, shall we?'

'Could you just give us a moment?' Anna said, glancing at Sam.

'Of course,' Nigel replied. 'I'll be outside.'

When he had closed the door, Anna turned to Sam.

'Sorry about that,' he said. 'Jim can be a little abrasive at times. I think he's just worried about getting this nailed down.'

Sam's skin still had a deep glow, having returned from Capri a few days earlier. But the actor looked far from relaxed.

'It's only natural to be anxious at times like this,' said Anna. 'But what I said was true, it really is only a formality. I have done lots of injunctions like this; if a judge is prepared to grant a temporary gagging order, there's no reason for him to change his mind about the permanent one.'

Sam nodded, but he didn't look reassured.

'Well, there's nothing else we can do now,' he said, standing. 'I'll push off so long as you call me the second it's done.'

'Of course.'

She felt for him, but she was confident that his worries were unfounded. The important thing was that he understood how close he had come to disaster. Experience told her that some clients never learned their lesson, but she suspected that this episode had put Sam Charles off parties and tequila for life.

'Did you tell Jessica?' she asked suddenly. She still didn't approve of his unfaithfulness, of course, but she felt invested in his future. She wanted him to do the right thing.

'No, I bloody didn't,' he said, looking at her incredulously.

'But what about the chat we had in Capri? About you being happy?'

'Anna, I hired you to sort this out and keep it quiet,' he said, a note of anger in his voice. 'Yes, I made a mistake, but I don't plan on making it again, so why rock the boat?'

She held up her hands.

'I'm on your side, Sam.'

'I know, and I'm grateful for everything. But I just want to put this behind me.'

'Of course, I understand.' She paused, thinking of something else to say. She knew that this was probably the last time she would see him.

'Well, I'd better get off to court,' she said briskly, moving towards the door. 'I'll call you the moment it's over.'

Suddenly he stepped in front of her.

'Look, can I take you for lunch?' he said. 'To say thank you when it's all done, a little celebration? I can book a table for one o'clock and I can get a car to take you back to work.'

Her heart began to hammer. After their night in Capri, when their taxi ride had made her feel happy and heady, she had convinced herself that it was just Sam's star quality pulling her into its tractor beam. But the truth was, she was attracted to him. It was impossible not to be. You're such a cliché, she chided herself.

'Lunch?' she said vaguely, playing for time.

'You know, the meal between breakfast and dinner.'

Get a grip, girl. Say yes.

'Okay.' She had to stop herself from laughing. 'Just a quick one. That would be lovely.'

'You can even bill me for it, if it means you won't be running off after an hour.'

She smiled.

'I might hold you to that.'

The Royal Courts of Justice, situated at the far end of the Strand, were housed in a huge Gothic wedding cake of a building a short walk from Nigel's chambers. Anna trotted after him, her long stride still struggling to keep up with the six-foot-five barrister. As he walked, Nigel chatted cheerily about the case and the judge, who was an old friend of his, every now and then glancing around to make sure Anna was keeping up. It was only a small gesture, but for Anna it separated Nigel from the rest of the pack. The law was certainly better than it used to be, but there was still a macho, old-boy superior culture hidden under the long black gowns. Half the time barristers thought solicitors – and particularly female solicitors – were the hired help, just there to carry the files and get them coffee, even though she was effectively their boss, having instructed them to do the job.

I bet they don't treat Helen Pierce like that, thought Anna ruefully. She wouldn't want to be in their shoes if they did.

At court, they filed in through the scanning machines, and into the huge vaulted foyer lined with oil paintings of judicial luminaries. As a student, Anna used to come down here and watch the trials. They had twice the reality and drama of the soap operas that transfixed most students, and she still felt that excitement whenever she stepped inside.

It's just a formality; that was what she had said to Jim Parker, and she had meant it. The UK privacy laws protected a celebrity's indiscretions if they were hidden behind closed doors, and there was no reason for a judge to challenge that. Even so, there was a lot riding on this. Not only Sam's reputation, but her own standing at the firm. It would be a big win – a few more like this and she could make partner by Christmas.

'What court are we in?' asked Nigel, his bespoke brogues tapping up the marble staircase. 'Eight, isn't it?'

But Anna wasn't listening. Waiting outside the courtroom with Blake Stanhope was Martin Bond QC. She groaned inwardly. It had to be him, didn't it? she thought.

At thirty-six, Martin Bond was one of the youngest silks on the circuit; public school, arrogant, entitled, he had asked Anna out for dinner almost immediately her break-up with Andrew had become public knowledge. Even if she hadn't felt so emotionally raw, she would have turned him down anyway: she found him unbearably patronising and self-important. Evidently Martin had not forgotten her rejection, and made a point of making her life difficult every time their paths crossed.

'Moving up in the world, aren't we, Anna?' he said with a sly grin as she walked up. 'Come to play with the big boys?'

'Big boy, Martin?' she said. 'That's not what I've heard.'

She saw with satisfaction that the barb had hit its target, but immediately cursed herself. Much as she liked to puncture his pomposity, it was a bad policy to upset opposing counsel just as you were going into court.

She took her seat in a wooden pew behind Nigel just as Judge Baker swished in through a back door, his black cape billowing behind him like Batman, a small red collar around his neck indicating he was from the High Court's Queen's Bench division.

A handful of people were sitting on the back row, including a blonde woman Anna recognised as a court reporter for one of the broadsheets.

'We request that the court be cleared,' said Nigel, standing and opening his file.

The judge knew the form; injunction matters were private. He nodded towards the court usher, who made sure the room was empty except for those directly involved.

As they shuffled out, Anna turned her attention to the pretty girl sitting next to her solicitor on the other side of the courtroom. Katie Grey, I presume, she thought, surprised. She had imagined a busty blonde, someone who had overpowered Sam with her overt sexuality, but this girl looked like a redhead version of Grace Kelly: glacial and elegant in a grey dress, hair tucked back behind her ears like a choir-girl. And she was certainly beautiful, she noted with a pang of disappointment.

'Well, here we are again,' said Judge Baker, peering at them over his half-moon glasses. It was Friday afternoon and he looked as if he'd had enough. By five o'clock he'd be on the golf course in Surrey.

Nigel Keyes rose to his feet and cleared his throat.

'My lord, we are here today to request that the injunction against Blake Stanhope and Katie Grey be continued on the grounds of privacy on the terms pursuant to the temporary injunction granted last week.'

Anna wondered where Sam would take her for lunch. She hoped it would be somewhere discreet. Then again, maybe somewhere press-friendly – the Ivy, Le Caprice – was a more obvious statement that this was a business meeting. She forced her thoughts to stop drifting as Martin Bond stood up.

'This injunction has been sought on the grounds of privacy, m'lord. And yet it strikes me that if Mr Charles was so concerned with his private life, he wouldn't have had sexual intercourse with Miss Grey in the first place.'

Arrogant shit, thought Anna, watching Martin smile smarmily at the judge.

'This case isn't about intrusion of privacy,' he continued. 'This injunction is about preserving Mr Charles's popularity and therefore his commercial worth. His sexual encounter with Miss Grey, which, may I add, involved him taking large amounts of alcohol, will not play well with the public, especially Mr Charles's substantial fan base in conservative parts of the United States. Mr Charles clearly wants to do everything in his considerable power to keep the Hollywood studios happy and to preserve his boy-next-door popularity. He is the face of Guillaume Riche aftershave, Sputnik vodka and Asgill's anti-ageing men's skincare range, to name but three. This isn't about privacy. It's about *business*, and the temporary injunction should be overturned on those very grounds.'

Bond was putting his case forward strongly, but Anna wasn't overly concerned. It was definitely a long shot. Judge Baker would have considered all this before he granted the temporary injunction. The judge waved his hand impatiently to indicate that he had heard enough, and Bond reluctantly sat down.

Nigel Keyes rose to his feet once more. Now it really *was* a formality. The barrister merely needed to mention a few cases where the same argument of privacy had been successfully used, which would establish precedent; it was a done deal.

Behind her the heavy courtroom door opened and closed with a bang. Turning, she watched a young man approach Blake Stanhope's solicitor with a look of nervous determination. He whispered into Martin Bond's ear while Judge Baker looked unimpressed by the intrusion.

'Can I remind our new arrival that this is a private session?'

Martin Bond raised his hand.

'Apologies, m'lord. It's one of our team with an urgent message.'

'Get on with it,' snapped the judge.

Anna felt her senses prickle as the young messenger handed Bond a bundle of documents that the barrister speed-read with ruthless efficiency. Then he looked up at her, a gleeful expression on his face. What the hell's he got? she wondered anxiously.

Bond turned his attention to the judge. 'Your lordship, I hardly need to remind you or my esteemed legal colleagues that an injunction obtained on the grounds of privacy is null and void if the facts of the injunction are no longer private.'

Nigel shot Anna an urgent look. Bond walked over to the bench and handed Judge Baker the bundle.

'I'd like to submit these documents – a printout of a news story that has broken in the last twenty minutes on the Scandalhound website and the *Daily News* Internet pages.'

He turned to Anna and Keyes with a flourish.

'The facts your client is trying to hide are now public.'

The judge had read enough. He looked apologetic as he addressed Nigel Keyes.

'I take it, Mr Keyes, that you have not yet seen this?'

'No, your honour,' said Nigel, looking unusually flustered as the usher handed him the file. 'If we could just have a few brief moments to confirm these facts?'

Anna rushed out into the corridor, turned on her iPhone and scrolled to the *News* and Scandalhound websites. Sure enough, there it was: 'Sam Charles Caught With Hooker: Exclusive Pictures'. Bile rose in her throat as she saw it was the lead splash on both sites. It was impossible to tell which one had got the exclusive as they both appeared to have posted within minutes of each other, although the *News* had published the mobile photograph of Sam and Katie in bed together.

I don't believe it – how? She felt her hands tremble as she turned the phone off again. I'm totally screwed.

She went back into court and nodded grimly towards Nigel.

Bond's expression was triumphant.

'Would you like me to read the story out for the benefit of the opposing counsel?' he crowed. '"Sam Nooky With Porno-Looky" is the headline on one.'

'That's enough, Mr Bond,' said the judge irritably before addressing Nigel.

'I find it hard to see how this is now a privacy matter when this story is all over the Internet. I think we would all agree that the law is clear on this issue.'

'Yes, your honour,' said Nigel, closing his file.

Anna could feel sweat beading at her temples and the room seemed to spin. All week the Internet had been clean of the story. After the *ex parte* injunction had been granted, she had spoken to both Katie and Stanhope to make absolutely sure they understood they were forbidden to say anything about it. So how had it got out? Surely they wouldn't have been so stupid as to go ahead and sell the story? She looked over at Nigel, who just gave her a shrug.

'Very well, the injunction dated last Thursday is lifted,' said Judge Baker, concluding the matter.

Nigel Keyes picked up his things and left the courtroom, with Anna following right behind.

'We've been pretty bloody unlucky there,' he said.

'Unlucky?' she said angrily. 'Someone has talked. There's no luck involved.'

She looked down the corridor and could see that Blake Stanhope was already on the phone. Without thinking, she stormed towards him.

'Anna! Wait,' called Nigel.

But Anna wasn't listening. She stopped in front of Blake, glaring at him.

He gave her a thin, weasely smile and pointed to the phone clamped to his ear.

'Darling, I'm on a call.'

'Does contempt of court mean nothing to you, Blake?' she snapped. 'Are you that determined to ruin people's lives you'll do anything?'

With a sour look, Blake flipped his mobile shut.

'What are you suggesting, Miss Kennedy? That I *leaked* the story? That's a pretty serious allegation.'

'Then why are two hacks from the tabloids here? Are they psychic?'

She pointed at a couple of blondes who were talking intently to Martin Bond.

'Darling, I simply told a friend that I was coming to court. Being strong-armed under the terms of the gagging order, I obviously gave nobody any details beyond that. I do this for a living, remember? I know the rules of the game, thank you very much.'

'Then why are they here?'

'Because temporary injunctions do get lifted. This isn't the first, you know.'

She shook her head slowly.

'I hope your lawyer is on a retainer, Blake,' she said. 'You'll be needing him.'

'No one likes a sore loser, Anna.'

She jabbed her finger at him.

'This isn't about losing "the game", as you so eloquently put it. This is about breaking the law, which you did when you leaked the story to the press.'

'No, Anna, I did not. Contrary to what you might think of me, I do have respect for the law. It's my sixtieth birthday next week. I don't want to spend it in jail for contempt of court.'

'Bullshit,' she said, turning on her heel. 'Total bullshit.'

She ran out on to the street, her heart thudding as she turned on her phone. If the story had broken online twenty minutes ago, then the media would already be closing in on Sam. Oh God, I wonder if Jessica's already seen it, she thought. What a mess.

Her throat was dry as she scrolled to Sam's mobile and pressed Call.

'Hey, Anna,' he said. His voice was cheery, expectant. 'All done?'

She closed her eyes. There was no other way to tell him, except bluntly.

'They've overturned the injunction, Sam.'

'What?' he croaked. 'What do you mean? They've turned it down? How? Why?' The confusion in his voice turned to fear, then anger.

She forced air into her lungs. 'The judge has changed his mind on the grounds that the story is not private any more.'

'Not private? What the hell do you mean, not private?'

'It's just been posted on the *News* online. On Scandalhound too.'

There was an ominous silence at the other end of the line.

'Sam?'

In the background, she could hear him tapping at a keyboard. There was another pause and then a loud clatter. 'Fuck,' he hissed finally. 'I don't believe it. I don't bloody believe it.'

'I don't know how they got hold of the story.'

'You don't *know*?' he cried. 'Isn't that what I've just paid you fifty thousand quid to know? Aren't you supposed to know everything? Your job was to keep this out of the news – well, great job, Anna.'

'Look, obviously Katie or Blake have talked to them. Of course they'd be in contempt of court and that's a criminal offence. We could try and pursue damages.'

'And how's that going to help me?' he shouted. 'The bloody horse has bolted, hasn't it? What the hell am I going to do about Jessica?'

Anna tried to remain calm, but her voice was trembling.

'Look, I heard she was filming in Boston. That means it's only five thirty in the morning so she's probably still asleep. At least you can tell her about this yourself before she finds out from the press.'

'Oh great. Just great,' he snapped.

'We can manage this, Sam,' she said, although she was honestly beginning to doubt that. He was right about the horse having bolted. She looked up to see Nigel standing on the court steps, talking urgently into his own phone. 'Our barrister's right here. I'll talk to him and see what can be done, then I'll go straight back to the office, talk to Helen Pierce.'

'Who should have handled this in the first place . . .'

Her cheeks stung with shame. 'This isn't ideal, but we can deal with it.'

'Yeah? Well, deal with this,' he said. 'You're fired.'

And then the phone went dead.

'Anna?' said a voice softly. Nigel Keyes was standing next to her.

'He just fired me,' she said, still staring at the handset in disbelief. It was only then that she realised Nigel was holding his own mobile out towards her.

'Helen Pierce,' he whispered.

Oh hell.

'Anna? Have you see the *News* online?' There was a sense of urgency in Helen's usually icy-calm voice.

'We've just left court,' stuttered Anna. 'We—'

'Look, this can stop right here,' said Helen, ignoring her. 'With the injunction in place, Katie won't be able to talk, and without her, no one will be able to prove that Sam had sex with her. We can sue for damages. I'm sure I can get a front-page retraction in tomorrow's—'

'Helen. The injunction was lifted,' said Anna finally.

'What?' The cold steeliness in her voice made Anna want to run and hide.

'Another few minutes and it would have been finalised, but Stanhope's QC got hold of the story as it was breaking. The judge overturned.'

There was no sound from the other end of the line. The roar of the traffic on the Strand seemed to engulf her. She felt as if she was walking on quicksand that was giving way under her feet, sucking her into a loud, claustrophobic hole she'd never be able to climb out of.

'Does Sam know?' said Helen, her tone cold.

'I've just told him. He was angry. He said I was fired.'

'Oh Anna,' said Helen. 'You stupid, stupid girl.'

But I did nothing wrong! Anna wanted to cry. How can I help it if someone decides to break the rules? Instead she just stood there, feeling as if she was being given the worst dressing-down by her headmistress.

Helen paused. 'I told you, Anna: no mistakes.'

'It wasn't a mistake,' she replied, fighting to keep her voice even. 'Stanhope and Katie must have talked despite the gagging order.'

'You should have served everyone with the injunction and shut the media down.'

'We had a strategy. We *all* agreed on it.'

She knew that her suggestion that even Helen Pierce was fallible was pointless. Although Helen, as Anna's supervising partner, had signed off the decision to gag only Blake and Katie, she knew that fact would be conveniently forgotten and that the failure would be hers alone. So much for partner by Christmas, she grimaced.

'Donovan Pierce is a boutique firm, Anna,' added Helen. 'We don't have a big rota of lawyers, but the ones we have are the best. We don't make mistakes. Our reputation is everything. Without that reputation, we are nothing.'

'I'll try talking to Sam again,' said Anna. 'I guess the *Standard* will run with the story this afternoon, but if we can get him to do a sympathetic interview with the *Sun* tomorrow, it will soften the impact.'

'I think you've done enough already,' said Helen. 'I will talk to Sam and do the firefighting myself. I'll see you when you get back to the office.'

Anna felt sick as she handed the phone back to Nigel. He looked sympathetically at her. 'Worse things happen at sea,' he said.

'Do they?' she said. She felt numb, as if she'd had all the air knocked out of her. 'Sorry, Nigel, I've got to go.' She saw a black cab approaching and stuck out her arm.

'Don't take it so hard. There will be other cases,' said Nigel kindly as he opened the door for her.

Don't be so sure, thought Anna as she sat back in the seat, dreading the inevitable face-to-face with Helen.

The cabby looked at her in the mirror.

'Where you going, love?'

'To face the music,' she said grimly.

11

Sam gripped the arms of his seat and tried to swallow. The pilot was banking the private jet to the right in preparation for landing, and Sam could now see Cape Cod peeking between thin, low clouds, a finger of land criss-crossed by roads and houses, surrounded by the flat grey Atlantic Ocean, completely oblivious to the tiny gnat flying overhead. If only he could just stay up here, permanently circling the earth, hermetically sealed from the rest of the world, he'd be happy with that.

Sam had always loved air travel; he'd been brought up in a bland working-class part of London, not far from Heathrow, where the planes roared so low over his house he could make out the name of the airlines: Air China, Thai Air, Air New Zealand, reminding him how easy it was to be transported, for the price of a ticket, away from your humdrum existence. And since he had become really famous, aeroplanes had become his sanctuary. A reclining seat thirty-five thousand feet above sea level was one of the few places he could truly relax, switch off and not be bothered by the millions of people who wanted a piece of him.

But tonight, despite the champagne and the tasty finger food the pretty stewardess had kept bringing over, he could not relax. Today he wished for storms and delays and the outbreak of bird flu, anything to keep them from landing, anything to keep him from the inevitable confrontation with Jessica.

He'd called her, of course. There was no getting around that. After Anna had given him the bad news – no, the disastrous news – about the injunction, he had been forced to wake Jessica up from the comfort of her luxury Boston hotel suite, where she was staying while filming the thriller movie *Slayer* in the city.

Their conversation had been excruciating. At first she had been tired and groggy, irritated that he was disturbing her. No, she hadn't heard the early-morning news. No, she hadn't been called by her agent.

So he'd been forced to tell her everything. At first there had been stunned silence, but when her emotional dam had finally burst, Sam had felt the full force of her confusion, disbelief and, finally, fury. No, she had said – or rather screamed – no, she would not like to meet up to discuss it in person. She never wanted to see him again. The conversation had terminated when Jessica's publicist had arrived at her hotel suite to take her out of the city.

He squirmed in his seat thinking about it. En route to Northolt airfield, where he had boarded the jet, he had seen images on Sky News of Jess's hotel besieged by paparazzi. He managed to avoid his own lynching by the press by a matter of minutes, packing a bag and leaving his Chelsea apartment before the media could make him a prisoner in his own home. His London agent had secreted him away in a house in West London until the earliest flight time had been secured. Helen Pierce had called him to assure him that everything was being done to crisis-manage the situation. Somehow he didn't believe her. The press coverage seemed wall-to-wall. There wasn't a news station, Internet site or newspaper in the Western world that wasn't gleefully reporting the story in lurid headlines. And this was only the first wave. The weekend papers would be dominated by the story. Ex-girlfriends, jealous colleagues and various conveniently unnamed 'friends' would come crawling out of the woodwork to add sensational details on Hollywood's hottest scandal. The celebrity magazines would come next – the story could run for weeks. Soon everyone everywhere would know what he had done, or rather the salacious version of it: Sam Charles Uses Hookers, Sam Charles The Cheat, and worst of all, Sam Charles Makes Jessica Cry. There would be nowhere to hide.

The jet's wheels jerked on to the tarmac at Cape Cod's

Hyannis airport, almost eight p.m. London time, three p.m. EST, sending a blast of oven-hot air at him as he stepped down. A limousine with blacked-out windows was waiting for him. He had no idea whose car it was – for all he knew it could be a hit man hired by Jessica – but there was no such luck. The window buzzed down and his manager Eli Cohen poked his screwed-up face out.

'Get in, you schmuck,' he growled.

Sam threw his overnight bag in the back and climbed in.

'Why did you bring me here?' he asked, looking around the flat, unfamiliar environment of the Cape. 'I need to speak to Jessica.'

'Yeah, I know that, Einstein,' said Eli. 'I brought you here because she's left the city. And lemme tell you, I had to call in fifty years' worth of favours to find out where she's gone.'

'So you've spoken to her?'

'Not in person, no. But you know Harry Monk and me go way back.'

Harriet Monk was Jessica's agent. She was an LA hotshot at the ITG talent agency, and had a reputation as one of the industry's most notorious ball-breakers.

'So where are we going?'

'Some compound on the Inner Cape. Belongs to a fancy-pants New York family. The daughter is one of Jessica's friends. So do you want to tell me what happened . . . ?'

As Sam recapped the events of the past week, his manager said very little, just nodding and grunting here and there. Sam was unsettled by his silence; Eli wasn't a man to keep quiet about anything.

'What do you think?' said Sam anxiously when he had finished.

Eli eyed him for a moment.

'All I want to know is one question. Why?'

'Why? I was pissed. You've seen the pictures, she's a good-looking girl.'

Eli snorted.

'I'm not asking why you *did it*,' he said, fixing Sam with a shrewd eye. 'I'm asking why you got *caught*.'

Sam shook his head and smiled ruefully. This was another reason why Eli was his manager. Most film stars these days had managers and agents who had MBAs from Yale and Harvard. They wore designer suits, ate Japanese food and plotted everything on a spreadsheet. But which of them could see through the clouds thrown up by this media storm and ask the one question at the heart of it? Eli was right. If Sam had wanted to screw some other girl on the side, he could have done it. Plenty would have volunteered and he could have found a discreet out-of-the-way venue for their trysts without much trouble. What Eli was getting at was that this wasn't about sex and it wasn't really about wanting to let off steam either. Had he wanted to get caught? Why else pick up a girl in such a public place? Why else dance the electric boogaloo with her in front of a gaping crowd? Why else get so drunk you were practically begging her to blackmail you? Sam let out a long breath.

'Okay, so you've got me,' he said. 'What should I do now?' Eli was old-school. He wasn't the most fashionable manager, but you could rely on him in a crisis, and right now Sam needed him more than ever.

Eli shrugged.

'These things will pass.'

'Come on, this is serious, Eli.'

'I know it's serious, son. I can tell you what movies to make, what commercial to do, which parties to avoid. I can guide you, advise you in all things professional. But this is your heart and I can't see inside it.' He turned in his seat and looked at Sam searchingly.

'Sam. As my client, I want you and Jessica to stay together and make lots more lovely money. As my friend, I want you to be happy. The two things really ain't the same. If you love her, then beg for forgiveness and get yourself to Vegas, tie the knot. If you don't love her, then tell her so. There's plenty of saps willing to take your place.'

Sam gazed out the window. Funny, wasn't that exactly what Anna Kennedy had been trying to tell him back in Capri?

'So you think I can get through this?'

'Hugh Grant did. But I'll be honest, it really depends on Jess.

Liz Hurley could have crucified Hugh but she chose to take the dignified route and that worked out for both of them. But Jessica? If she goes on *Ellen DeGeneres* on a revenge mission, you're dead. If Jess hates you, then America hates you.'

'Gee, thanks, Eli.'

'Hey, I'm just telling it like it is. You gotta do what's right for you. But remember, what affects your career affects my career. And I need a new pool.'

The car stopped outside a wide cedar gate and the driver pressed an intercom to announce them. When the gate opened and the car passed down the drive, an enormous white Cape house in an acre of lawns came into view.

Sam stepped out of the car. He'd half expected to see newsroom helicopters roaring overhead, but he could hear nothing except the swoosh of the sea crashing on the shore and the squawk of gulls above him. He closed his eyes, inhaling the warm, salty air – a moment of calm before the storm. Eli buzzed his window down.

'I'll wait for you at that bar just by the highway,' he said, leaning out. 'Gimme a call when it's all over. And Sam? Think of my new pool, huh?'

As the car's tail-lights disappeared, Sam took a deep breath and walked to the door. Just as he was lifting his hand to knock, the door was wrenched open.

'You've got a goddamn nerve!'

Barbara Carr, Jessica's mother. The style magazines were always tripping over themselves to say how much the two women looked like sisters, not mother and daughter, but Sam had always thought Barbara looked like a waxwork of Jess that had been left out in the sun.

'How dare you come up here, you cheap bastard,' she shouted. 'Hasn't she suffered enough?'

'If you'll just let me see her for a minute . . .'

'She doesn't want to see you,' snapped Barbara. 'She never wants to see you again.'

'I understand that, but we obviously need to talk.'

'Yeah? And what could you possibly say that would make this any better?'

'I just want to tell her what happened.'

'I think that's pretty goddamn clear.'

Behind her mother, Jessica appeared. She was looking pale and serious, no make-up, her green eyes red from tears, her famous body enveloped by an oversized jumper. In photographs of her on the red carpet, she looked toned and perfect in those curve-skimming dresses showing acres of tanned flesh, but today, the voluminous sweater emphasised how tiny her body really was.

'Hey, Mom,' she said. 'Just give us a minute.'

Barbara looked as if she was about to argue, then shrugged.

'One minute. He's not worth any more.'

Jessica turned and moved through the house, then out through glass doors that led on to the beach. Sam followed her and they walked on to the sand. Ahead of them there was a thin ridge of scrubby dunes to the left. Out to sea, across the sparkling Nantucket Sound, Sam could see Martha's Vineyard shimmering in the distance.

'Well?' she said.

'I'm sorry,' he replied, taking a step towards her.

'Don't touch me,' she snapped. 'I don't even like being this close. Say what you've got to say, then go.'

'Please stay calm, Jess. I just want to explain.'

'Explain? *Explain?* You want to explain that you've screwed a whore and humiliated me in front of the whole world? Excuse me if I can't stay calm, Sam.'

'It was wrong, I know that,' he began.

'Oh, it was more than wrong, Sam. It was career suicide, and I'm not letting you take me down with you.'

Sam felt his stomach turn over. He had seen people get on the wrong side of Jessica before and it hadn't ended well for them. He'd always known she had a vindictive streak, but he'd never been on the receiving end and he certainly didn't want to start now.

'For one minute can we stop talking about our careers? This is nothing to do with them. It's about me and you.'

Her eyes pooled with tears. 'This is everything to do with our careers. We're a brand, Sam. We stand for something. We're wholesome and happy, a perfect young couple; everyone wants to be us. But you've messed all that up, haven't you? All that work I put into it, it's all gone. And for what? Some cheap slut in London who massages your cock and your ego. Is that all it takes to spoil everything?'

She looked at him with contempt and he knew it was entirely justified.

'It wasn't like that. Jess, I never meant to treat you like that.'

He put out a hand to touch her arm, but she flinched back.

'Don't!' she sobbed. 'And don't think you can come crawling back to me with "I'm sorry" and think that's the end of it.'

For a moment he could hear Anna Kennedy's voice nagging in his head.

Think about why you slept with Katie in the first place.

His fiancée's exquisite, tear-streaked face made him feel so ashamed he could no longer look at it. But he knew his guilt and sympathy couldn't distract him from what he wanted, *needed* to say.

'I'm not crawling back, Jess,' he said finally, and felt a sweet, powerful relief as the words came out of his mouth. 'In fact, I'm not coming back at all. I just wanted to come here to tell you that. I am sorry, I really am. But it's over.'

She stopped still on the sand and looked at him.

'You bastard,' she growled.

'Maybe. Maybe you're right. But this is for the best.'

'How is this for the best, Sam?' Her voice was trembling. 'How can this possibly be for the best?'

'I hate how this has happened, but in a weird way I'm glad it did, because we don't want to end up at fifty still together and not in love. Not even close.'

The wind whipped at her honey-blond hair and for a moment Sam could see just how beautiful she really was, free from the make-up and the grooming, a real woman, not the Hollywood doll she had become since their stars reached the stratosphere. He remembered the day they had first met on the rom-com *Who Needs This?* It was the sort of movie that only worked if the leads had real chemistry, and they'd had it in spades. They were filming in the romantic paradise of Maui, they were young, free and single, and to be frank, they both knew an on-set affair never harmed any movie's publicity. Looking back, their relationship should have ended the moment they got back to LA, but by then it had caught the attention of the American public. Jess's TV series was taking off – the American public loved her, and they were all too happy to buy into the romance of her whirlwind courtship with this handsome Brit. Suddenly the two of them were hot. Everyone took Sam's calls. Directors, producers came knocking. And when *Who Needs This?* became a genuine smash hit, Sam immediately joined the A-list. It had all been too fast, too soon. He knew that now.

'Can I ask you a question?' he said quietly.

'So now you want to play quiz host?'

'Why have we never talked about our actual wedding? Why have we avoided setting a date?'

Sam had proposed twelve months ago, because it seemed the next logical step. By then, 'Samica' were one of Hollywood's most famous couples, and it seemed as though the whole world was holding its breath waiting for an announcement. But from the moment he had slipped the four-carat Harry Winston ring on her finger, he had felt unsettled. Now he knew why.

'Because we've been too busy for a goddamn wedding, Sam. What, you think we should have gone off to some shitty little chapel in Vegas?'

'Maybe.' He shrugged. 'Maybe we should have. Or maybe we never set a date because we both knew it wasn't right.'

'So now you're justifying the hooker with the fact that I wouldn't name the day? Screw you.'

He stepped towards her again.

'Jess, you deserve someone who gets you,' he said softly. 'We both do.'

'The only thing you deserve is herpes,' she spat.

He grabbed her arms and looked into her eyes. She struggled for a moment, then stopped.

'I'm lonely, Jess,' he said. 'Aren't you?'

She looked away, down at the sand. He thought she wasn't

103

going to say anything, then she suddenly turned back and met his gaze.

'Yes,' she said. She looked so fragile and vulnerable swamped in that huge sweater. Part of him wanted to put his arms around her and protect her, but he knew it would only make it worse.

'I'm sorry, Jess,' he said, 'I really am.'

She shook her head, tears rolling down her cheeks.

'Just go,' she said.

'Can't we—'

'MOM!' she shouted back towards the house.

He held his hands up in surrender. 'Okay, okay . . .'

He backed away, started walking up the beach, feeling the sand collect in his loafers. He pulled out his phone and called Eli. He could hear laughter and the tinkle of honky-tonk music in the background.

'Damn, that was quick,' said Eli. 'I'm guessing that's a big fat no, then?'

Sam sighed. 'Just come and get me,' he said.

'Hang tough, cowboy, I'm on my way.'

When Sam turned around, Jess had gone.

12

'First client?'

Helen popped her head around the door, her immaculate bob framing her smile.

Matt nodded. He had been at the firm two weeks and finally he had brought in some business of his own.

'Good,' she said briskly. 'And I want every nanosecond on that time sheet.'

For a moment, Matthew thought about pointing out that he was a shareholder and as such shouldn't be treated like a rookie, but he knew it would have little effect. Helen even talked that way to Larry.

'Oh, and remember, these are celebrities we're dealing with. The rich are different.'

'I think I read that somewhere,' muttered Matthew, but Helen had gone.

Jesus, he thought. It's like working in a fish tank.

Since he had started at Donovan Pierce, he had felt Helen's gaze on him every moment of the day, assessing him, criticising him. He'd thought that once he was starting to generate his own client list, she might ease off, but she was still 'popping in', dropping little titbits of advice, subtly undermining him. Maybe I'm being paranoid, he thought. But then what was that saying? 'Just because you're paranoid, it doesn't mean they're not after you.' It would certainly suit Helen Pierce if he decided to move on. 'Helen Pierce Associates' had quite a ring to it.

He had no more time to dwell on it, however, as his secretary Diane led a neatly dressed man into the room.

'Mr Beaumont for you, Mr Donovan.'

Matt stood up and shook his hand.

'Good to meet you,' he said. 'Please, have a seat.'

Personally Matt wouldn't have known Rob Beaumont if he had fallen over him in broad daylight, but a quick look at IMDB had told him that his new client was a film director with a string of critically acclaimed indie pictures to his name. To most teenagers, though, Beaumont was more famous because of his marriage to Kim Collier, the singer in a now-defunct girl band who continued to be popular, as far as Matthew could tell, by appearing in gossip magazines.

'It's a right bunfight outside your offices,' said Rob, settling into his chair. 'What's going on?'

Matt glanced towards the window, which looked on to the street. It was six o'clock, yet there was still a pack of photographers on the square.

'We had a high-profile case last week. The leading players are in hiding and the paparazzi seem to think we've got our client stashed away in here somewhere.'

'You weren't acting for Sam Charles, were you?'

Matt smiled thinly. He'd only worked in media law a fortnight, but even he could tell the failure of Sam's injunction was not good news for the firm. There had been some high-handed opinion pieces in the broadsheets about how the overturned injunction represented victory for freedom of the press. Secretly he thought they were right.

'So you're a friend of Erica's?' he said, as much as a way of distracting the client as opening conversation.

'Yes, but she's not the reason I'm here,' said Rob with a sardonic laugh. 'She's a friend. Not a *special* friend.'

'Of course not,' Matt said quickly.

'She speaks highly of you.'

'She does?' Matt couldn't help but be curious. He knew Rob had approached the firm on Erica's recommendation and had been contemplating calling her to thank her.

'When I told Erica about my marriage, she said you were the man for the job.'

'I'm flattered.'

Rob nodded and looked down at his hands.

'This is difficult, isn't it?'

'Divorce is never easy. I've been there.'

Twice actually, he thought. Despite insisting to Carla that he could not represent her in her divorce from David, his ex-wife had never been off the phone with lists of questions and requests for advice. It was proving impossible not to get dragged in.

'So do you want to tell me why the relationship has broken down?'

Rob sat back in his chair and began to tell his lawyer about his marriage to Kim. How they had met when he had directed one of her videos eight years earlier. About their son, Oliver, who was around the same age as Jonas. And the reasons why they had drifted apart.

'She wants to get a fashion label off the ground,' he said. 'She's seen Posh Spice do it and thinks she can too, so she's been travelling a lot. Next year she wants to tour, get her music going again. Kim is one of those sorts of people who always has to be doing something. I've always supported her in that, but sometimes it doesn't make for the most straightforward of marriages.'

He pushed an envelope towards Matthew.

'This is the petition she sent me last week.'

Matt speed-read the document inside.

'Unreasonable behaviour?' he asked.

Rob shrugged.

'I'm away a lot. Filming takes months, you see. And she'd get jealous of the actresses, but I told her, what am I supposed to do, just make films set in prison? And . . . well, there was a lot of conflict over money. I think Kim thought she was marrying the new Spielberg, but it's not quite worked out like that. I do my best, but I guess it's just not good enough.'

Matt glanced up and recognised Rob's sad, frustrated expression. He'd felt all those emotions himself.

'Do you want to get divorced?' he asked gently.

Rob paused.

'Not really, but it's a marriage that can't work. We want different things. That's what she says, anyway,' he added, trying for a smile.

'You could contest it.'

'Sure, but why be in a marriage someone else doesn't want to be in?' He shook his head sadly. 'No, I don't want to contest this. I just want to keep things as simple as possible. For my son's sake. For everyone's sake.'

They wrapped up the meeting and Diane showed Rob out.

Coffee, Matt said to himself, getting up and heading down to the space-age kitchen area at the end of his corridor. It was full of shiny machines and utensils, but he had no idea where the actual coffee was kept. As he searched around, opening cupboards, one thing Rob Beaumont had said kept going around in his head. 'I always did my best,' that was what he had said. Matt thought of that terrible day he'd found out about Carla's unfaithfulness. He should have gone straight to his lawyers and petitioned for divorce on the grounds of adultery there and then. He could see now that he'd been a fool, but love didn't work that way. If you got hurt, you still wanted to try and make it better. But Carla didn't want to make things better. At least not with him.

'Where is the bloody coffee?' he said irritably.

'Here,' said a voice. He turned to find Anna Kennedy holding up a tin that looked like a time capsule. 'In the coffee container.'

'Sorry,' he muttered. 'Bad morning.'

'I know how you feel,' said Anna, gently moving Matthew out of the way to get at the Gaggia.

'So how's things?' he asked, although he could predict her answer. Her pretty face looked tired and sombre. The feistiness that had scared him a little at Scott's restaurant was subdued, and with good reason, he supposed. The whole firm was still whispering about Sam Charles. He could only imagine the roasting Helen must have given her when she had come back from court, and she had barely left her office since.

'Bearing up. Although I could do without being followed home by any more paparazzi.'

'They're following *you*?'

She nodded. 'I'm convinced they think Sam's hiding out in my shed.' She handed him a mug. 'Speaking of which, I hope Rob Beaumont left through the back door.'

'Why?'

'Well the street is full of paparazzi and he just had an appointment with a family lawyer. They're not the brightest bunch, but even they can put two and two together.'

Matt felt a jolt of panic as he remembered Helen's quip: rich people are different. Should he have made arrangements to meet his client elsewhere instead of the office? Suddenly he felt very green and out of his depth.

'And have you been in touch with Piers Douglas?' She leaned on the cabinets as she sipped her coffee.

'Who's he?' asked Matt, feeling himself get defensive. This woman seemed to do this to him. He tried not to dwell on their Scott's lunch on their first day at the firm – after all, his father's heart attack had overshadowed everything – but he still hadn't forgotten her combative, cocky stance on privacy. He wondered whether she'd changed her mind about it recently.

'He's a media consultant we have on retainer. PR expert.'

'Why would I need him?'

She looked surprised.

'Because if Rob and Kim are having problems, that's front-page news. A media law firm has to offer a fully rounded service. Image management, that sort of thing. Plus you need to control the media when trouble's brewing, not just when the shit has hit the fan.'

This conversation was increasingly feeling like a telling-off.

'I thought we were a law firm. Not the offices of Max Clifford.'

'Well you'd better catch up,' she whispered playfully. 'Discretion is everything.'

He struggled not to frown. He was her boss and yet she was succeeding in making him feel stupid and embarrassed.

'I'm not entirely sure you should be the one dishing out expert advice on discretion, Anna.' It was a cheap shot, but she was annoying him. How was he supposed to know all this stuff about PR and image management? At his old firm, he'd just had to make sure they had a full box of Kleenex on the desk every morning.

'What's that supposed to mean?' she said, glaring at him.

'Nothing,' he muttered.

'I'd rather you came out with it.'

'Look,' he sighed. 'You don't need me to tell you that the Sam Charles thing was handled badly.'

'Handled badly? We all agreed on the strategy. How can I help it if someone decides to leak the story?'

'But they did.'

'Yes, and we should be doing everything in our power to find out who talked.'

Matthew raised his eyebrows.

'I'm no media expert – *clearly* – but I'd say that was next to impossible. All it would take would be an anonymous email, or maybe they texted that picture from a mobile. You can get a disposable SIM card for a quid these days.'

'Thanks for that insight,' she mumbled, walking to the door. 'I'll email you Piers' details; maybe you can brief him on how to go about leaking a story.'

Matt watched her go. He thought about following her to apologise but he was too tired and bad-tempered. *Women*, he grunted to himself. He was better off on his own.

13

Anna walked back into her office and closed the door with a slam.

How dare he? The patronising bastard! He'd worked in the media what, all of five minutes, yet he still had the nerve to lecture her.

She sat down at her desk, closed her eyes and rubbed her temples. She could have done without a confrontation with the new managing partner, who seemed almost as uptight and miserable as Helen Pierce, but then again, he was her boss even if he had been handed the firm by Daddy.

She looked at the piles of newspapers and magazines stacked up on her desk. The *News of the World*, the *Mail on Sunday*, the *Globe*, *The Chronicle*, each one of them running their own slightly different version of the Sam Charles story. And that was before you got to the gossip magazines and papers from the States and Europe. For the tabloids, of course, it was a perfect story: a sensational tale of celebrity debauchery supported by titillating pictures of a pretty girl in her bra, along with the bonus of being able to put the boot into media lawyers in the guise of stopping the madness of a legal system that protected rich, unfaithful rogues like Sam Charles. They certainly weren't going to drop this story until they had wrung every last drop of value from it.

She picked up Sunday's copy of the *News of the World*, which featured a large picture of Katie Grey in skimpy black lingerie next to the headline 'My Night With Sam: Exclusive Interview'. With everything else that was going on the world – soldiers being killed in Afghanistan, the situation in Sudan, Iran,

North Korea, the global recession – it was difficult to comprehend why even the broadsheets found the fact that Sam Charles had slept with an escort girl of such international significance. But they did. And what the British tabloids said had been repeated by every media outlet from twenty-four-hour satellite news programmes to worthy Internet discussion sites. There were even a batch of Sam Charles jokes going around. Q: 'How many prostitutes does it take to screw in a light bulb?' A: 'None. They're all too busy screwing Sam Charles.'

She threw the paper down angrily.

The last few days had been hellish. In her entire working career she had never felt more isolated and ashamed. Ashamed of her professional failure in getting the gagging order. Ashamed that she had promised Sam that everything was under control. Ashamed that her parents were watching the story – the bitter irony being that her sister Sophie's *Dorset Kitchen* show had aired immediately before her own appearance on *News at Ten*; although why anyone would consider footage of her leaving the office on Friday night news was still a mystery to her.

Anna leaned over and picked up the phone, dialling 1 for Sid, the trainee solicitor assigned to her.

'Sid, can you come through for a moment?' she asked.

She didn't really want to see anyone, but she had to do something. She had found it very difficult coming into work that morning; part of her had been tempted to phone in sick and go and live on a kibbutz. It would certainly have been the easiest thing to do. Helen Pierce hadn't said so in as many words – in fact, it seemed as though Helen was pretty much ignoring her – but Anna knew that this whole episode had been a PR disaster for the firm. After all, Donovan Pierce had been named in every newspaper from Brussels to Bangalore as the firm who failed to get the injunction. Whoever had said 'there's no such thing as bad publicity' had never worked in the law.

'Ah, come in, Sid,' she said at the timid knock on the door.

The redheaded trainee came into the room and Anna indicated the piles of papers.

'I'd be grateful if you could get rid of these. You'd better file them, although if it were up to me, you could go and make a bonfire out of them in Broadwick Street.'

'After I'm done with them, do you mind if I go?' Sid replied.

Anna glanced at her watch. It was barely six thirty. Most of the other trainees worked until seven, eight o'clock, eager to please and prove. Then again, Sid had recently found out that she was not one of the five trainees who would be kept on for a full-time assistant solicitor's job when they qualified in September. When Anna had joined the firm and found out that she had been assigned Sid as her trainee she had questioned the move, as Sid was only due to stay at the firm another few weeks. But right now, Anna realised that her own job at Donovan Pierce was not much more secure than Sid's was.

Anna nodded. 'Yes, you can go.'

Sid smiled gratefully and carried the papers out, taking care to close the door behind her.

With the papers gone, Anna realised how sparse her office looked. There was just a pen pot and a couple of files on her desk. She had barely made her mark on Donovan Pierce and there was a distinct possibility that she might not ever get the chance. When she had accepted the job, Helen had assured her that she would be considered for partnership at the end of her three-month probationary period. Now she wasn't sure she would even make it to the end of the three months. She could feel tears welling up. Since Friday she had held it all together, but there was only so much she could cope with.

'Don't be so bloody stupid,' she whispered to herself, screwing her fist into a ball. 'I'll be buggered if I take this lying down.'

She grabbed her notepad and flipped it to a new page.

'Right . . .' she said out loud, writing the word 'Strategy' at the top and underlining it twice. It was her favourite word. Positive, active, a word that said you knew where you were going. But which way? It was obvious to Anna that she had to fight back, but her pen paused above the paper, unsure of what to write next. She looked down at the space where the newspapers had been sitting and clicked her fingers. If they wanted a story, she would give them one.

'Blake Stanhope,' she scribbled. 'Sued for Contempt. Sam Charles Escort Girl Imprisoned for Leak.'

She smiled to herself. Matthew bloody Donovan was wrong; dead wrong. There were always ways to find out who had leaked the story. Of course Blake himself would deny it – as he said himself, he could go to jail for such a stunt. But someone, somewhere knew who had spilled the beans. In theory, the editor of the *Daily News* or the owner of the gossip website was unlikely to tell her the source of the story, but then again, Blake Stanhope had never been their favourite person. He was a parasite feeding on other people's mistakes and indiscretions, and Anna was pretty damn sure there were plenty of people who'd like to see him get a taste of his own medicine. Besides, she had bartered with editors on many occasions: one piece of information for another. The problem now, however, was that she had no leverage, no stories to swap, nothing to offer.

The phone began ringing and Anna glanced at it with irritation. For a moment she thought about leaving it. After-hours calls were never good news and she needed some randy footballer begging for an injunction like she needed a hole in the head. Sighing, she picked up the receiver.

'Anna Kennedy.'

There was silence at the other end.

'Hello? Anyone there?'

Finally she heard someone take a deep breath and a small voice said, 'Is that Sam Charles's lawyer?'

Oh God, not a crank call, she thought. Or even worse, a fan who wanted to ask what Sam was really like.

'Yes,' she said. 'I'm Mr Charles's representative. Or rather I was.'

'I'm sorry for calling so late,' said the voice. 'I wasn't sure whether to ring.'

'Who is this?'

The voice was young. Maybe teenage. They certainly didn't sound like anyone able to afford Anna's £250 an hour Donovan Pierce associate rate anyway. And too timid to be a journalist or another solicitor.

'You don't know me,' said the voice. 'But I really need your help.'

'Are you in legal trouble?'

There was another pause.

'I think my sister was murdered.'

Anna frowned.

'In which case I think you should be talking to the police,' she said.

'Oh, I've done all that – she died seven months ago, you see – but they don't seem to be interested any more.'

'In that case I don't see—'

'It was the inquest into her death last week,' said the girl quickly. 'The coroner didn't say it, of course, but I know she was murdered and I want – I need – to prove it.'

Anna took a sip of coffee. 'I'm afraid I don't understand why you are calling me.'

'You deal with celebrities, don't you? My sister's death made the newspapers when it happened so I thought someone might look into it a bit more, especially after the inquest. But now there's this big story about Sam Charles having an affair everywhere and it's as if my sister never even existed.'

Despite herself, Anna was intrigued.

'Who was your sister?'

'Amy Hart.'

Anna wrote it down, but it didn't ring any immediate bells.

'I still don't understand why you think I can help you,' she said.

'I called you because you know about the law and you know about celebrities. Someone famous killed my sister and they're trying to cover it up. Even the newspapers are in their pocket.'

Anna felt her heart beating faster.

'Look, I can prove that my sister was killed. Can't you meet me? Please.'

Anna knew she shouldn't touch this with a bargepole, but the pleading in the girl's voice did make her feel sorry for her. She sounded lonely, desperate, alone. It was no fun facing anything traumatic on your own; the last three days had taught her that. The girl's words rang around her head: *Even the newspapers are in their pocket.* Was it possible? Anything was possible if you had connections and money.

'What do you think happened to Amy?' said Anna softly. 'Who did this to her?'

'We should meet.'

The rational side of Anna's brain told her that this was a crazy, mixed-up kid who needed expert advice of the pastoral rather than legal variety.

'I can't help you unless you tell me what you think.'

'I need to see you in person.'

She finally relented. She was too curious.

'I suppose I could do coffee tomorrow.'

'I've got a summer job in Pizza Hut. I've got the day off on Wednesday.'

'Let's grab a sandwich. How about we meet in Green Park? By the fountain.' She didn't want this to be taking up office time. 'What's your name?'

'My name's Ruby. I've seen your photo, so I know what you look like.'

'Okay, Ruby. I'll see you then,' she said, grabbing her jacket and heading out of the door. Helen Pierce might have written her off, but there was fight in Anna Kennedy yet.

14

The beach was two and a half miles long, that was what Mike had told him. Sam looked back along the long white stretch of sand and wondered why he hadn't been here before. Eigan island, ten miles from the Scottish mainland, was so heart-stoppingly beautiful, with the pale sun glinting off the ripples of wet sand, the heather-fringed cliffs, even the sea eagles wheeling effortlessly above him scanning the waves for their dinner.

Sam kicked a piece of driftwood with his foot, but remembering that it made the best kindling, he stopped dead and stooped to pick it up. As he bent over, he noticed that the bottom of his two-thousand-dollar Tom Ford trousers had white rings left by the salt water. For a split second he wondered if anywhere on the tiny island offered a dry-cleaning service – as it didn't even have a shop, he very much doubted it – but as the sunshine shimmered like a spray of tiny diamonds over the clear Atlantic waters, he felt a surge of rebellion and ran to the edge of the shore, splashing through the tide until the fabric was truly soaked.

Laughing, he rolled the trousers up to his calves, realising that although he'd only left the pampered celebrity world two days ago, it already felt like a fading dream. Eli had suggested that Sam hide out in Mexico or at a director friend's ranch in Idaho – at least until the scandal had died down and the vultures had stopped circling. But Sam didn't want to be surrounded by strangers, he wanted to be among friends.

'Not many of those around at the moment, kiddo,' Eli had said. That was certainly true. Sam hadn't exactly been inundated with messages of support from his so-called buddies, the various actors and film people he hung around with in Hollywood. When you were dead, you were dead. They didn't want any of Sam's black marks rubbing off on them. So he had rung his old university friend Mike McKenzie, reasoning that he was one of the few people who would understand what he was going through. And Mike's oyster farm on Eigan was perfect when you were seeking blissful isolation.

Eli had driven Sam straight from Jess's Cape Cod hideout back to the airport. The jet had flown him to the tiny airport at Oban, where he had jumped into a four-seater prop plane, and he was skimming down for a juddery landing on Eigan's north beach before most people had even had their morning papers delivered.

Sam closed his eyes. He didn't want to think about the papers today, didn't want to ruin a lovely day just spent walking and enjoying the sun on his face, the sounds of the waves and the birds and the wind. There was time for all that later. Much later. Reluctantly he turned to head back towards Mike's place, the squat little crofter's cottage he could see in the distance, white smoke drifting from its chimney. There were worse places to hide out, he thought. In fact he could see himself staying here for a long time. Mike had managed well enough for the past six or so years; it had been his sanctuary, his salvation. Maybe a simpler, less vain life was what Sam needed too.

He walked up the little path to the cottage, smiling at the seashells and pretty stones that had been laid along the flower beds on either side. It was so totally unlike the scruffy, irreverent, disorganised Mike he knew. But then Mike wasn't the same man he'd known at uni, was he? Living out here, how could he be?

'The film star returns,' said Mike as Sam bumped in through the low door. 'I was worried that the seals had got you. What do you fancy for supper? Oysters. Crab. Scallops?'

Sam flopped down in one of the rickety chairs by the old iron range.

'You make it sound like bloody Nobu.'

'It is, except my stuff is fresher,' winked Mike. 'And I haven't got any chopsticks.'

Sam smiled. It had been years since he had seen his old friend and he had been nervous about calling him. After all, what would he say? 'Listen, Mike old thing, I've arsed up my life and my career and I need to hide out somewhere the paparazzi will never find me. I know I've been too important to so much as send you a postcard in the last five years, but can I come and stay?'

In the end, that was pretty much exactly what he had said.

Mike had left a dramatic pause, then said: 'Can you pick up a Snickers on your way through the airport? I'm desperate for one and the boat doesn't come over from the mainland for another week.'

At least he hadn't changed all *that* much. In fact, in many ways he was the same cocky bugger Sam had met on the second day of Freshers Week at Manchester University. Discovering they were on the same drama course, they'd bonded over a shared love of bitter and Seventies comedy. The summer after they'd graduated, they'd taken a two-man show to the Edinburgh Fringe and been a surprise hit. But Sam had always been the Dudley Moore straight man to Mike's Peter Cook comedy genius and they had amicably gone their separate ways six months afterwards: Sam to serious theatre, darhlink, Mike to massive acclaim at the vanguard of a new generation of indie comedy, followed by his own chat show, a BAFTA-winning comedy drama and something of a reputation as a hell-raiser and a ladies' man.

Sam watched as Mike shovelled more coal into the fire, his dark fringe hanging down. His hair had always been on the Byronic side: Mike always said he used it like a hypnotist's pendulum to lure girls into his bed.

'What are you looking at?' said Mike.

'You, you great jessie. You look like someone from a BBC Thomas Hardy adaptation.'

'Bugger, I was hoping for more of a David Essex gypsy troubadour look.'

'More "Come On Eileen" than "Winter's Tale", mate.'

'So says the limp-wristed thesp. I'm not the one getting my back waxed, am I?'

'Hey, if it's in the contract, I have to wax,' laughed Sam.

He loved how they could fall straight back into their banter as if no time had passed at all. He just wished he hadn't left it so long; he still felt guilty that he hadn't been there when Mike had needed him the most.

Sam hadn't been entirely surprised at the news that Mike had had a breakdown just when his star was at its highest. He'd always been mercurial and slightly manic, but that was just Mike. He would always be involved in some weird fringe play or organising a huge themed party. He painted and grew cacti and cooked curries for twenty people at a time; he was a powerhouse that never stopped. But Sam knew him well enough to see that he was just running to stand still; Mike once confessed to him that he feared that if he ever stopped, he'd fall into the empty space at his centre.

Finally, seven years ago, Mike had fallen into that hole. He'd been discovered wandering naked around Loch Ness, mumbling that he was looking for the monster. He had just finished a record-breaking sell-out run of his solo show at Wembley; he should have been basking in the glory. Instead, he was sent to a discreet psychiatric clinic in Wales. When he was released two months later, Sam had offered him a room in his LA home and introductions to his Hollywood contacts, but Mike had other ideas and moved out to Eigan. Since then, whenever Sam was in the news – an acting award, a starry premiere – Mike would send him mocking postcards reading: 'Heard about the nomination. I spent the day digging up potatoes'; or 'Loved you in the new film, we have foot and mouth here.'

But Sam's packed schedule coupled with the strain of maintaining a relationship with Jessica had meant that he barely remembered to send Mike a Christmas card, let alone come out to visit his old friend.

Mike took two tins of pale ale from the cast-iron fridge and handed one to Sam. 'Tell you what, Mr Bojangles. Let's go for lobster tonight. Then you won't feel so homesick.'

'What about you, Mike? Don't you get lonely out here?'

'How could I get lonely? There are twelve sheep per acre here.' He smiled. 'Plus there are six families; we even have a school – eight kids on the register, I believe.'

They ducked through the low-slung doorway to head outside, sitting on a low stone wall facing the sea. Sam tipped his head back, loving the feel of the warm breeze on his face. On a nearby bluff there was the ruin of a small chapel, covered with a colony of nesting seagulls. It was just perfect.

'I can see why you wouldn't want to leave. How did you find it?'

'My cousin Lucy moved to Mull. After the clinic I came up to visit, and one day I was walking past an estate agent's and saw this advert reading "Oyster farm for sale". I wanted some peace and quiet, and oysters aren't known for answering back. Plus I always fancied myself leading the *Good Life*. It was just all that fame that got in the way. And the girls, and the cars and the money.'

'Do you miss it?'

'No,' he said bluntly. 'Twice a year I go and do stand-up in Oban in a pub where they serve cockles and a pint for three quid. Mostly they just throw the cockles at me. But I think secretly they know my stuff is good.'

'I believe you. So you're still writing?'

Mike stepped inside the house and came back out holding a dog-eared notebook.

'This is a script about a priest who goes to work in Hollywood. I've written dozens of 'em. Some of it's the best stuff I've ever done. Must be the sea air.'

He threw it into Sam's lap and Sam flicked through it, feeling a rising excitement.

'Laugh a minute, old son,' said Mike confidently. 'I should know, I've timed it.'

Sam didn't have to read Mike's script to know how brilliant it would be. The word 'genius' was bandied about a lot in LA, but an on-form Mike McKenzie was the real deal. He wasn't just funny, he was sad too; he made the thoughtful seem so throwaway – you'd catch your breath and realise the impact of his words long after he'd moved on to something else. Sam had never been able to write anything even close to Mike's output, which was one of the reasons he'd gone off to become an actor. It was hard living in such a tall shadow.

'Why did we split up again?'

Mike gave a wry smile.

'Creative differences. That's what your Wikipedia entry says anyway.'

'The truth is, I just wasn't funny.'

'At least you had the balls to admit it.'

Sam gave him a sideways glance. 'It was tempting not to.'

Mike shaded his eyes and peered down at him. 'What do you mean?'

'I thought you were my meal ticket.'

Mike snorted and threw a pebble at him. 'The international movie star thought I was his meal ticket?'

'It's true. You were so fucking funny. I could so easily have tagged along as your Ernie Wise, but . . .'

'But you wanted to be the star?'

'Yep,' said Sam, sipping his tea. 'And look where that got me.'

'So do you want to talk about it?'

Sam laughed.

'Jesus, Mike, I know you're casual about things, but I didn't think you'd wait a full two days to bring it up.'

'Well, apparently the whole world's talking about it. I wasn't sure you'd want anyone else chucking their ha'penny's worth in.'

'The difference is you're my friend.'

'Okay, seeing as you ask, I think you've been a right knob. Shall we move on?'

Sam chuckled.

'That's what I love about you, you always find me hilarious.'

'Me and about a million other people.'

'Ah, you're talking about the past there.'

'Come on, Mike. You miss it.'

His friend was quiet for a moment and all they could hear was the bleating of a lamb on the hillside behind them.

'I miss making people laugh,' he said finally. 'Mentally I'm better, strong enough to do it again, but I'm wary of stepping back out there. I mean, look what's happened to you. You wanted to act. You've become a circus show.'

'Cheers.'

Mike gave a low, thoughtful laugh.

'They were good, the old days, though, weren't they?'

'I knew you were tempted, you sneaky sod. Why else have you been writing about priests in Hollywood when you could be chatting up the local milkmaid. I tell you, Mike, you could be the next Will Ferrell if you wanted to be. You're certainly tall enough.'

'Give me the Edinburgh Fringe over Tinseltown any day.'

Mike's eyes glazed over as if he was lost in the nostalgia of their twenties. 'Remember that first show we did straight out of uni? You were bloody funny, by the way.'

Sam shrugged to accept the compliment. He knew the sharp comic timing that had won him some of Hollywood's best romantic comedy roles had been honed in rehearsals for that very show.

'We should do it again.' Mike's voice was quiet and nervy.

'Do what again?'

'Edinburgh Fringe. Me and you.'

'Come on, Mike. You know I can't.'

'Why not? Too famous?' he chided. 'Your fragile movie-star ego not able to handle a few gentle hecklers?'

'Don't be daft,' blustered Sam. 'It's just not what I do any more. It never really was.'

'Don't look at it as stand-up. See it as entertainment. And no one does that better than you, Sammy boy. Look, it will be too late to get in the official Edinburgh programme, but you know there's not a promoter in town who wouldn't bite our hands off if we said we wanted to do a two-man show.'

Mike's mercurial temperament had undergone one of its mood swings, his reluctance to step back into the limelight, so obvious just a couple of minutes earlier, replaced by a euphoric desperation to make it happen. Sam hated to disappoint his old friend, but the thought of cranking out jokes to a roomful of pissed students seemed as alien to him as joining the astronauts on the next space mission.

'I can't. But you do it,' he said with encouragement. 'The comedy world needs a new hero.'

'What's stopping you?'

'I have a career. In Hollywood.'

'Then why do you look so shit-scared when I ask how long you're staying on Eigan?'

Sam felt embarrassed to be caught out. Eigan *was* idyllic, but that wasn't the reason why he wanted to stay on the island indefinitely. Its remoteness and solitude protected him, and made him feel so disconnected from reality it was as if the events of the previous few days – Katie, the court case, the showdown with Jessica – had never happened.

Mike looked at him sympathetically, as if he was reading his thoughts.

'I know how much your career means to you. Go back to LA. Sort things out. Make some decisions. You can't hide away here for ever.'

'You did,' Sam said softly.

'I'm not you,' replied Mike, and deep down Sam knew that his old friend was right.

15

'So I got the anti-harassment order against named paparazzi agencies this morning,' said Anna, explaining her morning in court to Grammy Award-winning singing sensation Chantal Elliot. 'They can't come within a hundred metres of you and we'll put a notice to that effect outside your house, your mum and dad's place and at these offices. They're not allowed to approach or follow you either. It's not perfect, but it should make things better.'

The tiny star leapt off the sofa in her manager Ron Green's office and threw herself around Anna.

'Thank you, thank you, thank you. You've saved my life,' she said, grabbing her tightly.

Anna froze, not knowing how to respond. She couldn't believe how bony the girl felt in her arms. The twenty-year-old peroxide blonde was like a tiny doll that might break if she hugged her back.

'Does this mean it's going to stop? Like, for ever?' sobbed the singer, black make-up running down her face. ''Cos I just can't cope with it any more. If the paps keep chasing me, I'm going to kill myself. I mean it.'

Anna nodded. Chantal was well known for her struggles with drink and drugs and seemed to be in the papers on a weekly basis for various hysterical outbursts on the pavement outside nightclubs.

'The paparazzi will have to back off for now at least,' she explained gently. She could understand how the constant presence of photographers would be hard to handle if you were so highly strung. 'But you have to know we can never stop it all. Not if you keep . . . well, putting yourself in the news.'

Chantal pouted, wiping her eyes vigorously and smearing her mascara even more.

'But I've been in rehab, I've been clean for two months now.' She shrugged. 'I mean, why are they still so interested in me?'

Because you're a one-woman headline machine, thought Anna. She looked at the fragile girl dabbing her eyes, all scrunched up on her manager's sofa, and wondered if it was all an act. Could she really be so naive? In the weeks preceding their application for the anti-harassment order, Chantal had complained about journalists and photographers peering in through her windows and going through her rubbish, following her to the off-licence and waiting for her when she stumbled out of a club. It was as if she genuinely couldn't connect the two parts of her life: Chantal the performer who thrived on and desperately needed the attention, and Chantal the damaged little girl with the multiple addictions who couldn't stand the pressure of living in a goldfish bowl. The final straw had been two days ago when she had popped out for a packet of Rizlas and been besieged by half a dozen paparazzi. As she had run across the road to escape them, one photographer had run over her foot on his moped. Chantal had had a complete meltdown and sat on the pavement screaming until someone had called an ambulance. This, of course, had been splashed across every front page in the country: 'Chantal Finally Loses It', 'Pop Star Taken To Nut House'. Anna had actually been shocked at the complete lack of sympathy the papers had shown her. But then she supposed this was just another in a long line of breakdowns for Chantal. If you couldn't get this close to her and see just how vulnerable she really was, it could easily look as if she was cynically courting the publicity, then crying wolf when she didn't like it.

Chantal forced a smile, then started skipping around the office like a child.

Ron touched Anna on the shoulder to beckon her out of the room.

'Are you sure they are going to leave her alone? You can see how unsettled she is.'

Anna folded her arms in front of her and looked doubtful.

'Right now, she's a meal ticket for the media. She's an addict, so it's a story. She kicks the habit. Another story. She falls off the wagon – another story right there. The press are just waiting, watching, and if they want pictures, they'll get them. We've got the order against those named agencies, but there's nothing to stop them employing freelance photographers and cutting a deal.'

Ron smiled.

'Well, the main thing is that Chantal feels as though the pressure has been lifted for a while. So thanks for that at least.'

Anna shook her head. 'No, Ron, thank *you*.'

She knew that Ron had particularly asked for her when he needed legal help, and it had been just the boost Anna had needed. After all the publicity with the Sam Charles case, clients were giving her a wide berth; no one wanted her bad professional luck to rub off on them. But Ron was a good friend. She'd done a lot of work for his management company when she'd been at Davidson's, and he'd stayed loyal when he'd needed help with Chantal.

'You don't know how much it means to get back in the saddle and nail a successful injunction for you,' she said.

'Come on, don't get all teary on me, Anna,' said Ron with a wink. 'I've got enough of that on my hands with madam through there. I came to you because you're the best, no other reason.'

She blushed slightly.

'Thank you.'

'And don't let the bastards grind you down, all right?'

No chance of that, she thought to herself. I'm back in the game.

She left Ron's Hammersmith office and got a taxi to Piccadilly. It was a baking-hot day and she pulled the window down, feeling the warm air on her face. Donovan Pierce was a relaxed firm but not so relaxed that she could wear shorts, vest and flip-flops. Her fitted light wool Armani dress had looked good in court, but it wasn't exactly ideal for walking through the park.

It was almost one o'clock. She'd give herself half an hour here – tops. The up side of her reduced workload was that she had more time to figure out how to get Blake Stanhope for contempt

127

of court. So far she'd hit a brick wall. Neil Graham, the editor of the Scandalhound website, had finally taken her call but had been typically obtuse and difficult. Perhaps he was still miffed about the photo-doctored picture of the actress Serena Balcon she'd sued him for last year. Regardless, there was no way he was going to confirm that Blake had leaked the story. Not yet anyway.

What the hell am I doing here? Anna thought as she paid the cabby and walked through the gates of Green Park. Meeting this strange girl had seemed to make sense yesterday. It had certainly been a left-field conversation with Ruby, but she'd been intrigued by the girl's story. Perhaps the truth was that she'd been feeling isolated and vulnerable and Ruby's desperate need had struck a chord with her. Oh well, let's get this over with, she thought. Ruby Hart, where are you?

Scores of office workers and tourists were teeming on to the parched yellow grass, to sunbathe or have lunch under a shady tree. She glanced at the photo of Ruby that the girl had emailed her, so she could recognise her, but no one seemed to fit the bill.

Anna looked at her watch. She had to be back in the office by two o'clock or Helen Pierce would start asking questions. Although the frosty atmosphere had lessened a little – Ron Green's business had no doubt helped in that regard – she still felt like a pariah in the eyes of the senior partner, but she knew there was no point in dwelling on the injustice of it all. She just had to pick herself up and prove to Helen that she had been right to hire her in the first place.

'Anna?'

She turned; she had been so caught up in her thoughts, she hadn't seen the girl approach.

She was small, and her dark-blond hair was scraped back in a ponytail. Despite the heat, she had thick black leggings on under canvas shorts, and she was chewing nervously on a painted nail.

'You must be Ruby,' said Anna, shaking her other hand. 'Shall we walk? It's too hot to stand around.'

Ruby nodded shyly.

'Sorry I didn't want to meet in your office. I didn't think I'd get past the receptionist.'

Anna smiled. 'No, you don't look like our average client. How old are you?'

'Seventeen.'

God, you look much older, thought Anna, observing the girl's hard, care-worn look. Don't jump to conclusions, Anna, she scolded herself.

'So where have you travelled from?' she asked as they began to walk around the lake.

'Near Doncaster.'

'Are you at college?'

Ruby nodded. 'I'm doing my A levels. I'm applying to uni when I get back,' she said with a hint of pride.

'Great. Which one?'

'Cambridge.'

'Well done you.' Anna smiled, hoping it hadn't come out as patronising. Which it was, she thought. You had her down as a teen mother on crack, didn't you?

'So what do you want to do? When you finish your degree, I mean?'

Ruby shrugged.

'I used to think about journalism, but maybe it's too corrupt and deceitful.'

Anna couldn't help but give a cynical laugh, thinking immediately of Andrew and how he'd got Sophie a food column on his newspaper, then begun an affair with her soon after. Deceitful wasn't the half of it.

'What's so funny?' said Ruby.

'Sorry, it wasn't you,' said Anna. 'I deal with the papers for a living, remember? And yes, you're right, perhaps there are some deceitful journalists. But then again, there are lots more very good, very honourable ones too. People who make a difference and who risk a lot to make politicians and companies accountable.'

'Does that sort of journalism even exist any more?' said Ruby doubtfully.

Anna thought about the endless debates she and Andrew used to have about the state of the media. Andrew's complaints about the overstretched budgets. The pressure on the news team to get the most up-to-date stories, not necessarily the most probing ones. 'It's the death of investigative journalism,' he'd once told her. 'With our budget cuts and media lawyers strangleholding us every two minutes, how can we ever get the world-class scoops we used to?'

'It exists. Perhaps not as often as it should,' she said guiltily, knowing that Andrew blamed lawyers such as herself for the demise in reporting. 'But it does.'

They reached a patch lined with trees and sat on a bench in the shade of a poplar.

'I still haven't quite worked out how I can help you,' said Anna, turning to Ruby.

'My sister was murdered and no one believes me.'

'Then why should I?'

'Maybe you won't, but I thought you might at least pay attention to me.'

Is that what this is about? thought Anna with a sinking feeling. This poor girl just wants someone to talk to? She glanced at her watch and took a deep breath.

'Okay, so perhaps you should start at the beginning.'

Ruby glanced away and began chewing her nail again. A flake of black polish came off and stuck to her lip.

'I told you,' she said. 'My sister died six months ago. The inquest took ages. Finally they ruled an open verdict.'

'And you're unhappy with that?'

'She was found dead at her flat by her landlord. Apparently she'd fallen down the stairs. She was wearing heels and the steps were steep.'

'It sounds plausible. What was the cause of death?'

'A broken neck.'

'Because she'd fallen down the stairs?' said Anna, trying to work out the sequence of events.

Ruby nodded. 'That's what the coroner said. But I think she was pushed.'

Anna leaned closer.

'Is that a possibility?'

'The pathologist spoke at the inquest. He said it was

impossible to know for sure, but the injuries that caused her death were "largely consistent" – she put up her fingers to denote quotation marks – 'with a tumble down the stairs.'

'Then why did the coroner not pronounce accidental death?'

'No one knows for sure what happened. And the coroner admitted there were some things out of character. For instance the amount of alcohol she'd taken. Amy rarely drank. Plus a neighbour in her apartment building saw a man in the stairwell near her apartment the evening she died. The police followed it up, but nothing came of it. They didn't think it was suspicious.'

Poor Ruby, thought Anna. She was clearly just a traumatised kid looking for something to cling to. Anna couldn't blame her for that, but she wasn't sure how she could help her either.

'Ruby, I can't even begin to understand how awful this has been for you,' she said gently. 'Sometimes trying to make sense of something helps us work through the grief. But I have to say that this sounds like a very tragic accident.'

Ruby nodded. It was as if that was the reaction she had been expecting.

'That's what my mum says. She says it's my coping mechanism. She wouldn't even let me speak at the inquest. No one ever takes a seventeen-year-old seriously anyway. But it just doesn't sound right.'

'So what makes you think this wasn't an accident?'

'The police report says that Amy was wearing high heels when she was found at the bottom of the stairs. But I'm not sure she was wearing them when she fell. For a start, she only had one nail painted and it must have been wet when the shoe went on because there was polish on the inside leather of her shoe.'

'What does that prove? She could have been painting her nails and then had to rush out. She grabbed some heels, she was in a hurry, she stumbled.'

'She was in leggings and a T-shirt when they found her. Stuff to lounge around in. Not to team up with a pair of Jimmy Choos. My sister would never wear her Choos with her comfy clothes.'

She looked back at Anna with embarrassment.

'I know, it sounds like I'm clutching at straws, doesn't it? I can see no one's going to believe any of that in court or anything, but I knew my sister and it just doesn't add up to me.'

'So why didn't the police treat her death as suspicious?'

Ruby shook her head sadly.

'I don't know.'

Anna looked at her watch again. She felt bad letting the poor girl down, but she really didn't have time for this.

'Listen, Ruby, I'd love to be able to help you,' she said, trying to keep the irritation out of her voice. 'But this isn't my area of law and besides, you really haven't given me anything I could work with. You said on the phone that someone famous killed your sister. Either you tell me everything or I'm really going to have to go.'

'I don't know who to trust.'

Anna put her hand over Ruby's.

'You can trust me, Ruby. Just tell me what happened.'

Ruby took a deep breath.

'My sister had started going out with a famous actor, I told you that. I was excited at first. Asked her to get me his autograph. But then after they'd been out, she didn't want to talk about him. She told me he was an idiot and that they'd had an argument and she didn't want to see him again.'

'So?'

'So she rejected him. And I bet famous people don't like that. I bet he went round to her house and they had another row and, well, the next thing we know, Amy is dead.'

'You know he went round?' she asked, puzzled.

'No. But it all makes sense. People are usually killed by people they know, aren't they?'

'Yes, but . . .'

'What about the shoe? The nail polish? I think he went round to her flat, and at some point he pushed Amy down the stairs. Maybe it was an accident but he wasn't going to take the blame for it. I think he put the high heels on her feet to make it look like she fell, and left the flat.' She was twisting her hair furiously around her fingers.

'Was Amy's boyfriend interviewed at the inquest?'

She nodded.

'He claimed they had split up by the time she died.'

Anna's hopes of this turning out to be anything worth skipping lunch for were rapidly dwindling.

'You've not told me. Who was Amy's boyfriend?'

'Ryan Jones.'

Anna just blinked. The name meant nothing to her.

'You know, Ryan Jones,' said Ruby. 'He plays Jamie in *Barclay's Place*.'

Barclay's Place was a low-budget suppertime soap aimed at students. It wasn't even on terrestrial TV. Anna had been expecting Ruby to name a Hollywood A-lister with top political connections, at the very least a theatrical 'sir' with some pull with the papers.

'I want to challenge the inquest,' said Ruby finally. 'And I want you to do it for me.'

Anna felt disheartened. 'Look, Ruby, I'm sorry for your loss, I truly am. But I think this is just a very, very sad accident, however hard that might be to accept. And I'm not sure challenging the inquest is going to help you and your family move forward.'

'But you can challenge an inquest?'

She shrugged. 'Well, yes. You'd have to apply to the High Court for a judicial review, although you're going to need more of a reason than "Amy didn't wear high heels in the house".'

Ruby ferreted in her bag and pulled out a tatty-looking purse.

'Listen, there's over a hundred quid in here,' she said, trying to press it into Anna's hands. 'I want you to be my lawyer. You know about the law and you know about celebrities. When I read about you in the papers I knew you were the person who could help me.'

Anna had to smile. 'You're one of the few people who probably does believe in my legal capabilities right now.'

'Take the money,' said Ruby.

Anna shook her head. 'Oh Ruby, I can't. I can't do this for you. This isn't what I do.'

'Please,' said Ruby, tears pooling in her eyes. 'My sister was beautiful and clever. She came from nothing, my dad beat us up, but she made a nice life for herself. And now she's dead. I don't know if you have a sister, Miss Kennedy, but if you do and she got killed, you'd want to know why, wouldn't you?'

'Obviously I would, but . . .'

Ruby's eyes challenged hers.

'I know what sort of law you do, Miss Kennedy. You cover things up for rich people. Why don't you do the right thing for a change? Why don't you help uncover the truth for once?'

The words sat with Anna uncomfortably. She looked at Ruby kindly.

'Go back to Doncaster. Go back to college. Get into Cambridge and make your sister proud.'

'Can you at least do me one favour?' said Ruby, handing Anna a brown envelope. 'At least take this. Everything I could find out about Amy's death is in there. Just read it.'

'All right,' said Anna, stuffing it into her bag. 'But now I really have to go.'

'Even if you don't want to help me, thanks for seeing me at least,' Ruby said. 'Most people would just think I'm some nutter.'

The thought had crossed my mind, thought Anna.

She turned away and practically ran towards the gate, praying that there would be cabs on Piccadilly. 'Helen Pierce is really going to kill me,' she muttered to herself. 'And to be honest, I wouldn't blame her.'

16

Helen was in the shower when the phone rang. It was 7.30 a.m. but her day had started an hour and a half earlier with a tennis lesson at her club; it took discipline to maintain both a body and a career. She snapped off the jets and called out through the steam.

'Graham, can you get that?'

The telephone continued to ring in the bedroom next to the en suite.

'Graham!' she shouted, then under her breath: 'Where is that bloody man?'

Grabbing a fluffy robe, she strode out of the en suite, leaving wet footprints on the cream carpet, and snatched the phone from the bedside cabinet. She stabbed the button to accept the call, glaring at her husband still slumbering in their bed, his mop of grey hair just visible above the duvet. It had been a long time since Graham had risen this early. In the months after he had lost his seat as a Home Counties MP, he would have been up before her, reading, researching, determined to carve out a new career as a political historian. But when the book deal and the accompanying television series had not been forthcoming, his drive had ebbed away and now he spent his days pottering in their Kensington garden and talking vaguely about 'shaking things up on a local level'. Not that Helen minded; she had enough ambition for both of them. She was simply irritated because this early in the morning, the call was bound to be work-related.

'Helen Pierce,' she snapped.

'He's back,' said a voice.

Helen recognised Jim Parker's West Coast drawl immediately.

'Sam?' she said.

'Who else?'

'Well it's about bloody time.'

'You don't have to tell me, sweetheart.'

Sam's LA agent had been furious when his headline-grabbing client had gone missing three days before. Well, not missing exactly. Eli Cohen, Sam's manager, knew where he was hiding, but was refusing to tell anyone, even Helen or Jim, for fear his location might leak out. Helen could understand Jim's anger – after all, they desperately needed to get to work on Sam's damage-limitation plan as soon as possible, as the column inches weren't getting any less.

'So where is he? And where are you?' she demanded, towel-drying her hair.

'Sam is back at his country place,' said Jim. 'And I'm on my way. I got into Heathrow an hour ago.'

'Fine, I'll meet you there in an hour,' she said and hung up without waiting for an answer. Jim Parker was smart enough to know that Helen Pierce would move heaven and earth to fix this situation: she had to. In truth, Helen didn't give two hoots about Sam Charles's career – that was the risk you ran when you were famous and unfaithful – but what she did care about was the reputation of the firm, which was why she had to be on top of her game not just to firefight the situation but to turn it around. And that was why Jim had kept her on the team despite Sam's sacking of Anna.

She walked into her dressing room and ran her hand along the line of clothes, loving the way the hangers knocked gently together. In the calm orderliness of her dressing room, she took a minute to take stock of the situation. It had actually been fortuitous that she had assigned the Sam Charles case to Anna. She had been sorely tempted to take it herself, for the glory, the spoils. The way things had turned out, it had been Anna's reputation that had been damaged. Over the next few weeks, Helen would assess how bad that damage had been; she didn't want to get rid of the smart, ambitious girl – she still thought Anna had potential – but if she had to sack her, then she would do it without a thought.

Finally Helen selected a starched white shirt and a tight navy pencil skirt. Usually she'd only wear such formal, highly tailored clothes on court days; the stiffness of her shirt collars and the structure of her skirt were like a suit of armour. For years the legal community had been debating the pros and cons of getting rid of the barrister's horsehair wigs, winged collars and gowns. The naysayers thought they were too haughty and ceremonious, relics of a Dickensian era, but Helen could understand why so many lawyers were fond of their regalia – it was protective clothing, a shield and helmet for when you went into battle. Today was going to be one of those days, except instead of the courtroom the battleground was Sam Charles's country manor. And Helen was an expert in military strategy; she knew she couldn't afford to lose this one.

'What time is it?'

Graham stirred, rolling over on the pillow to look at her, his face lined with creases from the linen.

'Almost eight.'

He grunted and snuggled back under the duvet. 'Another five minutes then I'll get up and make you coffee.'

'Don't bother,' said Helen, striding past, picking up her leather briefcase from the desk as she went.

'Whatever you say, darling,' he mumbled, and turned over.

Helen looked at him with a mixture of irritation and pity. So strange to think that just a decade earlier, Graham had been the perfect catch. She'd been thirty-eight when they'd met at a cocktail party in Mayfair. Helen had never felt any strong desire to be a wife, and certainly no ticking biological clock, but as she climbed higher up both the professional and social ladder, she'd observed that a husband was a desirable accessory. Singles were viewed with suspicion on her high-flying society circuit. It was fine for men, of course; single men were playboys, dashing roguishly around town, playing the field. Single women, on the other hand, were seen as either predatory or dysfunctional.

Graham was well bred, connected and handsome in that ruddy-cheeked public-schoolboy way. His grandfather had been a leading light in the sixties Conservative government, an old-school-style politician with money, power and an aristocratic lineage, and there were whispers that Graham's political career could have a similar trajectory. When they had married after a nine-month courtship, Helen had genuinely held high hopes that one day their marital home might be 10 Downing Street. But humiliatingly, Graham had turned out to be a one-term MP. In the new political climate, his style was seen as old fashioned and fuddy-duddy, and he lost his seat to an articulate Lib Dem fifteen years his junior. And that had been it. Graham had spent his life having everything laid out in front of him; he didn't know how to cope when something didn't fit the script.

She could have divorced him, of course. *Should* have divorced him, in fact. If Helen had had any close female friends, this might have been the sort of thing they discussed over long, commiseratory lunches in San Lorenzo. But she had no time for lunch – and no time for divorce. Not yet, anyway.

'Well, see you later,' grunted Graham. 'What time you back?'

Why? she thought. Are you thinking of whisking me off to Rome?

'Oh, late probably,' she sighed instead. 'I'm at a client's in Wiltshire. I'm not sure how long it will take.'

He pulled the duvet down, his interest evidently piqued.

'This the Sam Charles thing?'

Everyone was talking about the scandal; the fact that it had penetrated into Graham's clubby upper-class world was an indication of what big news it was. Helen nodded.

'Crisis-management talks at his house.'

'Well, it's nothing you can't sort out,' he said encouragingly. 'You got that chap Svurak off, didn't you?'

Just a month earlier, Helen had extracted the Premiership footballer from an even tighter spot. The bad boy of the pitch had been caught with a sixteen-year-old girl in a seedy hotel room. Not only had he gleefully filmed the whole event, he had thought it hilarious to send the footage to all his friends – one of whom had thought it even more funny to send it to a red-top in exchange for a large stack of cash. Helen had only avoided the complete destruction of Svurak's career by going straight to the top. She had struck a series of deals first with his club, who had agreed to trade the hotel footage for an exclusive – and uncharacteristically candid – interview with the team's captain for the tabloid. On top of that, the paper was given the scoop on Svurak's surprise marriage to the ambitious singer of a struggling girl band. The wedding would be held at the luxurious Carlos Blanco hotel in Marbella, whose owner, another client of Donovan Pierce, was only too happy to lap up the publicity.

They should call us cleaners, not lawyers, thought Helen. That's all we do: clean up the shit before anyone even knows it's there.

'I think it's going to be a long day,' she said, checking her phone for more messages. 'It might even run into tomorrow, so if I decide to stay out there I'll call you tonight.'

'You go get 'em, darling,' said Graham as she walked out.

One of us has to, she thought as she closed the door.

'Jesus! Can't you leave me alone for one second?' shouted Sam. He pulled back behind the curtain as the helicopter hovered over the trees at the bottom of his garden. Could they see him? he wondered. Would Sky News viewers see him cowering next to his Smeg fridge and read the guilt on his face? What did they even want from him? It was like a dream he couldn't wake up from.

Even in LA, Sam had never thought he needed to live in a fortress. At his Hollywood Hills home, he'd rejected Jessica's calls for a twenty-four-hour armed guard and made do with a state-of-the-art alarm system and a gated drive. Here at Copley's, his Wiltshire manor house, security was even more lax: just some electric gates and CCTV, which was currently showing him the dozens of reporters and photographers on stepladders crowded around the gate. He'd never needed anything before, even when Jessica had been visiting. The locals in the village had been respectful of his privacy and his attitude had always been, why turn yourself into a prisoner when you didn't have to? Besides, he'd have felt a fraud with all that movie-star nonsense – it was only pretentious LA wankers who bought into that kind of 'I'm so important' bollocks, wasn't it? But it was at times like these, times when you didn't dare look out of your kitchen window, that you could see the wisdom of 'better safe than sorry'.

'I wish I'd put bloody landmines around the drive,' he muttered as he watched the helicopter finally turn and spiral off into the clouds. The real shame of it was that Sam usually adored his time at Copley's. He loved the glorious eighteenth-century house with its honey-coloured façade and its own trout lake and woodland. It was his very own Neverland, with a five-a-side pitch beyond the ha-ha and a rope swing in the woods instead of Jacko's rollercoasters and carousels. Sam had felt safe at Copley's, he'd felt at home, even if it did have a dozen bedrooms he never went into. But now . . . now would it ever feel safe again?

He frowned as he became aware of an insistent buzzing. He hadn't heard it until the helicopter had gone, but now he could tell it was coming from the intercom.

'Josh,' he yelled. 'Is that the bloody reporters again? And where's Jim?'

His PA scurried in from the study, where he'd been fielding calls. 'Sorry, Sam,' he hissed, holding his hand over the receiver of his mobile. 'I'm on the phone to New York. You wanted me to get Harvey for you? And I think Mr Parker's in the media room monitoring the TV coverage.'

'Bloody hell,' muttered Sam, running over to the silver box on the wall. 'What's the point in having staff if you have to do everything yourself?'

He stabbed angrily at the button.

'Who is it?' he said, immediately jerking back as a roar filled the room: a hundred voices shouting, the chaotic whirr of camera shutters; it sounded like a riot going on out there.

'Hel . . . Pier . . .' said a crackly voice. Sam could barely make out the words over the racket.

'Who?' he shouted.

'It's Helen Pierce. Let me in.'

Jim Parker shouted down the stairs, 'It's the lawyer. Buzz her through already!'

As Sam pressed the switch that would open the gate, he could hear a plummy female voice coming through the intercom.

'If any of you puts so much as one foot on this property,' it said with schoolmistress authority, 'I'll have you in the nick faster than you can say "parasites".'

I like this chick already, he smiled.

His new lawyer was surprisingly sexy. Older, more severe than the last one and dressed in a crisp shirt and very high patent pumps, she looked like a 1940s pin-up. Or maybe I just go for uptight chicks, thought Sam as he watched her walk into his dining room accompanied by Eli and Valerie Lovell, the PR powerhouse who had also flown over from the States for this council of war. They all shook hands as they sat down around his redwood dining table. This was Sam's favourite room in the house, a modern addition to the three-hundred-year-old architecture designed to soften the antique edges of the house. A wall of glass overlooked a grey slate fishpond and the lawns beyond, although today the blinds were drawn to discourage any long-lens photography.

'Busier than I thought out there,' said Eli with his usual understated humour.

'Busy like a war zone,' sniffed Jim Parker.

'Sam, I don't think you've met Helen Pierce,' said Valerie, peering over the top of her horn-rimmed Chanel glasses. 'I've worked with her before and there's no one better at crisis management from the legal end.'

Sam snorted. 'If it wasn't for Donovan Pierce, there might not even be a crisis.' He knew he was being rude, but he was still angry at Anna Kennedy – and Donovan Pierce as a whole – for letting him down with the injunction. It would take more than sending their top attack dog – the lawyer he should have had in the first place – to placate him.

Josh came through with strong coffee and Sam slugged it back gratefully. The sleeping pill he'd taken at 3 a.m. to stop the endless questions running around his head was still making him feel groggy and detached.

'Where have you been, Sam?' asked Helen.

Sam lit another cigarette. It wasn't even 10.30 a.m. and already he'd smoked a packet. Terrible habit, he knew, but he felt justified today. He needed something to quiet his nerves.

'Eigan island,' he said. 'A tiny place near Mull. You won't know it.'

'Actually I do,' said Helen. 'It's a little piece of paradise, isn't it? I'm surprised you came back.'

Maybe I should have stayed, he thought. It had certainly been tempting, but Mike had urged him to 'get a grip and go and sort things out at home'.

Instead he was hiding here in his dining room, the table strewn with papers and magazines, all of them boasting 'exclusive' takes on the story. 'Sam and Jess Split: The Inside Story!', 'Why I Walked Out, Jess Speaks!', 'I Always Knew He Was A Cheat, Jess Tells Friend'. It was mostly speculation; thankfully Jessica had yet to speak publicly about it, although the fact that Sam was here, a thousand miles away from his 'heartbroken' fiancée, was a fairly large clue as to what was happening between them.

'So I guess we all know what's going on in the press,' said Jim Parker, indicating the table. 'I've just been scanning the satellite channels; the news media's pretty much taking the same stance.'

Helen Pierce opened her notebook. 'What's the support from the industry like?'

'Hard to tell,' said Jim. 'Everyone's making the right noises: "Tell Sam we're thinking about him", all that crap, but the only way to judge LA is by the movie offers that are on the table.'

'And what's that like?'

Jim glanced at Sam, then shrugged.

'It's summer. It's quiet. They'll be in a wait-and-see position until we know box office on his next movie. But honestly . . .' He pulled a face. 'I think we should be worried.'

'Oh great,' said Sam. 'Kick me when I'm down, why don't you?'

'Hey, buddy, we gotta get real,' replied Jim. 'You're nothing in Tinseltown unless you're making money, you know that. If you were making the studios half a billion a picture, we wouldn't be having this conversation. No one would give a damn who you screwed.'

'It's true, look at Charlie Sheen,' nodded Valerie. 'He had to really *really* screw up before they cancelled his show.'

'And we ain't in Charlie's position,' said Jim. 'He was the star of America's biggest sitcom. Sam? Well, let's be frank, his last two movies tanked.'

Sam hated his career being talked about as if he wasn't even in the room. He found himself getting defensive.

'Jim, you were the one who told me to do those movies.'

Jim turned his hands outwards.

'I get the offers. You and Eli take the decisions. If you choose to make the turkeys . . .'

'Hey, this is a team effort, Jim,' said Eli. 'Don't pass the buck just because the shit's hit the fan.'

It was no secret that Eli and Jim disliked each other, both of them fighting for the upper hand in the steerage of Sam's career.

'All right, gentlemen,' said Helen firmly. 'Let's focus on what we can control. Sam's next movie is premiering in a week or two, yes? So the industry is out of our hands until then. I think we should concentrate on the media. Valerie, this is your area.'

'The weakest link in the chain is the girl Katie,' said the PR, sweeping back her black bob. 'We could definitely go after her. Spin it as a set-up, release the story about her trying to blackmail us.'

'Wouldn't that just look like Sam was trying to wriggle out of it?' replied Helen.

'Isn't that what we're trying to do here?' snapped Jim. 'I don't think it's too late to persuade people that Sam didn't even have sex with her. She doesn't really have much evidence, so we threaten to sue, major damages, scare her into a retraction.'

Helen looked thoughtful. 'It's possible, but we should have come out with denial immediately. Sam's all but confessed.'

'I haven't said anything!' he managed to splutter.

'Yes, and that's the problem. If you'd denied it and Jessica had stood by you, we could have weathered it, but as it is, she's effectively kicked you out and now we have all this . . .' Helen grabbed a copy of the *Sun* and held it up, showing the headline that read: 'Kinky Sam Forced Himself On Me'.

'But that's just rubbish!' said Sam.

'Is it?' said Helen, scanning the text. 'Sam was a sex pest, always badgering me for sex . . . Sam wanted sex all the time, we did it five times a night.'

Sam winced. He couldn't bear to look at it himself and it sounded even worse when someone read it out. The funny thing about show business was that you needed the toughest skin just to get your foot in the door. The auditions, the knock-backs, the humiliations, you couldn't do it without tunnel vision and an iron will. But once you made it, that rhino hide disintegrated. Suddenly everyone was telling you how wonderful you were, how funny, how handsome, every single day of your life. And you came to expect it, your self-esteem was all wrapped up in the constant barrage of love, even if deep down you knew it was pure sycophancy. So when all that was taken away, the insults and the criticism hurt more than ever.

'Well, is it true?' pressed Helen.

'Yes and no,' he said uncomfortably.

'Yes and no to what? To being a sex pest?'

'No! That girl is an old girlfriend from when I was at university *fifteen years* ago. Yes, we had sex, of course we did. And yes, I was keen on it – who isn't when they're nineteen?'

'I hear that,' said Eli. Helen just glared at him.

'But this story makes me sound like some sort of rapist. And there's no timeline on it, so readers might think it happened last week.'

Valerie shrugged.

'Clever reporting. It's what they do.'

'Can't we sue?' said Sam desperately.

'What for? Turning back time? Anyway, this is all taking us away from the main problem,' added Helen.

'Which is what?'

'That your reputation is in the toilet and it's open season on you now. With your disappearing act, the media had nothing real to report on, so they went trawling for dirt and it's no big surprise that they found ex-girlfriends and disgruntled rivals who were happy to take a few quid to say bad things about you. The trouble is, this is going to run and run unless we give them a better story.'

144

Sam felt his heart start to pound and tried to calm himself. He really shouldn't have taken that sleeping pill; they always put him on edge the next day. Everywhere he turned people seemed to want to bring him down, ruin all the hard work he'd put in.

'A better story?' said Jim. 'What are you suggesting?'

'How about this?' said Valerie, holding up her hands as if she were imagining the front-page splash. ' "Sam and Jess: The Second Honeymoon".'

'We haven't had our first honeymoon yet,' said Sam.

'What I mean is that a reconciliation story could be all we need. All is forgiven, you both get a huge flurry of publicity and we're back on track.'

'It'd certainly put an end to all the Sam-bashing,' said Helen. 'What do you think, Eli?'

'Unlikely,' he said gruffly. 'I've spoken to Barbara, the mother. She's still talking about wanting Sam's balls on a platter.'

'But the buzz on Jess's latest movie is that it stinks,' said Jim. 'If it's really that bad, she may want a positive spin to deflect the attention.'

Sam's mouth almost dropped open. He couldn't believe they were being so cynical about something as important as his life.

'Look, this is my relationship we're talking about here,' he said angrily. 'It's not some smokescreen for a box-office turkey.'

Helen turned to him.

'Do you want to have a career in films?'

'Of course!'

'Then you will do whatever is necessary to get back on track. Now, have you spoken to Jessica? Is a reconciliation an option?'

Sam paused for a moment.

'I don't think so,' he sighed. 'You know I flew to the Cape to see her. Plus I've spoken to her friends. It hasn't changed what she's saying.'

'Which is what?'

'That it's over.'

'Well, of course she's gonna play hardball,' said Jim. 'The people who read US Weekly want Girl Power. They don't want her rolling over too quickly. She's got to let you roast for a while.'

Sam glared at him.

'Or there's always the possibility that she is genuinely heartbroken about being cheated on and wants nothing more to do with me. Besides, I think splitting up was maybe for the best . . .'

His team looked at him, their eyes wide.

'How is this for the best, Sam?' said Jim.

'Because I'm not sure I was ever in love with her.'

Silence rang around the room.

Valerie whistled between her teeth. 'I hope the press aren't bugging this room.'

'Have you actually said this to her?' asked Eli.

'I mentioned it in Cape Cod.'

Jim Parker went pale. '*Mentioned* it. Sam, this is your career.'

'*This is my life*,' he snapped, feeling his chest tighten.

Helen looked down at her notes, tapping the page with her gold pencil.

'Okay, well, if a reconciliation is out of the question, we need to think rehabilitation. Ideas, everyone?'

Sam looked at Helen as she took control of the meeting. She was certainly impressive. His agent, manager and PR were the best in the business, ass-kickers all, but they were deferring to Helen Pierce without a murmur. Sam had met plenty of players in his time – Hollywood was the natural home of arrogant egotists – but this woman had something more: control and authority. You felt she knew what she was doing and, more importantly, that she could make it happen.

'I think we send him to Hazelden,' said Jim Parker. 'Six weeks in rehab could be just what we need.'

'Rehab?' said Sam, appalled. 'What for?'

'Who cares? Booze, drugs, sex,' said Jim. 'It's a strong move because it shows you're admitting you have a problem and that you want to put it right.'

'Hazelden's great but is mainly substance abuse,' said Valerie. 'I know another clinic. Very small. Very discreet. Sex addiction is their specialty.'

'But then people will think I'm a sex addict!' protested Sam.

Eli patted his arm. 'There's worse things to be, buddy.'

'But it's not true. Before that girl Katie, I'd only had sex twice in the last six months. Me and Jess weren't exactly active in that department.'

Valerie looked up at the light fittings. 'I hope to God we're not being bugged.'

'I agree with Sam,' said Helen. 'If we can, we want to stick to the "one night of madness" story. I'll be frank, I don't think the public – and women in particular – really buy the sex-addict story. Michael Douglas got away with it because it was a new angle, but we've since had Duchovny, Charlie Sheen, Tiger Woods; it's become the get-out clause for anyone caught with their pants down.'

'We need to do a high-profile interview,' said Valerie. 'The biggest possible numbers. Letterman's already been in touch, so has Ellen DeGeneres.'

Helen nodded. 'We need to present Sam as penitent. I'm think-ing Hugh Grant after Divine Brown. Can you do tears, Sam?'

'Can he do tears?' scoffed Eli. 'Sam is one of the greatest actors of his generation.'

'Yes, I like this,' replied Valerie. 'We can go with how you didn't know she was an escort, you thought she was just a nice ordinary girl. You love Jessica, but you were lonely because you spend so much time apart. And you're just an ordinary boy who made a big fat lousy mistake.'

Sam could see the sense of what they were saying, but he had stage fright just thinking about it.

'I don't care what we do. But can we just be careful that I don't end up looking more of an arsehole than I already do? And can we keep Jessica out of this as much as possible? This is my fault, not hers.'

'That's exactly it,' said Valerie enthusiastically. 'That's what your public want to hear – you're sorry, but you still care.'

'Great,' said Helen. 'Let's set up one of the talk shows. In the meantime, we'll give the *Sun* an exclusive interview. It should make it more difficult for them to publish sex-pest stories when they've run three thousand words on "My Loneliness Hell".

And Valerie's right, you should use that line, Sam. "It's my fault. Not hers." That comes across well.'

'Let's play up your trip to Scotland too,' said Valerie, her Botoxed face looking almost animated. 'Some sort of wounded-artist-in-the-wilderness angle. Maybe hint at an interest in green issues, that sort of thing. Moving forward, we need to get visiting some soup kitchens, children's homes, maybe some refugee camps. Haiti perhaps. Sudan. Get you papped doing it.'

Sam flinched. 'I like that stuff to be private.'

'Not any more,' said Helen tartly.

Eli looked at Jim. 'What do you think about finding Sam a killer script? Nothing's going to help him like a shitload of good reviews. But we should avoid the lovable rogue thing. We need vulnerable bumbling Brit, like Grant in *Notting Hill*.'

'Good luck with finding that one,' sniffed Jim, adjusting his shirt cuffs. 'Great rom-com scripts are like gold-dust.'

Suddenly Sam had an idea, an idea he knew could work. He saw light appear at the end of a very long tunnel.

'Why don't I write a script myself?'

He looked around the room. Everyone was nodding, but he could tell they were just humouring him.

'Seriously, why not? I did write a show we took to the Edinburgh Fringe, you know.'

'Sure, buddy,' said Eli. 'You give it a shot.'

Screw them, thought Sam as his agent, lawyer, manager and PR got on with the business of arranging the life of this character called Sam Charles. I can do this, I really can. It was time for Sam, the real Sam, to get on with the business of being himself.

17

'So. Tell us *all* about it.'

Anna took a long drink of her wine. Oh God, she thought, the last thing she wanted to do on her night off was relive the nightmare of the Sam Charles debacle for the amusement of her two best friends.

'Come on,' said Cath. 'It's not every day your best mate makes the *News at Ten*.'

'Besides,' added Suzanne, her eyes wide, 'we want to hear about your new friend Sam.'

They were sitting around Anna's small dining table, drinking Sauvignon Blanc as Anna transferred Chinese takeaway from silver-foil dishes on to china plates. It was just like old times, when the three girls had shared a house in Bermondsey when they were at King's College. They weren't students any more – Suzanne was now a GP at a practice in Balham, Cath worked for one of the high-street newsagents 'sourcing bloody Christmas decorations', as she put it – but they still enjoyed teasing each other and mining for gossip.

'There's nothing to tell,' said Anna, trying to deflect the conversation. 'Sam Charles was a client, we got stitched up with the injunction. And now I'm being filmed taking my bins out.'

'I can't believe you were acting for Sam Charles and didn't even tell us,' said Suzanne with mock-offence. 'I mean, Sam Charles!'

Anna laughed.

'These things happen really quickly. You get instructed by the client, you get the injunction – or not. That's it, end of story. It's not like I'm getting invited to the Oscars, is it? Besides, client

149

confidentiality and all that, I'm not really supposed to tell you in the first place.'

Cath drained her wine and reached for the bottle. 'To think we actually feel sorry for you sometimes. You always seem so busy, you never have time to come out any more. We think you're being worked into the ground and then we find out about this exciting clandestine life you've been leading the whole time.'

'Exciting? It's hard work and stressful,' insisted Anna.

Cath pouted. 'Oh, is it hard for you? All the paparazzi and the film stars? I spent the week looking at tinsel snowmen.'

'Is he as gorgeous in the flesh?' asked Suzanne. 'He was so hot in that *Blue Hawaii* remake. His six-pack is amazing.'

'Yes, it is,' said Anna absently, thinking back to the moment when they were standing on the yacht together, the intimacy of the situation, the flash of tanned torso peeking out from under his towelling robe. She felt her neck prickle red.

Cath didn't miss her discomfort. 'Hang on, you've seen his six-pack?' she replied, her mouth dropping open.

Anna held up her hands.

'I had to go and interview him in Capri, on this yacht . . .'

'Hold on, hold on,' said Cath. 'Rewind. You've seen his six-pack? On a yacht? In Capri? I knew I should have studied law.'

Anna sipped her Sauvignon, trying to keep cool.

'Come on. Here we are, three successful, intelligent women, and we're talking about six-packs.'

Cath snorted. 'You've been hanging out with the world's most famous philanderer, Sam Charles. What do you expect us to talk about? Tolstoy? Come on, how gorgeous is he?'

'He's very attractive.'

'You fancy him.' Suzanne grinned.

'I do not,' she lied. 'He's a client.'

'Why did he shag that hooker?'

'What part of client confidentiality don't you understand?'

Suzanne topped up Anna's glass.

'Let's come back to this later when we've plied her with booze, eh?'

Anna was glad her friends had come over. Cath was right:

she *did* work too hard, always making excuses whenever they asked her out for a drink, and she had missed the banter and the cameraderie, especially after the isolation of the past week. In fact, she had been so stressed and grumpy, she had almost cancelled their gossipy night in. She was glad she hadn't.

'So, other than the Sam Charles case, what else have you been up to? Is the new firm better than the last place?'

Anna dug her fork into her noodles.

'Well, both the senior partners hate me. Which I suppose you could see as progress; only my direct supervisor hated me at Davidson's.'

'Balls to the boss,' said Suzanne. She had always been a lightweight; she'd only had two glasses of wine and already her can-do doctor façade was melting away.

'What else?' said Cath. 'And you're not allowed to talk about work.'

'Well, Sophie's getting married,' said Anna. The casualness with which she dropped it into the conversation surprised even herself.

Cath and Suzanne put their glasses down at the same time, instantly seeming to sober up. 'Oh no,' said Suzanne. 'Why didn't you tell us? How? When?'

Anna puffed out her cheeks, then shrugged.

'My parents told me a couple of weeks ago. The wedding's next month in Italy.'

'Not at that amazing villa?'

'The very same.' She nodded.

She tried to think about it in a detached way, like a news item or a piece of gossip about some remote acquaintance, but it was still difficult to actually say out loud. It must be the wine, she thought.

'Are you going to go?' asked Cath.

'No. I've told them I'm too busy at work, even though most of my work has actually dried up since the Sam Charles balls-up.'

'I think you should,' said Suzanne decisively.

'Yes, I agree,' said Cath. 'Don't give her the bloody satisfaction.'

'You two sound like my parents.'

Suzanne ignored her. 'It'll be hard, but sometimes you've just got to run at it and hope you make it through to the other side. 'Cos it's a better place over there, you know. Through it. Over it.'

Anna took a long swig of wine, focusing on the taste of cherries and gooseberries as it slid down her throat.

'I don't want to talk about it,' she said finally. Part of her was desperate to discuss Sophie's wedding with someone – deep down she knew that one of the reasons for inviting her friends around was to offload this tangled mess of feelings, to sort them out, work out how she really felt. But now she had voiced it, she knew she was in danger of getting teary, and had no intention of letting her old friends see that.

'Oh, did you hear that Maggie McFarlane has got some hot new banker boyfriend?' she said, moving the conversation to safer ground.

'Maggie? Yes, she met him on Match.com.'

'I thought she said she'd never do Internet dating.'

'Never say never.' Cath smiled. 'Not when there are hot bankers out there.'

Suzanne looked at Anna over the top of her glass. 'I think you need to get back out there. Dating, that is.'

Anna snorted, trying to ignore the remark.

'Knowing Anna, she's dating George Clooney in the secret life she's not telling us about,' said Cath.

'I'm too busy for a man.'

'I thought you said work had dried up after the Sam Charles injunction.'

'Stop hassling me or I'm going to have to injunct you.'

Suzanne sat forward and squeezed Anna's hand.

'Honey, it's been two years. How much sex have you had in that time?'

Anna felt her stomach clench. That was the sort of question she really didn't want to answer.

'What is this?' she said, trying to deflect their concern. 'Some sort of NHS survey?'

'I knew it. None,' said Cath with disapproval.

'I thought you were over him,' said Suzanne finally.

Anna knew immediately what she meant.

'I am,' she sighed. 'The fact that he's getting married to my sister in four weeks doesn't make me want to do cartwheels, but he's not the reason I'm single.'

'So you've got a month to find someone,' said Cath.

'I'm not going to the wedding.'

'But if you really are over him, then what better way to tell the world than by turning up in Tuscany with some sexy young hunk on your arm. Stop being the victim. Get off your bum and make things happen.'

'What about Sam Charles?' said Suzanne.

Anna threw a felt cushion at her.

'What?' said Suzanne, protecting herself. 'You've hung out in Italy with him once. Ask him for a rematch.'

'First, he's my client. Secondly, he hates me. Thirdly, he's a movie star. Oh, and a cheat.'

'You're prettier than that escort girl,' said Cath.

'Oh, thanks. Is that supposed to be your idea of a motivational speech?'

'Yes, and my catchphrase is "Think of the six-pack".'

It was 10.30 p.m. by the time her friends finally left. Anna scraped the plates into the bin, drained the leftovers from two bottles of wine into one glass and returned to the sofa. Outside, it had finally gone dark, and the solitary lamp in the corner cast a low glow around the room. She'd overstretched herself, three years earlier, buying Rosemary Cottage, a tiny whitewashed terraced house in Richmond, but it was the best decision she'd ever made. She couldn't quite hear the river, and the frequent roar of the aeroplanes on their way to nearby Heathrow wasn't ideal, but sometimes she would just close her eyes, pretend she was in some gorgeous little village in the Cotswolds and let all of her worries fall away. Not that it was quite working tonight. There was one worry that was overriding all the others at the moment: the fear of losing her job. And after such a public failure, would she find another one? Media legal work hadn't been hit as much as some sectors in the downturn – you could always rely on actors and sportsmen to make a mess of their lives – but firms were certainly tightening up, making do with the employees they had rather than taking on more staff. And if she had no job, there was the real possibility of losing this wonderful little house. The thought of how things could unravel so quickly made her shiver.

'Come on, Anna,' she whispered to herself. 'Stop being the victim.' That was what Cath had said, and it was solid advice. What was really so bad? She had a fab house, nice legs and a good brain, didn't she? She smiled to herself. That could be her dating profile for Match.com.

Pulling her iPad off the coffee table, she switched it on, typing 'Match.com' into Google.

'Start Your Love Story!' it instructed.

'I need a fag,' she mumbled, reaching down for her handbag at the foot of the sofa. Rummaging inside, her hand immediately touched something crammed in the top. It was the brown envelope Ruby Hart had given her in Green Park. She'd meant to sift through its contents back at the office, but by the time she'd got back to her desk, Ruby's claims had seemed more ridiculous and irrelevant to her own life than they had when she had spoken to her.

She lit her cigarette and hesitated a moment before she put the iPad beside her, and tipped the envelope out on to her lap. There was surprisingly little inside. Some newspaper cuttings, a copy of Amy Hart's post-mortem report and a photograph of a pretty blonde girl, no more than nineteen or twenty. She speed-read the document and immediately saw that Ruby was right: the tabloids *had* shown some interest in Amy's death in the days after it happened – 'Soap Star's Girlfriend Tragedy' – but after the inquest there was nothing in the press except a tiny story in the *Globe* reporting that there had been an inquest into the death of 'a party girl linked to soap star Ryan Jones'.

Anna looked at the date of the story: the Saturday that the whole world had run with the Sam Charles exposé. Amy Hart's death was lucky to make page seventeen. Anna knew only too well that the *Globe* had devoted most of the paper to Sam and Jessica.

She stared down at the newsprint, hearing Ruby Hart's words in her head. *I know what sort of law you do, Miss Kennedy. You cover things up for rich people.* She smarted at the memory. She knew she hadn't gone into media law for any more noble purpose than that it had seemed exciting, well paid and interesting. She was a news junkie – it was one of the things she had in common with Andrew – and life as a media lawyer was a thrilling way to be in the heart of it.

But Ruby had made her professional life sound so immoral; and it embarrassed her to know that that was what the young girl thought of it.

What harm can it do to look into this a little? she asked herself, studying one of the early stories more closely. It had run a photo of Amy walking hand in hand out of a nightclub with Ryan Jones. She was barely recognisable from the natural girlie blonde in the family snapshot. Her hair was longer, a brassier blond. A micro-mini showed off long legs in towering heels. This girl was confident, glamorous, in control.

What a waste, thought Anna, feeling a sudden desire to help Ruby Hart. She stubbed out her cigarette, picked up her iPad and typed 'Ryan Jones' into Google. There were dozens of tabloid stories about him: a dalliance with a busty reality TV star, a recent drink-driving conviction, an involvement in a punch-up in a west London pub, even a racist outburst at the Notting Hill carnival.

Hmm, nice guy, she thought, sipping her wine as she read on.

In a rare case of life imitating art, soap bad boy Ryan Jones was accused yesterday of attacking a musician and 'hurling racist insults' at her during a fracas at Sunday's carnival. Ryan Jones, who plays car mechanic Jamie Doyle in *Barclay's Place*, has been at the centre of a controversial storyline in the soap following the arrival of an Asian family in the street, culminating in the arrest of Jones's character for arson following a suspicious fire. 'People should not confuse what happens on their TVs with what happens in real life,' said Blake Stanhope, Mr Jones's PR representative . . .

155

Anna felt herself miss a breath. She reread the last line of the news item more slowly. Ryan Jones was represented by Blake Stanhope.

Time seemed to stand still as the significance of what she had just read sank in, then her pulse started racing. She Googled Blake Stanhope's own website and scrolled through his clients section. Ryan wasn't listed. Then again, Blake would have had hundreds of clients over the years, some of whom he dealt with personally, others who'd be handled by his team.

She stared at the grainy photograph of Amy and Ryan in the newspaper cutting. He was a thug and a bully if you believed the stories about him. But could he have been involved in Amy's death? Was Ruby Hart right that he'd pushed her down the stairs? And had he instructed Blake to minimise the press coverage of his summons to the inquest?

Her mouth had gone dry as she'd thought it through. If Blake was acting for Ryan and had wanted to bury the story, why not kill two birds with one stone by leaking the Sam Charles story to the press? That way he netted himself a fat fee for the exclusive on Katie and Sam's sexploits while also ensuring Ryan Jones would be kept out of the spotlight.

Anna frowned. Was she being paranoid? A little voice in her head told her to calm down. But no. This was exactly the sort of win-win PR coup that Stanhope could pull off.

She felt angry, used. A spike of injustice swelled in her throat.

You bastard, she thought, staring at Blake Stanhope's earnest black-and-white photograph on the website.

Her eyes drifted to the photo of Amy Hart. Pretty, smiling, hopeful.

She hadn't been able to help Sam Charles, but maybe she could somehow help Amy.

She picked up the phone and called the number that had been scribbled on the back of the brown envelope.

'Ruby? It's Anna Kennedy.'

'I knew you'd get back to me.' She could almost see the young girl smiling down the telephone.

'I want to help you, Ruby. I want to help you find out the truth about your sister.'

'Did you read everything I gave you?'

'I did,' said Anna, already wondering how she could achieve her next step. 'And I think it might be worth me meeting with Ryan Jones,' she said, realising it was her turn to kill two birds with one stone.

18

He was in a suit. And a tie. God, how long was it since he'd worn a tie? Sam leaned into the bathroom mirror and adjusted the knot. Maybe he should have used a Windsor knot? Or was that too formal? He knew he had to get it right, because tonight was the Big One: his appearance on *Billington*, his own personal walk into the lion's den. He had watched the tape of Hugh Grant on *Leno* over and over, noting how the actor sat, what he said, even what he wore. Hence the suit. Hugh had worn a white shirt and an orange tie like a public schoolboy. He'd looked respectable, respectful. Penitent, that was the word Valerie had used. Do I look penitent? Or just like a cheating love rat?

Uncomfortable in the stifling heat of the hotel suite, he pulled the tie off and undid his top button. What did it matter? he thought defiantly. People had already made up their minds, if the endless column inches over the last two weeks were anything to go by. He was going to get savaged in the press no matter what he said or how he looked on *Billington*. Wasn't that what the public demanded of their celebrities these days? They wanted to see him torn apart before they would let him crawl back asking for forgiveness. The only upside was that David Billington was one of the more elegant, cerebral interviewers on the talk-show circuit. Just the other week he'd made a televised chat with Paris Hilton feel like Frost/Nixon.

If there was any man for the job, it was Billington. With a bit of luck, it might even turn into the definitive interview.

'It's so hot in here,' he said, striding back into the suite's living area, where his manager was sitting. 'Can't you do something about the temperature?'

He knew he was just anxious. The show taped at 3 p.m. for a 10 p.m. transmission and they were due to leave at any minute for the Times Square studios.

'Relax,' said Eli, flipping through the TV stations. 'The heat's fine. Just first-night nerves is all.'

'First night?' said Sam. 'You think I'm going to make a habit of this?'

'Figure of speech. Sit down, eat some fruit. Jeez, you're making me nervous.'

Sam paced over to the window, staring out at the Manhattan skyline from his room in the discreet Upper East Side hotel his manager had checked him into. It all seemed so distant, like a city drawn in a child's storybook.

'Come on, Sammy,' said Eli, coming up behind him and massaging his shoulders like a boxer's trainer before a big fight. 'Be yourself. Say you're sorry, tell everyone how much you love Jess, smile when Dave breaks your balls, then we're out of there. Just like we practised, huh?'

Eli had hired a media coach called Monica Glenn, an expert in non-verbal communication, and they had spent the past few days doing mock-run-throughs of the interview. Of course, it was one thing being both charming and humble in Monica's workshop, quite another to pull it off under the bright lights and high pressure of a TV studio.

Still, the *Sun* interview had gone down well. 'Sam Charles: I Was An Idiot', screamed the headline. He'd been humble, he'd said how sorry he was for letting everyone down, he'd said he understood how angry Jess – and his fans – were. But the writer had been sympathetic and much was made of Sam's previously unsullied reputation and the fact that only one ex-girlfriend had come forward to dish the dirt on him. Actually, that was more to do with Valerie and Helen's work behind the scenes; the few women who had attempted to sell their stories had been paid off before they'd had a chance to give any damning interviews. He could only hope that David Billington would be equally sympathetic.

'Guys, news about *Billington*,' said Valerie, strutting into the room, waving her BlackBerry.

'Good or bad news?'

'I won't bullshit, it's not good,' she said. 'David Billington was in a car accident this morning. Nothing serious, but he's going to be off the show for a week at least.'

'So who's standing in?' asked Eli.

Valerie pursed her lips.

'Neil Peters.'

'Peters?' Sam groaned, sitting down on the bed. 'Fuck.'

'I know, I know, it's not ideal,' said Valerie. 'But they won't shift on it. Apparently the network's got big plans for him.'

Sam felt all hope drain from him. He was screwed. Neil Peters was a British comedian who'd somehow managed to break into TV Stateside. There was no question he was a mover and a shaker; he seemed to have graduated straight from Cambridge into a weekly satirical news show on BBC2, his own anarchic chat show on Channel 4, and after somehow landing one of the top agents at CAA, was now making waves in the States. He'd been branded overly smug by some sections of the British press, but with his irritatingly self-confident manner he was a master at getting headline-grabbing quotes from celebrities. Which was why Sam's instinct was telling him to run for the hills.

'Can't we put the interview back a few weeks?' he asked.

Valerie shook her head.

'It's now or never, Sam. We need to get your public back on side; we need to change people's opinion of what happened, give your side of the story. Right now the story's hot and we have a chance to get a fair hearing.'

'That's what I'm worried about. Is Peters really going to give me a fair hearing? He's standing in for Billington and wants to impress the executives, so he's going to go all out to get some fantastic exclusive, isn't he?'

'So give it to him,' said Eli.

'What?'

'Give him the old waterworks. Cry your little heart out. That's what the fans want to see.'

'I can't just cry,' he said. 'It would look so staged.'

'It *is* staged, Sam,' said Eli. 'What do you think this whole three-ring circus is about? It's just entertainment, bud. Give people what they want.'

Sam gaped at them. They made it sound as if he was just some juggling seal who'd been booked to jump through hoops for the amusement of the American public.

'I don't know if I can be that . . . dishonest.'

'It ain't dishonest, it's just acting,' said Eli. 'And that's what you're best at, huh?'

Valerie's phone was beeping. She glanced at it and then threw it back in her Birkin.

'Car's here,' she said, throwing Sam a look. 'Showtime.'

Sam shifted uncomfortably in his seat and gazed at a spot of fluff on his knee. The lights were uncomfortably hot and he was aware of the studio audience collectively holding their breath.

'She . . . she wasn't a prostitute,' stuttered Sam. 'I mean, she seemed to be a nice girl.'

He knew from the look of triumph on Neil Peters's face that he had said the wrong thing, but he had to say something. Anything.

'A nice girl?' Neil smiled as a ripple of titters went around the audience. '*This* nice girl?' he said, sweeping his hand up to a video screen behind him.

Sam winced as a picture of Katie the escort was flashed up. It was from a photo shoot she had done for some men's magazine where she was reclining on a bed clad only in black lingerie. The audience burst out into laughter.

Sam slumped further down in his seat. He knew this was exactly what Monica had told him *not* to do. 'Sit up straight, look him in the eye,' she had said again and again. 'Look as if you have nothing to be ashamed of and that's what people will read in your posture.' He could imagine exactly what people were reading in his posture right now. Guilt. Guilt and shame.

'Naughty but nice,' Neil smirked, clearly enjoying Sam's discomfort.

'Hell no!' shouted someone from the front row. 'Girl's a ho!'

This brought another wave of titters from the audience.

'Was she as *nice* as Jess?' asked Neil.

Immediately the studio fell silent. This was the killer question; this was why the network rated Neil Peters so highly. On the face of it, the question was innocuous, but everyone knew what he was really asking. Was this girl as good as Jess in bed? Had Sam turned to some pretty escort girl because Jessica, the nation's sweetheart, just didn't cut it in the sack?

Sam froze. What could he say? The truth? That she rarely even let him near her bed, let alone into it? No, the American public didn't want to hear anything bad about Jess, that much was clear. But he had to say something. What? Be charming, that's what Eli had said.

'A gentleman doesn't talk about a lady that way,' he said, desperately trying to make a joke of it.

'Come on, Sam. Tell us. Has this sort of thing happened before? It's lonely at the top, you're a long way from home. It must be tempting to want a pretty girl to escort you back to your room.'

Peters had a knowing way of delivering that made people want to smile. Sam glared out into the studio audience, squinting in the lights at the sea of faces that all seemed to be laughing at him. He was glad his collar was loose. He could feel sweat trickling down the back of his neck.

'No. This has not happened before.'

'So what did you get up to at the Playboy Mansion?'

'Sorry?' He'd been to Hugh Hefner's pleasure palace a few times. With Jess and some of his LA friends. It was a great place for a drink and a catch-up with industry acquaintances.

'I saw you there about a year ago,' pressed Peters. 'Having a *good* time, as I remember it.'

Sam felt his brittle emotions snap.

'Hang on. I was invited to a party there.' His voice was quavering with anger. 'I went with Jess. You make the leap from *that* to me being some sort of sleazeball?'

'That's not what I said at all.' Peters gave one of his trademark shrugs: protesting his innocence – hey, he'd only asked a question, right? – but at the same time drawing the viewing public in, making them complicit, making them feel as if they'd all got one over on this dumb Brit actor.

162

More laughter.

'What's your agenda here, Neil?' Sam snapped. 'Ratings? David's Billington's job?' He couldn't help the words pouring out of his mouth. He had a vague thought that Monica, Valerie and Eli would be having kittens about now, but he couldn't stop himself.

'Please don't start jumping on the sofa. Not on my first day.' Peters's smug smile seemed to melt into a grotesque mask. The laughter of the audience rang mockingly around the studio.

Sam stood up and ripped off the microphone that had been threaded through his shirt.

'Sod this.'

'Come on, Sam.'

'You think this is entertainment?'

Peters gave another shrug and the audience howled.

A studio manager scrambled from the wings to stop him. Sam swept past her only to run into Valerie. Her expression was frantic.

'Take a breath and get back out there,' she hissed.

'Pull the show.'

Valerie's hard, usually controlled face was pale with panic. 'I'll see who I can speak to.'

Sam knew it was pointless. The show would run. He would be humiliated.

'You were supposed to protect me,' he said bitterly, shaking his head. 'Get me out of here.' He broke into a jog down the long, narrow corridor as he spotted a fire exit ahead of him.

'Sam. Wait . . .' Valerie's voice faded.

He was at the door. Breathless, he pushed it open and bright sunlight popped in his face as he stepped on to the street. He was surrounded by noise, people, camera lenses being forced into his personal space.

'Fuck off,' he shouted, covering his head with his hands.

'Come on, Sam. Just a couple of shots.' A photographer pushed his Nikon right into his face.

'Just sod off.'

The photographer was relentless. The camera smashed against Sam's ear, the whirr of the shutter echoing around his head.

'Smile, lover boy,' leered the paparazzo.

Without thinking, Sam grabbed the snapper by the scruff of his shirt.

'Get off me,' Sam bellowed, pushing the man away from him. The photographer staggered back, then crumpled to the floor, his camera clattering to the concrete as he fell.

'Sam. Stop.'

Someone in the studios was calling him. The crowd was building. A siren roared up to the scuffle and he heard a door slam.

The photographer stumbled noisily to his feet. Through the crowd, Sam could see a police officer's face, blank, shiny and unsmiling.

'Oh shit,' he said, almost breathless.

Valerie ran up behind him. The snapper was talking to the officer.

'We can deal with this,' she hissed.

Sam shook his head. Right now he wasn't so sure.

19

The crowd roared as the pony thundered down the rail, its rider leaning out of the saddle, windmilling his stick to crack the ball between the posts. Matthew sipped at his plastic glass of Pimm's enthusiastically, partly because it was so damn hot out there on the grass, partly to cover his smile. Two years ago, you wouldn't have caught him dead at a polo match – and if pushed, he'd have muttered something about privileged idiots with more money than sense – but he had to admit, he was enjoying himself. It was like a royal wedding mixed with a rock festival: everyone dressed to the nines, but hell-bent on getting trashed and lying about on the emerald lawns watching the entertainment. He wondered if he was the only one who didn't have a clue what was actually going on. What a chukka was. At which end of the pitch the yellow team were supposed to score. Then again, he wasn't here to learn the finer points of polo. He was here to *network*, as Helen had instructed him, forcing him to attend on her behalf as one of their clients was sponsoring the event.

'Another drink, Matthew?'

Matt turned to find the tall blonde who had introduced herself earlier as Emily smiling at him.

'Go on,' he said, knocking back the rest of his Pimm's. He warned himself to go easy. Then again, this didn't really seem like work. It was a Saturday afternoon, and all day he had been surrounded by pretty posh girls, none of whom had the slightest interest in talking shop and all of whom seemed fascinated by him. He had never really experienced corporate hospitality like it; occasionally there'd been a wealthy client at his three-man practice in Hammersmith who would send him a bottle of Scotch, but at Donovan Pierce schmoozing with clients, a lavish fiftieth invitation, the cricket at Lord's, a corporate box at Wimbledon with captains of industry and their attractive co-workers seemed par for the course.

'I'll be back,' said the blonde, her high heels sinking into the grass as she disappeared to the bar.

Matt grinned wolfishly as he watched her go.

'Shit,' he muttered as his mobile began to vibrate. *Private number*. It was work, then. He tutted to himself, but secretly he was pleased to be in demand, important. He had surprised even himself by how quickly he was slipping into the role of senior partner at the firm.

'Matt Donovan,' he said.

'It's Rob. Rob Beaumont.'

'Hey. How's things?' he said, surprised to hear his client's voice.

'Things aren't so good, Matt, to be honest.'

Matt walked around the back of the hospitality tent to find a quieter spot.

'What's wrong?'

There was a long pause and then a stutter of breath. Matthew didn't need to see Rob Beaumont to know that he was very upset.

'I thought we could handle this in a grown-up manner; you know, for Ollie's sake. But she couldn't do that, could she? Had to try and get one over on me.'

'What's she done?'

'She wants to move to Miami, Matt. She wants to take our son and move to Miami.'

Matt put his Pimm's down and tried to concentrate.

'Do you know that for sure?'

'I saw Oliver's headmistress. She wished me luck and said she'd just written Ollie's reference for his transfer to some school in South Beach. I confronted Kim. She said nothing was definite but that it was an option. She says she wants to take a break from England. Too much media pressure,' he said, his voice trembling.

Matt doubted that was the reason. He had a stack of press cuttings in his office about Kim Collier and knew she was a woman who relished the media gaze.

'You'd better come into the office first thing Monday,' he said, knowing he could clear some things in his diary.

'She can't do it, can she? She can't just take him to Florida.'

Matthew felt a strong pang of pity for the director, but it was his policy to be as honest as he could with his clients.

'It's a difficult situation, Rob. We should talk about it more on Monday.'

'Can she take our son?' he said with a desperate staccato bark.

'Probably,' Matt said finally. 'Eventually.'

'How is that fair?'

He didn't need Rob to remind him how unfair British divorce law could be: a 'no blame' law in which the circumstances of the break-up had no bearing on the division of the assets. That was often what people found hardest to take; he certainly had. Carla had run off and had an affair with some slimeball with a stucco-fronted house, and yet she still got half of everything; in fact, she got more: she got Jonas.

'How often do you see your son, Matt?' asked Rob so quietly that he could barely hear him.

'Every weekend.'

'Once a week. You're lucky. If Kim goes to Miami, how often am I going to see my Ollie?'

Matt could hear him beginning to sob; a grown man struggling with big, breathless gulps.

'We can work through this.'

'How? When the law favours the mother?'

'Short-term, we can think about a Prohibited Steps Order to stop Kim taking Oliver out of the country. Moving forward, we can fight for a residence order, in custody if you want that battle.'

He didn't have to tell Rob how high the odds were stacked against him. Right now, his client wanted to hear that there was some glimmer of hope, some slim likelihood that he could at least keep his son in the country after their divorce.

'I'm ready,' said Rob with defiance.

'Then so am I,' said Matt, ignoring the flicker of self-doubt that reminded him that despite his experience, his talent, his passion, he couldn't even keep his own son.

20

If Anna was honest, Ryan Jones was a bit of a disappointment. She'd been expecting someone much better-looking, more imposing, a Cockney wide boy dripping with charisma, turning heads and joking with the ladies who lunched in this buzzing Notting Hill restaurant. Ryan's character in his teatime soap was a ducker and a diver, a lovable rogue, whereas the real-life Ryan Jones looked . . . well, a bit short.

She watched as the maître d' pointed him towards her table. He was wearing an expensive-looking shirt unbuttoned too far and had flashy sunglasses perched on top of his head. He was cocky too, rolling his shoulders and pouting like a model, clearly expecting people to look up from their linguine. Anna noted his irritation when none of them did.

'You Anna?' he said, shoving one hand into the back pocket of his drooping jeans.

Charmed, I'm sure, thought Anna, standing up to shake hands.

'Yes, I'm Anna Kennedy, I work at Donovan Pierce – I'm sure Hugh filled you in?'

Setting up this meeting had actually been far less difficult than she had expected. Ryan was represented by Archer Dale Management, a company Anna had worked with before, so all it had taken was a tiny white lie to her old friend Hugh Archer, managing director of the agency. 'People have been whispering about Ryan's appearance at that dead girl's inquest,' she had told him. 'We should nip this in the bud before the noise gets louder.' She had no intention of helping Ryan Jones in any way, but it was a plausible excuse to get him where

169

she could ask him about his dealings with Blake Stanhope.

'What's all this about?' he said, sitting down and ordering a beer from the waitress. 'You're a lawyer, right? Am I in trouble?'

According to a recent *Hello!* article Ryan was twenty-eight, but up close he looked at least five years older. The wonders of make-up, she thought. His Facebook fan page had over fifteen thousand members: young girls really did fancy anybody they were told to these days.

'It was about the inquest you appeared at two weeks ago.'

His eyes narrowed.

'Shouldn't Hugh Archer be here?' He looked tired and truculent; like a teenager woken up for breakfast after a night on the town.

'Hugh and I have worked together in the past; he trusts me. Besides, this is probably nothing,' she said, willing herself to remain blank and calm. When she had arranged the meeting, she hadn't anticipated feeling so nervous in front of him. Ruby had accused him of killing her sister, and while she still thought it was incredibly far-fetched, the connection with Blake Stanhope had made her anxious.

Ryan's lip curled into an angry sneer.

'Nothing? This has been a complete pain in the arse.'

'What has?'

'Amy bloody Hart.'

He saw Anna frown and sighed.

'Listen, I'm sorry the girl's dead and all that, but let's be frank here: Amy was just a quick fuck.'

Anna struggled to keep her face neutral.

'She wasn't even that. She was just some bird I took back to my gaff, then the next thing I know, she's dead, I've got my picture in the papers, and these coppers are asking all sorts of questions. Don't get me wrong, I like getting press, but I can do without the "Dead Girl" headlines.'

The waitress arrived with Ryan's beer and tea for Anna, and she used the distraction to take a deep breath and control her emotion. She needed to keep him talking, make him think she was on his side, however loathsome she found him. Poor Amy Hart, she thought. Was that how she'd be remembered? A quick fuck, just a bit of fun to round off a night out? Anna didn't really know much about Amy, just what her sister had told her, stuff she'd found on Google: a swimwear shoot in a men's mag she'd done a couple of years before, a two-line biog on her model agency's website and a handful of mentions in gossip sheets, and that was it until her death. Even then, the meagre reports on 'Party Girl Tragedy' revealed very little more. One paper had referred to her as a 'brainbox beauty' because she'd managed a year's study at university before she'd dropped out to model. Anna was never judgemental about how people chose to make a living; if Amy Hart wanted to wear lingerie and hang out in nightclubs hoping to snare a footballer or soap star, then that was her right to choose.

But even though she hadn't known Amy, Anna felt sure that she had never wanted to be used, to be thought of as that night's plaything, just because she was pretty and blonde and liked the odd glass of free champagne.

'You know what?' said Ryan, taking a swig of his beer. 'I really thought I'd got away with it . . .'

Anna looked at him, startled.

'Yeah, I mean I owe that guy Sam Charles a pint or two. After all those stories when she died, I thought the inquest was going to be big news, but then he gets caught shagging the wrong bird and' – he clicked his fingers – 'my story disappears.'

She looked at him closely.

'Thanks to Blake Stanhope,' she said casually.

Ryan frowned. 'Stanhope? What about him?'

'Oh, I thought Hugh had said something about Blake handling your PR. I assumed he had helped you with the Amy Hart thing.'

'Nah, that old wanker's too bloody expensive.'

'I thought you were a client of his . . .'

'I was. Ages ago. I was young and I got stitched up, didn't I? Racist thing. I needed help. But I don't trust that dirty old bastard any more. Set me up with a dolly-bird once. One of his clients. Next thing I know, I open the *Screws of the World* and there it is. "Ryan's a flop in bed" or some crap. Load of bullshit, it was. Never had any complaints in that department.'

Anna looked at him. Ryan Jones was clearly not an upstanding, trustworthy young man, but she believed him when he said he no longer dealt with Stanhope. The casual, dismissive way he had spoken about Amy was even more telling. Was he really so cold-blooded, so duplicitous that he could be flippant about someone he had killed? It felt impossible.

She put down her teacup.

'The reason I'm here today is just to find out what you said at the inquest, so I can play down the whispers if we need to.'

'You think it will flare up?' he asked, looking alarmed.

'I think the story's probably passed,' she said with more conviction. 'You were lucky. The Sam Charles thing happened at the right time.'

'To Sam Charles.' He smiled ruefully, raising his beer bottle.

'So tell me,' she pressed.

'I told them the truth,' he said with a hint of bravado. 'I met this blonde piece in a club last December. We met up a few days later. I took her back to mine, but it turned out she was a cock-tease so I never saw her again. That's it. The next thing I know, she's dead. Police interviewed me about it a couple of days after I read it in the papers.'

'Did you tell the police or the coroner that you thought Amy was a cock-tease?'

'I didn't phrase it like that. Why do you ask?'

'Because it sounds a bit angry.'

He ordered another beer without asking if Anna wanted a top-up.

'What are you saying, Anna? You think I pushed her down the stairs because she wouldn't fuck me?'

'No.'

'You're right she pissed me off, though. I didn't tell that to the police either.'

'Why were you pissed off?'

'Because girls like her don't know how to keep their end of the bargain.' He wiped his wet top lip with the back of his hand. 'They're happy to get all the attention when they're out with people like me. The free drinks, the VIP area, all that. And they love getting papped when they come out of a club with me. Amy

172

was lapping it up that night, sticking her tits out for the flash-bulbs. But back at my flat, she was just a prick-tease. Suddenly she's not interested. So I kick her out.'

'Nice,' said Anna, unable to hide her feelings.

'Don't give me that lawyer-takes-the-moral-high-ground crap. I know you lot are only in it for the money. Same as we all are.'

'Just because you bought a girl a few drinks, it doesn't mean she has to have sex with you,' she said, unable to bite her tongue.

'You one of these feminists, then? You think I was using her?'

Anna stayed silent, and Ryan laughed.

'She was using *me*, sweetheart,' he said, slapping his own chest. 'Amy was a nobody. Sorry, but she was. She wouldn't have got her picture in the papers without me. And that's what she wanted.'

'I wasn't aware that she was so press-hungry.'

He flapped a dismissive hand.

'Ah, they all are. Anyway, her mate told me she wanted to make someone jealous.'

Anna looked at him sharply.

'Really? Who?'

'I don't know, some bloke she wanted to get back at. Look, who cares about whether I was using her or she was using me? The fact is, I just want this gone. It's been more trouble than it was worth. And I got a reputation to think about, haven't I?'

'We'll do our best, don't worry,' said Anna, signalling for the bill. 'No promises, but I'll have a quiet word with a few editors, see if we can't get this hushed up once and for all.'

To her surprise, Ryan reached over and took her hand. He looked into her eyes as he held it.

'Thanks, Anna,' he said. 'No, I mean it. You've really helped me out and I appreciate it. Maybe I can pay you back in some way?'

She gently pulled her hand free.

'Don't worry, I'll settle up with Hugh Archer,' she said.

Ryan just sucked his teeth and made a gesture that clearly said 'your loss, darling'.

'So who was Amy's friend?' she asked, as they walked out towards the entrance.

He shrugged.

'Oh, some blonde model. Mandy. Molly. Can't remember,' he said, pushing through the door and out on to the street. 'She had cracking tits, though, even better than Amy's. I still see her around at parties, actually. She's with that modelling agency half the page-three girls are with. FrontGirls. I've had a few of them before, if you know what I mean.'

'Yes, I think I do,' said Anna, turning away. And they all have my complete sympathy.

21

She moved across the room, gliding from group to group. Helen was always elegant and graceful, but tonight she was at her shimmering best. Her blond bob shone from a three-hour session with Marcus, her stylist at James Worrall, and her lilac silk dress showed off her figure perfectly. Moving between the rooms of her Kensington townhouse, swapping anecdotes and clinking glasses, she positively glowed. You'd certainly never guess this was her forty-ninth birthday, unless you walked through to the kitchen where, behind the forest of champagne flutes, you would see the huge birthday cake emblazoned with the numbers. Many women of Helen's age would have kept it quiet or shaved a few years off their official age; they certainly wouldn't have thrown a glitzy party for their most influential clients and friends. But Helen Pierce had nothing to hide: not in that department, anyway. She was proud of what she had managed to achieve in a male-dominated industry, and proud of how she looked.

The room flickered in the low, flattering glow of candles in silver holders, soft jazz oozed from concealed speakers and the chatter and laughter of her illustrious guests was like a cool stream bubbling over rocks. Still, it was only a select gathering: maybe seventy, eighty people. Next year she'd have to pull all the stops out. That cake would have a big five-oh, but what the hell, you're only young once. She smiled to herself, wondering idly if she'd ever enjoyed her birthday parties growing up. She could barely remember them. A vague memory of cheap cake and orange squash, the smeared faces of a dozen children crammed into the kitchen of her parents' small Rochester semi.

What were their names? She couldn't remember. She'd left most of them behind when she'd gone to the local grammar. She'd worked hard to leave them all behind.

Through the crowd she could see the arrival of her newest colleague. 'Matthew, so glad you could make it. Not brought a date?'

'Well, I thought I might ask Sandra Bullock, but I think she's busy,' he answered, smiling. It took Helen a moment to see that he was joking. It was easy to forget that this was all so new to Matthew.

'Happy birthday. You look great,' he said, kissing her awkwardly on both cheeks.

'Thank you,' she replied, wishing she could return the compliment. He was wearing chinos and a denim shirt that hung loose over his waistband; it didn't even look as if he had shaved.

'So how was the polo?' she asked, wondering if he'd worn tonight's outfit to the Guards Club. 'Did you speak to Leonard Payne?'

'Yes. He's a good bloke.'

She didn't want Matthew getting too close to her top clients. That was her domain.

'So can we get you a drink? There's plenty of champagne.'

Matthew shook his head.

'I'm on the bike. I can't stay long. My son's round first thing in the morning.' He looked around the room. 'So who else is here?' he asked with a note of anxiety.

'From work? Just you. If I invite junior partners, then the associates want to come. If they come, we have to invite the assistants. Then the trainees start getting all uppity. We might as well have the party in the staff canteen.'

'Well, I'm glad you didn't,' said Matthew, looking around. 'This place is amazing.'

She appreciated the reaction, but she doubted that Matthew had ever been anywhere he could compare it with. His father's place in Cheyne Walk, perhaps. More spoils of law.

'It's a shame Larry couldn't make it tonight,' she said.

Matthew shrugged. 'Yeah, well, I think Loralee will be keeping him away from parties for a little while at least.'

Helen smiled tightly. She had too many fresh memories of Larry careering around her social gatherings insulting people and making a scene. As far as she was concerned, he could stay away for ever. Larry was out of her hair, but now she had to deal with his son. Not that Matthew was anything like as formidable an opponent, but even so, he was a partner and a shareholder. Helen really needed to keep him on side. For now at least.

'I must go and circulate,' she said. 'There are some very eligible women in the room tonight who would just love to meet you, I'm sure.'

Matthew looked at her with surprise, as if he hadn't been expecting the compliment. Interesting, she thought, filing it away. It never did any harm to keep track of your opponents' psychology. She moved out through the library, nodding and smiling, then stepped out on to the first-floor terrace. It was a small space, but it had an amazing view of Kensington Gore, and tonight in the balmy evening air, lit by ribbons of twinkling fairy lights, it was magical.

'Helen, darling! Do come over,' said a tall woman in a deep-blue backless gown, drenched in jewellery. Fiona Swettenham was the closest thing Helen had to a real friend, possibly because she was married to Viscount Swettenham, the hugely wealthy landowner, with the best house in north Oxfordshire and host of the most fabulous New Year's Eve parties.

'You are looking good enough to eat tonight,' gushed Fiona, fingering the delicate silk of Helen's dress. 'Doesn't she look fabulous, Simon?'

Fiona was standing with Simon Cooper, the managing director of Auckland Communications, the corporate PR giant. He was handsome, tanned and aloof, and Helen felt irritated to see him glance over her shoulder for someone more powerful to talk to. She demanded everyone's full attention, especially on a night like tonight.

'I saw you talking to Larry's son,' said Fiona. 'He's rather delicious, isn't he?'

'Fiona!' said Helen, teasing her. 'What would Charlie say?'

'My husband would say I had impeccable taste. Now don't tell me you don't think he's good-looking?'

'I haven't really thought about it,' said Helen. 'We didn't hire him for his looks.'

'You didn't hire him at all,' said Simon with a smirk.

Helen flashed the PR a warning glance.

'Yes, I heard he'd been foisted upon you by Larry,' said Fiona gleefully. 'Everyone thought that when Larry retired the firm was going to become Pierce's.'

Helen didn't want to make her professional frustrations obvious. 'Clearly Matthew is a fine lawyer in his own right; we wouldn't have brought him in as a partner if he hadn't been very capable . . .'

Simon raised his eyebrows to Fiona. 'I think that's what you call "damning with faint praise".'

Helen was about to reply, but Fiona gave her arm a squeeze.

'I'm sure he's very good,' she said quickly, throwing a look at Simon. 'Anyway, I love that shabby-geography-teacher-chic thing he's got going on.'

Helen rolled her eyes.

'I don't think it's deliberate. I think this is his idea of smart. When it's his birthday I might have to send him to Savile Row. Or at least for a shave.'

'Is this how you ladies talk about men when we're not there?' said Simon.

Helen returned his gaze, challenging him.

'What makes you think we talk about you at all, Simon?' she said, flirting gently with him.

Fiona insisted on introducing Simon to a Cabinet minister, and as they drifted off, Helen saw Graham staring at her through the crowd. She tried to smile back openly, and Graham reciprocated by nodding. She'd be damned if people could see the strains in their marriage tonight. Then again, they weren't the only ones. She could count a dozen couples in this room tonight who, behind closed doors, slept in separate bedrooms, had affairs, but to the outside world were devoted, successful couples.

'Why so glum, young lady?' Helen turned to see a rather stout man in a navy blazer and cravat smiling at her. 'This is your party, isn't it? You can't go around moping at such a splendid bash.'

Helen laughed. Timothy Hartnell was a former banking lawyer on the board of one of the big City investment giants.

'Sorry,' she said. 'You know how it is, you never enjoy your own parties, always worrying whether everyone's having a good time.'

'Look around, dear girl,' said Timothy, gesturing with his brandy glass. 'It's the party of the season, so have a drink and relax.'

Helen saluted him with her champagne and smiled. 'To relaxing.'

'Which brings me to dear old Larry,' said Timothy. 'How is it without him bellowing in your ear every five minutes?'

'It's quieter, I'll give you that.' She wanted to add that it was also cheaper; the cigars Larry had couriered to the office from Davidoff in St James's, the cases of claret he would send out to favoured clients, the mysterious entries for 'fruit and flowers' on the company accounts – Helen was sure they would save hundreds of thousands before the end of the year. But of course Timothy had often been a recipient of Larry's largesse, so she bit her tongue.

Timothy took her elbow and pulled her closer.

'What I want to know is why you didn't buy him out,' he said with a hint of mischief. 'We all thought the firm would become Pierce's.'

'You're the second person to say that in five minutes.'

It was another painful reminder of her corporate blindsiding earlier in the summer. Of course Larry had given her the opportunity to buy out his shareholding – he had to; it was in the partnership agreement. But the clause had given her just a twenty-one-day window to agree to the deal and come up with the money. With a bumper year in profits, the firm had been valued at twice the amount she had anticipated, and in the current financial climate she hadn't been able to get her hands on the requisite cash fast enough.

'I didn't even know he had a son in the business.'

'Matthew's background is family law. He's very good,' she said thinly. 'We want to provide a wrap-around service for our high-net-worth individuals.'

Timothy chuckled and took a sip of his brandy.

'Save it for the brochure, m'dear.' He smiled. 'I can imagine it's a pain in the bum. After all, you don't want to cloud your brand, do you?'

Helen frowned. 'Cloud the brand?'

'Oh, I've seen it happen with other firms,' said Timothy. 'They start taking on too many areas of practice and dilute the reason people come to them. Donovan Pierce are a specialist defamation practice, top of the pile in your field. But start adding too many other bits, Johnny Footballer might get confused.'

Helen took a deep breath through her nose, not wanting Timothy to see how furious all this made her. Was that how people were beginning to see Donovan Pierce – as a diluting brand?

'I don't think that will happen, Tim,' she said quickly.

'Really? People are starting to talk.'

Hartnell's opinion was one of the few she valued. She'd have fought harder against Matthew's appointment to the firm, but she had secretly seen the value in growing the business. Her ego wanted the firm to be Pierce's, but her business smarts told her it was better to have a forty per cent stake in a much bigger pie.

'Having Larry Donovan head up the firm gave you muscle. But having his lightweight family-law son on board doesn't bring much to the table, does it?'

Helen was furious at the suggestion that she couldn't bring enough gravitas to the firm for both of them.

'Per employee, Donovan Pierce is one of the top-performing law firms in the country.'

'Then what do you need Donovan for?' Timothy said sharply. 'Get rid of him. He's not growing your business, he's harming it.'

The thought that one of Europe's top financial brains thought that about her firm made Helen shiver.

22

According to the latest issue of *Vogue*, Danehill Park was the most exclusive day spa in the country. Set in a hundred acres of Surrey parkland, the grand stately home had been converted into a beautifully furnished hotel for mini-breaking couples and savvy tourists looking for a taste of rural England without the inconvenience of the mud and the creaky floors.

Anna settled back on to her poolside sunlounger and sighed. She'd booked the day trip to the spa as a present for her mother, but she couldn't deny she was enjoying it too. The spa was a modern addition in a glass and steel extension at the back of the house, built around a mint-green kidney-shaped swimming pool; with the gentle pan-pipe music and the aromatherapy, it was hard to do anything except just lie back and feel your stress float away.

She glanced over at her mother, lying next to her in a towelling robe, a lavender sleep mask over her eyes. According to her father, Sue Kennedy had been working herself into the ground revamping and extending the Dorset Nurseries's dining room while also running the gardening business. 'She needs a break, hon,' he had told Anna on the phone. 'If she doesn't slow down, she's going to blow a gasket.'

'This is wonderful, isn't it?' said Sue, lifting one corner of her eye mask and peering at her daughter.

'It was such a good idea of Dad's.'

When she had booked the trip, Anna had taken on board her father's concerns, but she was grateful for the quality time alone with her mother. They had always had an uneasy relationship. Even when the girls had been small, Sue Kennedy had seemed to dote on the prettier, girlie Sophie, who shared her feminine wiles and breezy popularity. She had never seemed to understand her older daughter's efficient bookishness, used to tease her for preferring to take long walks across the fields and hills with her father than spend time indoors braiding hair with Sophie or playing with make-up. But recently Anna could sense her mother drifting away from her in a vapour trail of disappointment and frustration. She had got used to not having Sophie in her life, but to add her mother to the mix would be unthinkable. She was determined to stop the rot in their relationship and knew that this day out was as good a place as any to start.

'How about lunch?' she said, uncurling herself from the lounger.

Sue glanced at her dainty gold watch.

'Not yet, darling. I wish you would just relax.'

Anna chuckled. 'You're right. We've got a big libel trial starting tomorrow, so I should chill out before the fun starts.'

'You mean *fun* as well, don't you,' Sue said, teasing her.

'Honestly, it is quite exciting.'

It was Sue's turn to laugh. 'You always found the funniest things to get excited about. Those books about Mount Everest you used to love. You were always so enquiring. It's probably why you turned out so clever, so successful.'

Anna realised that this was the nearest thing she'd had to a compliment in a long time. Then again, Sue had been good-humoured, less snipey all morning, and hadn't even mentioned Sophie or the wedding once.

'Come on then. Let's go and try out this restaurant.'

'I hope you're not going to complain about the food.' Anna grinned.

'Of course I'm going to complain, darling,' said Sue, knotting her robe tighter and slipping on her white slippers. 'It's just professional interest.'

The restaurant was beautiful. The interior was all scrubbed pine and stiff linen, just the right balance between formality and casual; you felt you were in a sophisticated restaurant, but it didn't seem weird to be wearing a fluffy robe. The double doors were open, leading on to an outdoor seating area around a small pond that shimmered invitingly in the heat.

'Let's eat outside,' suggested Anna, feeling lifted by the warm, scented breeze drifting into the restaurant and realising this was the nicest day out she had had in ages.

She snaked through the wrought-iron chairs and then stopped dead as she saw a familiar figure seated under a parasol. Sophie was reading a magazine. She was dressed casually in leggings and a T-shirt, her hair all piled up like some nymph emerging from a grotto.

'I don't believe it . . .' Words seemed unable to form in Anna's throat.

Sue looked at her wearily. 'I couldn't let it go on, Anna. It's so silly. At least speak to her.'

Sophie looked up, her expression papered with the same wide-eyed anxiousness she'd had as a child when she knew she was about to be in trouble.

Anna couldn't stop staring at her. Of course she'd tuned into her sister's TV show, more often than she'd liked. Sophie was a culinary Jessica Rabbit, all seductive curves and painted face, the perfect wife who could whip you up a luscious pie then take you to bed for an hour of mind-melting sex. That was how she remembered her sister in the flesh, too. A lusty temptress.

But the woman in front of her was slimmer, softer, less dangerous. Thin arms poked out under her black T-shirt; her face, leaner thanks to pounds lost for the television and her wedding, looked different, yet familiar. Her sister looked just like a slimmer version of herself.

'Go on,' hissed Sue.

Anna resisted her mother's forceful hand against her back, then put one foot in front of the other and moved slowly towards Sophie's table.

'Hello,' she said awkwardly. 'It's been a while.'

For a second she remembered the same words that were spoken almost four years earlier. She could see quite clearly the night Sophie had turned up at her flat, suitcase in hand, looking for a place to stay, having just washed back up from three years of travelling, with a sprinkling of tattoos, an empty bank balance and a vague ambition to get into telly.

Anna had been glad to have her sister back. Glad to have someone to laugh with, cook with, go out drinking with. They'd shared their love dilemmas: Anna's frustration with Andrew, Sophie's complaints about the lack of decent men in London. And after three months of Sophie's unsuccessful attempts to find work, Anna had pleaded with Andrew to give her a job at the newspaper, where he was on the fast track to editorship. He'd delivered: an assistant's job in the features department, which had turned into a food column when Sophie had charmed the editor and regaled him with stories about the Dorset Nurseries.

The rest was a history Anna had tried hard to forget.

A waiter had begun fussing around them, offering bread, hummus dips and sparkling water.

'Have you had any spa treatments yet?' asked Sophie finally. 'I believe they're heavenly.'

The benefits of the relaxing floral facial Anna had had an hour earlier seemed difficult to recall.

'It's a lovely place,' she replied coldly.

'How was the journey over?' asked Sue, trying to fill the silence.

'A bit of a rush.'

'Sophie's been filming the new show,' said Sue proudly. 'We'll never be able to cope with the demand when it's on in the autumn.'

Anna watched her mother beam at Sophie. Sue Kennedy never stopped mentioning how grateful she and her husband were to their younger daughter for driving business to the Dorset Nurseries. Anna tried not to feel too resentful that no one ever mentioned that it was her idea in the first place to transform the disused conservatory into a restaurant, or that she had spent many hours compiling her parents' business plan and helping them get the finance to do it. But it was hard not to feel slighted.

'So have you looked at the menu?' she asked.

'What do you recommend, Sophie?' asked Sue.

Anna almost smiled. Everyone in Sophie's inner circle knew that the delicious recipes in the best-selling *Dorset Kitchen*

Cookbook and on the show were Brian Kennedy's creations rather than Sophie's, but even her parents went along with the little white lie.

'Oh, um, probably the field mushrooms,' she said, picking up the stiff card. 'Or the sea bass with fennel.'

'I'll have the risotto, then the sticky toffee pudding,' said Anna.

'Gosh, I wish I could eat all that,' said Sophie. 'If I so much look at a dessert, it jumps straight to my hips.'

'Sophie's already lost eight pounds in the last month,' said Sue. 'For the wedding.'

'And she looks great,' said Anna politely.

Her gaze met Sophie's and they exchanged a look: rolling eyes, raised eyebrows, a look that said, 'Mum's put her foot in it again.' It was a familiar look, a code from their childhood, just one of many secrets they'd shared growing up in the same room, and it made Anna suddenly terribly sad. Her anger had passed. But it was regret now that nearly took her breath away. Regret that every happy memory of childhood – singing along to cheesy pop on their bedroom stereo, birthday parties, trips to the movies – now seemed tainted. Regret that the whole sorry episode of Sophie and Andrew's betrayal had changed her; she didn't want to be a cold, bitter and lonely person, but she knew that it was the reason she hadn't had a relationship since. She felt herself getting emotional. She didn't want her mother or sister to see that.

The waiter was approaching again. Anna took a deep breath.

'Look, I'm sorry,' she said, getting up. 'I can't do this right now. I need to get back.'

Sue Kennedy looked incredulous. 'But we haven't even ordered yet.'

'I'm not that hungry,' said Anna, pushing her chair in. 'You two enjoy yourselves.'

She turned and walked out, squeezing her nails into her palm, desperate not to cry. She returned to the pool area as fast as her spa slippers would allow, needing to grab her book and trainers from where she'd left them. And then she could get the hell out of there.

She was just gathering her things when Sophie came up behind her, looking upset and concerned.

'Anna, please wait. Can't we just talk?'

'About what?' she said simply.

'I know how hurt and angry you must have been . . .'

Anna closed her eyes and the whole horrific scene leapt towards her, as if she was seeing a slideshow of images. The key turning in the lock as she let herself into the flat. Glancing at the stereo on the sideboard, wondering why Coldplay was playing so loud. Walking through to the bedroom and bending to pick up Andy's shirt that he had dropped in the corridor. And then opening the bedroom door. Legs entwined on the bed. Sophie's face, her eyes wide. Andrew chasing Anna down the stairs on to the street. 'It didn't mean anything,' that was what he had said. But it had. It had meant everything.

'No you don't,' she said quietly. 'These things don't happen to you, Sophie. You can't possibly know how it feels to have your heart stamped on, to feel so betrayed that you don't know if you will ever really trust anyone again.'

Someone at the far side of the pool looked up from their daybed.

'I'm sorry that we hurt you, Anna, but we fell in love,' Sophie said, lowering her voice to avoid a scene. 'And ask yourself this: did you really love Andy? I'm not sure, because if you did you wouldn't have put your career above him.'

'Don't try and make out that this is my fault.'

'I miss you, Anna.' For a moment her words sounded heartfelt. 'I miss you and I can understand why you don't want to come to the wedding, but please, at least come to my hen party.'

'To celebrate the happy occasion,' Anna said bitterly.

'Because you're my sister.'

Sophie's voice trembled, and Anna felt a wave of regret so strong she felt as if it could knock her down.

How bad could it be? a little voice in her head reassured her. *It's time to move on.*

'Please,' pleaded Sophie. 'There are lots of people coming and they're going to wonder why you're not there . . .'

Anna snorted.

'You almost had me there again, Soph.' She shook her head ferociously. 'You know, I don't believe you're a bad person. Just an extremely selfish one. You expect people to give, give, give. And you take, take, take, even things that aren't or should never be yours, and you don't care what depths you have to plumb to get what you want, because you *expect* them to be yours. The food column you lied to get your hands on – the editor told me all about your *years* of work in the Dorset Nurseries restaurant, which is funny, because I thought you were in Thailand while you were apparently sharpening knives in Dad's kitchen. But then those came in handy, didn't they, for when you stabbed me in the back and slept with my boyfriend. How many times did you tell me it happened? Once, twice? Funny, I don't believe that any more.'

'It was a handful of times,' Sophie said sheepishly.

'How long?' Anna snapped, the details that she had never dared broach again suddenly seeming of urgent importance.

'We were together for about two months before you found us.'

Anna inhaled sharply, and when she breathed out, she felt an enormous sense of relief.

'I know all I need to know now. You can't hurt me any more.'

'Anna, please,' said Sophie, grabbing her sister as she pushed past her at the side of the pool. Anna tried to shake her off, and as she did so Sophie slipped. In slow motion Anna saw her falling away from her, her arms waving, hands clutching at the air, her mouth in a perfect 'O', landing in the swimming pool with a huge splash.

'Anna!' shouted a voice. It was her mother, full of anger and disapproval and disappointment. 'What have you done . . . ?'

Anna ran so fast out of the spa, she didn't hear another word of what her mother was about to say.

23

'I assume you've seen page eleven of the *Sun* this morning?'

Helen watched with satisfaction as Anna Kennedy flinched. It was 7 a.m. and the Donovan Pierce boardroom already had half a dozen people sitting around the table; Helen's team for the Jonathon Balon libel case. They were in court first thing and she wanted a counsel of war before they started.

Well, at least she has read the papers, thought Helen as she watched Anna sip her coffee, obviously trying to appear unruffled. Interesting. Perhaps there's more to this than the story suggested.

Helen spread the newspaper out on the long walnut table.

' "Celebrity Chef in the Drink",' she read aloud. The story was accompanied by a grainy photograph of Sophie Kennedy emerging from a swimming pool – bedraggled, but still sexy. 'So what's the real story?' she asked, silently noting two trainees who craned their necks to read the piece. She expected her employees to be completely up to date with all media – TV, papers domestic and foreign, even reading the wires from AP and Reuters. These two would be made to pay for their slackness, even if it was early.

Anna put her coffee cup down and shrugged.

'I was at the spa with my mum and my sister. My sister fell in the pool and someone must have taken the shot with a mobile phone. There's nothing more to it than that.'

Isn't there? thought Helen. She hadn't got to her lofty position in the legal profession without being able to sniff out a lie. Usually she wasn't interested in the private lives of her employees, unless they were doing something that might impact on the firm – and this could quite easily fall into that category. Anna Kennedy had been castigated over the Sam Charles debacle and Helen really hadn't been pleased to see her name in the tabloids again: 'sister of the bride-to-be and solicitor for shamed actor Sam Charles'. She knew it could have been worse, of course. Only last week she'd seen Donovan Pierce referred to as the lawyers behind 'the bungled Charles injunction'. That had put her in a bad mood for days.

'All right,' she said, looking around the table expectantly, 'any ideas what damages we could seek for Anna or her sister here?'

Trainee Sid Travers raised her voice nervously.

'Breach of privacy? Her sister thought she was in a secure area.'

'And the citation for that?'

Sid fell silent.

'Sienna Miller versus Xposure Photo Agency,' suggested Toby Meyer more confidently. 'She'd been on the movie set and the paparazzi had taken nude photos of her with a long lens.'

'Correct,' said Helen, pleased that her trainees weren't complete idiots, but careful not to show it. 'Although privacy damages aren't huge, so sometimes it's not worth the client's time.'

She stabbed her finger down on to the table.

'But the case we are going to win is this one,' she said, turning her gaze on each of the team one by one. 'Jonathon Balon is relying on us. He employed us because he believed we could prove in court – and to the public – that these charges are groundless and malicious. We have a reputation to uphold, both ours' – she looked directly at Anna as she said this – 'and his. It's not enough that we win this case; we need to destroy the opposition's arguments and prove ours beyond a shadow of a doubt. This is war, people.'

She tapped her hand on the desk.

'Okay, let's go to work.'

Anna leaned over and handed a twenty-pound note to the cabby. What was this? Her sixth cab journey today? And it was only 3.30 p.m. She felt as if she was on a piece of elastic. In the course of the morning she'd shuttled back and forth between court and the offices twice, grabbing another stack of files or looking up some vital piece of case law. So far they'd only scratched the surface of the Balon case, but at least they were under way; after weeks of intensive preparation, the whole team was hyped up and full of energy, keen to win at all costs. The day had begun with Nicholas Collins QC delivering the claimant's opening statement, and right now the barrister for the defence was putting his initial case. She'd drunk a gallon of coffee and had at least three blisters from speed-walking along the marble corridors of the High Court, but Anna was in her element. This was exactly the sort of work she'd joined Donovan Pierce to do. Meaningful, exacting work that required meticulous preparation, but which nevertheless was edge-of-the-seat stuff: most libel cases settled long before they got to court and if they didn't, both sides must believe they had a decent chance of winning. The courts were buzzing, because you never knew exactly what the other guy was going to throw at you.

Anna walked across the road to the office, skirting around a flaming red Ferrari that was parked halfway onto the pavement, and took the stairs to the Donovan Pierce reception.

'All right, gorgeous? Buried any good actors lately?'

Her heart sank as she saw Wayne Nicholls coming her way. Wayne was an East End wide boy who owned one of the most notorious picture agencies in town. He was rich, cocky and had the sort of unshakeable self-regard that allowed him to wear cowboy boots and sunglasses indoors. They had crossed swords more than once: the photographers contracted to Wayne's agency seemed to take gleeful pleasure in flouting the privacy laws firms like Donovan Pierce were there to protect.

'Pleasure to see you, Wayne,' she said, knowing the sarcasm was wasted on him. He kissed her on the cheek, almost overpowering her with his aftershave.

'Nice picture of your sister in the *Sun* this morning,' he said with a wink. 'I wish we'd had it, could have made a few quid on that. Hey, how about winging some exclusive little wedding snaps of her bash in Italy over to me? I'll make it worth your while.'

'Wayne, what are you doing here?' Anna said, changing the subject. 'I'd have thought it was like Dracula walking over consecrated ground.'

'Doing a job for your boss, aren't I?'

'For Helen?' she said, wondering why she hadn't heard about it.

'The other one, Matty D,' said Wayne, tucking his shirt into his tight jeans.

'Really? What sort of job?'

Wayne tapped the side of his nose.

'Privileged information, darling. You wouldn't want me to abandon my principles, would you?' He glanced at his chunky Jacob & Co. watch. 'Must fly, sweetheart. Car's on a meter.'

'Let me guess – the badly parked Ferrari?'

'That's her. Any time you fancy a quick spin, my door's always open.'

Anna couldn't help laughing.

'I'll bear it in mind,' she said, watching him prop up reception to try his luck on Sherry, the telephonist.

Anna walked slowly, thoughtfully, past her own office towards Matt Donovan's and lingered at the door. She hadn't really spoken to him since their showdown in the kitchen and had no desire for a rematch, but given that he was, as Wayne had helpfully reminded her, the boss and she needed to hold on to her job, it would be good politics to try and help him out. She looked inside – Matthew was bent over his computer screen, tapping away at the keys, his brow furrowed.

'Dipping your toe into the shark-infested waters of media law, are we?' said Anna with a smile. Matthew glanced up.

'Why do you say that?'

'I've just seen Wayne Nicholls, puppet-meister of the paparazzi, hanging around the entrance.'

'He's helping me with something,' said Matt casually, looking back at his computer. Anna knew she was being dismissed, but curiosity had got the better of her.

'Anything I should know about?'

He looked at her, unsmiling. 'Checking up on me again, are you?'

Anna flushed. He was obviously still annoyed about her advice regarding Rob Beaumont's visit to the office, but she was bothered he was about to make the same mistake twice.

'No, not snooping, just wondering if I could help. I know Wayne and he's not, shall we say, the most trustworthy of individuals.'

'I think I can make up my own mind about that, thanks,' said Matthew, not looking up.

'Yes, of course, it's just—'

'If you must know, I've been trying to track down some information about Kim Collier.'

'How come?'

'Kim wants to take their son to live in Miami. Rob has no idea why, so we're trying to find out in the hope that it might give us some leverage in the divorce, which is turning nastier by the second.'

'And you want *Wayne* to help you?' said Anna, trying not to sound judgemental.

'Actually he's done a bloody good job,' said Matt, sliding some photographs across to Anna. They were shots of Kim Collier in a car, coming out of a shop, having lunch in a restaurant, the usual paparazzi fare you found in celeb mags.

'Well, there doesn't seem to be much here,' said Anna.

'Exactly,' said Matt. 'She's had five meetings over the last forty-eight hours. Her manager, her friend from school, her make-up artist, nothing at all controversial. Certainly nothing Wayne Nicholls can sell on to the tabloids, if that's what you're worried about. Besides, I made it clear that if he screws us over, we'll come down on every single set of pictures he takes like a ton of bricks.'

Anna frowned. Paparazzi were better at following celebrities than conventional private eyes as they had a network of drivers, waiters and doormen to tip them off, but it was a risky strategy.

She hesitated. 'I'm just worried that Wayne will have worked out that you're a divorce lawyer, and as you have him following Rob Beaumont's wife, he'll put two and two together and "Kim and Rob Love Split" will mysteriously be all over the the *Sun* tomorrow morning.'

Matthew gave a small smile.

'I had, of course, thought of that,' he said. 'I've drafted a confidentiality agreement so tight not even Houdini could get out of it.'

'I still don't like using Wayne Nicholls, though,' she said.

'As it happens, having her followed has paid off.'

He leaned over and tapped one of the photographs; a middle-aged man in a leather jacket was sitting with Kim in a café.

'Fabio Martelli. Hotelier. Businessman. Old friend of Kim's.'

'So?'

'That's what Wayne said. Why shouldn't she be having a drink with an old friend? You could see from Wayne's face that he was secretly pleased his paps hadn't found anything; that way he was getting ten grand from me while I got nothing. But Wayne doesn't have the other piece of the jigsaw.'

'Which is?'

'Martelli owns four homes, in New York, London, Milan and Miami, where he's opening a live entertainment venue at Christmas and where he intends to base himself full-time in preparation for the launch.'

'*Miami*. Where Kim Collier's taking her son.'

'He doesn't know it, but your pal Wayne has been very helpful.'

Anna couldn't help smiling to herself as she left Matthew's office. Wayne Nicholls *helpful*. That was a first. She had to admit, however, that she had underestimated Matthew. Maybe there was more to him than met the eye after all.

As she walked into her office, she frowned. Her windows overlooked the street and she could hear yelling and swearing coming from that direction. She peered down and was pleased to see the irate figure of Wayne Nicholls standing next to his Ferrari, waving his arms at two burly men in overalls. Behind them in the street was a pick-up truck labelled 'Secure Towing Co.'.

Giggling to herself, she ran back down the stairs and out into the sunshine.

'Little problem?' She smiled innocently.

'Thank God! A lawyer!' Wayne said. 'These meatheads are

refusing to release the Ferrari from this bleedin' truck. Tell him I'll sue them.'

The first clamper merely raised his eyebrows. He'd clearly heard it all before.

Anna was tempted to let them carry out their threat, but she had an idea forming in her mind, and for that she needed Wayne on side.

'Listen, Wayne, let me have a word,' she said. 'I'll see what I can do.'

She went over to talk to the clampers. What Wayne didn't know was that the towing company was employed by Donovan Pierce to prevent people parking outside their office building – Larry had wanted it kept clear so he could park his Bentley.

'Yeah, and don't come back, either!' shouted Wayne as they drove off. He turned to Anna and winked. 'Cheers, darling.'

'Actually, I need a favour.'

If Matthew Donovan could use the pap boss to his advantage, why shouldn't she? Anna knew a lot about Wayne's organisation. When she'd sued him as often as she had, it paid to know the background. Thanks to the explosion in demand for celebrity pictures over the past few years, he had expanded and diversified: a photographic studio and a model agency that specialised in glamour girls.

'It'll cost you,' he said playfully.

'How about you do it just to get on my nice side?'

'How nice is your nice side exactly? Because I actually quite like the uptight bitch thing.'

'Your model agency, FrontGirls? Do you know many of the models yourself?'

'Shagged half of them,' he said proudly. 'I mean, what's the point being the boss otherwise?'

'I need to speak to someone. A blonde called Mandy.'

'Mandy Stigwood? Incredible knockers?'

Anna smiled thinly.

'What do you want to speak to Mandy for? What's she done?'

Anna leaned in, whispering. 'It's just one of my clients fancies her. I thought I could have a word. Play Cupid.'

'You? The ball-breaker. Playing Cupid? Come on, I wasn't born yesterday.'

'Is she one of your girls?'

'Yes, she is.'

'How often do you see her?'

'Not often. But she's got a shoot at my studios sometime this week, I think. Always make a note of which girls are popping down to the studios. I like to welcome them. Give it the personal touch.'

'I'm sure. Can you sort it out, then? A quick chat between me and Mandy.'

He sighed deeply. 'Go on. Seeing as you just sorted out the motor. We've got each other's number. I'll call you.'

'Thanks, Wayne, you're a star,' she said, pecking him on the cheek.

He looked genuinely flustered.

'And go easy on me next time you're trying to stiff me in court, all right?'

'Only if you don't go trying to stiff Donovan Pierce,' she said, resuming her cool.

'What are you talking about?'

'Your job for Matthew. He might think a non-disclosure agreement will hold you, but we both know you've got the morals of a jackal.'

Wayne gave a wicked laugh.

'That's what you love about me.'

'I mean it. Don't mess with me or I'll come after you, and I won't stop until the damages you have to pay to my clients run your business into the ground.'

Anna turned on her heel to go back to the office. She glanced behind her and watched Wayne disappear into a coffee shop. She didn't trust him. There was no way she was going to let him shaft Matthew. It was time to fire him a warning shot.

Seeing a council parking attendant in his green uniform, she crossed the square to speak to him.

'Excuse me?' she said, pointing over at Wayne's Ferrari. 'That red car's been parked up on the pavement for hours. It's blocking a fire exit too. I think you should call a tow truck.'

She took out her mobile and texted Wayne.

'I'm watching you. PS. Stop drinking coffee and get to your car.'

24

'You ready?'

Lauren Silver stood at the door of Sam's house in the Hollywood Hills, an architectural triumph on stilts that overlooked the whole of the LA bowl.

Sam whistled through his teeth. She was wearing a black silk cocktail dress that hugged her curves and had a see-through mesh back panel that hinted at a smooth, creamy expanse of skin.

'Someone's looking very va-va-voom tonight,' he laughed, not attempting to hide the soft spot he had for the vice president of marketing for Oasis, the studio behind his latest movie.

'Don't get any ideas, lover boy,' said Lauren, turning on her heel and heading back towards the limo waiting on the drive. 'I'm your babysitter, remember, not your date. And we're late, so hop to it.'

Sam looked at his watch as he pulled on his suit jacket, a bespoke Anderson & Sheppard that felt like a suit of armour. It was already five o'clock. The premiere was due to start in an hour and the traffic was usually chaotic when there was an event in town. He jumped into the car beside Lauren and sat back as they raced down the windy lanes towards the City of Angels.

'So are you prepared for this?' Lauren asked, giving Sam a sideways glance. 'This will be your first time out in public since *Billington*. The press are going to go crazy.'

'They won't be looking at me, not with you by my side,' said Sam, sounding more confident than he felt. For the past forty-eight hours he'd felt so sick with panic, convinced that the crowd were going to pelt him with eggs, that he'd even suggested hiring a stand-in from the lookalikes agency to make a quick appearance on the red carpet. The studio chiefs had other ideas, and had sent Lauren along to hold his hand.

'I'm serious, Sam,' she said. 'You need to be on your A-game tonight. All charm and smiles.'

'What do you think I'm going to do? Try and touch up the reporter from Fox News?'

'Who knows? The last time you went out in public you were arrested on battery charges.'

'That was different,' said Sam sulkily. He was still smarting at having been charged with assault for the supposed attack on the paparazzo backstage at the *Billington* show and had to return to court in New York at the end of the month.

'We just want to keep things tight. Secure.'

Sam looked out of the window.

'You make it sound like I rob banks.'

Lauren's expression was firm. 'We just can't afford any more bad press on this movie, Sam. You know how it works. This isn't about you, it's about the money. The studio needs a hit and so do you.'

Sam fell into a brooding silence. He knew he'd be feeling more relaxed if he had actually seen the movie in question. Despite shooting *Robotics* almost twelve months earlier, he'd yet to view a final cut. He'd been shown a worrying version of the sci-fi film two months earlier, and had not been surprised when he'd been told that it had gone back into the editing suite for revisions and additional CGI. Ordinarily that would have worried him, but he knew *Robotics* was one of the studio's 'tent-pole' movies; it had cost over two hundred million dollars to make, and apparently had another hundred million spent on marketing. No, the studios could not, would not let it fail.

The butterflies in his stomach kicked up a gear as the limo slid in front of the Village Theater in Westwood. From the protected womb of the car he could hear the screams of a thousand fans pressed up against the crash barriers. The driver opened the door and the heat and sound crashed over him like a tidal wave. As if on autopilot, his face lit up with his thousand-watt smile and for an instant he was overwhelmed by the moment. It was impossible not to be. Over the past decade he'd been to so many of these things they were almost routine, but the thrill of turning up to your own movie premiere never lost its magic.

The photographers were going crazy.

'Sam! Sam! Over here!'

'Give us a smile, buddy.'

'Where's Jessica tonight? Can you look sad for us?'

Keep it together, he said to himself, trying not to flinch as the whirr of the camera shutters filled the air like gunfire. Just do what you always do.

'Keep moving,' said Lauren into his ear.

'Who's that? Your new hooker?' shouted a voice from the back of the crowd. Sam tried to turn back, but Lauren kept a grip on his arm.

'Keep smiling,' she hissed. 'Charming and lovable, remember?' She tugged at his hand, pulling him towards the theatre's entrance. 'Perfect,' she whispered in his ear.

Sam was glad to be inside the foyer, away from the gaze of the public.

'There he is, the star of the show.' Jim Parker strode over and tapped him playfully on the cheek. 'You ready to see some kick-ass action?'

'Let's hope it does kick ass, Jim,' said Sam quietly, as they walked towards their seats at the front. 'Because we're in trouble if it doesn't.'

Usually at events like this, the stars who walked the red carpet were discreetly let out the back of the movie theatre, but this time Sam couldn't wriggle out of it. He was already under scrutiny and they couldn't afford a 'Sam Snubs Premiere' headline.

Then again, no one could have blamed him if he had chosen to walk out. The movie was worse than he had suspected; in fact it was a full-on disaster. He sat there almost mesmerised as scene after clunky, unbelievable scene played out before him in full Dolby Surround Sound. He could hear people sniggering in the darkness behind him. It was the biggest, fattest turkey he'd ever seen. As his character ran across the battlefield – ironically enough, a CGI version of downtown LA – to save his girl from the distinctly unscary robot killers, Sam shrank further and further down in his seat, dreading the moment when the lights would come up and he'd have to face yet another humiliation. No one would say 'Jeez, what a crap movie,' of course. This was Hollywood; everyone was relentlessly upbeat to your face. But no one could have watched that train wreck of a film and not seen it for what it was: the death knell for Sam Charles's career.

'Come on,' whispered Lauren, as the final scene played out. 'Let's get out of here.'

Gratefully, Sam followed her towards the side exit, Jim tagging along behind.

'What's up?' Jim asked as they reached the street door. 'I thought we were hanging around to press the flesh.'

Lauren shot him a look.

'Can it, Jim,' she said. 'Hasn't Sam put up with enough recently without hanging him out to dry?'

'I loved that goddamn movie,' Jim said earnestly.

Lauren shook her head. 'Right, Sam, you and Jim go off to the aftershow at Momo's – the studio needs you to go, I'm afraid: united front and all that. I'll stay here and firefight as much as I can, then I'll see you there.'

Sam tried to give her a smile, but he felt utterly miserable. Even Jim had picked up on the mood, and for once sat silently as an SUV carried them to the restaurant on Wilshire Boulevard. They both flashed smiles and waved at the waiting photographers, then ducked inside quickly, being ushered to a booth at the back. Thankfully they were alone for the moment, with the rest of the partygoers still back at the theatre. Jim unfastened the buttons on his tux and let out a deep breath.

'Okay, so it wasn't *Casablanca*,' he said. 'But they can't all win prizes, can they? Tomorrow morning we'll find you some-thing else. The next one's going to be dynamite, I promise you.'

Sam looked up at him.

'What do you mean, "find you something else"? I've done three back-to-back movies. I start on that Dreamscape thing next month. We agreed that's enough until the next knockout script comes in.'

200

Jim's mouth flattened into a line.

'About that . . .'

Sam felt his stomach turn over.

'Oh no,' he said. 'Don't tell me there's a problem.'

'Sorry, Sam, the Dreamscape movie has fallen through.'

Sam blinked at him. This was meant to be his big payday. No one won an Oscar for doing voice work on a cartoon, but the financial rewards could be phenomenal. He had been promised ten million for what amounted to a week's work, plus all the extras for the merchandise: licensing his voice in the talking dolls, mugs, greetings cards, the whole caboodle. After all his hard work, this was supposed to be his golden pay-off, his retirement fund. And now it was slipping through his fingers.

'It's fallen through?' he said, panicking. 'What do you mean – that it's not happening at all?'

Jim shook his head slowly.

'Course it's happening. Animation's almost done. The problem is you voicing the lead . . .'

'But we signed a contract.'

Jim picked up a handful of nuts from a bowl on the table and tossed a couple into his mouth.

'Look, they're not happy about the publicity you've been getting. Dreamscape is a family company and they can get very jumpy about that sort of thing.'

'But by the time the movie's out, this is going to be old news.'

Jim shrugged.

'Right now they're pointing at the morality clause in the contract and they're saying they don't want to take their chances. It's Hollywood, baby. They don't want to add any risk to their investment.'

By now the restaurant was beginning to fill up. There was still a party atmosphere – lots of shouted greetings, air-kissing and shoulder-clasping – it was LA, after all. If an alien had stepped into the scene, they would have concluded that the people gathered at the party were the closest friends imaginable, rather than deadly rivals prepared to stab each other in the back for the next movie deal. People were glancing in Sam's direction, but most were looking away again, embarrassed looks on their faces. Two-faced wankers, he thought angrily. Half the people in the restaurant had done exactly what he'd done at some point in their career, probably on a regular basis. But Sam had got caught.

'Look, we need to talk,' said Jim, sipping a fruit juice.

'More bad news?' said Sam cynically.

'Just a strategy.'

'What is it?'

'It's Jessica.'

'Jim, enough of that.'

'Seriously, I know she didn't want to speak to you a few weeks ago, but I think you should try again and make it work.'

'Why?'

'Because you need her. You need stability. A wife. Even a family.'

'What I need is you getting off my back.'

'I mean it, Sam. You have a credibility problem. You need goodwill on your side and you need it fast. Hollywood loves a love story. I can make this work for you. Let me talk to her.'

'I mean it, Jim. No.'

As the VIP area started to fill, Sam felt as if the walls of the restaurant were closing in on him. He stood up.

'Where you going?' snapped Jim.

'The bathroom.'

'But Evan Black is coming this way. You need to network.'

'I need the bathroom.'

His agent tutted.

'The damage limitation starts in five minutes. You got that long to get back here.'

Damp patches of sweat were collecting on the back of Sam's shirt and the drag of champagne had made him feel heady. Blaming the sudden onset of nausea on a shrimp roll he'd had five minutes earlier, he pulled at his shirt collar as he fled to the bathroom.

He felt a little better in the cool, quiet warren of store cupboards and corridors. Pushing open the bathroom door, he saw a slim blonde in a tiny black Lycra dress bending over the sink, a rolled-up dollar bill in her hand.

'Sorry,' he said, holding up a hand. 'Think I've got the wrong room.'

'No, this is the men's,' said the girl, giving him a glassy smile. 'The queue was too long in the ladies'.'

'Well, I'll just wait outside, then,' began Sam, but the girl stood in his way. 'Don't go on my account,' she said, holding up the note. 'D'ya want a bump?'

'Not for me, thanks,' said Sam.

'How about we try something else, then?' she said, running a finger down his chest.

He backed up against the wall of the small enclosed space. 'No, I just . . . I just wanted to use the, uh . . .'

'I know what you wanted,' said the girl, taking Sam's hand and putting it on her breast. 'But I've got something else for you to try.' She sank to her knees, expertly unzipping his fly and reaching inside with a firm, determined grip.

'Hey, no!' he said. 'You can't . . .'

'Yes I can,' murmured the girl, sliding back his boxer shorts and taking the tip of his cock into her mouth.

'Stop it,' said Sam, slapping his hand against the wall. Despite himself, he was getting erect.

She pulled back a fraction.

'I didn't think *you'd* play hard to get.'

Sam could feel his heart hammering, the blood banging in his ears. What if someone came in? All these influential people, he'd never live it down.

He scrambled away from her, zipping his trousers up, stumbling back to the bathroom door. He tugged at his collar, panting. His head was swimming now. What was going on? Had he been drugged? His pulse was racing and he felt faint. He had to get away, but how? He was cornered, trapped.

'NO!' he yelled, pushing the girl as hard as he could. She toppled backwards, with a baffled look that twisted to anger.

'Fuck you, you Limey fuck,' she hissed. 'My dress. This cost me a thousand goddamn bucks!'

'Listen, I'll get it cleaned, I'm sorry . . .' he spluttered, realising the worst thing he could do was hand her money.

The girl's spiteful laugh followed him as he bounced off the walls into the corridor.

'Yeah, you run, you goddamn fruit,' she yelled. Clawing at his throat, gasping for air, Sam fell into a store cupboard and crumpled to the floor. He fumbled in his pocket for his phone and, squinting down, thumbed to Lauren Silver's number.

'Sam?' said Lauren, her voice concerned. 'What's up?'

'Lauren, thank God,' he gasped. 'I think I'm having a heart attack.'

'Shit, where are you?'

'I'm at the back of the restaurant.'

'Find a quiet place and stay there, I'm on my way . . .'

He clutched his knees in front of his chest and forced himself to breathe. Closing his eyes, he felt the rise and fall of his chest regulate. He looked at the phone gripped between his fingers, and knew immediately what he had to do. He scrolled to another number, and when Mike McKenzie finally answered, he felt an uplifting sense of relief.

'Meet me in London,' he said simply. 'I'm coming home.'

25

Matthew glanced at his watch as the lift door closed. It was two minutes to nine and he really didn't want to be late for his first conference. He cursed himself; he never should have stopped off at his father's Cheyne Walk place on the way to work, but he was a little concerned. Larry hadn't replied to any of the messages he had left on his voicemail over the past few days. There was nothing unusual about that in the normal scheme of things; in the past, whole years had gone by without a whisper from his father, but now he was convalescing from his heart operation, Matthew had assumed that Larry would have a little more time to keep in touch. As it happened, there had been no reply when he had rung the bell at the house either, not even a housekeeper to answer the door. It was curious, but Matthew resolved to put it out of his mind. Loralee would have let him know if there were any problems, and knowing his father, being out of the loop meant he had probably gone to convalesce in Vegas.

The aluminium doors were just about to close when a hand shot through the gap, jamming it open.

'Sorry,' said a flustered Anna Kennedy, slipping inside holding a coffee cup in one hand and a huge pile of files in the other. 'Morning,' she said as she struggled to balance them.

'Let me help,' said Matthew, grabbing the files just as they were about to slip to the floor.

'Thanks,' she said. 'I need to get these to Helen or she'll lynch me. Again.'

He smiled.

'So how's the Rob Beaumont thing coming on?' she asked.

'Actually I have a meeting with him and Kim Collier at nine. It's the first time we've had them in the same room together, so it could go either way.' He glanced at her with a smile. 'And before you tell me off, they're arriving separately through the back door.'

'You've mastered this celebrity thing,' she laughed as the door pinged open.

'Speaking of which, you've got a fan,' said Matthew, helping her carry the files down the corridor into her office.

'Oh yes? Who?'

'Wayne Nicholls.'

'A dream come true,' she said playfully.

'I mean it. He sent me an email that said something like "she's a tough bitch", which I think is the highest level of praise in his world.'

'Well, I can use that as a reference if Helen still wants to fire me.'

Matt laughed as he walked quickly towards the boardroom, glad that the atmosphere between them had thawed, but his fleeting good mood vanished as soon as he opened the door. Rob was sitting across the table from Kim Collier and her solicitor Chris Snell; the atmosphere in the room was icy, and Rob's angry expression suggested that there was going to be none of the grown-up, sensible approach to the divorce he had wanted only a few weeks before.

Matt extended his hand towards Snell.

'Matthew Donovan,' he said. 'I don't think we've had the pleasure before.'

'No indeed,' said Snell, his eyebrow raising just enough to convey his disapproval.

The London family law circuit was a small world, and Matthew had gone up against the main players countless times, but Chris Snell was top of the food chain. Dark-haired and skeletal, he had been nicknamed 'The Vulture' by the broadsheets, as much for his client base of gold-digging trophy wives as for his reputation of being forbiddingly aggressive in his methods.

Matthew glanced at Kim Collier as he sat down next to Rob and pulled out his files. She was certainly beautiful, there was no denying that, but she was clearly furious at being here. Matthew wondered how much that was anger at her soon-to-be-ex-husband and how much was annoyance that, for once, she wasn't getting her own way.

'So I think we all want to keep this simple and uncomplicated,' said Snell briskly.

Matthew nodded.

'Hopefully we're not completely past that. But things are definitely more complex than they once were. As I think we all know.'

Snell shrugged. He clearly wasn't going to give an inch.

'My client and yours have had initial conversations about the welfare of Oliver and they both agree that it's in his best interests for him to stay with his mother. Ms Collier has no objections whatsoever to weekend visitation rights. Possibly even one evening visit on a school night.'

'Like that's going to be easy when he's in Miami,' said Rob, his voice laced with sarcasm.

'I believe you live within fifteen miles of Heathrow airport, Mr Beaumont,' said Snell with a wintry smile. 'I'm sure Ms Collier would welcome you in Miami at any time.'

Kim leaned over and whispered something into Snell's ear. He nodded.

'With prior and convenient notice, of course,' he added.

Matt glanced at Kim. Had that really been necessary? If his reading of her cuttings files were anything to go by, Kim Collier had a reputation as something of a diva and a bitch. He wasn't sure whether show business attracted bitches, or whether clawing your way to the top made you that way. Certainly it followed that someone as ambitious as Kim would want to win whichever game she was playing, even if it meant trampling on everyone else along the way. Who knew what a nice bloke like Rob had seen in the woman; then again, he too knew the masochistic appeal of a beautiful and difficult woman, which had also ended in tears.

'As I said, things have become a little more complicated,' said Matthew, passing a document across to Kim, taking his time as he enjoyed the moment.

'What's this?' she asked, picking it up.

'Perhaps you should let me look at it first,' said Snell, snatching it from her. 'You're cross-petitioning?' he said, looking up startled.

Kim glared at Rob, who gave her a weak shrug. If he was enjoying this, he certainly wasn't showing it. In fact he looked completely miserable.

'What is it?' Kim snapped at Snell impatiently.

'It's a petition,' said Snell. 'Your husband is divorcing you for adultery.'

'He can't do that!' she gasped.

'I'm afraid he can,' said Matthew, sliding a ten-by-eight photograph across the table. It was a grainy long-lens shot, but it was clear that it was Kim on a balcony wearing only a bedsheet. She was being embraced by a silver-haired man in his fifties. After the tip-off via Wayne Nicholls, Matthew had handed the more intimate discovery work back to a trusted private investigation company. Kim Collier wasn't a big star in America and, ignored by the paparazzi, she had clearly let her guard down.

'For the record,' said Matt as coolly as he could, 'the man in the picture is Fabio Martelli, the international hotelier and playboy.'

'Oh please,' spat Kim, but she looked away from Rob. Matthew had broken the news to him the evening before and it hadn't been one of his favourite meetings of all time. Whatever had gone on in their relationship, Rob Beaumont clearly hadn't anticipated that his wife would cheat on him. He had been devastated.

'Mr Martelli is based in Miami, I believe,' continued Matthew. 'His primary address is about a mile from the Sacred Heart School where Ms Collier has enrolled Oliver.'

Chris Snell pushed his chair back and stood up.

'I would like a moment with my client,' he said.

'Certainly,' said Matthew, showing them into an adjoining room and closing the door.

'I hate this,' said Rob, rubbing his temples.

'We have to play hardball to get leverage,' Matt said as reassuringly as he could.

Rob nodded sadly. 'I get all that,' he said. 'I just wish it didn't have to hurt so much. What did I do?'

Matthew didn't answer. He suspected Kim was with Fabio for the same reasons Carla had gone off with David; not because they loved them more but because they could provide a better, more comfortable life. Or so he liked to think.

Kim and Snell walked back in, their previous air of confidence slightly dented as they sat down.

'Regardless of the reasons for the breakdown of this marriage, we both know that when we are considering the arrangements for the child, his welfare must come first. Mrs Collier is his mother. She can provide a stable, loving environment for Oliver.'

'Five thousand miles away from his father with some bloody playboy?' snapped Rob, leaning over the table and pointing his finger. 'I'll fight you every step of the way. I'm not going to roll over and let that dirty old sod play daddy to Ollie.'

Matt took Rob's arm, and as gently as he could, sat him back down.

Chris Snell was busy scribbling a note on the pad in front of him.

'Of course any episode of volatility or aggressive behaviour will be taken into account by the judge when deciding on the remit of any residence order.'

Matt felt sick; no wonder they called Snell the Vulture. The man was genuinely enjoying picking over the bones of this relationship. It wasn't about getting the best settlement for his client or making sure the children were well cared for; it was about power, about using anything to gain an inch of ground. It was a game. It was his career. Cases like this one were just another case victory at any cost to the people involved, another step on the ladder towards a bigger partnership, the judges' bench or even a title. Who cared who got hurt along the way?

'I think we should call this meeting a day, don't you?' said Snell, slotting the petition and photograph into his briefcase. 'We have plenty to go on here.'

'As you wish,' said Matthew, his mind already wandering to the next step. He looked at Rob; at the bags under his eyes, the jittery manner. He was taking this hard. He thought back to their first meeting; what was it Rob had said? Something about how he wanted a straightforward divorce. 'Let's keep this simple', wasn't that what he'd said? No, simple was one thing divorce never was.

26

'Your boss fucked me over.'

Anna stopped in her tracks, surprised to hear Wayne Nicholls' voice as she walked into Strawberry Studios just across the road from the Roundhouse in Chalk Farm. Nicholls was sitting in an office behind the reception, his feet up on the desk, cigarette dangling from the side of his mouth.

'Slumming it a bit, aren't you?' smiled Anna, putting her head around the door. 'I didn't think you left trendy Clerkenwell these days.'

'Don't change the subject,' said Wayne. 'That snake of a boss of yours has done me out of an exclusive.'

Anna perched on the edge of his desk. 'Okay, what's your beef this time?'

'Kim bloody Collier,' said Wayne, stubbing out his cigarette angrily. 'Ten measly grand for following that bag around for a couple of days. I'd have asked for fifty times that if I'd have known it was heading for this.'

He tossed a copy of the *Evening Standard* on the desk bearing the headline 'Kim And Rob Love Split: Exclusive'.

Anna crossed her arms and smiled. 'Like you're not rich enough.'

'That's not the point. I feel stitched up.'

He looked so dejected, like a little boy being denied his favourite toy, that Anna couldn't help herself: she cracked up with laughter.

'Hey, it's not funny, this is my reputation here.'

'Come on, Wayne, even you must have guessed there was something going on. Matthew Donovan, a divorce lawyer, asking you to follow Kim Collier, see who she talks to?'

'Course I twigged,' said Wayne, pouting. 'But there was no story – she didn't meet with anyone, only her leg-waxer and a couple of fruits. I thought it was just Rob getting paranoid or something.'

'And you didn't think to tip off the papers about that? That's very principled of you, Wayne.'

He looked down at his waste basket. 'Yeah, well I'd signed one of them confidentiality wossnames, hadn't I? Had to stick to it. As I told Donovan, you're a tough old bitch.'

'Well at least you're in my good books.'

'Then how about dinner?'

'How about you show me where the shoot is?'

He sighed, shook his head, then got up from behind his desk. Anna had to grudgingly admit that she did owe Wayne Nicholls. He'd been true to his word the day before and called with the time and place of the shoot Mandy Stigwood had been booked for. In the meantime, Anna had sent Ryan Jones a photo of Mandy to confirm that she was indeed the girl he had met with Amy Hart that night in the club.

'See?' he had replied. 'Told you she had great tits.'

Anna glanced at her watch as Wayne led her along a white corridor. Ten thirty already. Helen would be wondering where she was. Anna had managed to fob her off, saying she had urgent work of her own at the office, but she knew that Helen would be watching her time sheets like a hawk. Certainly if she wasn't in court within the hour she'd have some serious explaining to do. Even so, Anna was prepared to risk her boss's wrath. Over the past week, since her meeting with Ryan, she'd been unable to shake the thought of Amy Hart's death from her mind.

She might know her case law inside out, but Anna knew that what made her a really great lawyer was her instinct, and it was her instinct that was telling her that there was more to Amy's death than met the eye.

'Check this shit out,' said Wayne proudly, pushing through two massive double doors.

The studio was enormous, like an aircraft hangar. You could easily have fitted three double-deckers and Evel Knievel inside.

'It's huge,' gasped Anna.

Wayne winked. 'That's what they all say, darlin'. But enough about me. The studio's thirty thousand square feet of space, all within London's Zone Two. It's full every day. Catalogues, magazines, corporate work. No fashion yet; they're so up their own arses they're snooty about what studio they use, let alone the models and photographers. But they'll come around when they realise how close we are to Soho.'

'Remind me not to feel too sorry for you next time I get a two hundred thousand damages settlement out of you,' said Anna slowly.

'Yeah, well, the *Heat* years have been good to me, haven't they? Everyone's mad for celebrities. You know people slag off the pap agencies, but I'm just providing a service, satisfying a demand.'

They opened the door of Studio 5 on the top floor. Dance music was blaring out and the whole room was full of stylists fussing around rails of clothes, make-up artists laying out their wares and a whole crew of technical staff setting up lights, reflectors and camera triggers.

One end of the room had been decked out in red drapes, at the centre of which was a huge circular bed covered in black satin sheets. Nice, thought Anna. Classy. Wayne's voice boomed across the studio.

'Mandy, my darling. You have a visitor!'

A platinum blonde in lacy white lingerie stepped out from behind a screen and tottered towards them on stacked heels, pulling a short robe around herself.

'Hi, baby,' she said to Wayne, stooping down to his level to give him a kiss on the cheek. Wayne whispered something to her and she giggled, glancing in Anna's direction.

'Mands, we need you to jump on the bed in five, all right?' shouted a man in a waistcoat.

'Of course, babes,' cooed the girl. 'Just talking with the boss.'

'*I'm* your boss today,' said the man.

'Course you are, sweetie,' she pouted. 'But Wayne's special.'

Wayne slapped Mandy on the bum and sent her over towards Anna.

'All right?' she said, looking Anna up and down warily. 'Wayne said you're a lawyer. What's this about then?'

Anna led her over to a quieter corner of the room, where three sofas were positioned round a coffee table laden with sandwiches.

'Something about a date, was it?' said Mandy, sitting down. She had perfectly even white teeth and a slender Barbie physique with a hand-span waist and cantaloupe-melon-sized breasts.

'No, not exactly a date,' said Anna. 'Although I do have a lot of high-profile clients. I actually wanted to talk to you about Amy. Amy Hart.'

'Amy? God, that poor cow,' said Mandy, glancing over towards where Wayne was laughing with two other blondes. 'Awful, isn't it?' she said sadly. 'I mean, it could of been any of us, couldn't it? Slipping on her heels like that.'

'Were you good friends?' asked Anna.

'Not especially,' said Mandy. 'We used to hang about at parties and that, but we weren't really close. I was sad to hear about it, though. She was pretty and clever, and she was a good girl.' She glanced over at Wayne and the models again. 'A lot of them girls can be right bitches, but Amy was always nice.'

'You didn't get called to give evidence at her inquest?'

She shrugged. 'I didn't know nothing about an inquest. Why did she have one of those?'

'They have inquests to work out exactly how someone died. Sometimes they call witnesses.'

'But I thought it was an accident, wasn't it? She fell down the stairs.'

'Probably,' nodded Anna.

Mandy pulled the tiny white robe tighter around her waist and frowned.

'Don't you believe them?'

'I'm just looking into it for someone.'

'Who, the police?' Mandy said with wide eyes.

'No,' smiled Anna. 'Amy's sister Ruby, actually.'

'Oh, her,' giggled Mandy. 'Amy brought her down one of the clubs once. I think she wanted to meet a footballer or something. But she was sweet. How can she afford a fancy lawyer like you?'

Anna smiled. 'She can't. I just want to see if there's anything in what she says.'

'And what's that?'

Anna paused for a moment before she spoke. She had no idea whether she could trust Mandy, or where a conversation like this might lead.

'Ruby thinks Ryan Jones killed her sister.'

Mandy gave a low, slow laugh.

'Ryan Jones?' she chuckled. 'Ryan's an arsehole, there's no doubt about that. But a killer? He hasn't got the balls.'

Anna smiled. Mandy had given a pretty accurate assessment of Ryan's personality, in her opinion.

'I spoke to Ryan at the weekend and he thought that Amy might have had another boyfriend. He was saying that he thought Amy used him to get back at someone. Do you know what he meant by that?'

Mandy pulled a face.

'Like I said, we weren't close, but I do think she was unhappy about some guy. That night we met Ryan, Amy had had a few drinks – she wasn't usually a drinker but I think she was upset. I remember she asked me: "Do you think I'd get in the papers if I shagged Ryan?" At the time I thought it was weird, because she was never one to go boasting about her boyfriends.'

'Why do you think she was discreet?'

Mandy shrugged.

'There's different reasons why we do this job,' she said quietly. 'People think we're tarts, slags. And yes, some girls like showing off, they like the attention and all the parties. When you're living in the back arse of nowhere, with no hope of getting out, it looks pretty nice dating people off the telly and that. But Amy wasn't like that; she was smart, savvier than most. She wouldn't do glamour or topless like this, only swimsuit stuff, because I think she had plans to get out.'

'What plans?'

'Sorry,' said Mandy. 'We never really had many heart-to-hearts, and like I say, she was a private sort of person. Don't get me wrong, though, she did like the modelling and the partying, because of the people it could introduce her to.'

'The men it could introduce her to?' prompted Anna.

'Yeah, sure. Amy just wanted a better life for herself. We're all looking for a meal ticket,' said Mandy, glancing at Wayne again. 'And I actually think Amy had found hers.'

'So who was it?'

Mandy looked down at her long, squared-off nails.

'About twelve months ago we were driving past the Houses of Parliament. We were in a taxi going from one party to another one in Chelsea. Amy was drunk. She told me that she'd had sex there.'

'In the Houses of Parliament?'

Mandy nodded. 'Saucy, hey? Of course I asked who. She said it was that MP Gilbert Bryce. Always on telly. Bit of a wanker.'

'And you think that's who she was seeing just before she got together with Ryan?'

'After she told me about it, I only saw her maybe twice a month. When I asked her about it, she totally clammed up. The only thing she said was that she was seeing someone but she couldn't talk about it because if she did he might finish with her.'

'And you think it was Gilbert.'

'He's a twat but he's ambitious. If it came out about a relationship with Amy, the press would have spun it as "Bryce Dates a Glamour Girl". He'd definitely want her to keep quiet about it.'

'Oi, Mands!' shouted the man in the waistcoat. 'We're ready for you.'

'Okay, lover!' she called, then rolled her eyes at Anna. 'It's a living,' she said.

She stood up and Anna shook her hand.

'Sorry I couldn't help more,' said Mandy.

Anna smiled at her.

'Oh, I think you've helped a great deal.'

27

Sam looked at the phone, willing himself to pick it up. He hadn't felt this way since he was a teenager, trying to pluck up the courage to call some girl, but even then he hadn't felt this anxious. Then, as ever, girls always said yes to his invitations. 'Come on,' he said to himself. 'You're Sam Charles. Everyone wants to talk to you.' Yet somehow it was hard to convince himself. Just six weeks ago, he was one of the world's biggest stars, engaged to one of the world's most desirable women. He'd never tried, but Sam suspected that if he'd called the White House, they'd have taken his call.

And now? Now he was standing in the living room at his Chelsea Harbour apartment, crapping himself about calling an Edinburgh comedy venue and speaking to the manager about the possibility of hiring out the space.

'Stop being such a knob,' he said out loud, striding over to the phone and snatching up the receiver. Unused to making his own professional phone calls, he quickly tapped in the number and waited, wondering what he should say.

Hello, it's Sam Charles. No. That didn't cut it. That phrase used to open doors, get him reservations in the best restaurants; now it sounded grubby and embarrassing. 'Sam Charles' used to be synonymous with 'top actor' and 'British heart-throb'; now it was synonymous with 'love rat' and 'thug'. He couldn't have buggered it all up more if he'd actually tried.

He jumped as the front door opened and Mike McKenzie almost fell in, carrying two straining carrier bags of shopping. 'Hey there, bro,' grinned Mike. 'Thought you'd gone out. I'm doing fish pie for lunch, that okay?'

Sam put the phone back in its cradle and watched Mike thump the bags down on the kitchen counter and start unloading: celery, a bunch of basil, some fancy olive oil, free-range eggs. Sam winced. It was only a bag of shopping, but it seemed to be loaded with criticisms of his life. His empty kitchen, his single status, his inability to cook. In fact, if he was honest, he wouldn't have had a clue where to find the nearest supermarket – it had been years since he'd bought a pint of milk. And now his friend – the famous burn-out and mental case, no less – was here looking after him, making him a pie because he couldn't be trusted to do things for himself.

But that was why he had come back. To change. To make a fresh start, to begin a new way of living. Back in his London flat, everything felt more real. From his wrap-around penthouse window he could glimpse the King's Road, Battersea Park and Stamford Bridge, home of his beloved Chelsea Football Club. And while he couldn't exactly go shopping, watch a match or go for a run – he'd been besieged by paparazzi when he had popped out for a packet of cigarettes – it still felt more like home than LA had ever done.

He felt a pang of regret at how he had neglected his birth city in the pursuit of fame. When he had moved to LA seven years ago to star in a short-lived pilot for ABC, he had promised himself he would return to London every three months. But as time slipped by, and he got bigger, more successful, there seemed increasingly little reason to do so. His parents had both died a decade earlier, which had severed his greatest tie with the country, whilst he had less and less in common with his old friends from the capital's acting circuit, most of whom had disappeared into non-acting jobs whilst they were 'resting' from their sporadic theatre and soap-opera gigs.

'I'll just get this in the oven and then we can get back to work,' said Mike breezily. 'How have you got on this morning?' he went on as he busied himself at the stove. 'Any blinding inspiration?'

'A few ideas,' said Sam, smiling.

'Ah-ha!' said Mike, pointing at him with his spatula. 'I knew it. You've come up with something good, haven't you? I can see it on your face.'

It was true. The one good thing to come out of all this mess was the two-man show that Mike and Sam had decided to do for the Edinburgh Festival. The two men had arrived back in London within hours of each other, and had got to work on the script immediately. Predictably, Mike had come up with a dozen brilliant gags and situations. But slowly Sam had found that he was having his own ideas – ideas that were actually making Mike laugh. So far they had written dozens of gags and set pieces, many of them Sam's, send-ups of their status as fallen stars.

The project had distracted Sam from the savage reviews for *Robotics*, which had taken three million bucks in its opening weekend; great box office for a small indie movie but a disaster for a major studio summer release. Jim Parker was being bullish out in LA, but Sam could tell that the scripts and offers had stopped coming, and Eli was talking about making a shift over to TV. 'Look at Glenn Close, and Forest Whitaker in *The Shield*,' he said. 'They had Emmys coming out the wazoo. We get you something like that, we can write our own ticket when you go back to the studios.' *When you go back*. Was it really all over already?

But if Hollywood was closing its door to him, why shouldn't he go back to doing the thing that, looking back, had made him most excited? The early days of his career. The buzz from the stage after a live performance. Okay, so Mike's comic genius had overshadowed him back in uni days, but things were different now – actually, he and Mike were on level pegging: the world saw them both as massive fuck-ups.

Scripting the Edinburgh show was hard work, but he was enjoying it more than anything he'd done in years, and best of all, he wasn't doing it as a career move; he was doing it for fun, for the hell of it, to help Mike out – whatever. But still, there was a nagging thought . . .

'So did you make the call to the Hummingbird Club?' asked Mike, chopping an onion.

'Not yet,' Sam replied vaguely.

'Why not? The festival's already bloody started. We'll have to pitch up at the bottom of Arthur's Seat and perform there at this rate.'

'You should do it.'

'Why? Your name opens doors.'

'I think we should keep my involvement under wraps. Until the gig starts anyway.'

'What for?'

'Because it could get hairy. Hecklers, press.'

'I see your point.'

'But what if no one comes?' he asked suddenly. 'What if they come and walk out?'

'Thanks, mate. I know I'm not a big draw any more, but still . . .'

'This isn't about you. It's about me. Trouble is following me around at the moment. Jess believes in karma, and maybe there's something in it. I've been a bastard. The way I treated Jessica. Firing that lawyer, who, to be fair, probably hadn't done anything wrong. I didn't even treat you properly. When you had your breakdown I should have flown over, brought you back to LA. But no, I was filming in Queensland. If no one comes to the show, it's what I deserve.'

Mike put his knife down.

'So what?' he said. 'So what if no one comes to the show so long as we enjoy it? You've got enough money to last ten lifetimes. For me, this is just a holiday from Eigan.'

'But it will be embarrassing,' said Sam uncomfortably.

'No it won't. You're just missing the thought of an adoring crowd, people laughing hysterically at every word you say.'

'No I'm not.'

'You are,' laughed Mike. 'You've been seduced. And right now is a chance to stop this silly life you've been sucked into.'

'What silly life?' Sam replied, affronted.

'Look at you, mate. Your three-hundred-dollar haircuts. Your waxed chest. Your concierge on speed-dial. Where does it stop, Sam? A facelift at forty, a Pekinese dog on the passenger seat of your Aston? A circle of friends, an entourage, that you pay for?' Mike shook his head. 'Don't get me wrong. I know being a celebrity can be a really great gig sometimes. The free stuff. I especially liked the free stuff. But it turns your head, mate. Turns it away from all the important stuff. You should be hanging out with people you have a connection with. Not people who are connected. Doing work that you feel passionate about, not stuff that pays the biggest cheque.'

'You're right,' said Sam, thinking about the string of bad, soul-destroying rom-coms he'd made, compared to the thrill of appearing at the National Theatre for the first time.

'Mate, this is the best thing that could have happened to you. Sometimes when you hit rock bottom – and in this penthouse flat I'd say you're hardly there – when you come up for air, it's in calmer, less shallow water.'

Sam's phone was ringing.

'I'd better take it,' he muttered.

For a moment, he didn't recognise the plummy voice on the other end of the line.

'Helen Pierce,' she prompted.

'Oh, Helen, sorry. I was miles away. How are you?'

'Well, thank you. And how are you, Sam? I enjoyed *Robotics*.'

'You saw it?'

'Yes, I took my nephew. It was wonderful.'

Sam smiled to himself. He would put money on the fact that Helen Pierce didn't even have a nephew, and if she did, they would not enjoy a movie that had been universally panned by the critics. Then again, Helen Pierce was part of his entourage; one of the sycophants and yes-men who agreed with everything he said and thought everything he did was fabulous.

'So, Helen . . .'

'Just a heads-up about a story that was going to print about your latest house guest.'

Sam frowned.

'My mate Mike.'

'Well, the *Bugle* were going to splash with "Sam Charles Moves Hunky Male into Chelsea Penthouse". You can see where that story was heading. Fortunately we managed to head it off at the pass.'

'Thank you.'

'What is Mike there for?'

Sam had no intention of telling the lawyer about their proposed Edinburgh show. Word would get back to Jim and Eli, both of whom knew nothing about it on the grounds that they would vigorously oppose it.

'Just a holiday.'

'Very good. Anyway. We should meet. Have a catch-up while you're in town.'

'How's Anna Kennedy?' he asked suddenly as the female lawyer sprang into his head without warning.

'Fine.'

Sam looked at Mike, then walked into the bedroom to continue the call.

'I want to apologise to her,' he said. 'I went a little over the top. I was rude. Very rude, in fact.'

'It's not necessary,' said Helen coolly. 'You're our client. You were dissatisfied. These things happen. You know how sorry I am for the way she dealt with it. She was suitably reprimanded.'

'Is she in the office today? I should say hello.'

'She's busy at court.'

'Could you give me her mobile number?'

'She'll be busy.'

'Well, for later then.'

Helen sighed. 'Very well. I'm sure she'll be very relieved to hear from you.'

Sam peered out of the window, watching as the silvery curve of the Thames snaked away below them. Sloping away to the left of the road was a long green hill; beyond that, water meadows running down to the river.

Anna certainly lived in one of London's smartest areas, he thought, surprised that he had never noticed how beautiful the city was before. Idly he wondered if he should have chosen a more sedate, stable career like the law. He could see that his acting skills – such as they were – might come in useful in a courtroom, but he was useless on the details, and that was everything in the law, wasn't it?

They turned off the main road into a network of residential streets, dozens of tiny chocolate-box cottages crammed together. On the corner of one was a cute little deli-cum-general-store, and for a second he wondered if he should take her anything.

Flowers? Bottle of wine? As Mike had pointed out, he had a concierge service on speed-dial; he felt sure they could get an albino peacock delivered to Anna's house if he asked them to.

However he did it, apologising to Miss Kennedy had suddenly become important to him. He'd never believed in Jessica's New Age claptrap before now, but it was worth a shot. Treating people a bit better might bring a turnaround in his own luck.

'Here we are, sir,' said the driver. 'You want me to wait?'

Sam looked up at the little cottage with the wisteria climbing around the door, wondering what sort of reception he was about to get.

'Yeah, better had,' he said, climbing out.

He paused on the path, glancing left and right.

'Don't worry. The coast is clear,' said a voice.

Sam looked up in alarm. Anna Kennedy was standing in her doorway, a wry grin on her face.

'No paparazzi in Richmond,' she said. 'Too posh and refined for that.'

Smiling, Sam walked up the path, but Anna didn't move aside to let him in.

'I was surprised to get your call,' she said slowly.

'I wanted to come and apologise for the way I treated you after the injunction,' said Sam in a rush.

'Well I wasn't fired. Not by Donovan Pierce, anyway.'

'I was feeling emotional,' he said to justify his sacking of the young lawyer.

'I would have done the same.'

'I bet you would. Feisty little thing like you takes no messing, I bet.'

They grinned at each other and his shoulders slumped in relief.

'Want to come in? I've just got home. About to open a bottle of wine.'

'If you've got beer, you've twisted my arm.'

Sam stepped into her living room. It was like a little box. He thought back to his spacious five-thousand-square-foot Hollywood home, and wondered how anyone could live in such a tiny space.

The kitchen led off the living room through foldback wooden doors. Anna poured them both a beer and handed him a glass, perching on a stool at her breakfast bar.

'So how's things?'

'Career on the skids, a gay lover moving into my house . . .'

'Really?'

'Not really. About the lover, anyway. I have my mate staying with me and the press have found another angle.'

'I heard about the arrest,' said Anna.

'Yeah. Me – the hard man of Hollywood.'

'You should get off. Aren't Stein and Kotter repping you in New York? They're really good.'

'Should we go outside?' he said distractedly. 'It looks like a little sun-trap out there.'

She led him out to her courtyard garden, where the early-evening sun warmed his face. He felt as if he was on a first date in some pretty country pub, an idea that somehow excited him.

They sat for a while, watching a pair of yellow butterflies spiral around a lavender plant.

'So what are you doing back in London?'

'Can I tell you a secret?'

'That's what I'm here for.' She smiled.

'I'm putting on a show. A comedy show, with my friend Mike McKenzie.'

He was surprised at himself for telling her, especially when he had kept his plans so under wraps from Helen Pierce.

'Mike McKenzie the comedian?' said Anna, her eyes wide. 'I love him! I went to see his stand-up show at Wembley. I had all the videos and everything. Such a shame he gave it all up.'

'Well he's back.' Sam puffed out his cheeks, feeling a rush of dread race through his body. It was the first time he had told anyone about his plan with Mike, and it was almost as if saying it out loud had made it real.

'Amazing,' she said, looking genuinely excited. 'So what is it? A two-man show?'

'Two men and their gags. It's so far out of my comfort zone, it's not even funny. To think I have entered into this arrangement willingly.'

'I think it's a great idea.'

'I know you're paid to be nice to me, but if you think it's a crap idea, then I want to know.'

'It's a radical change in direction, but that's why it's so clever and exciting.'

Her words, spoken so bluntly, her expression, so sincere and open, fortified him.

'What about you? I hope you didn't get into too much trouble after what happened.'

She suddenly looked distracted. She sipped her beer, and when she looked at him again, it was with her usual can-do efficiency.

'I'm glad you came,' she said finally. 'I want to talk to you about that. The injunction.'

Sam waved a hand. 'It's old news. Let's just get pissed and pretend we're back in Capri.'

'I think you might have been set up,' she replied flatly.

He pulled away from the table in disbelief.

'What? Katie Grey was a set-up?'

'I don't know.'

'Well what do you know?' he said, leaning back in.

'Wait there.'

He watched her disappear back into the cottage, returning with a bundle of documents, which she spread out over the table.

'Newspaper cuttings?' he said, puzzled. 'But not about me.'

'For a change.' She smiled.

She had beautiful hands, he noticed, as she traced a long finger over the newsprint.

'They're about the death of a model called Amy Hart.'

'Never heard of her.'

'You won't have.'

'So she died falling down the stairs,' Sam said, leaning closer to Anna to read the text.

'Found six months ago at her apartment with her neck broken. It was an open verdict at her inquest. Her sister maintains lots of little things don't add up.'

'So what's this got to do with my injunction?' he asked, frowning.

'The inquest was held on the same day as your story came out in the press. Consequently it went unreported. Convenient, don't you think, considering Amy Hart's love life?'

'What love life?'

'Before she died, she dated a soap actor called Ryan Jones.'

'So?'

'Ryan Jones was one of Blake Stanhope's clients.'

Sam looked up with interest. 'Now that is a coincidence.'

'I thought it was odd. But I met Ryan and I think he barely knew Amy. I did some digging and he was filming in Wales the week she died. He didn't have anything to do with her death, I'm sure of it. At first I thought Blake Stanhope was covering for him, but a job like that would be expensive. Too big, too expensive for Ryan Jones.'

She looked up at Sam, big limpid eyes searching his.

'But Blake acts for more heavyweight people too. Politicians, billionaires, big, rich companies. Under-the-radar stuff. Big-money reputation-management jobs. He's not just in the business of brokering stories. He hides them too.'

'So what else was Amy up to?' Sam asked with a raised eyebrow.

'According to one of her friends, she was having an affair with a high-profile MP.'

'Who you think got in touch with Stanhope to hush it up?'

'I don't know,' she said quietly. 'But it's possible. We both know that the truth isn't always what we read in the newspapers. Sometimes, what we see in the media is what someone somewhere *wants* us to know.'

He viewed her carefully. The serious expression, the sober blue dress, the flash of red lipstick, which gave her – he found his mind wandering – a touch of the bad-girl look. From the get-go he'd found Anna Kennedy the sort of pretty, sensible bluestocking girl he hadn't met since he'd joined the May Ball committee at university to score. But now she was beginning to sound like some conspiracy theorist. Still, who was he to spoil a nice evening in the sun? He looked at the red lips again and decided to run with it.

'This MP. You don't think he killed her, do you?'

'Probably not. More likely he doesn't want the embarrassment of having a dead glamour girl on his hands. It's not exactly career gold, is it?'

'So the MP needs a smokescreen. Stanhope leaks one story at the same time he covers another one up. Paid twice for the same job, eh? Even my agent couldn't sort something like that.'

He was beginning to feel pulled in by her story.

'Who is this MP?'

'Gilbert Bryce.'

'Who?'

'I know. Not exactly the Prime Minister. But look . . .' She handed him a sheet of paper. 'Here's a list of all the select committees he's on.'

Sam looked at it, and suddenly Anna's wild theory didn't seem quite so crazy. Defence acquisition, energy resources, aerospace development, foreign tax policy – it was as if he had deliberately picked the committees that would give him influence over the wealthiest people in the country. Sam had no idea whether this man was corrupt or not, but he was certainly in a position where he could be involved with bribes and favours.

'Even if this is all true, how are you going to catch Stanhope out?' he asked, intrigued. 'I know you're after him for contempt of court, but how are you going to do that? I suppose the *News* online editor and Scandalhound haven't fessed up.'

'No,' she admitted. 'We have some investigators we use, but they cost money we have to sign off to a client.'

He looked at her playfully. 'So, you want me for my money. Wouldn't be the first.'

'And I want to speak to Gilbert.'

'Can't help you there, love. Brad Pitt I could introduce you to. MPs aren't on my Rolodex, though.'

'Well my ex is a broadsheet journalist. He owes me a few favours.'

Her face tightened at the mention of her lover. He suspected there was a story there as good as the yarn she'd just told him.

'Don't you want to know?' she said, touching the top of his hand. 'Don't you want to know if you were stitched up to cover up for what someone did to Amy? Not just for you, but for her.'

He wasn't sure he did. After all, the horse had bolted. Whatever Blake Stanhope had or had not done to cover up the wrongdoings of some MP didn't matter any more, because the damage to his life – or blessing in disguise – had been done. And yet as he watched Anna's face, her soft scarlet bottom lip trembling with anticipation, he felt an electric rush of panic that he might never see her again unless he helped her.

'Okay, let's do it,' he said suddenly. 'Let's look into it a bit more. I can pay for the investigator. Whatever you want.'

She grinned at him and gathered up her papers, and for a moment Sam felt like Jack Bauer. He was already so far out of his comfort zone, what did it matter if he was off on another left-field adventure?

28

'Mom!' Jessica Carr walked into the cavernous living room of her Malibu beach house, a furious scowl on her face. 'Mom! Where are you?'

She hadn't had her blueberry pancakes that morning – gluten-, wheat- and dairy-free, obviously, which made them mainly blueberry – and it was making her grouchy in the extreme. Well, that and the ordeal she had to face in half an hour.

'MOM!'

A small Vietnamese woman appeared from the bedroom holding a feather duster.

'Mrs Carr goes jogging,' she said with a grin. 'You want me make pancakes?'

'Yes, Mai, thank you,' said Jessica hurriedly. The housekeeper was a godsend, but she still found it slightly unnerving how the woman seemed to be able to read her mind.

Jessica walked out on to the balcony, looking up and down the beach before she spotted Barbara Carr, power-walking in a pink Lycra sweatsuit.

'Jesus Christ, she looks like a frankfurter,' she muttered, sitting down at a glass table.

Her mother had moved into the house right after the Sam story had broken. They'd spent a couple of days at her friend's place in Cape Cod, then come back to Malibu. Jessica might have been heartbroken, but she wasn't going to let Sam Charles keep her away from the parties and restaurants of West Hollywood; that was where business was done. But it hadn't been going so well cohabiting with Barbara. While she was supportive and gung-ho about everything Jessica did, her constant rants about Sam and how he'd destroyed her career, which Jessica had initially revelled in, were now starting to wear her down. Yes, he was a bastard, but he had been part of her life for four years and they'd shared . . . what, exactly? Their lives? Not really. It was rare for them to spend two nights in the same house together. Or maybe she was just feeling vulnerable today. In twenty minutes, Sam's removal guys were coming to take away his personal possessions. Not that there were many of those: a few clothes, a hideous ceramic coffee table, a running machine. He'd barely left a shaving kit in the bathroom. Maybe he'd been right when he'd said they weren't – hadn't been – in love. But what the hell did that have to do with anything in this town?

Sinatra, her golden retriever, came and nuzzled his wet nose against her leg.

'Come here, boy,' she pouted, crouching down and wrapping her arms around the neck of her beloved dog. 'We don't need Sammy any more, do we?'

The dog licked her face, apparently in agreement, and feeling much better, Jessica went to sit down on the white suede sofa overlooking the ocean. Sighing, she grabbed a red folder from the table and flipped it open: a collection of this week's Jess-related press cuttings assembled by her PR company. It was thick with news features and gossip pieces from every magazine and paper that counted: everyone from *People* to *US Weekly* in the States, and the big Euro titles like *Heat*, *Paris Match* and *Bunde* across the pond, all running different versions of the same story: 'My Pain, by Jessica'. 'Bowed but unbroken', as *In Touch* put it, Jessica was being portrayed as a strong woman who was rising above her heartbreak. And it didn't hurt that they all had shots of her looking sad but sexy in a white Eres bikini to show that she still had it.

'Like there was any doubt,' she said, tossing the file on to the table and walking back inside.

The Malibu house was one of the more impressive ones on the PCH strip, the road that snaked north from LA and hugged the coast behind some of the most expensive houses in America. She loved being on this private strip, with the glass foldback doors down the beach side of the house that let in the scent and sounds of the ocean, but it had been Sam who'd gone crazy for the stark John Lautner-designed aesthetic. She'd always preferred something more lived in.

Jessica cursed as she heard the intercom buzz. There was no point in shouting for her mother, and Mai was in the kitchen.

'Do I have to do everything myself?' she muttered, picking up the phone.

'Hey, Jess, Jim Parker.'

Rolling her eyes, she pressed the button to let him in.

'Jess! You're looking fabulous as ever,' cried the agent as he swaggered in, looking as much a movie star as the actors he represented: perfect white teeth, a tan Armani suit and a white T-shirt underneath. He looked hip, slick and powerful. 'So how you doing?' he asked, glancing around the house with greedy eyes.

'I'm fine, Jim,' said Jessica, crossing her arms across her chest, 'and I don't mean to be rude, but can we just get on with this?'

'Sure thing,' he said, taking his cell phone out of his pocket and barking some orders into it. Seconds later, two men came through the back door, each holding a large cardboard box.

'It's all in the den, straight ahead as you go down the stairs,' Jessica said to them, then turned to Jim. 'How long do you think this is going to take?'

'Depends how much has been done.'

Jess clenched her jaw. When Jim had called to say he was sending a removal team to clear the detritus of Sam's stuff, he'd had the royal cheek to tell her to pack it up. She had thought of making a bonfire on the beach, then telling him to pack that, but she had wanted the job done, so she had taken both her personal assistants off their existing duties the day before.

'It's all ready,' she said with a cold smile. 'You want to wait outside?'

As if by magic, Mai appeared with a tray bearing fresh papaya juice, and Jessica and Jim moved on to the terrace.

'So I hear you've moved your mother in,' said Jim, leaning on the balcony as if he owned the place.

'Doesn't every girl need her mom at a time like this?'

'I'd say you've been holding up pretty well. I mean, if the press is anything to go by.'

'Press?' she said innocently, hoping he wouldn't see the folder of cuttings still lying on the table.

'The *Enquirer* last week?' Jim prompted. 'Those shots of you looking sad and sexy by that spa pool in Los Cabos. I noticed Jeff Benton at Pacific did the photos.'

'Really? I didn't see it.'

Jim raised his eyebrows.

'I use him sometimes for set-up pap shots,' he said knowingly. 'It's worked for you, hasn't it? Every wronged woman in America is rooting for you.'

Jess took a deep breath, hiding her anger. She knew that Jim was on to her. After all, he was one of the smartest, sharpest, most convincing agents in the business. Sometimes she envied Sam for having Jim on his team.

'What are you saying, Jim? That I set those shots up?'

'Of course I wasn't saying that, honey,' he said, holding a hand up. 'I was just pointing out that you looked beautiful. A beautiful wounded little bird. That's all. But I wouldn't overplay it, if you know what I mean.'

Jim was right, of course. Jeff Benton was the top paparazzo in Hollywood and he had done a fantastic job on the long-lens shots. It had taken two hours of careful choreography and three bikini changes, complete with hair and make-up people fussing around her between shots. They didn't take that much care on her publicity shoots for her hit TV show, *All Woman*.

Jim was also right that it had worked beautifully. To every disappointed housewife and lovelorn teenager in America, Jessica Carr was not some pampered distant superstar, she was one of them, a real woman who suffered heartache just like them. And the fact that she looked so good while she was doing it too had got every red-blooded male panting.

'I hope you're not planning on ten per cent for this advice.'

'I could do if you wanted me to,' he said playfully. 'You know I'm the best agent in town, Jessy.'

'I have the best agent in town, Jim. No offence.'

'Old Harry. She's the greatest,' he said with a touch of sarcasm.

'Hi, honey, you okay?' Barbara Carr walked on to the terrace, her pink sweatsuit now clinging to her with perspiration.

'Hey, Barb,' said Jim, waving his juice glass at her. Barbara looked at him suspiciously.

'Everything all right, hon?' she said, not taking her eyes off him. 'It's gonna be tough, but you'll feel better when that bastard's completely out of your life.'

'All right, Mom,' said Jessica with irritation. 'Go have a shower. I'll be fine.'

'You sure?'

'I'm sure.'

'Hey,' said Jim. 'Do you two ladies want to go out, grab a coffee, while I supervise the workers?'

'He's right, honey. This can't be easy for you.'

Jess rolled her eyes.

'Okay, okay. Let's drive over to the Plaza.'

Twenty minutes later, Jessica and her mother slid into her dove-grey Aston Martin and swung out of the underground garage, carefully avoiding the furniture truck standing at the rear entrance, its door open, stacked with boxes. Jess felt a single traitorous teardrop swell in her eye duct, and she blinked it away fiercely.

'Don't look,' said Barbara. 'Never look back.'

Jessica nodded as she turned the car and slipped into traffic. For once, it was good advice. She gunned the engine and drove away, that part of her life shrinking in the rear-view mirror.

29

Anna came out of the Royal Courts of Justice and leaned on the wall of the ancient building, breathing in the fresh air. The courtroom inside had been stuffy and crowded, crammed with barristers, their pupils, staff and rubberneckers, all breathing the same stale, dry air. They had been in there for five long hours with only a short break for lunch; after that, the sunshine on the court steps was like being released from a cell. Not that it had been entirely a chore. Part of her was excited to be involved in the Balon case; after all, there were only a handful of libel jury trials a year, and that alone brought its own glamour and energy. But did it have to be so damn slow?

Perhaps she'd been spoiled; her area of media law was one of the few where things moved fast. A client came to you at 4 p.m. having 'misplaced' some dirty pictures, and by 9 a.m. the following morning you had served your injunction and sent out your bill. On the other hand, very few trials were as drawn out and pedantic as a libel trial; it was too expensive. Only the very rich could afford the full letter of the law.

'Whoo! They go on, don't they?'

Anna looked up to see Sid, her trainee, joining her. She laughed.

'It is a bit long-winded, yes. The sort of thing that gives lawyers a bad name.'

'I wouldn't mind,' said Sid, 'but the QCs seem to be loving every minute of it. I've never seen someone get so worked up about the implied meaning of the word "businessman" within a certain context.'

'Ah, that's because they're getting paid for every minute they're in there. The longer they can stretch it out, the higher the fees.'

'All this to keep them in golf shoes, eh?' replied Sid honestly.

Anna laughed. She would be sad to see Sid leave. She hadn't been at Donovan Pierce long enough to really bond with the girl, but she was one of the few employees who seemed human. Maybe that was why they were letting her go.

'I'm going in to get a drink. You want anything?'

Sid shook her head.

'I think I'll stay out here in the sun for a while. Make the most of it.'

Anna walked back inside, her heels tapping on the marble floor. She put a few coins into the vending machine and sat down on a bench in the atrium, gazing up at the sculptures and paintings, enjoying the calm.

'Anna Kennedy? Not working? Never thought I'd see the day.'

She looked up and frowned when she saw Blake Stanhope.

'Back in court, Blake? Who have you stitched up this time?'

Blake pulled a look of mock hurt. 'Don't take that tone with me. I thought we were friends.'

'I wouldn't go that far.'

'Come on, Anna,' he said, more evenly. 'We're in the same game, aren't we?'

'Blake, you belong in jail.'

His shoulders slumped.

'I know you think I'm some sort of unprincipled rat, and maybe I have my moments, but believe me when I say I didn't leak that story. And I don't appreciate you quizzing every editor in town asking them if I shared the Sam Charles story with them.'

'You heard about that?' Maybe her discreet enquiries weren't so discreet.

He nodded.

Anna looked at him, trying to read his face.

'Well, someone did, and we only have two in the line-up: you and that girl Katie Grey. Or maybe someone in your office.'

Blake paused, looking up at the dark portrait of a rather forbidding-looking judge in ceremonial dress.

'It was no one in my office,' he said defensively. 'I was the only one who knew about it. As for Katie . . . She's not a bad girl. Just a frustrated one. It's often the way with kiss-and-tell girls. It's not just about the money. Someone they slept with makes a heap of promises to them and then doesn't deliver. Speaking out is their way of lashing out. Katie felt rejected, hurt. But she understood the injunction had gagged her, and she wasn't going to break the law.'

'You all sound so moral.'

He took a seat beside her.

'Have you considered phone hacking?'

She had.

'We take every precaution. Our phones are swept regularly. We avoid leaving voicemail messages. Don't you?'

'Never been stung yet.'

'To your knowledge.'

'I'm careful. Besides, do you think the papers are going to take the risk of phone tapping after the last scandal?'

She downed her drink, deep in thought.

Silence rattled between them.

'Have you ever considered that the leak might have come from your end?' he said finally.

'Don't be ridiculous.'

'You don't think it's possible? One of Sam's staff, a driver, a PA? Or someone at your office. A temp. A cleaner.'

'Don't make ridiculous accusations just to get yourself off the hook.'

'For a smart girl, you're very trusting,' he said casually.

For a second Anna thought about Sid. Struggling for cash, with a job about to end. Or Josh, Sam's PA. Sam was convinced his young assistant didn't know the details of his indiscretions, but Josh had that smart competence that suggested he knew everything.

'I trust everyone on our team one hundred per cent,' she said defensively. 'We run a tight ship.'

'Just a little food for thought, some free advice between old friends,' said Blake playfully. 'You lawyers do rather think in straight lines, don't you? Maybe it's time to take off the blinkers. Who would benefit from leaking the Sam and Katie sex story, if it wasn't Katie and it wasn't me?'

30

He was already there when Anna arrived, sitting alone at a table facing the street. The front windows of the bistro had been folded back to the evening air and she paused at the corner watching him, a glass of red wine in front of him, making a big show of tapping away at his BlackBerry; he was always so concerned about appearances, desperate to show he was busy and in demand. They had been here together once before – she wondered if he remembered. Probably not; he would never have agreed to the meeting here, it would have been too loaded and intimate.

She looked at his face, so familiar yet so distant. He was tanned, his blond hair lighter than she remembered, his eyes more blue. It was strange how people could be such a big part of your life, how you could become accustomed to their habits and tics, their every crease and wrinkle like your own. And then, just like that, they could slip away completely.

'Anna,' he said, standing up as she walked over.

'How are you, Andy?' she said, sitting down, allowing him to push her chair in. In the early days, she had been charmed by his little old-world customs. She'd met plenty of people from Andrew's background at law school – wealthy parents, public school, Oxbridge – but none with his effortless polish. And yet he had been so normal in many ways: he liked football, Britpop, wore his shirts untucked. But every now and then there was a little reminder of the privileged upbringing a world away from the Cumbrian pub she had been brought up in.

The waiter brought her a glass and Andy poured her some wine from the open bottle. She noticed the menu face down on the table.

'You're not eating?'

He shook his head.

'Not hungry. Are you?'

'Not really,' she lied. She was actually starving, having been stuck in court all day, but Andy was clearly telling her he had no intention of staying longer than he had to.

'So how's things?' he said, carefully rearranging his two forks on the tablecloth.

'Don't you read the papers?' she said. It was meant to be a joke, but came out wrong.

He glanced at her.

'Of course. Always nice to see my fiancée half drowned. Honestly, Anna, what was all that crap at the spa about?'

'If you ask me, she got off pretty lightly,' she said, standing her ground. 'I'm amazed the media haven't found out that we haven't spoken for two years. "Cosy cake-maker is home-wrecker" type thing.'

She'd had this conversation with Andy in her head a hundred times since they had split up – their first proper sit-down discussion – and she'd always been witty and cutting and amazingly beautiful, not bitter and sarcastic like this.

'Look, Anna, if you've just asked me here to rake over all that again, I've got better things to do with my time.'

'I don't want that either.'

She was being honest. She'd seen him a handful of times since That Night; she'd tried hard to avoid him, but it was difficult to do so in the worlds in which they moved. It was always awkward, but sitting opposite him today she felt strangely unmoved.

'Does she know we're meeting?' she asked.

He looked away.

'No.'

Anna felt a surge of triumph. Childish, pathetic even, but it made her feel better.

'I didn't know whether I should tell her,' said Andy. 'Although I've hardly seen her all week. She's been filming.'

'At the nurseries?'

'No, she was finding all that travelling too difficult. It's filmed in Notting Hill now.'

'That well-known rural idyl.'

He laughed. 'They're shooting in the most rustic central London location house they could find. Poured concrete floors, Aga, imported Provençal knick-knacks, you know the sort of thing.'

'Which will of course be passed off as your own?'

'Well I wasn't having a bloody camera crew round at our place.'

Our place. Andrew and Anna had never had their own place. He had his bachelor pad in trendy Wapping. Sterile and manly, all black leather and chrome with damp towels left on the bathroom floor. Anna had tried to make her mark, but she was swimming against the tide, and with their long work hours, it was so much easier to go back to their respective homes. Another sign she had missed.

He sipped his wine.

'So what's this favour you need?'

'It's for a case I'm working on.'

'The Balon case? Did he get funded by those mobsters like they're saying?'

'As if I'd tell you, even if I did know.'

'You always were so secretive.'

'Secretive? Andy, this is my job. I get paid to keep secrets. And you're a journalist.'

'I was your partner, wasn't that more important?'

'You tell me,' she said, meeting his gaze.

It was no surprise to Anna that Andrew was now associate editor at *The Chronicle*, effectively number three, within striking distance of the top job. He'd risen effortlessly from news reporter to business editor to his current position. Not bad for someone not yet thirty-five. They'd met at the Islington home of a senior BBC news executive. It had been his daughter's party, a law school friend of Anna's, while Andrew was a family friend. Anna had felt so grown up talking to a serious journalist in this high-ceilinged room, full of books and pictures, the sort of place she wanted for herself. They'd talked for hours, getting drunker and drunker on the fruit punch, until suddenly he'd taken her hand and pulled her outside, kissing her in the doorway of that

240

tall white Georgian house. Their jobs had provided common ground; both workaholics and obsessed with current affairs. But the nature of her work, her clients' indiscretions to have to keep quiet, her battles against the papers, built a Chinese wall between them that had often made Andrew feel resentful.

'This isn't about Balon. It's about Gilbert Bryce, the MP. I need to talk to him.'

'What do you want to meet Gilbert for?' His expression clouded. Gilbert Bryce was a well-known womaniser but Anna didn't flatter herself it was jealousy.

'It's something I'm working on for a client. I can't tell you.'

She had no idea how interested *The Chronicle* would be in the story of a lingerie model's death. Probably not very. They didn't usually go for stories about the Chinawhite set at the broadsheets.

'Of course not,' he said, not hiding his exasperation.

'Please, Andy, this could be important.'

'I'm not asking for any gory details, I just want to know what you want to speak to him about.'

'I can't tell you,' she said firmly.

'Then I can't introduce you. Gilbert is a contact; I have a relationship with these people. I can't just fix you two up without knowing what it's about.'

'Can't you? I'd have thought it was the least you could do.'

'Oh Anna . . .' he said, shaking his head just enough to register his disappointment.

'Sophie told me how long you'd been having an affair. Before I caught you. Not quite the once or twice you claimed, was it?'

He looked down. She was sure she saw him colour with shame.

'What point was there in telling you the truth?'

'You made me look a fool by sleeping with Sophie. But you kept on making me look like a fool when you didn't tell me the truth.'

She hated the thought of Sophie and Andrew pitying her with the little secret they had carried between them. 'You owe me, Andy.'

'If I introduce you to Gilbert, will you come to the wedding?'

241

'Unbelievable,' she said scornfully.

'I want you to come to our wedding.' He shrugged. 'Why not? I do you a favour, you do us one.'

'Forget it,' she said taking a five-pound note out of her purse to pay for her drink. 'I thought you might want to do the decent thing and help me, I thought you might think you owed me something for the time we spent together at least, but obviously not.'

She got up to leave, but he caught her arm.

'Don't go. Please,' he said.

Reluctantly Anna sank back into her seat.

'Look, Parliament has closed for the summer,' said Andrew finally. 'But I happen to know where Gilbert lives, some chocolate-box village in Sussex. I'll see if I can set up a meeting, but don't piss him off, okay?'

'Thank you,' she said honestly. 'I'll try not to be my usual offensive self,' she added with a half-smile.

She watched her ex-boyfriend's face soften.

'I'm sorry. For everything.'

'I'm a big girl, Andy. I get it that two people have to move on because their relationship isn't working, because they meet someone else . . . But why her?'

'Because she was like you, only simpler.' He looked down and then met her gaze intently. 'Soph makes me feel *good* about who I am, not bad.'

Anna looked at him with puzzlement.

'What did I do wrong?'

'You're so smart, so always on the money about everything. I guess I wasn't up to the challenge. You deserve someone in your life who is.'

She waved her hand to order the bill, feeling lighter and more free than she had in years, because she knew she agreed with him.

31

Jessica opened her pale green eyes and sat up, propping herself up on her elbows. God, these hospital beds were uncomfortable, and she'd been lying in it most of the day. Who'd have thought a death scene would need so many takes? She caught a glimpse of herself in a prop mirror: pale make-up, darker around the eyes, a few dribbles of fake blood on her cheek where she'd been coughing it up to dramatic effect. Exactly how I feel, she thought. She was drained, exhausted. For some reason, since Jim Parker had removed Sam's treadmill and shaving kit, the house had seemed empty and she'd been finding it hard to sleep. Normally she would have taken a Xanax, but she had to stay sharp for the reshoots. Although sharp wasn't the word. She felt lethargic and moody all the time. Maybe she was coming down with something.

'All right, people,' said Judd Spears, the director of *Slayer*, the serial killer thriller that Jessica was filming. He beamed with pride as he stepped away from the monitor. 'I think we can say that's a wrap!' He slapped Jessica on the shoulder. 'We nailed it, baby. You were a sensational stiff.'

'Great,' said Jessica, forcing a smile as she slid her legs off the gurney.

Joe Kennington, the leading man, walked over.

'Good work, Jess,' he said with a smile.

'Thank you.' She blushed. Joe had a reputation for being exacting with his own performances and consequently very critical of his co-stars, with stories of on-set dust-ups and subsequent freeze-outs of the offending actors, so she was chuffed with the compliment.

'Hey guys, there's a party in the Hills,' said Judd. 'Wanna come?'

Jessica's heart sank. She wasn't sure she'd be able to keep her eyes open, let alone have the necessary sparkle at an industry networking gathering.

'Not for me,' said Joe, holding up a hand. 'I've got some interview with *Rolling Stone* in the morning.'

Judd bounded off and Joe turned to Jessica, raising his eyebrows.

'He makes me feel really old,' he laughed.

'Rubbish. You're the hottest, fittest guy in Hollywood.'

It wasn't strictly true. Joe was pushing fifty; not even a facelift could stop the dying of his looks. But it was never a bad idea to suck up to industry grandees like him.

'How about dinner? Catering wasn't up to much today, was it?'

Jessica smiled prettily. What a wonderful idea. And if the paps spotted them, it would only add weight to the rumours of an on-set romance that were already fluttering around.

'That sounds good,' she said. 'Just let me wash this blood off first.'

Maki Soba was a low-key Japanese restaurant off Melrose. Lit inside by glowing pink and yellow paper lanterns, it had the most flattering lighting this side of the studio lot.

'Try the tempura,' said Joe, pointing to the bowl with his chopsticks. 'It's so light.'

Dutifully Jessica popped some in her mouth and pulled a suitably ecstatic face. 'This place is amazing,' she said. 'How did you find it?'

'I've been coming here for years,' said Joe. 'It was a favourite of Sia's.'

Jessica nodded solemnly. Sia was Joe's ex-wife. They'd been married for twelve years – a lifetime in Hollywood terms – and only separated the previous spring. Rumour had it Sia had run off with her personal trainer and that Joe was still in mourning.

'So what do you think about Judd landing *Purple Skies*?' he asked, referring to the hot new project their director was attached to.

'I'm not sure,' she said honestly. 'Do you think he's sensitive enough to pull it off?'

'Ah, so you've read it too,' grinned Joe. 'I didn't think anyone else in Hollywood had actually heard of it. I love that book.'

'Doesn't everyone?' She laughed lightly. In actual fact, she had only read the PEN Award-winning novel because Sam had practically forced her. He had gone on about how clever and moving it was, and she had finally given in.

'Well that's what I was worried about. Can Judd do it? When you have a property that delicate, that personal, it would be so easy to turn it into some hokey thriller, but I was at Tori Adams's house at the weekend. Apparently she thinks Judd is the new Spielberg – that he can turn his hand to anything from *Schindler's List* to *Indiana Jones*.'

Jessica wasn't convinced. Not if the rushes of *Slayer* were anything to go by. But if Tori Adams rated him, well, that was a different matter. Tori, who was producing *Purple Skies*, was one of the most powerful women in Hollywood, notorious for her tight inner circle of influential friends, including studio bosses, directors and, of course, top stars like Joe, who all helped each other.

'How long have you known Tori?' she said casually.

'Thirty years.' Joe smiled, picking up a shiitake dumpling. 'We shared a flat in Venice Beach when we were just starting out.'

'I wonder who they'll cast?' she said nonchalantly.

'I think Tori's keeping a tight rein on it. At least Judd's ego isn't so big yet that she can't still control him. She's having a party on Saturday, so I'll get the inside track on what she's thinking then.'

'What's the occasion?'

'Oh, you know Tori, she's just dropped some huge bundle on three Matisse sculptures and she wants to show them off. We're supposed to turn up and drool with jealousy. Which we will, of course.'

'I never saw you as an art aficionado,' said Jessica.

'I started collecting five years ago. Mainly Twombly, Warhol, Clemente.'

'I have a Francesco Clemente at the beach house,' Jessica said, wide-eyed, happy to compete. She had worked out a few years earlier that collecting was a signifier of status, intellect, particularly when you didn't have any, or were working on it.

'You must just sit and stare at it for hours,' Joe said earnestly.

Jessica shook her head sadly.

'No, not any more. It . . . well, it reminds me of Sam too much, you know?'

He nodded, perhaps thinking about his own break-up.

'Are you looking for a buyer?'

'Maybe,' she said. 'The Gagosian are interested . . .'

'Perhaps we could cut out the gallery?'

'Why don't you come and have a look at it after we're done here? You don't have to be anywhere, do you?'

He hesitated for a moment, then clicked his fingers for the bill.

'Not until my *Rolling Stone* interview, no.'

She was glad of the forty-minute drive out to Malibu. Joe had been a tough nut to crack on set, but she knew he was someone worth getting to know a lot better.

Oh shit, she thought with a jolt as they pulled up at her home. My mother. She couldn't take Joe Kennington back to her Malibu love nest and have him walk in on Barbara lying on the sofa in her velour sweatpants eating potato chips and watching *Jersey Shore*.

She slid her key into the lock and before she even had time to push the door fully open she could hear her mother's sing-song voice.

'Hi, honey. How was it being dead?' said Barbara, appearing in the hallway.

'Hi, Mom,' Jessica replied, glancing back at Joe. 'Not at the gym?'

'At this time?' she scoffed, stopping as Joe stepped forward.

'And you must be Jessica's sister,' he said, offering her his hand. 'I'm Joe.'

Cheesy bastard, thought Jessica, smiling despite herself.

Barbara looked like a hooked fish, her eyes staring, her mouth opening and closing.

'Joe Kennington. How *are* you?' she said greeting him as if he was a long-lost friend.

'Of course you're at Sarah's tonight, aren't you?' prompted Jess, hoping Joe hadn't seen the warning glances she'd flashed at her mother.

Barbara winked at Jessica with all the subtlety of a brick. 'Sarah? Oh yes. Friend of mine, having a few problems, you know. I'll just grab the car keys. See you again, Joe, *hopefully*.'

With relief, Jess listened to the engine of Barbara's SUV gun away, then calmed herself, listening to the gentle background swoosh of the ocean.

Joe was standing with his arms crossed in front of him, smiling with a gentle look of amusement.

'It's great you have such a close relationship.'

'It has its moments. So. Drink? Vodka? Tequila?'

'Not for me. Just a soft drink.'

Another teetotaller, she thought wearily.

She pulled a carton of juice from her Sub-Zero fridge, filled a tumbler and added a large measure of vodka when he wasn't looking.

'To the movie,' she smiled, raising her own glass. 'I'm sorry I took so long to die.'

Joe chuckled as they clinked the glasses together.

'Well I guess you'd better show me this Clemente,' he said.

'This way.' She snaked through the house to the top floor, swaying her hips just a little more than usual, knowing that Joe's eyes were going to be glued to her ass.

'This place might be too big now I'm on my own.'

'How you holding up?' he said with concern.

'Truthfully, Sam and I had run our course. We'd both agreed that. But I wish it could have ended in a different way. The press intrusion has been tough.'

He nodded.

'I can sympathise. When Sia and I separated, we were hounded for weeks. I didn't even think the press were interested in us.'

'You're the biggest movie star in the world,' said Jessica. 'Of course the press are interested in you.'

He shrugged. 'I'm fifty years old and my face isn't quite as pretty as it once was.'

'Men just appreciate with age,' said Jessica. 'Like good art.'

'Talking of which, where is this painting?'

'I thought you'd never ask,' she said, beckoning him with one finger into the master bedroom. '*Et voilà*,' she smiled.

The painting was on the wall right above her eight-foot bed. Seven feet wide, it depicted a naked woman stretched out. It was powerful, provocative, but at the same time it had a delicacy and vulnerability to it. She hoped Joe would recognise those same qualities in the painting's owner.

'Wow,' he said quietly, his eyes glittering as he gazed at it. 'That is amazing.'

'Isn't it?' she said, looking at Joe's tall frame, his swimmer's physique. He was separated after all. It was only his Catholic faith that stopped him being officially on the open market, and that meant he was fair game. And if *In Touch* were already spreading rumours about their supposed romance, why not make it real?

'I'll be one moment,' she said, touching his arm. 'I'll leave you to view.'

She slipped into her en suite and quickly took off her vest, kicked off her jeans and, after a moment's hesitation, pulled off her bra and panties too. Leaning in to the mirror, she licked her lips so that they had a tiny hint of glistening shine. Smiling to herself, she switched off the main light of the en suite and opened the door. She knew that she'd be backlit by the glow from the illuminated mirror behind her: sexy, beautiful, totally fuckable.

'What do you think?' she purred.

He didn't move his eyes from the painting.

Dismissing a moment's irritation, she moved over to him. 'I can think of a better nude than the one you're looking at.'

He turned to look at her in stunned silence, his eyes wide.

'Jess . . .'

She put her finger to his lips, then, pressing her bare breasts against his shirt, looped her arm around his neck to pull him closer.

He resisted.

'I'll do anything you want,' she whispered.

He was as still as a statue. She lifted her face to his, expecting to see desire and excitement. Instead she saw disapproval. Deliberately, he took her arm from around his neck.

'Maybe you should put some clothes on,' he said, his eyes averting from hers.

She took a furious step back.

'You're kidding?' she snapped.

'Jess, you're confused. This . . . this isn't right.'

'Confused? Don't make me sound like I'm crazy. You want this as much as I do.'

'You're a beautiful woman, Jessica, and I know if we did hook up it would be good for the movie.'

'Yes, it would,' she smiled, seeing an opening. She grabbed his hand and put it on to her warm breast, but Joe snatched it away.

'Stop it,' he said, his voice trembling.

She grabbed the sheet from the bed and wrapped it clumsily around her body.

'What *is* your problem?' Her voice was quivering with anger.

'Don't you know?' he said finally.

'Know what?' she whispered.

'It's not you, Jessica. It's me.' He dipped his head and played with his hands, pushing the knuckles into the opposite palm.

'Tell me, Joe. What's wrong? Because I'm feeling pretty stupid at the moment.'

'Look,' he said, rubbing his hand across his mouth. 'I'm gay.'

'Gay?' she repeated. It just wasn't possible. Joe Kennington was the most macho man in America, an icon of straight-ahead masculinity – he was a father of two, for God's sake! Jessica wasn't naive; she knew at least a dozen Hollywood leading men who were hiding in the closet, but *Joe*? That was just crazy. She wanted the ground to swallow her whole.

'But you and Sia . . .' she said, sitting down next to him.

'I love her, don't doubt that,' he said. 'And we were a real couple when we got married.'

'So your kids . . . not out of a tube, then?'

He laughed, and the atmosphere lifted a little.

'No, they're all natural. And completely wonderful. So is Sia, but I guess she wasn't enough.' He sighed, shaking his head. 'I've always preferred men, but I knew I'd have to hide who I was when I came out here, that's just the way it is in Hollywood. But when I met Sia, I really did fall in love with her. I thought it was the real thing, and in a way, I was glad. It made life so much easier. Until I met Greg. He's a teacher from Montecito. We share a house together now, right by Tori Adams's weekend place.'

'Shit,' whistled Jessica, and he laughed.

'Exactly. I'm older now, but not old enough that people wouldn't care.' He turned to look at her. 'And you know what? It's not about the money; I've got enough of that. It's because I love what I do and I want to keep on doing it. Does that sound selfish?'

She smiled.

'What the hell are you asking me for? I'm an actress in Hollywood, it doesn't get more selfish than that.'

He smiled and touched her bare shoulder.

'I was wrong about you, Jess.'

'What do you mean?'

'I thought you were just another one of those hard bitches who'll do anything to get where they want to go. But you're okay.'

'Thanks,' she said, but she knew he was wrong. She would have fucked him and milked it for all it was worth. And she wouldn't have given it a second thought. What was it he had said? *That's just the way it is in Hollywood.* Damn right.

'Still interested in the Clemente?' She smiled.

'Too right. It's beautiful. I'll get my art consultant to give you a ring this week, get a valuation.'

Jessica nodded. She really didn't care how much it was worth, she just wanted it out of her bedroom. It had been a gift from Sam and held nothing but bad memories.

'Hey, you know what?' she said. 'I'd love to see those Matisse sculptures of Tori's.'

Their eyes met for a moment. Joe knew what she was saying: a favour for a favour. An invitation to Tori Adams's party in exchange for her silence. Now that was what made Hollywood go round.

'Sure,' he said smoothly. 'I'll set it up.'

32

Andrew had been right: the village of High Marple was perfect, especially on a warm summer afternoon like this. Thatched roofs, flint walls, tidy little front gardens overstuffed with foxgloves and marigolds. The drive down had taken ninety minutes but had seemed quicker, with the windows wound down and the radio tuned to a cheesy eighties station as the meadows zipped by. Anna realised that the pressure she had been feeling over the past few weeks had been mostly self-inflicted. Yes, Helen Pierce had been watching her more closely than the Stasi, just waiting for her to slip up again, but Anna was fairly confident her work on the Balon libel trial had been spotless. And then there was Amy Hart. The rational side of her brain told her she was wasting her time, quizzing models and soap stars about the death of a party girl she had never even met. Yet there was an emotional pull to this case she had never felt in her working life before, and she knew that Amy's death was something she wouldn't stop thinking about until she had got to the bottom of what was going on.

The Honourable Member for Derrington East lived in a large double-fronted former rectory on the outskirts of the village. Anna had been surprised that Andrew had arranged the meeting so promptly; then again, guilt could be a very powerful call to action. She parked the Mini as close to the verge as she could and pushed open the garden gate, which gave a satisfying creak.

'Over here! It's Ms Kennedy, isn't it?'

Gilbert Bryce was sitting on a garden chair underneath a parasol reading a Robert Harris novel. He was wearing beige chinos, a navy polo shirt and chunky boat shoes, the sort they sold in M&S. Most people considered Gilbert Bryce a bit of a joke. Unmarried, with a colourful romantic life including two long-standing relationships, with a celebrity clairvoyant and a fifty-something character actress, he was a sitting target for *Private Eye* and the political columnists, who seemed to be incensed that someone like that could become an MP. But in the flesh, he certainly had something: not quite charisma, perhaps, but he was one of those people with an unshakeable belief in his own abilities, and that was a quality that instilled confidence. Anna could see why people would vote for him. He certainly was not a conventionally good-looking man, but his teeth were perfectly straight, his fingernails manicured, and his dark brown hair precisely clipped. Gilbert Bryce understood the power of image, even if it was a slightly ridiculous one.

'Beautiful village you have here,' said Anna, walking across the lawn towards him.

'I like to think so,' he said, gesturing to the chair opposite him. 'It's a shame you're not here next weekend. I'm due to host the village fete. The locals love it.'

'I'm sure they do.'

'Speaking of the village, I thought we might have our chat here, if you don't mind?'

'Of course,' said Anna.

'Normally I'd take you to the Crown – lovely place, by the way – but I do find that the locals start to ask questions.'

'Questions?' said Anna, suddenly nervous that he knew exactly why she was here.

'You know, lunching with an attractive young woman,' said Gilbert. 'Believe it or not, that counts as news in these parts. Last week I heard a rumour that I was having an affair with the girl in the butcher's; I'd only popped in for a chop.'

Anna laughed. She had to admit he had a certain charm.

Gilbert reached over to the table and poured her a glass of lemonade.

'Sorry, I really should offer you Pimm's or something, but it's my housekeeper's day off.'

He looked at her curiously.

'So you're a friend of Andrew Barton's?'

'That's right. He's my future brother-in-law actually.'

'Then you must be the sister of that delightful television chef. What's she called?'

'Sophie.'

'Yes, Sophie Kennedy, of course.'

Anna handed him her business card.

'Oh, but you're a lawyer, not a journalist,' he said with a hint of disappointment.

Gilbert was a legendary self-publicist. He had been on *Celebrity Big Brother* despite the grave misgivings of his party whips, and had survived two weeks on *Strictly Come Dancing*.

'Yes, I'm acting for the family of Amy Hart,' she said, watching his face closely for a reaction. He gave nothing away. 'She was a model who died about six months ago.'

'Oh dear. I'm sorry to hear that.'

'Doesn't the name mean anything to you, Mr Bryce?'

He shook his head slowly, as if trying to recall.

'Amy Hart? Was she a constituent?'

Anna pulled a photo from her bag and handed it to him. He looked at it for several seconds, then glanced back at Anna. She knew he was deciding whether to call her bluff.

'It's my understanding, Mr Bryce, that you knew Amy rather well.'

'Heavens,' said Gilbert, handing the photo back. 'You really are a lawyer, aren't you?'

Anna smiled politely. She had known all along he would deny the relationship; if Mandy Stigwood was right, he had kept his fling with Amy completely under the radar. Indeed, Anna only had Mandy's word that there had ever been a relationship, and Mandy was what a judge might call an 'unreliable witness'.

'As you can imagine, Ms Kennedy, in my line of work I meet a lot of people. I'm generally good at remembering names and faces, though. I find it helps at election time if you keep things personal.'

'So you do remember Amy?' she pressed.

'Possibly, yes. But as I said, in my line of work . . .'

'She's dead, Mr Bryce.'

'So you said.'

Anna laid the photo on the table so Gilbert could not help looking at it.

'And you say you're involved with the family?'

'Yes,' said Anna. 'The inquest into her death was held the other week. It was an open verdict, but her family aren't convinced it was an accident.'

She paused for a moment, searching his face. If the news had rattled him, he gave no indication.

'I'm speaking to people who knew Amy, putting together her movements . . .'

'So you think it was foul play?'

'Perhaps.'

'Well I wish you the best of luck with it,' said Gilbert, reaching for his drink. 'But I still don't see why you'd want to talk to me.'

He's very clever, thought Anna. Much sharper than people give him credit for. He hadn't specifically denied or confirmed that he knew Amy, leaving himself room for manoeuvre either way. Time to push a little, she thought.

'I'm sorry to have to ask you these questions, Mr Bryce,' she said. 'But it has been suggested that you and Amy had an affair. My source wasn't sure of the seriousness of the relationship, but was convinced that the two of you had been involved. Can you tell me if this is true?'

He looked immediately uncomfortable. Drawing a hand up to his neck, he rubbed it nervously.

'Yes, I knew Amy. No, we did not have a relationship.'

'How well did you know her?'

He shook his head.

'Barely. Now that you mention it, I had heard that she had died. It was a terrible tragedy. But really, I hardly knew her.'

'Did you ever sleep with her?'

He flashed her an angry, impatient look. 'Really, Miss Kennedy, this is not the sort of thing I'm happy to discuss. I am a public figure, yes, but I am entitled to some sort of private life, am I not?'

She knew she was treading towards thin ice. For all she knew, Gilbert was a friend of Helen's or Larry's, and the last thing she needed was for him to voice a complaint.

'I don't want to make you feel uncomfortable. I'm just helping a family come to terms with their grief. To help make sense of it all, if you like.'

'It sounds more like you're in the business of finger-pointing. Does Andrew Barton know the real reason you're here?'

'No.'

Relief softened his expression.

'Although it would make a great story. "MP Had Affair with Dead Model".'

'Are you threatening me?'

The atmosphere was now decidedly hostile.

'I'm just trying to get a picture of Amy's life in the months before she died. Were you having an affair with her?'

'No I was not!' he said angrily, then stopped himself. 'I met her once at a party as I recall,' he continued more evenly. 'Perhaps we flirted, I don't really remember. I'm a single man, it's hardly the stuff of news.'

There was a long pause. Anna heard Andrew's voice nagging at her. *Don't piss him off.*

'Who was it said I'd had an affair with her?'

'I'm afraid I can't tell you that.'

He gestured towards the garden gate. 'Then I think this discussion is at an end, don't you?'

She couldn't believe she had failed to gain any information from him. Then again, the man's a politician, she reminded herself. He's hardly going to break down and confess, is he?

She leaned across the table, picked up the photograph of Amy and put it back in her bag.

'You asked me if Andrew knows anything about this case,' she said as coolly as she could. 'The answer, for now, is no. I'm one solicitor, looking into this on behalf of a family. But as you can imagine, I've got a lot of heavyweight media contacts . . .'

'Who all love the lawyers at Donovan Pierce, I'm sure,' he said sarcastically.

'What if the family go to the press? Then it's out of my hands. They think Amy was murdered, and for someone this is a really big scoop. Tell me what you know, Gilbert. So I can manage it.'

'Look, as I said, I barely knew her, but from what I saw, she was a good-time girl. Isn't it more likely that she was drunk and slipped on the stairs?'

'I never said she slipped on the stairs. Or that she was drunk.' She searched his face for a sign that he had been caught out, but there was nothing.

'I suppose I absorbed the news story more than I'd thought.'

'Her inquest got barely a few column inches.' She paused. 'You're a smart guy, Gilbert. You know how bad this could look for you.'

He held up the palm of his hand. A cabbage white butterfly hovered around it.

'All right,' he muttered. 'But don't play with me, Anna, because I have lawyers too.'

'Tell me about Amy,' she said quietly.

It was a few moments before he spoke again. 'I met Amy at a house party in Knightsbridge. We had sex that night and a few times after that in London. I suppose you could call it an affair, but it was a very short-lived thing.'

'Why did it finish? Was she not good for your image?'

'No, she wasn't really appropriate. I know my love life is flamboyant, but a party girl like Amy on my arm would give *Private Eye* a field day.'

'So you finished with her.'

He shifted in his seat.

'Plus she'd met someone new.'

'Who was it?'

A red rash had begun to flower from the opening at Gilbert's neckline.

'I'm not sure.'

'But you have an idea.'

He shook his head slowly, puffing out his ruddy, jowly cheeks.

'I think it was someone who runs with that set.'

'Which set?'

Another long pause.

'I don't want to get into this.'

'Gilbert, you're already in it. Help me out and lead me somewhere new.'

'The party I met Amy at was thrown by James Swann. He has a crowd, a circle of friends. They're tight with each other, go to parties at one another's houses. They're all influential, very rich.' His confidence, his bluster was deserting him.

'How did Amy know them?'

'Through the parties. They have them once every couple of months. Sometimes it's little more than a dinner party, other times it's more lavish. Lot of pretty girls attend. Out-of-work actresses, models, students.'

'Friends of the set?' probed Anna.

'Not exactly. They get invited there to pep up the party, show the men a good time.'

'Prostitutes?'

'Generally not. Not to my knowledge, anyway. I'm certain Amy wasn't a prostitute.'

'She wasn't,' said Anna, feeling defensive about the dead girl.

'The night I met her, it was her first time at one of these parties. She'd been invited, *recruited* she later called it, by Johnny Maxwell, the society photographer. He gets attractive, discreet girls to the parties. Girls who know they can make the right sort of connections by going.'

'How do you know Amy's new boyfriend was part of the set?'

'Because we went to a splashy big party at Swann's country house together. The week after that she finished our affair, saying she'd met someone else. I'm certain she met him there.'

'Do you know who it was?'

'Anna, please.' His face looked in genuine pain. 'I had nothing to do with Amy's death. Nor did any of Swann's lot. And to be frank, I wouldn't go suggesting they did. They're powerful people.'

'How can I speak to him?'

'Who?'

'Swann.'

Gilbert laughed.

'You'll be lucky.'

She felt a surge of determination.

'Maybe Andrew and his news team will have more luck.'

Gilbert downed his lemonade in one anxious swoop.

'Bloody hell, you're not going to let this drop, are you?'

'No.'

His shoulders sagged with exhaustion.

'Then you should meet Johnny Maxwell. I'm not introducing you directly, but I can find out where he is this week. Which parties he'll be going to. The rest is up to you, but he'll like a pretty girl like you. In fact Swann's summer party at his Oxfordshire place is sometime around now. Play your cards right, don't tell him what you do for a living, and I bet Johnny will invite you.'

'To be a Swann set plaything? I'm not sure I'll take that as a compliment.'

'You'd better go.'

'I will. And thank you.'

'She was a lovely, lovely girl. I swear I had nothing to do with anything you're suggesting, so please keep me out of this.'

His voice was trembling, desperate. Anna believed him. She walked down the path out of the garden, and when she turned round, his gaze was blank and regretful, lost in the memory of what was, what might have been, and what now never could be.

33

Jessica slipped on her oversized Tom Ford sunglasses and glanced about nervously. The Primrose Gym on Mulholland was LA's workout space *du jour*, and as such it was exactly the sort of place you'd expect the paparazzi to be lurking. Not that Jessica usually minded; in fact she'd often had her publicist tip them off that she would be there at a certain time, looking lithe and lovely. Today, however, had been a particularly strenuous and sweaty Bikram yoga session, and her beet-red face was not the sort of look she wanted to project to the outside world.

Satisfied the coast was clear, she walked as fast as she could to her car and leapt inside, only allowing herself to relax when the doors were firmly locked.

Rigorous exercise always made her feel fantastic, as if her whole body was being purged, and today was no exception. In fact today was the first day in ages she had felt a surge of optimism that life was returning to normal.

She smiled as her mobile rang and she saw the caller was Joe Kennington. She hadn't heard from him about her invitation to Tori's art party and was beginning to worry she'd pushed it too far.

'Joe, honey,' she purred into the phone. 'How are you?'

'Not so good, Jess,' he said. She noticed the panic in his voice immediately. 'Have you seen *US Weekly*?'

'No, I came straight to the gym this morning. What's the matter? Is it about the reshoot on *Slayer*?' She had been worried that the industry would read 'reshoot' as 'disaster'.

'No, it's about you and me,' said Joe. 'About how we went out for a romantic meal and then . . .'

'Then what, Joe?' she snapped, a familiar flutter of panic rising in her belly.

His rich baritone sounded meek, apologetic.

'And then they're saying you came on to me and I turned you down. Honestly, Jess, I didn't tell anyone about it.'

It was like a fierce sideways blow. A dozen different thoughts leapt into Jess's head. None of them good.

'*Didn't tell anyone?* Then how the hell did they get hold of the story?'

'Who knows? We didn't exactly go to the most discreet place for dinner.'

'Not that,' she snapped. It was a fairly standard procedure for gossip magazines to link two stars on a movie, especially if they were both single and seen out in public. 'I want to know how the hell they found out about . . . the thing at my house.'

'I swear to you, Jess, I didn't tell anyone.'

'Well neither did I!' she growled. That wasn't strictly true. Her mother had seen Joe arrive at the house, and when she'd returned she'd found Jessica moping on the balcony with a joint, all alone. As for Mai, she was always sneaking around the house like some silent ninja. For all Jess knew, she was making a packet on the side selling her secrets. 'You must have told someone, Joe.'

'Why would I?' said Joe. 'I mean, if they found out the truth, I have more to lose, don't I?'

'Not in this case,' said Jessica, her voice rising. 'According to this story, you look like a goddamn stud and I look like a pathetic, needy reject.'

'I'm sorry, Jess,' he said. 'I promise you I didn't—'

'Bullshit, Joe!' she yelled, throwing the phone across the car. She twisted the ignition of the Aston and stamped her foot to the floor, fishtailing out of the parking lot.

'I sound like some stupid desperate bitch who can't even get a man by begging.' Jessica threw the copy of US Weekly on to Sylvia's desk in floods of tears.

'It could be worse,' said her publicist in her usual measured tones. She leaned over and tapped the paparazzi picture of

261

Jessica in a bikini. 'At least they used the Jeff Benton pictures. You look amazing.'

'And what does that matter?' Jessica sobbed. 'The story says Joe turned me down; anyone reading that is going to ask themselves why. Because I'm disgusting to look at – or because I'm half-crazy.'

'Come on, it's not the end of the world,' said Sylvia. 'The rest of the press has all been supportive of you.'

Jessica barked out a laugh.

'For a PR expert, you don't seem to have much understanding of how these things work. I'm screwed and you know it.'

It was true that the magazines had got behind Jess during the Sam fiasco, but that had been weeks ago, and in celebrity terms, four weeks was a lifetime. The press needed a new angle and the Joe story gave it to them on a plate. Jessica wasn't just heart-broken, she was desperate, unfuckable. Unlovable. Now all the stories about her bravery and strength would morph into stories about weeping fits and needy tantrums. She had seen it happen with so many other A-listers going through break-ups. The public's sympathy was finite; they quickly became bored and wanted something else to gossip about.

'Look, I can talk to Joe's people,' said Sylvia. 'We can put a counter-story out there. Maybe how you too have become just close friends and he's been supporting you through your ordeal.'

'It's too late for that. Millions of people have already read this shit.' She snatched the magazine back and began reading out sections of the text.

' "Jessica lured the Oscar-nominated actor back to her luxury Malibu home." See? I "lured" him back there like some deranged serial killer. Or how about this: "Jessica split from her fiancé Sam Charles a month ago." They don't mention that the prick cheated on me; it's like I drove him away! And they even say Joe's trying to get back with his wife, like he'd prefer that old hag over me!'

'We can spin this,' said Sylvia. 'To be honest, it's good early press for *Slayer*. If people think there is chemistry between the leads, they're more likely to go out and see it.'

'The movie isn't even released for eight months!' cried Jessica.

'And I want people to go see it because I'm a great actress, not because I'm part of some Brangelina-type sideshow.'

Sylvia looked at her, her eyebrows raised.

'Did anything happen between you and Joe?' she asked.

'You've read the feature,' snapped Jessica. 'No, nothing.'

'But . . . *did* you try to seduce him?'

Jessica looked away.

'He's about ninety, Sylvia.'

'Come on now, Jess, this is me.'

Jessica glanced at her. Sylvia had been around the block three or four times, she had dealt with – and hidden – more celebrity scandals than you could imagine. It was no use lying to her.

'I might have tried to kiss him,' she croaked. 'I'd had a drink, I was feeling emotional; about the end of the shoot, about Sam. It's been hard for me, you know.'

Sylvia came over and put a motherly arm around her shoulders.

'We'll sort this, okay?' she said. 'We'll get to the bottom of it.'

Jessica was now genuinely emotional. Everything that was happening to her was so unfair. She hadn't done anything to warrant any of it.

'He's a complete bastard,' she said, her hands balling into fists. 'He's just using me to keep the real story out of the press.'

'What real story?' said Sylvia, frowning.

At the time, Jessica had felt genuinely sorry for Joe. She could see how difficult it must have been for him trying to make it as a leading man when the industry still saw being gay as a problem. But that was before he had tried to screw her over.

'You *do* know why he rejected me?' she said.

Sylvia shrugged.

'Because he's a gentleman?'

'Because he's a *gay* gentleman.'

If Sylvia was surprised by the news, she didn't show it.

'You want a counter-story? Why don't we just tell the world why Joe turned me down?' said Jessica.

Sylvia shook her head.

'We should leave Joe's private life out of this.'

'Why? His private life is my public humiliation.'

'Jess. Leave it,' said Sylvia firmly. 'Joe is a national treasure. You screw with his image, this town will come down on you like a truckload of horseshit.'

Jessica had rarely heard Sylvia swear. It was so at odds with her steely, matronly persona.

'Look, what's done is done,' Sylvia said. 'Let's just think about how we can turn this to our advantage.'

Too right, Jessica thought, a plan forming in her head. It was so obvious, she wondered why she hadn't thought of it earlier.

'Could I just have one moment alone? I need to make a call.'

Sylvia looked reluctant until Jessica flashed her a fiery look.

'Fine,' she said, closing the door behind her.

Jessica took out her cell phone and scrolled to Joe's number.

'It's Jess,' she said without preamble.

'How are you?' he asked, his voice guarded. Hardly surprising, seeing as she had screamed at him then hung up the last time they had spoken.

'I just wanted to apologise for how I spoke to you,' she said. 'I was upset, but there's no excuse for behaving like that.'

'No, I totally understand,' said Joe.

'Yes, and I also wanted to say that of course you can count on me to keep your secret. One friend to another.'

'I appreciate it, Jess. And if there's anything I can do for you, like that Tori Adams party . . .'

'Well, it's funny you should bring Tori up,' she said.

'What do you want?' he said cautiously. He was experienced enough in the ways of Hollywood to know that everyone was after something.

'I'll cut to the chase, Joe. I want the role of Daisy in *Purple Skies*. I know you're tight with Tori and I know she has the power to decide who's chosen.'

'But I can't—' he began.

'Oh I think you can, Joe,' said Jessica, her voice hard and clipped. 'I think we both know how much this favour would mean to me. And how much pain it would avoid.'

'I don't respond well to threats, Jessica,' he said, his voice low.

264

'It's not a threat, Joe, it's a business transaction. You know what I want, I know what you want.'

'You didn't let me finish. I was about to say I can't ask Tori to cast you as Daisy, because they offered it to Angelina Jolie this morning.'

Jessica felt the room tilt.

'I would have tried to help you. One friend to another,' he said sarcastically. 'Maybe I could have pushed Tori to give you something else in the movie. But now? I don't think so.'

Jessica moved her mouth, but nothing came out.

'I know you youngsters all think the industry is dog-eat-dog,' said Joe, his voice quivering with anger. 'You'll climb over anyone to get what you want. But actually, it's all about friendship, about helping each other out where you can. That's how I've been friends with Tori Adams for so long, that's how I've got to the top.'

'Yeah, that and sucking cock,' snapped Jessica and stabbed the End Call button.

She stood there staring down at the phone in her hand. She couldn't take it in. The part had gone. She had been so sure she would get it, that it would be her way out of girl-next-door TV star and into the realms of being a proper serious actress. She was screwed, royally screwed. She turned and walked out of the office, straight past Sylvia, who was waiting in the corridor.

'Jess, what's the matter?' she called. 'Where are you going?'

'Home,' she said. 'To get more stoned than I've ever been before.'

34

The courtroom was packed; Helen looked around with satisfaction. It had been her idea to push for a jury trial, and so far it had all gone exactly as she had planned. She wanted – needed – the case to be high-profile to maximise the effect when her client won: Jonathon Balon's reputation would be restored and Donovan Pierce would once again be the top media law firm in the country. Helen sat next to Balon; to his left was their QC, Nicholas Collins. Behind them were Anna Kennedy and her team, and the rest of the pews were packed with reporters and that weird breed of judicial groupies who brought their own sandwiches and seemed to relish a juicy trial. They were certainly getting their money's worth this time. Libel jury trials were rare enough, but the Balon trial had extra glamour in the form of the defendant, the glossy society magazine *Stateside*, and the claimant himself, Jonathon Balon.

Helen watched as Balon stood and walked to the witness box, where he would be cross-examined by Jasper Jenkins, the barrister for *Stateside*. Balon was the ideal claimant; good-looking but sober, intelligent; jury-friendly. Still, it was hard to read the jury in civil cases of this nature. It was not like a criminal trial, where you could see the horror on the jurors' faces as they looked at grim photographs of abuse, or listened to the testimony of a battered teenager. But Helen was confident they would win. *Stateside* were not trying to prove that Balon took money from mobsters. Instead, their lawyers were arguing the 'Reynolds defence'; that the media could publish information that turned out to be false, so long as it was in the public interest and written in a responsible, balanced manner.

Nicholas Collins had done a fantastic job of pulling *Stateside*'s case to pieces. Over the past week he had presented a persuasive argument that while Jonathon Balon denied taking money from a powerful London crime family, whether he had or not was irrelevant. Balon was a private businessman who had no dealings with the general public, and therefore it was not in the public interest to expose him. The *Stateside* piece was just a hatchet job; a scurrilous story for their readers. And that was against the law.

Helen glanced at her watch. It was almost 3 p.m., Friday afternoon. They'd been at it since 10 a.m. this morning and the judge was showing signs of weariness. She hoped that would spur him to cut proceedings short, as she was planning to retreat to Seaways, the Devon home she had bought five years earlier. Graham had been pestering her to go since the trial began: 'You need a break, darling,' he'd said. 'Even you need to relax sometimes.' He was right, of course; she just hoped he wouldn't suggest coming along too.

Jasper Jenkins rose to his feet, fluttering through the stack of case notes in front of him.

'Your honour,' he said, 'we request permission to submit additional evidence we did not provide in discovery.'

Helen's eyes opened wide. What? She immediately sensed danger and her eyes flicked to the judge. Mr Justice Lazner frowned.

'We have allowed plenty of time for discovery on this case,' Lazner stated coldly.

Jenkins was undeterred. 'M'lord, as you are aware, this trial was brought forward by almost one month. We conducted the most thorough discovery exercise we could in the time allotted and thought we had supplied all the relevant documentation. But we can't let this trial be hampered because of things found out after the expedited timeline.'

Nicholas Collins immediately jumped to his feet in reply.

'Your honour, last-minute disclosure is both highly unusual and extremely detrimental to the fairness of this trial.'

The judge held up a hand.

'In view of this trial being brought forward, I'll allow it.'

Dammit, thought Helen as the court usher took a sheaf of documents from Jenkins and handed them to the judge.

'I would like to submit into evidence documents obtained from domain registration agency Netstuff.com,' said Jenkins.

This definitely wasn't good. Surprise witnesses and evidence were very unusual in any trial, let alone a libel trial. How many times had Helen told her team in the discovery process: 'Don't find out everything we need to know. Find out *everything*.' Worse, she didn't like the self-satisfied look on Jasper Jenkins's face. She'd seen that confident, cocksure expression in QCs before. It meant they were going for the sucker punch.

'Your honour, we have always contested that the *Stateside* story on Jonathon Balon was a fair reporting of facts in the public interest.'

Mr Justice Lazner looked unimpressed. 'I'm aware of what the Reynolds defence is, Mr Jenkins.'

'Mr Balon's defence team have spent an entire week attempting to prove that the *Stateside* story is not in the public interest. They argue that Mr Balon is not a public figure.'

Get on with it, thought Helen with a grimace. Barristers were like actors with a law degree, and this smug bastard was enjoying himself on his little personal stage.

'But our evidence will show that Mr Balon is about to run for political position.'

Helen glanced across at Balon – had she seen him flinch?

'I contend therefore,' said Jenkins, 'that Mr Balon's business integrity and the origins of his considerable fortune are very much something the voters need to know about.'

Helen could only look on in dismay as Jenkins turned to Jonathon.

'Mr Balon,' he said, 'is it correct to say that steps have been taken to prepare for a campaign for a future London mayoral election?'

Balon looked over at Helen. Helen had met with him dozens of times over the past year and he had never seemed anything other than powerful and in control, but now? Now his dark eyes betrayed panic.

Oh God, thought Helen.

'I don't have any political ambitions, no,' said Balon cautiously. 'I'm a very busy businessman and right now all my time is taken up with growing that business.'

'So how can you explain the registration of an internet domain name' – Jenkins looked down at his notes – 'Balon4Mayor.com?'

'I'm not aware of any domain name.'

'So you are telling this court you didn't register the name Balon4Mayor.com with the web-hosting site Netstuff.com?'

Helen watched the colour drain from her client's face.

'No,' said Balon. 'I mean, this could easily be someone else called Balon, couldn't it?'

Jenkins nodded, as if he was considering the point.

'Yes, but Balon is a very unusual surname, isn't it? And I doubt there are many – or should I say *any* – other people with that surname who are qualified to run for the city's mayor. Wouldn't you agree?'

Balon opened his mouth as if he were about to deny the fact, then changed his mind. He just sat there, evidently stunned. Helen wondered idly if the judge would understand if she strangled her client there and then.

'This is a bloody disaster!' shouted Helen. 'A total and utter bloody disaster.'

Anna sat silently in Helen's office, scribbling notes as her boss paced the room. She was certainly glad that it was Jonathon Balon and not her who was currently on the receiving end of Helen's fury. Not that the legal team had escaped her wrath; far from it. Immediately after the judge had called for an adjournment, Helen had taken everyone back to her office and gone ballistic. 'Unprofessional', 'embarrassing', 'criminally unprepared' were just a few of her more generous observations. None of the team had said a thing: what could they say? They had missed a vital piece of evidence that could potentially undermine the whole trial. No wonder Jasper Jenkins had been looking so pleased with himself.

But in truth, it was Jonathon Balon himself who had scuppered their case. He'd had ample opportunity to tell Helen all about his plans to run for mayor, but he hadn't. Certainly Helen would have used a completely different strategy in approaching the libel trial had she known, but now it was too late. They could hardly change tack without looking stupid at best, possibly even dishonest. It was indeed a total disaster, and part of Anna was enjoying the fact that Jonathon Balon was getting it in the neck.

'I can't believe you didn't mention this to us,' said Helen. 'What possible reason can you have had for keeping it a secret?'

'I didn't think it was relevant,' said Balon, shifting in his seat like a naughty schoolboy.

'Not relevant?' snapped Helen. 'It's completely bloody relevant, as *Stateside*'s learned counsel has just ably pointed out. It completely destroys our whole case!'

'But I'm not running for London mayor,' said Balon loftily. He clearly wasn't used to being talked to in such a manner.

'So explain this domain name.'

'It was just an idea I had kicking around.'

Helen picked up the evidence file she had been given by the defence team and leafed over a few pages.

'And who is this "Paul Jones" the site is registered to? Is Paul Jones in any way connected to you? Jenkins and his team clearly haven't established that he is, otherwise they would have brought it up.'

There was a pause as Balon picked at a piece of fluff on his trousers.

'Paul is an acquaintance,' he said finally.

'Oh shit,' whispered Helen.

'He was a freelance business consultant I employed a year or so ago,' continued Balon. 'I wanted to look into new projects outside the core areas of Balon Properties.'

'So less of an acquaintance and more of a close, valued colleague,' replied Helen tartly. There was no point in mincing words. The defence team would say exactly the same thing.

'Paul is Australian and he'd worked in corporate PR over there, where industry is more closely aligned with the legislators. He suggested a move into politics might be good for me – good for the business.'

'And London mayor is perfect for an ambitious businessman like you,' said Helen. 'Someone who has no intention of working their way up through the lowly ranks of MPs but who could stand as an independent mayoral candidate and have a good chance of winning one of the most powerful public offices in Europe. Like being PM without any of the hassle.'

Anna couldn't help admiring her boss. She was talking to Balon as if he was back on the stand. It was the quickest way to break down his defences and get the truth out of him, no matter how uncomfortable the atmosphere in the room, no matter how many millions he was paying her in fees.

'It was only an idea, for Christ's sake!' said Balon. 'It was just one conversation over a round of golf or drinks, I really don't remember. Yes, for a minute I was interested in the idea, but then we won the contract for a huge build in Russia and all those plans for diversification were shelved.'

Helen stood looking at him, clearly trying to process the information, trying to get one step ahead.

'So where's Paul Jones now?' she asked.

'He lives between London and Sydney.'

Helen looked at Anna. 'Paul Jones,' she said. 'Get everything you can on him. Names, dates, inside leg measurement, I want everything: *everything*.'

'I'm on it,' said Anna, with what she hoped sounded like confidence. Helen was already pacing again.

'Thankfully Paul Jones is a common enough name. If he's not still on the Balon payroll' – she looked enquiringly at Jonathon, who shook his head – 'then maybe the defence team won't be able to make the connection.'

'And if they do?' asked Balon uncomfortably.

'The fact that you're a potential mayoral candidate, however vague those ambitions might be, gives *Stateside* a case for publishing the story in the public interest.'

Anna raised her pencil.

'Provided they knew about it,' she said, and was relieved when Helen gave her a thin smile of acknowledgement. The magazine could only claim they were reporting in the public interest if they had known about Balon's political ambitions

271

when they published the article. In which case, why hadn't they mentioned it in the feature?

'Precisely,' said Helen. 'And that's what we're going to spend the next forty-eight hours working on.'

35

Matt sat back in the cream leather passenger seat of Carla's Range Rover and smiled.

'Why are these windows tinted?' he asked, watching as the wide-open moorland outside the car was slowly swallowed by the tall trees of the New Forest. It was Jonas's birthday, and every year they did something as a family, even after the divorce. Usually it was just a meal at a local burger place or a walk around the park, but today Carla had suggested getting out of the city.

'Privacy glass,' said his ex-wife vaguely as she overtook a Porsche, the speedometer hitting eighty. 'I'm sensitive to the sun and I hate it when people peer into the car as we're driving. It unsettles Jonas.'

'Unsettles Jonas?' teased Matt. 'It makes me feel like a pimp.'

She took her eyes off the road and looked at him with annoyance.

'A pimp?' she huffed, glancing in the rear-view mirror. Thankfully Jonas was watching a DVD and had his headphones on.

'All right, not a pimp,' said Matthew, laughing at her reaction. 'Maybe a rap star.'

'And I suppose that makes me your ho?' she replied tartly.

Four years of marriage and Carla had never quite got Matt's sense of humour. She always took things so literally, he couldn't help winding her up. In her preppy white jeans, navy T-shirt and a silk scarf tied loosely around her neck, she couldn't have looked less like a gangster's moll if she had tried.

She looked particularly beautiful today, he thought glancing at her. Of course he didn't flatter himself that she had made a special effort for his benefit. In fact these days Carla dressed like she'd just stepped off the catwalk: the cocktail dresses that cost as much as his car, the little fur coats, the cavernous leather handbags, all very Chelsea, darling. But today she looked just like the girl he had met in a bar in Fulham almost ten years earlier, the girl he'd fallen in love with and who he couldn't quite believe had fallen in love with him.

Obviously feeling his critical gaze, Carla glanced up at him.

'What are you looking at?' she said nervously. 'Is it my hair?'

'No, nothing,' chuckled Matthew. 'Just keep watching the road.'

But his eyes kept being drawn back to her hands, so tanned and elegant on the steering wheel, the milky-white band of skin where her wedding ring had been only a few weeks earlier stirring up a range of emotions he knew he was unwise to dwell on.

'Dad! Dad! Look, we're almost there,' said Jonas, spotting the Beaulieu Motor Museum sign at the side of the road. Car-mad, he had been looking forward to the trip for months.

Carla parked up in the Beaulieu grounds and they went into the big hangar that housed one of the most impressive motor collections in Europe. Matt watched with delight as his son darted from one vehicle to the next, spouting impressive trivia on what he had seen.

'Hey, look, Dad, the James Bond Aston Martin!' he cried. 'I think you should buy it.'

'I don't think it's for sale.' Matt smiled.

'Well maybe buy one just like it. You've only got that silly motorbike.'

'My bike is cool,' laughed Matt, leaning over to tickle his son, loving the pure joy of just being with him.

'The motorbike,' said Carla with a touch of disdain. 'And you say you're not having a mid-life crisis.'

He let her comment pass; he wasn't going to allow anything to ruin the day, especially as their trip to the New Forest had made such a welcome change from the snatched hour in Pizza

Express, which was what had happened on Jonas's birthday last year.

'Mum knows all about cars; she can help you choose one,' said Jonas.

'You can afford it now,' said Carla, looking as if she approved of the idea.

'Think about it, Dad. Please, think about it. It would be so cool if we went out looking for sports cars together.'

'Maybe,' said Matt, beginning to feel some discomfort.

They left the exhibition hall and went into the sweet-smelling manicured grounds. Jonas walked between his mother and father, holding hands with each of them, so that they formed a reassuring chain.

'I'd love a stately home,' said Carla wistfully, looking at Palace House, home of the aristocratic owners of Beaulieu.

'Really? All those ghosts and draughts?'

Jonas ran off ahead of them. 'I'm just going into that exhibition over there,' he said excitedly. 'It's all about spying in the war. They've got guns and everything!'

'Okay, we'll wait for you here,' said Matt, but Jonas had already gone, his trainers scuffing on the gravel path.

'Well I think the birthday boy is enjoying himself,' he said as they sat on a bench in the shade of a laburnum tree.

'He just loves seeing you, us. Together like this, I mean,' said Carla. 'I think we underestimate how important it is to him. We should have done it more often.'

'I would have been up for it,' said Matt. 'I never got the feeling you . . .' He left the comment hanging in the air.

'It was complicated, Matt,' sighed Carla.

'How was it complicated? I'm his dad.'

The twenty-four hours a week he had had with his son since the divorce had never been enough. Every weekend had been an exhausting round of the cinema, football and rugby in his effort to show Jonas a good time, fearing that his son might start comparing him to David. Every weekend they did something together, but there was never enough time to do *nothing* together. Walk, talk, watch TV. There was certainly never any opportunity to involve Carla, who always used to drop Jonas off at the flat with a polite wave before disappearing back to her Notting Hill life.

Carla looked embarrassed.

'David didn't like it. Didn't like me spending any time with you. He always felt threatened by you.'

Matt looked at her over the top of his sunglasses.

'David? Threatened? By me? Does he not remember that you *left* me?'

She laughed. 'I think he was jealous.'

'Of what?'

'About the way you look. Being so good-looking. David's the first one to admit he's no oil painting.'

'*You* saw something in him,' muttered Matt. He wanted to add, 'the thirty-million-pound bank balance', but decided against it.

'I told him once that the night I first met you, I thought you were the sexiest bloke I'd ever seen.'

Her compliment caught him completely off guard. She'd always made him feel witty and charming. She was good at that. That knack of making you feel like the most important person in the room. He willed himself to deflect the remark.

'You don't have to be nice to me just because I'm giving you some free legal advice,' he said, trying to make light of it. Carla looked embarrassed and turned away.

'Are you going away this summer?' she asked after a pause.

'I doubt it, what with the new job and everything. I feel like I'm running at a hundred miles an hour just to stand still.'

'So no girlfriend tugging at your sleeves to take her somewhere hot?' She made the word 'hot' sound provocative.

'No holiday. No girlfriend.' He wasn't sure if she was fishing, and if so, to what end. 'The only woman pulling at my sleeve is Helen Pierce, wanting me back in the office. What about you?'

'Jonas and I are going to Ibiza in a couple of weeks.'

'Really? He didn't mention it.'

'I only just found out. My friend Sara has a villa and she's asked us out there. I think it's a sympathy invite.'

Matthew laughed.

'I doubt that. She'll have some handsome single banker

waiting for you at the pool, a rose wedged between his Zoom-whitened teeth.'

She giggled.

'Eww, that's enough to put you off your mojitos.' She picked a flower and began pulling off the petals. 'I'm not looking, anyway,' she said quietly.

'I can understand that,' said Matt.

She nodded, clamping her lips together as if she was afraid they would reveal something.

'I'm sorry, Matt,' she said softly. 'I know what it's like now. I'm sorry I made you feel like this.'

He looked up at her, just as she turned her face away.

'Carla . . .' he said, but just then Jonas came running back towards them, his arms stretched out to the sides like the wings on a fighter plane.

'Dad, Dad!' he cried, grabbing Matt's hand. 'You've got to come and see, there's a man with a parachute and these bombs they used to hide inside dead rats.'

'Wow,' said Matt, grinning. 'That sounds cool.'

'Can I have a parachute?' Jonas asked, dragging Matt towards the house.

'Ask your mother,' said Matt, winking at Carla.

Jonas slept all the way back to London. When they pulled up in a side street around the corner from Larry's Cheyne Walk house, it felt cruel to wake him. Carla switched off the engine and for a few moments they sat in silence. The sun was low in the sky. Across the river they could see the scratchy, inky outline of Battersea Park, and the water looked blue and orange where it rippled. Matt had been pleased when Carla had suggested bringing Jonas to visit his grandfather on his birthday, but then Larry and Carla had always got on. They were the same sort of people. Gregarious social climbers who both appreciated the finer things in life. Matthew could tell Carla was impressed by the tall Georgian house; who wouldn't be?

'This place is lovely,' she said. 'When did Larry move here?'

'Not sure. Some point between wives three and four.'

'Do you remember when we used to walk around here when

we were first married, dreaming about having a house on the river?'

Matt had always known that Carla yearned for a smart Chelsea address; it was just the way she was. He supposed he should have realised that she would be looking for a way to move up to the next rung on the ladder.

'We were happy then, weren't we?' she said quietly.

'Were we?' he replied. He didn't mean to sound bitter; it was a genuine question. Looking back, he had never been entirely sure why someone so beautiful and socially adept had chosen to marry him. Throughout their entire relationship he'd been waiting for her to change her mind, realise that she could do so much better. But when he'd asked her to marry him, as they walked across Albert Bridge one evening after a glorious meal in a little bistro on a sleepy Chelsea back street, she'd said yes and he hadn't thought to ask her if she was absolutely sure.

'I loved you, Matt,' she said simply, looking straight into his eyes.

'You had a funny way of showing it.'

The car filled with an awkward silence until Jonas woke up grumpily.

'Where are we?' he mumbled.

'We're at Grandad's,' said Matt, leaping out of the passenger door, glad to defuse the tension.

Loralee answered the door dressed in a miniskirt, flip-flops and a T-shirt that instructed the world 'Don't mess with me'.

'How are you?' said Matt, giving her the double kiss. Since their showdown in the hospital, he'd made an effort to keep the peace with Loralee for the sake of his father. She knelt down to look at Jonas.

'Gosh, and this is your son, Matthew? You're adorable.'

'This is Jonas,' he smiled. 'Oh, and this is Carla. His mum.'

Matt watched as Loralee gave Carla the up and down. Evidently she passed muster.

'Hi, Carla,' she said, offering a limp hand. 'You look so cute together.'

'Oh, we're not . . .' began Matt, then decided it wasn't worth the trouble.

'Is he in?' he asked. Loralee shook her head.

'I'm so sorry, Matthew. He popped out about ten minutes ago. Gone to see a friend. I could give him a ring if you'd like?'

'No, no. It's just good to hear he's out and about now.'

She nodded, her head on one side.

'Getting stronger every day.'

Matt ruffled Jonas's hair.

'Sorry, cowboy, no present today.'

'It's my birthday,' announced Jonas proudly.

'Oh, happy birthday, sweetheart,' said Loralee, stepping forward to give him a bear hug.

Matthew watched his son blush. Clearly Loralee's effect on men started young.

'I'll tell him you came by.'

'Do,' said Matt as she closed the door.

'I'd watch that one,' said Carla tartly as they walked back to the car.

'Oh, she's harmless,' said Matt.

'You know your trouble, Matt?' said Carla, getting into the Range Rover. 'You're a terrible judge of character.'

Maybe you're right, thought Matt, looking back up at the house. Maybe you're right.

36

Despite working in the media for almost a decade, Anna had never seen a printing press. She had imagined a hangar full of hot iron rollers smelling of wood pulp, the wheezing machines churning out the magazines and newspapers one by one to be collected up by inky-fingered paper boys at the end of the conveyor belt. The reality was much slicker and high-tech – everything automated, robotic and gliding on air like footage from a Japanese car plant. And the noise! That had been the biggest shock: even wearing the unflattering yellow ear-defenders, she could barely hear what her host was saying – or rather shouting – to her.

'I said I'm not sure I should even be talking to you,' yelled Bruce Miles, the general manager of the Colby Press, this huge printing plant in Leicestershire. He was leading Anna across a steel gantry, inspecting the printer below as he went. Her grip tightened on the handrail; her four-inch heels weren't ideal for this sort of environment.

'You know we do a lot of work for Steinhoff Publications?' shouted Miles. 'If they thought I was talking about things I shouldn't be, they could cut our contract, and do you know how many millions that would cost us?'

'I understand your position, Mr Miles,' said Anna into his ear. 'And I appreciate you seeing me, but this is the easy way to do it. We could give you a witness summons to attend court, and believe me, you wouldn't want the hassle of all that.'

He looked at her for a moment, then nodded.

'Come into my office,' he shouted, and opened a heavy door. When it was closed, the noise was reduced to a mere whine and

Anna gratefully took off her ear-defenders.

'Tea?' Miles said, sitting behind his desk. The office was strikingly disorganised after the shiny efficiency of the shop floor.

'No thank you,' she said, glancing at the clock on the wall. She had somewhere else to be and needed this to be as short and sweet as possible. 'I'll get straight to the point, if I may.'

Miles gestured to the plastic chair facing his desk. 'Please do.'

'Well, I know you print the UK edition of *Stateside* as part of your contract with Steinhoff,' said Anna. 'I just need to find out what day last October's issue of the magazine went to press.'

He reached behind him and took out a red hardback ledger.

'I've got that information right here,' he said, licking his thumb and leafing through the pages.

Somehow Anna found it strangely reassuring that a cutting-edge operation like the Colby Press still kept all its records in proper books rather than on some computer spreadsheet. She leaned forward as he turned it around for her to read.

'The content of the magazine comes to us as files. The magazine's production manager was supposed to send them to us on the eighth of June, but we didn't get them until three days later, on the Friday.' He sighed, as if this was something that clients did just to annoy him. 'So we actually printed here. The twelfth of June,' he said running his finger along the date line.

Dammit, thought Anna. That wasn't the news she was hoping for.

'Well, thanks for letting me know, Mr Miles,' she said, standing up.

'That's all you wanted?' He looked a little disappointed. 'Are you sure you don't want that cup of tea? It's a long way back to London.'

She glanced at the clock again. 'I'd love to, but I have another appointment.'

As she walked towards her car, Anna pulled out her BlackBerry and tapped in a message to Helen as she went: 'Stateside printed 12 June. Balon4Mayor registered 1 June. Enough time for magazine to know about it. Strengthen their argument public interest?'

Inside her Mini, she opened her road atlas, wondering if the detour she was planning was worth the risk. Travelling back to London at this time of day, she figured she could easily claim that traffic hold-ups had stopped her getting back to the office, although she wouldn't put it past Helen to check that with the AA.

'Sod it,' she whispered, firing up the engine. She pulled out of the industrial estate and, ignoring the signs to London, turned the car north.

Ruby Hart lived with her mother in a pebble-dashed semi on a council estate that showed all the signs of poverty and neglect. There was a skeletal Christmas tree still lying on its side in the small overgrown front garden, presumably marooned there since December, and a rusted baby buggy parked by the door, its seat filled with a leaking black bin bag. What a far cry it was from the sleek Thameside flat that Amy Hart had died in, thought Anna as she pulled her car up outside.

She sat in the Mini, hesitating, telling herself that she had about thirty seconds to start the engine and drive back to London. Eventually she got out and walked up the path with purpose. She was just about to press the bell when the door was opened by a tired-looking middle-aged woman.

'You must be Anna.'

'That's me. Are you Ruby's mum?'

The woman nodded.

'I suppose you'd better come in.'

Liz Hart shuffled inside, her manner unhurried and slightly weary. Anna supposed she was still a mother in mourning. Ruby had said she was forty-five, but the shapeless navy tracksuit, over-dyed hair and deep lines on her face made her look ten years older.

'Ruby's just gone to the Co-op to get some biscuits,' said Liz, showing Anna into an old-fashioned living room that smelled of boiled food drifting in through a hatch in the wall to the kitchen. The front door slammed and Amy walked in holding a packet of Garibaldis.

'Oh hi,' she said, suddenly shy. 'I didn't think you'd come.'

When Ruby had called Anna three days earlier to ask her how she was getting on, Anna knew it was the moment when she could have admitted that she hadn't found out anything concrete and finished all this amateur sleuthing right there. Instead she found herself volunteering to visit the Hart family in Doncaster.

'I wanted to give you both an update, although I'm not sure I have that much to tell you.'

Liz Hart pulled out a nest of tables and put out a teapot and a plate of sandwiches that remained untouched as Anna told them about her meetings with Mandy Stigwood, Ryan Jones and Gilbert Bryce.

When she finished speaking, she realised that Liz Hart was crying.

'Sorry,' said the woman. 'I'm finding this quite hard.'

Anna felt around in her bag and handed her a tissue.

'Thanks, love,' she said, dabbing at her eyes. 'I mean it. Thank you, for everything you are doing for us. For Amy.' She puffed out her cheeks to compose herself. 'It's just I can't help thinking how it could have been. You send your kids out into the world and you hope for the best, but who knows if they're making the right decisions?' She shook her head. 'When Amy got to university I thought she'd make a better life for herself. All those opportunities, all those nice people she'd meet, but as it turns out, she'd have been better off around here, wouldn't she?'

Anna knew what Liz Hart meant. Life on the estate would have been hard and her choices much more limited, but at least she would have been alive, and for a mother, the only thing that mattered was your child being safe and well. She felt a swell of resolve. Over the last two weeks she had asked herself many times why she was bothered with looking into Amy Hart's death. Of course she had been intrigued by a possible connection with Sam's overturned injunction, but as she sat and watched Liz Hart sob softly, she knew it was no longer her driving motivation. Finding out how and why Amy died might not bring her back, but it might try and help Liz and Ruby make some sense of it.

'When Amy died,' asked Anna gently, 'what happened to all her stuff?'

'Gary, my fella, has got his own window-cleaning round, so he drove us down to London in his van,' said Liz. 'We cleared her flat. I put everything in her old room. I couldn't bear to throw anything away.'

Anna looked at Ruby.

'Can we go and have a look?'

'For what?' asked Liz.

Anna shrugged. 'Maybe we'll know when we find it.'

She followed Ruby up the narrow staircase and into a tiny room only just big enough for a single bed, which was covered in a pile of overstuffed black bin liners and a stack of cardboard boxes. The boxes were filled with magazines, make-up and knick-knacks. Anna opened one of the bags and saw that it was full of clothes. Tiny skirts, sparkly tops and high-heeled shoes. Expensive, most of them, clothes that had seen many nights out. She felt a pang of sadness. All this life, all this potential, it was all gone, crumpled at the bottom of a flight of stairs.

'You're sorry you got into this, aren't you?' said Ruby, perching on the dresser in the corner. Anna gave her a rueful smile.

'When you first came to see me, I thought it was none of my business. Or rather, I didn't want it to be my business,' she said honestly.

'So why did you get involved? I mean, you didn't take my money, so what was in it for you?'

'I thought it might have something to do with Sam Charles. I thought maybe he'd been stitched up as a way of diverting attention from Amy's inquest.'

Ruby looked stunned.

'You think Sam Charles had something to do with Amy?' she said incredulously.

Anna shook her head.

'No, no, I don't think he had anything to do with Amy's death. But something you said on the phone made me think. When the news of Sam's affair hit the papers, it was as if Amy never even existed. I wondered if Sam might have been set up, but I've spoken to Mandy, Ryan and Gilbert Bryce and . . .'

She trailed off. And what? What had they all told her, exactly? Nothing very much, if truth be told. Ryan thought he was being used, Mandy thought Amy was hiding something, and Gilbert, well Gilbert was clearly just thinking about himself. Taken individually, it all added up to nothing, but taken as a whole, it was setting off an alarm in the back of Anna's head.

'You believe me now,' said Ruby quietly. 'You believe that someone killed Amy.'

Anna was only half listening, her eyes scanning the wall next to Amy's bed. There were lots of photos there, Blu-tacked reminders of good times, holidays and friends. You always smile in photographs, don't you? she thought sadly. However you're feeling, you always smile for the camera.

Suddenly she stood up and began opening the boxes on the bed.

'What are you looking for?' Ruby asked.

'Pictures, photos, letters, anything like that,' said Anna.

Ruby shook her head. 'I wouldn't bother,' she said. 'I packed those boxes and there's nothing like that. I thought it was a bit strange, actually, 'cos Amy was a bit like our mum, she was a hoarder, could never throw anything away.'

Anna frowned at her.

'You mean that in that whole flat, there were no photos at all?'

'No, should there have been?'

Of course there should, thought Anna. Amy was a model, and she spent her life in a social whirl. The place should have been covered in pictures.

'What about a computer? Did she have one?'

'I thought she did,' said Ruby. 'She definitely used to have a laptop and she'd send me emails all the time, so she must have done. But when we cleared her flat, we couldn't find it. Or her mobile.'

Anna frowned, while Ruby began rifling through her sister's chest of drawers.

'Before you ask, there were no mobile phone records or a diary, although who keeps one of those these days? But she did have this.' She took a battered address book out of the drawer and gave it to Anna. 'I had to use it to ring her friends about the funeral. Their numbers are all in there.'

Anna flicked through.

'How many of them came to the funeral?' she asked.

'About a dozen.' She rattled off the names, although none of them meant anything to Anna.

'The only one who didn't come was Louise, actually,' said Ruby. 'I was a bit sad about that because Lou was Amy's best mate in London. They used to be flatmates before she moved into that posh flat by the Thames. I met her a few times; she was nice, she worked at a magazine.'

'Why didn't she come?'

Ruby shrugged. 'Don't know. She sent my mum a really nice letter saying how sorry she was, but when I tried to call her, her number had been disconnected. I rang the magazine and they said she'd left to go travelling.'

'When did she leave?'

'Not long after Amy died.'

The sky was turning dark as Anna's car crept slowly along the inside lane of the motorway. At least she wouldn't have to lie to Helen Pierce about traffic snarl-ups – it seemed as if the whole of the M1 was being dug up tonight – and it certainly gave her time to think. Not that it was getting her anywhere. The further she delved into Amy's life, the harder it was to see clearly; it was like walking blindly into a dark wood. If only she had been able to go through Amy's missing laptop and mobile phone, she was sure she would have found something of interest: photographs, emails, texts. But then, of course, perhaps that was the exact reason she hadn't been able to check them. It was as if Amy's flat had been cleared before Liz and Ruby Hart had done the official job.

She pulled out her phone, wondering if it was too late to ring. No, men like Phil Berry were always on call. That was sort of the point. She scrolled to his number.

'Phil. It's Anna Kennedy.'

'Friday night,' said the man, his Irish accent softening the words. 'Ten thirty. Someone's been a bad boy if you're calling me now, Anna.'

She laughed. Phil Berry was a former consultant with Hill Securities – one of the private investigation giants that Davidson Owen had used for forensic accounting and chasing down witnesses. She'd worked with him on half a dozen cases before he'd left to set up on his own, undercutting his old firm. He was cheap, he was quick and he was completely reliable. If you wanted to find someone, he would find them. Anna thought of him as a human bloodhound.

'I need you to track someone down for me.'

'Don't you ever call to invite me to dinner?'

Anna chuckled.

'Not this time, Phil. I need the whereabouts of a girl named Louise Allerton. Twenty-four, works in fashion journalism. *Class* magazine. Left the country six months ago to go travelling, not been heard of since. I need to speak to her urgently.'

'I'll get on it straight away.'

She laughed. 'I appreciate the dedication, but as you point out, it's ten thirty on a Friday night. Don't you have a life, Phil?'

'This *is* my life, darling,' he said, and hung up.

Mine too, thought Anna, as the traffic ahead of her began to move once more.

37

Helen Pierce stared at the calendar in front of her, wondering if she could turn back time or somehow change the frustrating facts written down there in black and white. It had been deeply irritating to discover that *Stateside* had gone to press over a week after the registration of the Balon4Mayor domain name, but much worse, it was potentially fatal to her case. She seriously doubted that anyone at the magazine had really had a clue that Jonathon Balon had registered the web name or even had political ambitions when they had gone to press, otherwise they would already have used it as a big stick with which to beat him. After all, the article had been a hachet job, and 'Property Developer With Criminal Connections Wants To Run London' would have been ten times more sensational. The annoying thing was that none of that mattered. The fact remained that Balon4Mayor.com pre-dated the magazine's print date, and legally that was enough for the magazine to argue that the story was in the public interest.

She sat back and closed her eyes, going over the trial once more in her head. *Stateside* had called dozens of witnesses in the course of the week, most of whom had been humdrum: the writer of the piece, a selection of the people he had interviewed, most of them just there to nod and say 'yes, that's what I told him' – it was all par for the course in a trial like this. The only witness Helen had been worried about had been Spencer Reed, the magazine's flamboyant editor. Spencer was one of the most famous editors in the world, and he had an ego and swagger to match. In the past decade she'd represented a handful of clients in defamation actions against *Stateside*, and Spencer had always been an impressive witness: passionate, defiant, deeply protective of his magazine. But this time, he'd been different. He was still outwardly confident and eloquent, but you could tell he was just going through the motions. I wonder . . . thought Helen, walking across the office to the tall bookcase covering the wall opposite her. On the bottom shelf, neatly filed in boxes, were dozen of copies of the magazine. They had both the UK and the US edition delivered, as any given month there would be a few subtle differences between the two. Different advertising, occasionally a different cover.

She carried the magazines back to her glass desk and sorted them into two stacks, one American, the other British, then set about methodically going through each one, armed with a packet of pink Post-it notes.

Forty minutes later, the job was done. Helen stood back and smiled at her handiwork, then picked up the phone and called Anna.

Her associate was there in less than a minute, standing at the door like a schoolgirl summoned to see the head teacher. It was a Sunday, so Anna was wearing her weekend clothes – jeans, ballet pumps and a white T-shirt, but even so, she still had that clean-cut head-girl efficiency about her. Helen knew that Anna felt personally responsible for the Sam Charles debacle, and that was good; she had no time for 'clockers', people who just treated the law like a job they could clock on and off from. Like her, Anna lived and breathed her work, plus she was smart, sharp and hungry, and she had something to prove to her boss. Helen would never dream of saying as much, but for all those reasons, Anna was the member of her team she trusted the most.

'Do you know what I have always found strange?' she said, gesturing towards the piles of magazines. 'The fact that the Jonathon Balon story appeared in both the US and the UK issue.'

'I thought all features appeared in both issues,' replied Anna.

'Not quite. Only about ninety per cent of the editorial is the same. The UK issue usually has one major story pertinent to the British market, a couple of party pages and a handful of diary items to give a regional flavour, which are generated by their London bureau.'

'So the fact that the Balon story is in both issues means it was generated by the main editorial office in New York?'

Helen nodded. 'Which is the odd thing. Why run a five-thousand-word feature on a London-based property developer?'

'Because he's a billionaire and because he's politically ambitious?'

'They didn't know that when this piece was commissioned, I'm pretty sure of that.'

'Do you think that's enough reason to get the public interest argument thrown out?' asked Anna.

'Possibly,' said Helen, 'but possibly isn't good enough any more.'

Helen had no intention of taking any more chances with this case. She had been confident of a win, but they had been caught out by the defence: that couldn't happen again.

'See the pink notes sticking out of the sides?' she said. 'I've marked all the British-focused features that appear in both editions. They're British stories, yes, but stories with a real international impact. Stories that would interest you whether you lived in Manhattan or Manchester.'

Anna stepped closer, then looked at Helen in surprise. 'There aren't many.'

'There are just three,' smiled Helen. 'And there are eight years' worth of magazines there.'

'So it's unusual for *Stateside* to commission a story like the Balon profile, something with such a uniquely British flavour?'

'Unusual?' Helen corrected. 'Almost unheard of.'

She could see that Anna was interested now, thinking through the angles, looking for a solution: that was exactly why she had called her.

'Find out everything about the senior members of staff on the magazine,' said Helen. 'Start with Spencer. I want to find a connection, however small, to Jonathon Balon.'

Anna looked at her, the penny dropping.

'You think this is an intentional hatchet job?' she said. 'Something personal?'

'Did you notice the way Spencer was glaring at Jonathon in court?' said Helen, nodding. 'I thought it was because he was annoyed that Jonathon had brought the libel action, but what if it's something else? Spencer is famous for using his magazine to voice his anti-Republican standpoint; why wouldn't he go a step further and use it to trash an individual he didn't like?'

Anna's eyes opened wider.

'And a story printed with malice would stop *Stateside* from using the Reynolds defence in a libel case, because even if it's in the public interest, it has to be balanced and fairly reported.'

Helen nodded gleefully.

'Go and find out what this is really about.' She smiled. 'Then we'll give them a hatchet job of their own.'

38

As far as Matthew was concerned, the White Horse was the perfect London boozer. Dark, cramped, done out in chipped mock-mahogany and red velvet, the walls covered with pictures of boxers and racehorses. The gents' had grafitti and a broken mirror, and they still sold cling-film-wrapped cheese rolls behind the bar. It certainly wasn't the sort of place where you'd order a white wine spritzer.

Perhaps that explained why Matthew was the only Donovan Pierce employee in the pub at half past seven in the evening, despite the fact that the White Horse was by far the nearest watering hole to the office. He'd asked a few people, of course, but everyone seemed to be chained to their desks, still making calls and furiously writing reports. That was the kind of work ethic Helen Pierce demanded, and they were probably terrified of her coming back from court to find them drinking lager, but Matthew had been brought up to value his leisure time. His mother Katherine had worked long, hard hours as a lecturer at University College London, but when work was done for the day, she felt no guilt in letting her hair down.

'There's always time for fun,' she'd say with a smile, filling their weekends with trips to the beach, the cinema and London museums. When Matthew was just starting out as a solicitor, he'd still meet up with his mother for after-work suppers or her trademark G and Ts, dissecting their days and sharing the gossip.

Matthew smiled nostalgically as he sipped his bitter. It was warm, foamy and tasted of bracken. During his career as a family lawyer, he'd met dozens of men who'd turned to alcohol as a way of numbing the pain of losing their family. And after Carla had left him, he had almost gone the same way. But he'd taken hold of his heavy drinking before alcohol had become his crutch. He'd started rowing again, and bought a motorbike for long rides deep into the countryside that made him feel better than whisky ever could.

'That looks good,' said a familiar voice behind him.

Matt glanced up and saw his father standing there clutching a white plastic bag under his arm.

'Bloody hell. What are you doing here?'

It was actually quite a shock to see Larry. In Matt's mind, his father was always a charging bull. Maddening at times, yes, but always vital and strong. Now he was pale and thin, his shirt baggy and loose around the neck. Perhaps it was the dim light in the bar, but his hair seemed greyer, his skin transparent. But he still had the same twinkle in his eye.

'I'm allowed to come into pubs, you know,' he said. 'Laid off the heavy drinking but I can still breathe in the fumes.'

The chestnut-haired barmaid waved at him.

'Melinda, my dear,' he boomed, his voice as loud as ever. 'Just a vodka and tonic for me, hold the vodka, there's a darling.'

He carried his glass over to Matthew's booth and lifted it in salute.

'How did you know I was here?'

Larry shrugged. 'Sarah on reception said you'd gone to the pub. This was always my favourite place to sneak off to, so I figured, like father like son.'

'Well it's good to see you up and about,' Matt said. 'Were you coming in to work? The Garrick Club?'

'Absolutely not,' said Larry. 'I was shopping.'

'Shopping? You? I never thought I'd hear you say those words.'

Larry slid his plastic bag towards Matthew. It had a Hamleys logo on the side.

'For Jonas. I hope he likes it, but the receipt's in the bag – God knows what kids like these days. I felt rotten for forgetting his birthday. Not quite got used to not having a secretary there to keep a diary.'

293

'It was a shame you weren't in on Saturday,' said Matthew, peering into the bag.

'Saturday? What do you mean?'

'We stopped off to see you. Me, Jonas and Carla.'

'I didn't go out on Saturday. I was probably in the den watching the cricket and didn't hear the bell. Strange that Loralee didn't answer, though.'

Matt frowned. Why had Loralee turned them away? Perhaps Larry wasn't as well as he was making out and she wanted him to rest. Either way, he didn't want to press the point.

'Maybe she'd popped out for something,' he said.

'So you were with Carla?' said Larry, not missing a trick. 'I didn't know you were even talking these days.'

'We've always tried to keep up the tradition of going out on Jonas's birthday, however awkward it is, because Jonas loves it. But this time we actually had a lovely day. Went to the New Forest. Carla and I weren't even at each other's throats for once.'

'And what did her banker fellow think of that?'

'He didn't know. She's divorcing him.'

Larry guffawed, slapping the table.

'And now she's sniffing back after you, is she?'

'Don't be daft. That ship has sailed.'

His father looked at him probingly.

'So, I'm enjoying the firm,' Matthew said, to divert the subject.

'So I believe,' replied Larry.

'You have spies reporting back to you, eh?'

Larry chuckled.

'Something like that. Are you bringing work in yet?'

'I'm acting for Rob Beaumont in his divorce,' said Matthew casually.

Larry looked suitably impressed. 'Really? That's a good one. Very high-profile. And how's it going?'

Matt hesitated. He realised that he had spent twenty years pretending that his father's approval didn't matter to him, when really it mattered very much indeed. The last thing he wanted to admit was that the Rob Beaumont divorce wasn't going well, but he knew he would welcome his father's take on things.

'Actually, the poor sod is screwed.'

Larry laughed. 'Surely not, when he's got the best family lawyer in the country on his side?'

His father's words did little to reassure him.

'Kim – Rob's wife – is having an affair with an American and wants to move out there to be with him, taking the child with her.'

'This is Rob's child?'

Matt nodded. 'The courts will order the child lives with Kim, I'm sure of it. Rob can refuse consent to take the kid out there, but you know she'll get round that.'

'The law can be a bitch,' said Larry. 'So who's the boyfriend?'

'Fabio Martelli, some uber-rich Miami businessman.'

Matt watched as his father sipped his tonic, mulling the problem over.

'So what's your advice been so far?' he asked.

'I've been realistic with him,' said Matthew. 'Kim will eventually get the residence order to have her son with her, but if Rob withholds consent, we could keep Oliver in the country for another eighteen months.'

Larry nodded with approval. 'By which time Kim's affair might be over?'

'It's what I figured.'

'Good strategy. But if this guy Fabio's as rich as you say, Kim Collier's not going to walk away lightly.'

Matthew gave an ironic smile.

'You know Kim?'

'I've been in this business thirty years, watching people like Kim Collier keep their careers afloat. I know her singing career is on the slide. She tried acting too, and that didn't take off either. So my gut feeling is that a good marriage might be her next career move.'

'What are you suggesting?'

'Your problem is you're thinking too straight.' He leaned towards his son. 'Lawyers don't just use the law to get what they want, you know.'

Matthew frowned.

'So what exactly are you saying I should do?'

Larry's expression turned serious.

'It depends how much you want to win this – and how much Rob wants to keep hold of his son. Kim, Fabio, they'll have their weak points. Exploit them.' The glint in his eyes suggested ruthlessness, grubbiness.

Matt knew what sort of strategy his father was suggesting. He had no problem with playing hardball, but dirty tricks had a habit of rebounding and biting you on the backside.

'There is an eight-year-old child involved in this, Dad. I'm not sure that having his parents' names dragged through the mud is the best thing for him.'

'So you want to do the *decent* thing?' Larry mocked.

Matt smarted, remembering his mother, weak, near the end. When she had told him what a wonderful, decent son he was, it had been with a sense of pride not just in him, but in the way she had brought him up. And yet to Larry, the word was clearly an insult.

'Do you want to win this case?' snapped Larry. 'Donovan Pierce is a firm of winners. We do whatever it takes.'

'Under your regime, perhaps.'

'Well it's *my* name still on the letterhead.'

Matt flinched. He'd tried hard not to think too carefully about his father's motives for handing over the firm, wanting to believe the best of him, not see the worst.

'So that's why you gave me the job? To be your stooge?'

'Is that what you think?'

The jovial mood between them had gone.

'Something motivated it,' said Matt, voicing a thought that had troubled him since Larry had first made the offer. 'It was a pretty strange gesture for someone who hadn't even bothered with me for the last twenty-five years of my life.'

'I gave you that firm because you are my son and I wanted you to have it.'

'And not because you were so guilty about abandoning me and Mum?' queried Matt defensively. 'Not because your ego still wanted the Donovan name above the door?'

'You ungrateful little shit,' Larry muttered.

They glared at each other, and Matt was instantly reminded how fragile their relationship still was.

'I'm going,' said Larry, getting up to leave.

Matt wanted to stop him, but couldn't find the words to do it.

39

Loralee was standing in the hall looking at herself in the art deco mirror when Larry opened the front door. She was wearing a cherry-red mini-dress he hadn't seen before, and her hair looked fresh from the hairdresser's.

'Oh darling,' she cooed. 'You've just caught me on my way out. Where were you?'

'I've been to see Matt at work,' he muttered, still smarting about the argument he'd had with his son.

'Really?' she said, her face betraying a hint of worry. 'What about?'

'It was Jonas's birthday on Saturday. I took him a present.'

'That would be a first.'

She didn't say it maliciously, but the words hurt him. Angrily he flung the keys on to the hall cabinet.

'I'm trying, okay? Yes, I've been a shit in my time, but I'm trying to be a good husband, a good father, even a decent grandfather. Is that so wrong?'

She held up her dainty hands.

'All right, all right,' she said soothingly. 'Let's not get worked up; remember what Dr Strong said about your blood pressure.'

She was right, of course, and he could feel his heart thumping uncomfortably, but some things just had to be said.

'I hear Matt and Jonas came round on Saturday. Why didn't you tell me?' He'd made light of Matt's revelation in the pub, but the fact that Loralee had kept their visit from him had been needling him all the way back to Chelsea.

'You were resting, darling,' she said. 'I didn't think it was a good idea for you to have visitors just then.'

'Why the hell not? I was only watching TV.'

'How am I supposed to know when you're asleep, reading, or watching telly? You're recuperating. If you're in the bedroom or the den, I'm going to assume you don't want to be disturbed.'

'But this was my grandson, Loralee. It was his birthday.'

'Yes, you said,' she snapped. 'And I told you I thought you were asleep.'

Her expression softened almost immediately. She put her clutch bag under her arm and came over to give him a warm kiss on the lips.

'Let's not fight, baby,' she breathed seductively. 'It was only a misunderstanding, after all.' She trailed her fingertips down his chest and kissed his neck. She smelled of honeysuckle and the cosmetic waxiness of lipstick, and he instantly felt a stirring in his groin.

'Perhaps,' he murmured, sliding his hand up her leg.

'Let's save that until later,' she whispered, removing his hand.

'Where are you going?'

'Danielle is having a little supper,' she said, straightening herself up.

'I thought Danielle was in Sardinia.'

'Back yesterday,' she said, then turned and held out her hand. 'Did you want to come, baby?'

He shook his head. 'You go. I'm tired.' In reality, he couldn't think of anything worse than spending the evening with one of Loralee's gym friends. They were all so vacuous – and they brought out the worst in his wife. Last time Loralee had dragged him to Danielle's place, he had been forced to sit and listen as they discussed colonic irrigation – and that included the men.

As the front door slammed shut, Larry walked slowly to his study, standing in the doorway. He felt restless and unsettled. It wasn't just the confrontation with Matthew, when things had seemed to be going so well between them. He even felt vulnerable being home alone, wondering if another heart attack, like some seismic aftershock, could strike at any minute. It was the sort of discomfort he knew alcohol could settle. Back in the pub, the sight of Matt's bitter had made him almost drool, but however good it would have tasted, it wouldn't have been worth the inevitable lecture. He'd had enough of those when he was in hospital. The doctors had seemed to draw some sort of sick pleasure from reeling off the endless list of things he had to avoid. Cigarettes, gone. Cigars, banished. Whisky, vodka, gin, all off the menu. No wonder he was feeling so irritable these days. The only patch of blue in this blanket of grey sky was when his consultant had let slip that some studies had shown that an occasional glass of red wine might actually decrease the chances of a recurrent attack. Larry had seized on the idea with both hands.

A little of what you fancy . . . he thought as he opened the door to the wine cellar and descended the stone steps. The chill of the cellar felt good after the too-warm summer's day, and he smiled at the rows of sleeping bottles as if they were old friends. There were thousands of bottles down here. Over the last twenty years Larry had invested in art and in wine, and both had yielded impressive returns. Some of the oldest, dustiest bottles were worth upwards of ten thousand pounds.

As he ran his fingers along the racks, Larry thought of Matthew and felt a stab of pride. He knew his son was a better man than he would ever be, a fact that he had, disappointingly, very little to do with. He liked to kid himself that he had had a hand in Matt's accomplishments, but the truth was, Larry had spent more money tucking crisp fifty-pound notes into lap dancers' g-strings than he had on his son's education. He'd offered, of course, but Katherine had turned him down flat.

'We've managed very well without you so far. Why don't you spend it on your tarts?' had been her response, if he remembered correctly. She'd been a fiery one, his Kathy, he thought with a smile. In the end, Matty had gone to a good state-funded grammar and from there on to Trinity College, Cambridge. He'd done well, but then he had always been his mother's son; an idealist, and that was exactly the sort of lawyer he had become. A smart, nimble-minded one who used his considerable brain to work within the law. But Larry had meant what he said in the pub. Sometimes the law just wasn't enough. It hadn't been his knowledge of the law that had made Donovan Sr one of the best solicitors in London. It was his understanding of power, and how it was the only thing that mattered in any negotiation. And wasn't that all a divorce was? A negotiation on how to divide up the assets?

Feeling suddenly better, he carried the dusty bottle upstairs and decanted £400 worth of claret into a crystal goblet. Swilling it around the glass, letting it breathe, enjoying the ritual and the anticipation of pleasure deferred, he opened up his laptop. Matt wasn't his stooge. From the feedback Larry had heard within the firm, his son was shaping up to be a popular and competent managing partner. Still, everybody could use a little helping hand . . .

'Fabio Martelli,' he murmured to himself as he tapped the playboy's name into the search engine. Larry had employed people to do all the legwork of course, but he'd always enjoyed the research part of the job: finding out everything you could about both adversaries and allies, ferreting out foibles and weaknesses. Screw the law books and precedents, everything you needed to win a case was always in the details of other people's lives.

Finally he took a long sniff of the bouquet – apples, plums – and slurped up a mouthful, letting the wine run around his mouth.

Larry was certainly enjoying himself, but it only reminded him how much he missed work. Matt was wrong. There had been no sinister ulterior motive when he had given the firm to his son. But while he had loved the craziness of such a sweeping gesture, Larry knew he'd been hasty to retire. At sixty-five, his body had been telling him he couldn't hack the pace of a young man any more, but his brain still felt pin-sharp. Watching Sky Sports just didn't give him the stimulation he craved.

Half an hour later, he was sure he had enough. It was amazing how much information you could accumulate these days, but two details stood out. Firstly, it was Fabio's birthday in three days' time. According to *Paris Match* magazine, Martelli held a White Party every year in one of his many homes around the world. Secondly, FBC, his construction company, had begun a major expansion of his hotel and club empire into Dubai. According to reports, work on the site had already begun, with an opening date pencilled in eighteen months hence.

Larry's mouth curled into a smile as a plan formed in his mind. Yes, with a little luck, his Middle Eastern contacts and a compliant mutual friend, he could pull it off. He sat back in his chair and took a good glug of his wine. He might not have been able to help Matthew with his school fees, but hopefully this would be an education in how to get things done. And how winning was everything.

40

It was beautiful, there was no other word for it. Jessica walked barefoot through the sunken living room and through gently billowing voile curtains out on to the wide marble terrace, its gleaming white surface ending at a bright blue infinity pool. She stopped at the water's edge and took in the view, an uninterrupted sweep of dramatic volcanic coastline with a crescent of bone-white sand at its centre. Someone knew what they were doing when they made Hawaii part of the United States, thought Jessica with a smile.

'Here she is, America's most wanted!' Jose Silveira, the camp Brazilian photographer came towards her from the other side of the house, his arms spread wide. He was wearing a completely open silk shirt and tiny hipster shorts. 'How's this for a location, huh?' he said, evidently pleased with himself, and rightly so. Jessica had been on Maui for four days already – '*IIQ* magazine are paying,' Sylvia, her publicist, had said. 'Why not make a holiday of it?' – and she had fallen head over heels for its lush vegetation and dramatic landscapes.

Sylvia had initially been against the idea of Jessica doing the magazine's December cover, arguing that her client needed to draw more attention to her acting and less attention to her body, especially after the Joe Kennington incident. But *Utopia*, the sci-fi action movie that Jessica had shot in last year's summer hiatus, had been moved to a November release date, and the studio pointed out that Jessica's contract specified publicity support. It also specified that unless she did it, they were entitled to withhold her fee.

So Jessica, her mother and Sylvia had all flown out just before the weekend. There were only three weeks to go before season five of *All Woman* began shooting, so this was an ideal chance to recharge and tan. Freshly Botoxed, waxed and eight pounds lighter than she had been at the start of the summer, Jessica actually felt pretty good. She was happy that the magazine had agreed to use Jose for the pictures, too. He had a genius for producing gorgeous, glossy iconic shots of women – 'I could retouch a baboon's backside into a thing of beauty' he boasted – and she loved his over-the-top personality too: no flattery or sycophancy was ever enough for his subjects.

'Dahling, you are looking so gorgeous today,' he said, eyeing her up and down. 'So goddamn hot, I can even feel myself turning for you.'

She giggled.

'Just make me look even more hot, okay?'

'Don't you worry, I make you like the centre of the fucking sun,' he purred.

Jessica was about to say something else, but she was distracted by raised voices down by the pool.

'Your publicist, darling,' pouted Jose. 'She's have a blazing row with the creative director. She wants to keep this gorgeous body covered in a sack or something. I say to her, be free! Do not be scared of the sex! Let the world see how sensual my darling Jess is, but she just pull a face like an old cow.'

Jessica stalked over to Sylvia, annoyed that she was causing problems before they'd even started. She knew how mercurial Jose was; if he didn't feel the vibe was right, he had been known to flounce off the set.

'What's going on?' she said.

Sylvia was having a heated discussion with Daniel Moore, the creative director.

'The shirt would be closed, just a few buttons open at the top,' explained Daniel hastily.

'When we talked about this on the phone, they said shirt *dress*. Not shirt,' snapped Sylvia.

'But this is the sort of mood we were thinking of,' he said, holding up a film still of Julie Christie in the sixties movie *Darling*.

'I'm sure I don't need to point out that the character in *Darling* was an unscrupulous model who slept her way to the top?' said Sylvia coldly. 'I'm not sure we want to be channelling those undertones after everything that's happened this summer.'

Jessica looked at the iconic image of Julie Christie.

'Actually, I think it's a good idea,' she said, giving Daniel a coy smile. She knew it was as important to get him on side as Jose. He was just one tiny cog in the machine, but he was a useful cog. All it would take was a little flirting to make him feel wanted, and he would rush back to his dull little office, desperate to please Jessica by choosing the most flattering shot or making sure the retouching was perfect.

'Look, I know you're a men's magazine,' Sylvia said through tight lips, 'but Jessica is a respected actress, not some centrefold.'

Jose came behind Jessica and wrapped his arms around her waist.

'This woman is the sexiest bitch on the planet,' he declared. 'She makes all those so-called models look like cheap whores! And I, Jose, will make her look like an angel!'

Jessica laughed and showed the picture to Jose. 'Can you make me this beautiful, Jose?'

The photographer took her face in his dainty hands. 'Darling, I make all the men in the world want to fuck you,' he said sincerely.

'Oh Jose, you say the most wonderful things.'

Jessica breathed a sigh of relief; finally she was on her own, having slipped away to an empty bedroom in a far wing of the villa for lunch. She loved the attention, of course, being fussed over by hair and make-up girls, having everyone tell her how amazing she looked, but as the day wore on, it was beginning to make her feel anxious. I mean, what if they're wrong? she thought. What if I look hideous? After those lies that fag Joe had been spreading, she simply *had* to look like a goddess; nothing else would do.

The room was cool and serene after the blaring music and heat of the shoot, with a wrap-around balcony that overlooked the ocean, lying like a shimmering pool of mercury in front of her. She sat on a rattan sunlounger, legs placed on either side, and laid out her lunch: a slice of melon and a can of Diet Mountain Dew.

She wanted something to read. Sylvia had declared a ban on media while they were in Hawaii – 'we're here to relax, remember?' – and while Jessica could see the logic, it was making her jumpy to be so out of the loop. In her business, what people were saying was everything.

A young girl in shorts and a tank top popped her head into the bedroom; Jessica recognised her as one of the make-up girls.

'Jose wants to start shooting in ten,' she said nervously. 'Can I get you anything in the meantime?'

'Got any magazines?'

The girl looked awkward.

'We were told no media at the location house.'

'Really?' Jessica frowned. 'Why?'

The girl was chewing her lip.

'I think it said so in the contract.' As Jessica glared at her, the girl opened the satchel she was wearing. 'But I've got an iPad if you'd like.'

'Sure,' said Jessica, wondering why they'd been told no media. 'But let's keep it between the two of us, all right? Now leave me.'

She immediately logged on to the *New York Post*. Some scandal had broken about an East Coast politican. Yeah, like that's news.

She typed *National Enquirer* into Google, then rolled her eyes. Not Charlie Sheen again; didn't he ever take a week off? Tutting to herself, she logged on to *Celeb* magazine, and gasped as the page popped up.

'Tragic Jess Heading For A Breakdown?' it said.

'Tragic?' she gasped, staring at the screen in disbelief. '*Breakdown?*'

She quickly clicked on the article and began reading:

Friends fear heartbreak has driven *All Woman* star Jessica Carr to the edge, writes Lindy Snape in Los Angeles. Her split from hunky Brit actor Sam Charles was only the first in a series of career disasters, quickly followed by the news that Uniglobe Pictures have ordered a reshoot on her movie *Slayer* in which she stars alongside Joe Kennington. 'Jess just wasn't convincing as a romantic lead,' said an insider. 'There was zero chemistry between her and Joe, so Judd the director took the decision to kill her character off.' Friends fear this may have unhinged the highly strung actress, who was then revealed to have thrown herself at co-star Joe. 'She was drinking pretty heavily,' said a witness. The ageing starlet, 32, is said to be worried that she's losing her looks. 'When a woman begins to feel that she can't hold on to a man, that's got to make you desperate,' commented TV doctor Gillian Toomey, presenter of Channel Nine's *What's Your Problem?*

Rumours have also circulated that Jessica was spotted smoking what appeared to be a marijuana joint on the balcony of her Malibu beach house last Tuesday. LAPD declined to comment over whether they would investigate.

Jessica felt faint as she clicked on the four-page photo montage and timeline – stunning photographs of herself dated a year ago, that became increasingly unflattering as the story went on. 'Unhinged', 'ageing', 'can't hold on to a man'? Even worse, the article was illustrated with a huge long-lens pap shot of Jessica leaving the Primrose Gym on Mulholland, her face puffy and pink. *How the hell did they get that?*

Why hadn't she known about this? Why hadn't *Sylvia* known about this? Mentally she calculated how long she'd been on the island. They had arrived Tuesday – the day *Celeb* magazine hit the news stands.

'Holiday my ass!' she sneered. 'That bitch Sylvia knew all about this.'

She jumped to her feet and stormed through the villa and back to the pool, where she found Sylvia was on the phone. Jessica grabbed the cell from her hand.

'Jess!' squealed Sylvia. 'What the hell?'

'We need to talk. Now,' said Jessica, grabbing her arm and virtually dragging her back inside.

'What the hell's wrong with you?'

'I've just read the *Celeb* magazine story, that's what's wrong with me.'

Sylvia looked out towards the pool, where the whole crew were watching, then closed the patio doors.

'You knew, didn't you?' spat Jessica.

The PR glanced at her, then down at the floor.

'I heard they were running it, yes,' she said. 'I didn't think it would help to tell you about it – looks like I was right.'

'You think you can hide things from me? How dare you?'

'It's just a gossip story; there's no substance to it. All we need to do is keep our heads down . . .'

'Bullshit!' cried Jessica. '*Celeb* has like five million readers. The media are like sheep. One prints "Tragic Jess, she's losing her looks", the others are all going to do it.'

'This will blow over.'

'You said that three weeks ago, and it's only getting worse. Why don't you do something?'

'We have to stick to our strategy, Jess,' said Sylvia firmly.

'Oh yeah? Well it looks to me as if your strategy is to do nothing.'

'I'm doing the best I can, Jessica,' said Sylvia. 'And I'm not sure how much I can help you when you go off-piste, arranging your own long-lens photography. Do you think I am stupid? I know that was you.'

'So now this is my fault?' said Jessica, her eyes wide.

Sylvia sighed. 'Okay, we should both calm down here.'

'There's no "we" any more, Sylvia,' said Jessica, hands on hips. 'You're fired.'

The older woman looked at her in disbelief.

'Jessica, please . . .'

'I said you're fired!' she screamed.

Sylvia looked at her for a moment, then nodded, turned and walked out of the villa. As soon as she had left, Barbara opened the patio doors and stepped through.

'Honey, what's going on?' she asked, her face full of concern. 'Jose told me you were having some almighty screaming match with Sylvia. What's happened?'

'*Celeb* magazine, that's what happened. A four-page photo-montage of my misery.' Jessica began to cry through narrowed eyes. 'This is your doing, isn't it?'

'What the hell are you talking about? I never speak to the media, you know that. Not unless you ask me to.'

'Someone's been talking. How else would they know Joe Kennington turned me down, except from you?'

'I didn't know, honey.'

'You saw him at the house. You know he didn't stay over . . . Admit it, you've been selling stories to the press, haven't you?'

'No!'

'Well explain why all this has only been happening since you moved in, Mother?'

'It's a coincidence,' said Barbara, flustered. 'I swear to you . . .'

Jessica pointed her manicured finger towards the door. 'Take the next flight back to LAX and get out of my house,' she said, her voice trembling in anger.

'Honey, no,' said Barbara, tears beginning to run down her face. 'I'm your mom. You can trust me.'

'From now on, I trust no one. From now on, I'm going to be in charge of my life. Me.'

Jose put his head around the door. His eyes were sparkling and his cheeks were flushed. It was obvious he was loving every moment of the drama.

'Is everything okay in here?' he asked. 'Is just we're ready to shoot again.'

Jess inhaled sharply and looked at her mother.

'Barbara's just going,' she said, ignoring the other woman's sobs and stepping out into the sunshine. 'But I'm ready when you are. And why don't we try a few shots with that blue shirt?'

Jose clapped his hands with delight.

'Oh darling, that's a marvellous idea.'

Jessica went into the pool house they were using as a changing room and slipped out of her clothes. Naked except for her lace thong, she stared at her reflection in the full-length mirror. Long tanned legs, flat stomach, toned arms and the best goddamn tits in the business. Ha! Tragic Jess? Such crap. She had never looked more beautiful in her life.

She pulled on the shirt the stylist had left for her and rolled up the sleeves. The tails just skimmed the top of her thighs and, at the back, gave just a hint of her ass. She had to admit, that dorky guy Daniel was right: she did look pretty hot.

'Oh honey!' purred Jose as she stepped out. 'You look soooo beautiful.'

He came over and positioned her next to the pool, before stepping back to fire off some shots. 'Give me more tiger, baby.' He bent to check the shots on his laptop. 'Wow, you're sensational, Jessie.'

Jessica looked across at Daniel and fingered the material of the shirt.

'But is it sexy enough?'

'Oh yeah.' Daniel blushed, unable to take his eyes from her. 'You look great.'

'Only great?' she said. 'I think we can do a little better than that, don't you?' She reached up and, one by one, undid the shirt buttons.

As Jose carried on shooting, Jessica shrugged the shirt off one shoulder, flashing her golden flesh at the camera. She felt sexy, liberated. For once, she was in control, and that was all that mattered.

'How about a little more?' she laughed, turning away from the camera and letting the shirt slip from her arms and on to the floor.

'That's it!' said Jose. 'Give it to me, baby!'

She crossed her arms across her chest and looked back at the camera with a toss of her hair and a mischievous smile that said 'Come and get me.'

Tragic Jess? she thought, laughing. This would be the hottest, sexiest shoot of the decade. No one would be pitying her now.

41

'Pow, gotcha! Pow! Argh no, you're dead, you're dead. Haha!'

Matt groaned and threw down the video game handset in disgust.

'You're too good for me, Jonas,' he said, genuinely embarrassed at how easily his son had beaten him.

'Well if you come round more often, you can practise,' laughed Jonas. 'So long as you remember that I am still the king!' he added, leaping in the air and landing on Matt's back.

'Oh yeah?' chuckled Matt, wrestling the boy to the ground. Gosh, he was getting big. Matt remembered the days when rough-and-tumble tussles like this had been a daily occurrence. He would lift Jonas in the air and Jonas would pretend he was Superman, squealing, 'Higher, Daddy, higher!' Now it was all Matt could do to wriggle out from beneath him.

'Come on. Bedtime, young man,' said Matthew, ushering Jonas out of the playroom and up the stairs towards his room, a shrine to cartoon character Ben 10. Matthew had agreed to babysit in a moment of weakness, but he was glad he had. Initially he had been nervous about it; partly because he'd never been inside what he still thought of as David's house, having always dropped Jonas off at the doorstep, but mainly because he wasn't sure if it was a good idea giving Jonas all these mixed messages. For three years, David had been playing Daddy to his son, and as much as he had hated it, Matthew had been forced to accept the status quo, watching Jonas grow from a distance. But just because David had gone, that didn't mean Matthew would be stepping straight back into his old role. Indeed, Carla was out at some fancy party tonight and could well come home with another substitute daddy for Jonas – and there would be nothing either of them could do about it. Even so, he had loved spending quality time with Jonas in his own home, rather than at some café or playground. It was wonderful to see how he lived.

Matthew bent to tuck Jonas in and kiss him on the forehead, surprised but grateful when he didn't protest. His little boy's face was beginning to take shape; he had his mum's nose and mouth, but he had Matthew's eyes. Matthew liked that.

'I'm glad you've seen our house, Daddy,' said Jonas.

'I'm glad too,' said Matthew quietly.

Jonas's eyes widened in the dark. 'Maybe if David lets Mum keep the house, you could move in, 'cos it's loads bigger than your flat.'

'I like my flat,' he said, trying to laugh off the suggestion. 'But if your mum agrees, I'll be round to visit more often. I can't have you blasting me to death every time, can I? I've got to practise.'

'Good idea.'

His son looked at him more seriously.

'Are you and Mum friends again?' His face, that perfect combination of Matt's and Carla's features, looked hopeful.

'We've always been friends. How can we not be when we have such a brilliant thing in common as you?'

He hated lying to his son, but he knew there was some truth in his words. He and Carla had been getting on much better lately. More importantly, because of their son, there would always be a deep bond, a connection between them.

Jonas's eyes were starting to close.

'I love you, Dad,' he said drowsily.

'I love you too,' Matt replied, enjoying the simple, sweet moment of saying good night to his son in the place that he called home.

He closed his son's bedroom door softly and stood at the top of the stairs, listening to make sure Jonas was asleep. He peered up the stairwell to the second floor and beyond that, a third. This house is huge, he thought, padding towards the master bedroom and peering inside. I'm not being nosy, just interested.

And for Jonas's safety, I need to know where the fire exits are, don't I?

He moved from room to room, past a library, a bathroom with his-and-her wash basins and a dressing room as big as his corner office at the firm. He wasn't surprised that there were no photos of David in any of the rooms he looked in; Carla could be ruthless like that. Once she had moved on, she moved on. But there were reminders of the ex-master of the house everywhere. The study with his captain's chair and golfing memorabilia, the weights machine and the muddy green wellingtons by the back door. Even though David had gone, Matthew still felt as if he was intruding in a stranger's home – which he supposed he was.

He moved downstairs, to the basement and the gym, the laundry and the media room. His son had been living the life of luxury, he thought with bittersweet emotions, looking at the rows of velour seats in front of the cinema screen.

He walked over to the popcorn machine and turned it on. It hummed to life. He watched mesmerised as the kernels bounced along the bottom of the steel base, then began to pop like machine-gun fire, the glass drum filling with pale golden bubbles of corn.

'Waste not, want not,' he mumbled to himself, scooping the popcorn into a stripy red carton, then went over to the racks of DVDs and looked for something to watch, running his fingertip along the thin spines. Most were cartoons or children's movies, with a few mainstream action films thrown in, certainly nothing Matthew hadn't already seen. To one side were a group of boxes with neatly handwritten titles: exotic place names or occasions that had no meaning to him. Christmas – Barbados. Isabel's 40th, Cap Ferrat. The Hamptons – Jake's House.

'Who's Jake?' he wondered aloud, cracking open the case and putting the disc in the machine. The huge screen immediately came to life, footage of a blue ocean and creamy white sand, a much smaller Jonas running away from the camera, then stopping and waving, before disappearing behind a palm tree. Then a jump-cut to a new scene: David walking along a wooden pier, his arm around Carla; she wearing a poppy-red dress, he wearing a straw hat. Tinny laughter, shaky footage, the sign of an amateur home video.

'I'm not sure you should be watching those.' Matthew turned, startled, sending popcorn all over the floor.

'Bugger,' he muttered, grabbing the remote and punching the eject button. 'I thought I'd watch a movie,' he said, trying to scrape up the spilled popcorn. 'Wondered what Hamptons – Jake's House was. Don't get to the cinema much . . .' He cursed himself for getting caught out like this, but in the low light he could see a smile curling at the edges of Carla's glossy lips.

'You're early,' he quipped guiltily.

'I was tired. Or bored. Maybe both. How was Jonas?'

'We had a great time. You should have stayed here. Tiring and yet never boring.'

'I won't hear the last of it tomorrow.'

He stood up, suddenly feeling uncomfortable in the media room.

'Excellent popcorn machine.'

'Amazing what money can buy you.'

'I'm sorry for being nosy,' he said finally.

'I'd have done the same.'

'I doubt it. I've got no media room. A thirty-two-inch telly and some Sly Stallone DVDs, that's all you'll find at my place.'

'Don't give me the sob story. You're senior partner of Donovan Pierce now, you can afford the trimmings.'

She unbuttoned her coat and slipped it off, revealing a pale pink slip dress, silky, slim-cut and short, showing off her long, tanned legs to perfection. He tried hard not to stare too hard; then again, he defied any man to be able to tear their eyes away from Carla when she looked this good.

'So why was the party dull?'

'Everyone asking me about David, pulling faces like someone had died.'

She was drunk, he could hear it in her slightly slurred words and see it in her glassy eyes. He felt a pang of sympathy for his ex-wife. He knew how much she would have hated that: being pitied in some Knightsbridge society salon. She'd have knocked back the champagne to forget about it and then made her excuses as soon as it was polite to leave.

'Do you want me to make you a coffee?' he asked.

'That obvious, is it?' she said with a crooked grin. 'I'll do it, there's an espresso machine just over here.' She pressed the side of a cabinet and it popped open to reveal a bar. 'Open sesame,' she said. 'Just like magic.'

She perched on the back of one of the velour chairs beside him.

'Well I'm sure you won't be single for long,' said Matt, trying to make her feel better. He quite enjoyed having a pleasant conversation with his wife; being friends, as Jonas had rightly put it. It was a change from the years of bitter snipes and exchanges that invariably came when a marriage had gone sour.

'I think you're wrong,' she said matter-of-factly. 'Good men get snapped up so quickly. Women are ruthless. A whiff that a marriage is in trouble and they hover, console, move in before the divorce lawyers have been called in half the time.'

'I never had that.'

'Good,' she said softly.

Their eyes locked and he had to look away.

'I'm not sure how well I'd have taken it if you'd got married again,' she added as the coffee machine gurgled in the background.

Matt smiled to defuse the tension that was building in the confines of the dark room.

'Well, I'd like to think I'm not on love's scrapheap quite yet.'

'So you're looking?' She turned to face him.

'I never said that.'

She gave a little laugh, shaking her head gently. 'Why am I jealous?'

The pace of his heart quickened. 'We were married. It's only natural.'

There was a long silence. Matt knew it was time to leave, but he couldn't tear himself away from his spot beside her. He could sense she had something to tell him, and curiosity, ego, his pride that had been so bruised when she had betrayed him made him want to hear it.

315

'I was wrong to leave you,' she whispered finally.

When the words came, he could think of nothing in response.

She lifted her hand and brushed the back of her fingers across his cheek. He reached up to stop them, but as his hand gripped hers, the cool softness of her skin made something in his stomach flutter.

'Don't,' he said, feeling the situation galloping out of control.

'Why not?'

She stood up and stepped towards him. In her high heels they were almost face to face. At this distance he could see the tiny vein beneath her eye trembling like it did when she was nervous. He could smell the light scent of expensive wine and lipstick inhabiting the air space between them. Her mouth was inches away from his, her lips parted, waiting.

He couldn't think of a single reason why he shouldn't kiss her. Then again, logic always did fly out of the window when he was faced by the most beautiful woman he had ever seen.

His hand cupped the soft, silky curve of her waist, slowly, carefully, pulling her towards him, and he kissed her on the mouth, on the soft fold of her ear lobe, on her long, smooth neck. He had forgotten how sweet she tasted; and yet the smell and taste of her were so familiar, it was as if the three years since any physical contact had contracted into nothingness.

'I've missed you,' she whispered, responding to his touch.

His hand brushed the thin spaghetti straps of her dress off her shoulders, one and then the other, so that the flimsy fabric slid down over her slim body and rustled to the floor.

She was naked except for her thong and heels. He stole a glance, wondering if she had ever looked so forbidden and exotic, then held her waist as she arched her back, teasing each ripened nipple between his lips as she gasped in pleasure.

His own arousal was unbearable. With his free hand he unbuckled his belt and slid down the zip of his trousers. Carla drew herself up, her lean, Pilates-honed torso as strong and elegant as a ballet dancer's.

'Jonas,' he muttered as her fingers unfastened his shirt buttons. 'He'll hear us.'

'Media room. Soundproofed,' she said, raking her fingernails across his chest.

Their kisses were more urgent now. They stumbled back on to a two-seater sofa at the back of the room, the soles of her shoes crunching stray balls of popcorn underfoot. Matt kicked off his trousers and boxer shorts.

Carla lay back, propped up by some expensive-looking cushions, and parted her thighs, and he slotted his body between them, a perfect fit, as if they were made for each other. Her fingers pushed the wisp of thong to one side, and he guided himself inside her, slowly at first, but as she hooked one leg around him, he pushed deeper, groaning as they moved as one, in, out, *together*.

Somewhere in the back of his consciousness, he couldn't remember married sex ever being this good. Nor could he reconcile the brittle, frosty ex-wife with this hot, responsive woman. When she came, he felt her whole body tremble. Then he felt it too, white-hot electric desire pushing him closer and closer to the edge, and then a sweet release deep inside her.

They lay motionless for a few moments, listening to the sound of their breathing slowing, regulating, and then he pulled himself out of her.

'Not bad for a pair of thirty-something parents,' he smiled, collapsing back on to the opposite end of the sofa.

'I need another drink,' she said, laughing.

He said nothing.

The silence vibrated between them, and then she touched her fingers against his, as if willing him to say something.

'I should go,' he said quietly, putting his palm over the top of her hand.

She slid it out, her body pulling away from him.

'I didn't think that was your style,' she sniffed.

He felt a stab of guilt for all the other one-night stands he'd had over the last three years. The post-coital excuses he had made to other women he knew he could not commit to. But this was different.

'What do you suggest, Carla?' he said quietly. 'That I stay the night? That Jonas wakes up in the morning and sees us there, together in bed, as if the last three years hasn't even happened?'

'I'd prefer that to you getting up and walking out of the door the second after you've come inside me.'

He inhaled sharply, then looked at her.

'I'm sorry. I just didn't expect this.'

Her face softened.

'Me neither.' She pulled her knees up to her chest and rested her chin on top of them.

His son's words reverberated around Matt's head: *Are you and Mum friends again?* He owed her more than this.

'Maybe we should go out for dinner,' he said without thinking.

'We go to Ibiza tomorrow. But we could do something when we get back. The time, the space might do us good. Give us time to think.'

She tipped her head to one side, her blond hair cascading over her bare shoulder, and smiled so adorably that he felt himself start to get hard again.

He nodded his approval.

'You don't regret what we just did?' she said softly.

'That was the best sex since . . . since you,' he said truthfully. In fact it had been incredible, and that was what scared him.

42

'Darling, I could have told you he was a coke fiend. You didn't have to send me to St Tropez with a camcorder down my knickers to find that out.'

Sheryl Battenburg rested her chin in the curve of her palm and smiled at Larry. He was fairly sure that if they hadn't been in the rarefied environs of the Beaumont Bar at the Savoy, she would have come over and sat on his knee.

'Well, pictures were what I needed, Sherry, not rumours.' He smiled as the waitress brought his old friend a flute of Krug. It was one of the few places in London that did it by the glass; he didn't want to waste a bottle when he wasn't even drinking it.

It had only taken Larry a few phone calls to find someone who was going to Fabio Martelli's birthday party, held on a yacht and at the Nikki Beach Club in St Tropez. Sherry was an old-school Chelsea good-time girl with bleached blond hair and a deep tan. She and Larry had indulged in a short-lived affair between wives two and three. Now pushing forty, she had never married and Larry had no idea what she did for a living, other than attend parties and launches. He didn't think to ask where the money was coming from.

He looked down at his iPhone and scrolled through the photographs that Sheryl had sent him from the yacht party, stopping at a shot of a redhead lounging on the deck dressed in just a micro-bikini.

'Looks like it was fun,' he grinned.

'I hope they are okay. I know you said you wanted something really fruity, and there were obviously people having sex all over

319

the shop, but I could hardly go into the cabins and get piccies of them at it, could I?'

Larry nodded. He'd known that even someone as connected as Sheryl might have trouble getting snaps of Fabio actually taking drugs or in the act with someone other than Kim Collier, so he'd asked her to take pictures of people who were obviously part of Fabio's party. And as he scrolled through the photos, he had to say she'd done the job magnificently. She had managed to snap shots of Fabio draped over a variety of beautiful women in next to nothing; she'd even caught him evidently in conference with some burly men dressed in expensive loungewear and chunky jewellery. It was better than he could have hoped.

'Have you ever thought about going into spying?' he said with a chuckle. The single-mindedness and world-class schmoozing that had allowed Sheryl access to the highest strata of society were perfect transferable skills, should she choose to enter the field of espionage.

'Sorry the quality isn't that brilliant,' she said, leaning forward to peek at the photos – and give Larry a flash of cleavage.

'Don't worry, sweetheart,' said Larry. 'I'm not looking for David Bailey, just something to give me a bit of leverage.'

'This is nothing illegal, is it?' she said, looking at him earnestly.

He slipped his phone back into his pocket.

'How can you suggest such a thing, Sheryl?' he said with mock-outrage. 'I'm a well-respected lawyer.'

'You're a shark, Larry. If you weren't one of my oldest friends, I wouldn't trust you further than I can throw you.'

'Well you can rest assured that you've done a good thing here,' he said, leaning back in his banquette and scratching his stomach in a satisfied way. 'A father is going to keep his son because of this.'

'Oh, Larry, I always knew you were a big softie underneath it all,' she cooed.

Larry laughed. He wasn't entirely sure why it hadn't worked out with Sheryl while Loralee had managed to drag him to the altar. The more he experienced life and love, the more he was convinced that relationships were a matter of timing. True, Loralee was younger, and more beautiful, but if he was honest, Sheryl was more his type of woman: slightly worn around the edges perhaps, but fun and clever and wise in her own way. It was just that Loralee had been there at the moment that Larry had decided to settle down again.

'So. Are you going to take me shopping?' asked Sheryl as Larry waved for the bill. 'After all, it was a very, very big favour you asked of me.'

He looked at the two-carat diamond studs she was wearing; if he wasn't very much mistaken, those were the earrings he had bought her during their affair.

'I think we can safely say that you can expect a very nice Christmas present,' laughed Larry. 'But a married man taking another woman shopping might be interpreted the wrong way.'

'You've changed, Larry Donovan,' she grinned.

'I'm trying,' he said honestly. 'I really am.'

'Well don't try too hard,' said Sheryl. 'I quite liked that old rogue you used to be. How is the latest Mrs Donovan, by the way?'

'Fine. Beautifying herself at the Chelsea Day Sanctuary today.'

'Really? I thought that was closed for refurbishment.'

'Oh well, some spa in Chelsea,' he said, waving his hand dismissively as they got up to leave. 'Anyway, how's your love life?'

'I only have eyes for you, lover,' she giggled.

Larry gave Sheryl a sidelong glance, wondering at her true age. Was she too old for Matthew? He could certainly do a lot worse, Larry thought, feeling a sudden pang of affection for her.

He hurried through the foyer and out towards the cab rank. No matter how fond he was of Sheryl, he really didn't want to be seen loitering in a hotel lobby with a notorious party girl, especially after the task he'd set her.

'Find a nice fellow.' He smiled, kissing her on the cheek to say goodbye. 'I do want you to be happy, you know.'

'That's always been the trouble with men like you, Larry,' she said, jumping into a taxi. She wound down the window and winked at him. 'You all think we need a man to make us happy. It never crosses your mind that we're perfectly fine on our own.'

43

Dear Anna,

I just wanted to say how much I am going to miss you at Sophie's wedding. Of course, I understand your reasons for not wanting to be there. I can't begin to think how hurt you must have been by what she did and I'll always regret not being there for you more after it happened. For a soldier, I didn't handle it very well, did I? Burying my head in the sand wishing it hadn't happened and hoping that things would just get back to normal.

For the record, your mother and I were so angry and disappointed with Sophie for doing what she did to you. Maybe you needed to hear that sooner, but the conflict between you and Sophie has been hard for us. We are Sophie's parents too, and however much we disapprove of what she did, we still have to keep on loving her. I hope that one day you will forgive her too.

I know it will happen because you are the most big-hearted woman I've ever met. I know it because you are the smartest, shrewdest, most compassionate daughter a man could wish for. I've always been so proud of you, Anna. The clever, enquiring little girl you were. The strong, capable woman you've become. The incredible wife and mother I know you will one day be.

You're a wonderful sister, and I'm sure Sophie wants to tell you that herself too. If you are open to that opportunity, you should know that Mum has arranged a hen-party dinner at the Savoy next Thursday from seven o'clock, with dancing at some nightclub later on. No pressure at all, I just wanted you to know, because everybody would love to see you there. We're a family, Anna. We miss you and it doesn't feel right without you.

Anyway, I've said my piece. I completely understand how difficult this is for you, and I will respect your decision whatever you choose to do.

Love always, Dad

It was the fifth time she had read her father's email. For the last ten minutes she had been staring at it, hoping that the more she looked at it, the easier it would be to find the words to reply.

But here she was, the media lawyer, the voracious reader, the first-class communicator – or so the Legal 500 had once described her – struggling to work out what she felt, let alone what to write.

She wished she had a glass of wine or a cigarette. Wished she did not have to deal with this right now. Wished that this whole situation had not made her so bitter and angry, because she knew that before Sophie and Andrew had betrayed her, she was a different person, a better, nicer, happier one. She hated feeling like this, and hated making her father feel like this.

Her hand hovered over the Delete key, then she changed tack and pressed Reply. 'Thanks for the note, Dad, sorry I can't make it, have to go to Edinburgh Festival, speak soon. Ax,' she typed quickly, stabbing the Send key before she had time to think about it any more.

Anna knew her dad wouldn't try and contact her again about it. He was a quiet, wise man, respectful of other people's feelings, and he knew when to bow out. Living all those years with her mother had taught him that.

But as she turned away from her computer, she pictured him sitting in his kitchen office reading it, shaking his head with disappointment, and felt a flood of guilt and shame. Her breath quickened as hot tears collected and pricked the back of her eyes. Through the glass window of her office she could see Matt Donovan glancing over as if he wanted to speak to her. There was no way she was going to let him see her cry. She stumbled up from behind her desk and raced to the ladies', ducking into a toilet cubicle and closing the door. She pulled the seat down and sat on it, pushing her thumbs on to her eyelids to stave off emotion.

Outside the stall, she could hear the click-clack of court shoes entering the bathroom. Someone was talking; a one-way conversation as if they were on the phone. The voice was low, but she recognised it immediately: Sid Travers, her trainee.

'Look,' said Sid, 'I know they've fired me, but it still doesn't make it right doing it. I feel dreadful.'

There was a long pause, whilst Sid evidently listened to her caller.

'But I need the money.'

Anna's ears pricked up. *Money?*

A pause, then Sid continued: 'No, she doesn't know, of course she doesn't. She would go absolutely mad.'

The pitch of her voice rose with aggravation.

'Because I should have come clean but I didn't, did I?' she hissed. 'And now, after everything that's happened, now they'll never understand it and hate me for being a liar.'

Anna grimaced. The one-sided conversation made it impossible for her to know what Sid was talking about, but she had a slow, sinking feeling about what it could be. She recalled her conversation with Blake Stanhope, when he had said, 'Have you ever considered that the leak came from your end?'

Sid had definitely known about the injunction and about Sam's infidelity. They had openly discussed it in meetings with Helen in the boardroom. And something else too: Katie Grey's mobile phone photograph of her and Sam in bed had been sent to Anna's computer terminal. How hard would it have been for Sid to make a copy?

She strained her ears again. Sid seemed to be winding up her telephone call.

'All right, I'll come,' she said. 'But I don't know what I'm going to say to get out of work.'

The heels clicked back out. Anna shook her head in disbelief. Could it really have been Sid who had leaked the Sam Charles story to the press? And if so, then who the hell was she just talking to? The person who had paid her to do it?

325

She left the bathroom in time to see Sid disappear into the kitchen to make a coffee. Returning quickly to her office, she busied herself behind her desk as if she had never left.

A few minutes later, Sid appeared at the door with two drinks.

'Coffee?' she said, holding up a mug.

'Thanks,' said Anna, as breezily as she could.

Sid stepped into the office and placed the coffee on the desk.

'Listen, Anna, I need a big favour.'

Anna raised her eyebrows.

'Go on.'

'I have to go in twenty minutes. Is that a problem?'

'Well it's not great, Sid,' she said looking at her watch. 'It's not even three thirty. You know how busy we are with the trial. What is it?'

The trainee dropped her head. 'It's important.'

In normal circumstances Anna would have given her a hard time about it, perhaps even refused to let her go unless she had a very good excuse, but today wasn't normal. If there was any chance of finding out who was behind the leak, she'd have to let her leave. Still, she had to make it convincing.

'Fine, go if you must,' she said. 'You can make the hours up tomorrow night. That's if nothing "important" is going to happen then.' She felt a bitch, but she was angry.

'No,' said Sid gratefully. 'Thanks, Anna.'

Anna watched Sid pick up her bag and quickly leave the office. Whoever had called her was obviously in a hurry. As soon as she was out of the door, Anna grabbed her own bag and followed. As she came out of the revolving doors on to the street, she could already see Sid leaving Broadwick Street, heading into Soho.

Where was she going? Anna gave chase, keeping a decent gap between them in case Sid should turn around and see her. The Friday-afternoon commuter rush was building as they crossed Shaftesbury Avenue into Chinatown, but Sid's russet hair made her easy to spot in a crowd. Finally she disappeared into Leicester Square tube station. Anna walked cautiously down the stairs – she didn't want to run into her in the ticket hall – but Sid was already through the barriers, heading for the Northern Line. Anna prided herself on her intuition, and she had always known there was something wrong with Sid. Her work was good, excellent at times, but she didn't seem to have the dedication of the other trainees, lacked their willingness to work through the night on a case if necessary and never socialised or schmoozed. Which probably explained why she had been told they wouldn't be renewing her contract. Donovan Pierce was a firm made in the image of Helen and Larry and if you weren't prepared to match their twenty-four-hour commitment to the job, you were never going to climb the ladder there.

A train was just pulling in to the platform with a rush of air, and Anna saw Sid jump into a carriage towards the front. Anna took a seat at the end of the next carriage, just far enough to be out of sight, but close enough that she would see when Sid got off. She had to wait several stops. At Clapham South, she followed Sid up the escalator and out on to the busy crossroads. She had to trot to keep up – she couldn't lose her now. Crossing into a maze of residential streets, Sid turned on to a quiet road made up of Victorian terraces with tiny front gardens. To Anna's surprise, she turned and walked up to an ordinary front door and disappeared inside. Who the hell was she meeting in there?

Anna watched the house from the other side of the road. This is ridiculous, she told herself. Go and confront her.

Hesitantly she walked up to the door, but before she could knock, she heard raised voices inside. They were muffled, but she could hear the words 'selfish' and 'money': tempers were frayed. Suddenly the door flew open and a middle-aged woman came out, pulling on a cardigan. Seeing Anna, she stopped in her tracks.

'Is Sid there?' asked Anna quickly.

The woman looked over her shoulder.

'Sid. Here.' Her voice was slow, cautious.

Sid appeared in the corridor. Anna could barely see her, her eyes finding it hard to adjust from the outside light, but as she focused, she could see that her trainee was holding a small child.

'I have to go,' said the middle-aged woman, hurrying off.

Anna and Sid just looked at each other.

'Want another coffee?' said Sid finally. 'I don't suppose you drank much of the last one I made you.'

Anna closed the door and the child, a boy she noted, started crying. She followed Sid into the kitchen. Sid put the child down on a colourful mat strewn with toys, where he began to play happily.

'So now you know I have a son,' she said crisply.

'I didn't want to pry,' said Anna guiltily.

Sid looked unconvinced.

'Don't worry. I've been expecting this for months. And you know what? I actually feel relieved. It's been hard living a lie for so long. I had to keep going for Charlie,' she said, indicating the toddler.

Anna nodded, unable to think what to say. All the time she'd been following Sid, she'd been rehearsing a speech about loyalty and commitment and how she felt let down. But now she saw just how horribly wrong she'd been about the girl.

'Helen's not going to like it,' she said with a wry smile.

Sid laughed. 'Who cares what Helen thinks? I've only got two weeks left at the place anyway. The problem is I haven't found another job yet, and if this gets out . . . I might find it more difficult than I am already. Single mums aren't exactly top of corporate recruiters' lists, are they?'

Anna wondered if she had any sway at the firm. Maybe Matt Donovan might be receptive to finding Sid more work. After all, she'd heard he had a child of his own.

'That was my mum who just left,' added Sid. 'I still live with my folks and Mum looks after Charlie while I'm at work. She's brilliant, but sometimes she gets frustrated with it all, like today, when she's got other stuff to do . . .'

'I heard you on the phone at work. That's why I followed you. I wondered what was going on.'

'Why, what did you think it was?'

'I don't know,' said Anna quickly.

'Come on, you followed me for some reason,' Sid chided.

Anna felt on the spot.

'I heard you talking about needing money . . .'

Sid laughed. 'Thought I was selling secrets to the *Sun*, did you?

'Something like that.'

'Still pissed off about the Sam Charles injunction?'

'It's not a question of being pissed off, Sid, it's about finding out what went wrong.'

'Let it go, Anna,' said Sid passionately. 'People have stopped talking about it, the work is piling in for you, and I know you're speaking to Sam because he phoned the office for you the other day. Oh shit, I forgot to pass the message on . . .'

Anna laughed off her embarrassment. Sam had been ringing her every couple of days; checking in, he called it, but there was something about their contact that felt illicit.

She looked over at Charlie.

'He's beautiful, Sid,' she said, feeling a warm glow that surprised her.

'I know.' Sid grinned.

'Is his dad in the picture?' she asked as diplomatically as she could.

Sid shook her head.

'I got pregnant at law school. Max, Charlie's father, was a student at LSE. American, rich. Not sure what he saw in me.' She smiled. 'We decided to keep it, we were going to get married, set up home, all that romantic crap. He was going to live off his trust fund and look after the baby while I did my training contract.'

'So what happened?'

She gave a cold laugh.

'Have a guess. That bohemian romantic ideal lasted for about a nanosecond, until his parents heard about it and went bananas. He left me a note and buggered off back to America the second he graduated.' She shrugged. 'It was too late for an abortion. His family offered me a thousand dollars a month maintenance, but I told them to stuff it. They've never even met their grandson.'

'But I don't understand how you've kept it hidden all this time.'

'My closest friends at law college knew,' said Sid, 'but I didn't tell anyone else. I only started showing at six and a half months, and by then everyone was too wrapped up in their final exams to notice I'd got a bit porky.'

'Didn't you think people would find out?'

Sid raised an eyebrow.

'I'd landed the Donovan Pierce job before I got pregnant, and when Charlie was born at thirty-four weeks I realised that I could start work in the September after law school finished as planned. I wanted to qualify as quickly as possible and start earning some decent money so I could make a life for us. On the first day I joined the firm, I went to see Helen Pierce, ready to tell her I had a four-week-old baby, but I just couldn't. And the longer I left it, the more impossible it became to say anything.'

'But Sid, you should have. Instead, people think you're not committed to the job, when you've just got other commitments.'

'Wouldn't have washed though, would it, Anna? You must know how hard it is. How few women make partner. Are you telling me it's because men are better at their jobs than women? I don't think so.'

Anna felt both sad and relieved. Thankful that Sid had not been the source of the leaked Sam Charles story; yet depressed that this smart young woman had been booted from the firm for being twice as strong and resourceful as the other trainees.

Her phone was ringing. Helen Pierce would be back from court, wondering where her associate was. How was she going to explain that she was in the depths of south London?

'Can I just take this?' she whispered to Sid, walking into the next room. She was surprised to hear not Helen's voice but Phil Berry's.

'It looks like Ruby Hart was right,' he said without preamble. 'Louise Allerton left her job at *Class* magazine for no apparent reason three days after Amy died. As far as her old boss knew, she didn't have another job to go to, and actually he was very surprised she resigned because she'd just got a promotion to beauty editor. She seemed to be loving her job.'

'Any reason why she went?'

'I tracked down her mother, but she wasn't exactly

forthcoming. Claimed she didn't have a clue where her daughter was.'

'So she could be anywhere?' said Anna disappointedly.

'Not quite. Turns out Mum was lying through her teeth. She wired money to a bank in Alappuzha, Kerala, a month ago.'

Anna knew better than to ask him how he found this stuff out.

'Kerala? Is that India?'

'The southern tip. I phoned round all the hotels, hostels, backpacker places. A place called the Sea View Hotel says she checked in late January.'

'And is she still at the Sea View?'

'No,' said Phil. 'She stayed a month, then left.'

'And we've got no mobile phone number for her, no Facebook page, even?'

'No, she's lying low, this one.'

I wonder why, thought Anna. She was already convinced that this girl knew something about Amy Hart's death.

'So what now?' This couldn't be the end of the line. It just couldn't be.

'To be honest, Anna, it's difficult to do much more without going to India, but I don't know how much your client wants to find this out. How much he's willing to pay.'

'The client's got money,' said Anna slowly. 'I just need to find out if he's prepared to spend it.'

Sam had invited her to see him in Edinburgh. She would feel too much like a groupie if she just turned up, but now there was a reason.

She would go to him. She had to go to him.

44

Sam glanced at his vintage Patek Philippe wristwatch, willing it to run slower. Only two minutes to go until showtime. One fifty-nine. One fifty-eight . . .

He looked over at Mike, standing in the cool, dark wings of the Hummingbird, the peeling old comedy venue on Edinburgh's Cowgate. Surely Mike should be feeling the pressure? It was seven years since he had performed anywhere other than the Oban pub, and yet he seemed completely calm, serene even.

Sam crept forward, peeking into the theatre at the packed audience, already buzzing from a foul-mouthed Glaswegian warm-up who'd got his biggest laugh by hitting himself in the face with a rubber brick. God, there were hundreds of them. He realised that this was infinitely more nerve-racking than the time he had presented a gong at the Oscars ceremony. Three billion people had watched him read the autocue at LA's Kodak Theater, and right now there were fewer than three hundred waiting patiently for the ten o'clock headline act.

Back in London, when they'd been scripting the show, it had felt exhilarating. But right here, right now, with the second hand sweeping mercilessly round, he wasn't at all sure, especially as absolutely nobody in the audience was here to see Sam Charles. They'd billed it as 'Mike McKenzie: Back, Back, Back', a one-night-only appearance of the fallen comedy genius, and it had been the talk of the festival. Even without being listed in the programme – they'd arranged their gig far too late for that – the show had sold out in minutes, and tickets were changing hands on eBay for hundreds of pounds a pop.

But no one except Sam and Mike knew that Sam would be

part of the evening too – that in fact the whole show had been written around him, as a sort of comic satire on the perils of celebrity. Sam had been adamant that they should keep his name off the bill. They wanted the audience to be full of genuine Mike McKenzie fans, rather than press and rubberneckers there to see the notorious Hollywood fuck-up.

'You okay, buddy?' said Mike, clasping Sam's shoulder.

'I'll be honest, Mike, I'm shitting it.'

'But why? This show's the best thing either of us have written.'

'They don't want to see me. They're all here to see you.' Sam was having serious second thoughts.

'You're kidding. You're the hottest movie star in the world.'

'Most notorious movie star,' Sam corrected.

'Whatever,' said Mike. 'Their heads are going to frigging explode when you walk out.'

'Maybe.'

Sam knew that in theory there were a lot of people who would love to see him at close quarters on the stage; over the years he'd been inundated with requests to appear in the West End, where a major movie star in the cast could treble ticket sales. But comedy crowds were more demanding, unforgiving. Especially drunk comedy crowds, he thought as he heard them roar. The Hummingbird MC, a curly haired Scouser with a great line in withering put-downs for the hecklers, had stepped on stage.

'It's time for the main event . . .' he began, to delighted hoots and whistles.

Sam could feel his heart pounding. Usually he was surrounded by people reassuring him that he would be fabulous. But his manager, agent, publicist . . . none of them knew about the show. On a whim he had invited Anna Kennedy, but it was no surprise she hadn't turned up. She was his lawyer, an acquaintance more than a friend. Suddenly he felt swamped by loneliness.

'He's been on TV,' said the MC, 'he's been to Wembley, he's even been in the nuthouse . . .' The crowd crackled with excited laughter. 'But tonight, here on stage at the Hummingbird, he's back . . . back . . . BACK!'

Mike bounded on to the stage to a deafening roar. The applause went on and on as he bowed politely, then held his hands up in a faux-modest 'What, me? This is all just for me?' gesture. Finally he took the microphone from the stand.

'Two nuns go into a bar . . .' he said. The crowd were loving it.

Sam looked behind him to the illuminated Exit sign. It wasn't too late to bail out. Mike of all people would understand, wouldn't he?

'First nun says to the other, "What are you having?",' said Mike.

He paused, the audience tittering in anticipation.

'Second nun says, "Sam Charles, if I play my cards right."'

As they'd anticipated, the crowd cracked up. Everyone knew that Sam and Mike were old friends, but to hear him take the piss was exactly what they wanted from the edgy genius. And in that roar of laughter, Sam took a deep breath and stepped out on to the stage. There was an almost audible pause, then the crowd went bananas, yelling his name, stamping their feet – they couldn't believe their luck.

Grinning, his nerves all forgotten, Sam picked up his own mic and said, 'Remind me next time that there's no such thing as no-strings sex . . .'

The cheers from the crowd were still ringing in his ears as Sam ran into the dressing room and shut the door. A can of lager was waiting for him on the plastic counter and he opened it with a hiss, gulping it down greedily. The show had been an absolute triumph. From his first line, Sam had felt the crowd were in the palm of his hand. The jokes and routines they had written were pitched perfectly for this audience. They loved Mike's anecdotes about bumping into an eighties pop star in rehab and singing a duet together, despite the fact that they were both heavily sedated. They lapped up Sam's account of being trapped in a lift at the Chateau Marmont for an hour with Batman, Spiderman and the Incredible Hulk. And they clearly appreciated the effortless comic timing of two men who had been bursting each other's egos since they were unknown teenagers. Sam couldn't remember when he had felt so alive. It was partly the warmth and affection he felt from the crowd; after the endless outraged 'Sam Charles Is Cheating Scum' headlines, he'd convinced himself that he'd so pissed off Joe Public that his career – any career – was over, but now he felt them willing him on, a surge of goodwill perhaps born of the fact that they appreciated the huge risk he was taking. More than that, however, he was ecstatic at the reaction to his writing. They had been genuinely laughing. Yes, Mike's comic delivery added a strong following wind, but it had been his jokes that had started the chuckles. And that was a revelation to him. Maybe there was life beyond LA after all.

'Well, I think they liked that.'

He could see the reflection of his visitor in the illuminated mirror in front of him. Anna Kennedy was standing in the door frame, her arms crossed, a smile on her face.

'Anna!' he cried, turning around to embrace her like a long-lost friend.

'You're . . . choking . . . me,' she moaned before he released her from the bear hug.

'What are you doing here anyway?' he asked.

'You invited me, remember?' she said, looking a little embarrassed.

'Yes, yes, but I didn't think you'd come.'

'Well someone had to watch over you. You know what usually happens when you get in front of a crowd.'

'I'll have you know that the assault and battery charges against the photographer have been dropped.' He grinned.

'Does that mean I can't charge you for danger money any more?'

He laughed and motioned to a rickety stool. 'Sit down. Beer?'

She waved her hand. 'All yours. You deserve it.'

He watched her face, looking for traces of pity or sympathy, but she seemed genuinely excited. Even so, there was something reserved, impenetrable about Anna Kennedy; he never could quite work out what she was thinking. Handy for a lawyer, he supposed.

'So. What did you think?'

'Honestly Sam, you were brilliant. Both of you. And I'm not the kind of girl who gives compliments willy-nilly.'

'And it was funny?'

'Bloody funny. Smart, self-deprecating . . . I bet Eli and Jim are on the phone right now setting up Madison Square Garden and Caesar's Palace.'

Sam took a pull of his beer and grimaced.

'Actually they're not. They don't know I've done this.'

'You're kidding me! I thought you were joking when you said you weren't going to tell anyone.'

He shook his head.

'They'd have put me off doing it. Or even worse, turned it into a circus.'

'Hey, it *is* a circus out there, a total scrum.'

'So it was good?'

She chuckled. She had a lovely laugh. Knowing, tinkling, genuine.

'Sam, I'm not here to massage your ego,' she said. 'I think you've got enough people to do that already.'

Suddenly the door burst open and in stumbled Mike McKenzie, wide-eyed happiness oozing from every pore. 'We did it!' he cried, flinging his arms around Sam and spinning him around, laughing. 'You clever, clever bastard! I could never have done anything like this on my own. We fucking rocked out there!'

'No, you rocked,' insisted Sam. 'They all came to see you, after all.'

'But it was you they loved, you daft pillock,' said Mike.

Finally he noticed that Anna was in the room. 'Oh, sorry, not interrupting anything, am I?' he said, extending his hand with a playful smile.

'This is my lawyer, Anna.'

'Dammit,' joked Mike. 'I thought we'd got our first groupie.'

'I'm sure there's plenty to go round. They were practically drooling,' replied Anna.

'Excellent news,' boomed Mike, turning to Sam. 'You back off, pretty boy. I get first pick of the scrubbers, okay?'

Sam laughed. 'How about we get out of here and find a drink?'

'It's a bit mental out front,' said Anna. 'Is there a back way?'

Sam put his hand lightly on the back of Anna's shoulders and led her through the corridors towards the stage door. Already they could hear a rabble in the street behind the theatre. 'Mike! Sam!' came the chant. 'Mike! Sam!'

Anna turned to Sam, her face half frightened, half excited. 'What do we do now?'

Sam slipped his hand into hers, enjoying the feel of her smooth palm. 'When I say run, put your head down and leg it, okay?'

'Just like the old days, eh?' laughed Mike, flinging open the metal door and charging out, arms outstretched like some cult leader meeting his followers. He was immediately swamped by bodies patting him on the back, thrusting programmes at him to sign, holding up mobile phones to get a snap. For a moment Sam thought they had managed to hide in Mike's shadow, but suddenly the night was lit up by flashbulbs, hands were grabbing at his clothes, people were screaming his name. He'd been through this before, of course, only a matter of months ago, even if it seemed like a lifetime. But this was different. In Hollywood, he had been like some exotic creature paraded in front of the fans, something fantastic and unreal. Here the fans weren't just here to worship at the altar of celebrity; they wanted to speak to him, to make a connection, tell him how much they had enjoyed what he did. It was a completely different energy: supportive, encouraging, a sense of a shared experience. Sam wanted to cry with happiness.

'You go on, meet your public,' whispered Anna into his ear. 'I'll get a taxi.'

Sam looked around for her, but he was surrounded. Grinning, he took the proffered pens and began scribbling dedications, posing for pictures.

Then, above the hubbub, he heard a loud whistle and turned. Anna and Mike were standing next to a black cab, waving their arms.

'Come on, you twonk!' shouted Mike. 'I think we all need some booze.'

Muttering apologies to the fans, Sam dashed across the road

and jumped inside, laughing. Anna slammed the door as the cabby pulled away at speed.

'Well how about we head on down to the Midnight Mash?' said Mike, pulling a flyer from his back pocket.

'What's that?' asked Anna.

'"Irreverent humour in a crypt",' read Mike in a Christopher Lee-style baritone. 'Probably wall-to-wall goth birds mad for some comedy celebrity lovin'.'

Sam glanced over at Anna nervously.

'I should probably lie low, to be honest,' he said. 'Don't want to undo all the good work we put in tonight.'

'I don't know how you live like this,' said Mike, whistling between his teeth. 'Come on, I've been living on an island for seven years. The ladies have been pining for me. I can't let them down.'

Sam laughed.

'I would love to be your wingman tonight, but I'm in enough trouble as it is. I'm just waiting for my agent to call me and ask why I've gone rogue.'

'Come on, Anna,' whined Mike. 'Tell him he needs to come to the crypt.'

Anna pulled a face. 'I agree with Sam. "Hollywood Heart-throb in Vampire Sex Orgy" on the front of *News of the World* might be slightly counterproductive at this stage.'

'Right then, you pair of old fogeys,' said Mike as they pulled up outside the hotel where Mike and Sam were staying. 'Out you get. Mind you don't break your hips playing Scrabble,' he added, flashing Sam a mischievous grin he hoped Anna missed. Once they were standing on the pavement, Mike turned to the driver and cried, 'To the crypt, my good man! Adventure awaits!'

As the lights of the taxi disappeared around the corner, Sam turned to Anna. 'Do you think he's got his confidence back?' he asked.

'I think he'll do fine,' chuckled Anna as a couple walked past, nudging each other.

'Let's get in,' whispered Sam, feeling conspicuous all of a sudden. 'Do you mind if we go up to my room? The hotel bar will be swamped with tourists.'

'Okay, but behave yourself,' said Anna with a wry smile. 'I've heard all about you.'

They rode up silently, glad that the lift was empty. Anna was his lawyer, of course, so Sam could easily claim she was in his suite for a conference. *A beautiful lawyer, all on her own? Pull the other one, sunshine*, his brain mocked. He glanced at their reflection in the lift's mirror – they did look good together, he decided as the doors hissed open. Outside the Royal Suite, he fumbled with the key card, finally opening the door and letting Anna inside.

Anna cooed for a few moments as she looked around the elegant space. While Sam mixed their drinks, she walked over to the window and looked out at the skyline, the castle just visible towering over a city peppered with light.

'Mike's great, isn't he?' she said, gazing through the glass as if she was looking for him.

Sam surprised himself at how disappointed he felt. 'Oh, I forgot, you were his biggest fan, weren't you?' he said, trying to keep the jealousy out of his voice. He walked across and handed her a tumbler, the ice cubes chinking. 'Should I call him back? He is single, you know.'

She swatted his arm playfully.

'I meant that I liked his work. Not that I fancied him.'

'Don't feel bad. Everyone fancied Mike when we were at college.'

She gave him a sideways look.

'More than they fancied you?' she said sceptically.

He nodded. 'He had that tortured artist thing going. I was the pretty, stuck-up twat from the drama department. That's what one ex-girlfriend told me, anyway.'

She laughed, that tinkling bell of a laugh again. For some reason it made him feel sad, and he took a slug of his whisky. They fell into silence, just watching the humped outline of the capital, a sleeping giant.

'You know, in some ways, I feel like I've come full circle.'

'How do you mean?'

He gestured towards the city with his glass.

'The first time I came to the festival, we were straight out of uni. Mike and I had cobbled two grand together; you know, bar work, some modelling, scrimped and saved to put on a show. We stayed in a little hostel just down there,' he said, pointing beyond the Old Town. 'And you know what? I never thought I'd make it up here to the Royal Suite. Not deep down.'

'And here's me thinking all thespians were crazed egotists.'

'Oh, we are. But we tend to swing between hope and despair: one day we believe we're going to have a star on Hollywood Boulevard, the next we think we should chuck it all in and get a job in Starbucks. But in my more realistic moments, I sort of hoped I might get like a Persil ad or a part as the wacky neighbour in some Channel Four sitcom. You see too many failures and almost-theres to really believe you'll make it to the Oscars.'

'But you did.'

He nodded.

'Past tense.'

'You'll make it back,' said Anna.

'I'm really not sure I want to any more,' said Sam honestly. 'Not after tonight. It felt good, you know? Maybe when you come full circle, it's best to start a new adventure.'

'Perhaps you could go back to the modelling?' she said, her eyes twinkling with mischief.

He laughed. 'You don't want to see those photos.'

'I do,' she teased. 'Go on, give me your best Zoolander face.'

'Only if I can see your Blue Steel.'

Laughing, she sucked her cheeks in, put her hands on her hips and strutted across the carpet as if it were a catwalk.

'Terrible,' he said flatly. 'This is how an expert does it.'

He stuck out his backside, dropped one shoulder and began skipping around the room like a deranged Mick Jagger. Anna doubled up with laughter.

'Stop! Stop! You win!'

They sank back on to the huge sofas, laughing.

'I'm sorry,' said Anna as the giggles subsided. 'I'm your lawyer, I should be more professional.'

'Rubbish. I wish every lawyer was like you.'

Her gaze fluttered away from his and she took a nervous sip of her drink.

'I went to see Amy Hart's family,' she said, a little too quickly.

Sam's heart sank. Was this the real reason behind her visit to Edinburgh? Had she come to discuss her findings rather than to support his debut on the stage? If he was honest, he'd always found Anna's theory of a cover-up a little far-fetched. Nevertheless, he found himself getting drawn in as she spoke, her face becoming more serious as she told him about Amy's missing mobile phone and her best friend Louise who had gone travelling days after Amy's death. It was fascinating, and Sam began thinking what a good movie it would make, before he remembered that Anna's murder investigation was a real one, with an actual dead body.

'I'm convinced Louise knows something,' said Anna. 'If Phil can just call round a few more hotels, maybe he can find her.'

'But she could be anywhere,' said Sam frankly. 'India's a big place to get lost, and from what you're saying, that seems to be her plan.'

'I think she knows something about Amy's death,' said Anna passionately.

'Just because she skipped town after she died?'

'And left her dream job and her family . . .'

Sam considered it, sipping his whisky.

'You still think this has got something to do with me? The cover-up and all that?'

'Does it matter?'

'Well I am paying for this,' he joked.

'I'm aware of that, boss,' she replied, and when she smiled, Sam felt a sudden stir of longing. What was it about her? She wasn't even his type. She was too sharp, too knowing, too unforgiving of people's failures. Or maybe that is my type, he thought, remembering Jessica. But there was a controlled passion about Anna he found strangely attractive. He had seldom met a woman more difficult to work out. He'd spent over a decade in a city where women made 'shallow' a career; they were obsessed with money, fame and their own looks to the exclusion of everything else. But a woman like Anna? Sam suspected that you could spend years in her company and only begin to scratch the surface.

'Listen, I want you to get to the bottom of this, I really do,' he said.

He wasn't lying. He had never met Amy Hart, and could barely even remember what her photograph had looked like. But he knew the type of girl she was: the sort who mixed with powerful men and who suddenly found themselves disposable.

'Thank you, Sam,' Anna said softly. 'Phil thinks the best way to find out more would be for him to travel to India, but that's obviously going to cost money, and his fee is being billed to you.'

Sam looked at her, and all he could think about the next twenty-four hours was that he wanted to spend them with her.

He began to feel another surge of excitement: another adventure, another circle beginning.

'This girl, Louise. She's in Kerala, right?'

Anna shrugged. 'We think.'

'Have you got your passport?' he asked urgently.

'Yes.' She frowned. 'I flew up here.'

'Good,' he said, reaching for his phone. 'Then let's go and find her.'

'*What?*' said Anna, her eyes wide. 'How?'

'On my jet. Well, it's not actually my jet, I've got a share in it,' he said, waggling the phone. 'But I can call the pilot right now and check that it's available.'

'You're joking,' she gasped.

'I'm deadly serious. I think you're right. This Louise is lying low and her mum's telling porkies; why would she hide unless she knows something?'

'But I can't just go to India. I've got to be back in work on Monday.'

He grinned at her, feeling giddy and liberated. The thought that by this time tomorrow he could be on some unknown hotel balcony, sipping cocktails with a beautiful, complex woman made him feel like Cary Grant in his own real-life Hitchcock movie.

'Okay, it's Friday night,' he said. 'If the jet's fuelled and ready, we'll be in Kerala by tomorrow afternoon at the latest. We fly back on Sunday and you'll be at your desk at nine o'clock

Monday telling everyone that you had a nice quiet weekend.'

Anna still looked hesitant.

'I thought you wanted to find out what happened to Amy?'

'I do,' she said passionately.

'So let's go.'

'What time would we leave?' she asked, looking more confident about the idea.

'I'll need to speak to the pilot, but we'll get the first slot out of the airport.'

'So like, *now*?'

Sam could see this was freaking her out and didn't want to scare her off.

'Let me make a few calls,' he said, getting up. 'You just relax and have another drink. It might be easier if you stay here. There are two bedrooms,' he added quickly.

'But my bag and passport are at my hotel,' said Anna, with a look of panic. 'I'd better go.' She jumped to her feet. 'Call me when you know what the arrangements are,' she added, opening the door to the suite.

'But what about that . . .'

The door slammed.

'. . . other drink?' he said to empty space. Then he burst out laughing.

45

'So who is this Deena Washington exactly?' said Helen with irritation, flicking through the notes her private investigator had prepared. She looked up at Mark Carrington at the wheel of his SUV as they drove towards the Hamptons on the Sunrise Highway. Helen was tired, jet-lagged and annoyed that she'd had to come to New York at all: wasn't that why she employed PIs like Mark? Carrington was a forty-something former cop who had left the force to join Travis Sim, the prestigious global risk management firm. If you wanted anything found – a person, a computer file, a missing aeroplane – Travis Sim, and more specifically Mark Carrington, could find it for you. He was the best in the business. Which was why Helen was particularly annoyed with him. Previously, his work for her had been flawless: background screening checks, profiles on witnesses, finding evidence that had conveniently disappeared into the bowels of the US justice system, he'd done it all with speedy efficiency. But this time, he had failed.

By Mark's account, he had hit a brick wall trying to find something, *anything* that linked a member of the *Stateside* staff to Jonathon Balon.

'Everyone's clammed up,' he had told her over the phone, 'They all seem terrified of this guy Spencer Reed. No one will talk.'

Helen couldn't sit back any longer. They only had a few days to go until the end of the trial and she couldn't risk – wouldn't even consider the possibility of – losing the case. The whole reputation of Donovan Pierce rested on it, and she hadn't worked so long and hard to let that happen. So she had left court on Friday and flown straight to JFK, determined that she would return to London on Monday with a piece of information that would blow *Stateside*'s case out of the water.

But now, sitting in Mark's untidy car, watching his stubby fingers drumming on the wheel as he hummed along to Springsteen's 'Born to Run', she wasn't at all confident that was going to happen. She reached out and snapped off the radio.

'If you couldn't get any of the others to talk, why do you think this girl's going to tell anything?'

'Deena doesn't work in magazines any more. She's gone into TV,' explained Mark, turning the radio back on.

The car threaded along the highway, towards Long Island's South Fork. The traffic was slow; clogged by wealthy New Yorkers escaping the city humidity for the seaside towns. Helen had visited the area many times to attend parties or stay at the homes of powerful clients, but she could never see the appeal of spending a whole summer cooped up with so many snooty bankers, all playing the same game of one-upmanship: who's got the biggest house, yacht, bank balance. She herself was much more interested in making money than showing it off.

'Is this it?' she asked as they pulled off the main road and into the town of Bridgehampton. It was almost six o'clock and the sun was slinking towards the horizon, sending out flashes of orange between the large houses as they passed. Mark turned into a small private road, more sand than blacktop, and stopped the car in front of a dove-grey cottage, set back from the sands. Little more than a shack, it was still a shack with a view that Helen guessed rented at more than $30,000 a summer.

Mark and Helen got out and followed a path leading around the house. They could hear music and laughter coming from the side facing the pale-almond sands of the beach. As they turned the corner, they could see a small group: young men in chinos and blue shirts, girls in bikinis and sarongs, all standing around a huge barbecue pit, drinking wine.

'Deena's the redhead on the tiki seat,' said Mark.

Seeing the strangers, the girl stood up and walked over. She was petite, with delicate features and freckles across an upturned nose.

'Deena Washington?' said Helen.

'That's me,' she said, looking instantly defensive.

'Helen Pierce,' she said, putting out her hand. 'I'm an attorney with Donovan Pierce, a legal firm in London.'

Deena looked from Helen to Mark and back again.

'The Balon case,' she said. A statement, not a question. She turned and waved at her friends, calling, 'I'll just be a minute, save me a burger, okay?'

Raising his eyebrows, Mark excused himself and, slipping her shoes off, Helen followed Deena on to the sand.

'So I take it you're not surprised to see me?' she asked.

'Spencer has told every member of staff, past and present, not to speak about the case, so yes, I was kinda thinking you'd be in touch.'

'Why's that?'

Deena gave a low laugh. 'Because that Jonathon Balon feature was my idea.'

The waves were roaring on to the shore and a cool breeze whipped Deena's burnished hair across her face.

'I'm not sure it's worth my while to talk to you.'

Helen knew instantly what she was getting at. Everything was about money out here. She smiled.

'Do you want me to have to call you as a witness? I could easily force you to give testimony.'

Deena stopped and faced her.

'In a foreign trial?' she said. 'With a week to go? I don't think so.'

Helen was surprised at the girl's knowledge. She was a hustler, a deal-maker.

'Well I'm sure we can come to some agreement,' she said.

'It depends what you're offering me.'

'It depends what you're telling me,' replied Helen.

Deena turned to look out to sea.

'The magazine got this new commissioning editor,' she began. 'Joanne Green. Beautiful, ambitious, but she was an out-of-towner, had no connections at all in the city.'

She glanced at Helen.

'Look, she got the job I wanted, but I figured she was better

346

as a friend than an enemy, so I took her under my wing. We went to parties, and I introduced her to people. I thought that way I'd get more of my stories in the magazine. But I was wrong – at first, anyway.'

She paused.

'Jo wasn't a real decision-maker at the magazine; that was Elizabeth Krantz, the features editor. I'd never got on with Lizzie; I think she resented that I got invited to more parties than she did, so she took great delight in knocking back my features ideas again and again and again. Until . . .'

'Until what?' asked Helen.

'Until Jo started sleeping with Spencer.'

Helen felt her eyes widen, and Deena smiled. 'Suddenly it was easy for Jo to overrule Lizzie about editorial. Suddenly I was getting my stuff in the magazine.'

'And this was when you pitched the idea of the Jonathon Balon story?'

Deena nodded.

'My boyfriend at the time told me about this billionaire Brit and his property empire, which was built on his connections with London gangsters. It sounded a great story – it *is* a great story. So I pitched it to Jo, but she said it wasn't international enough.'

'Who was your boyfriend?' asked Helen, her excitement growing. Finally Mark had hit gold, she could feel it.

'He was from London. A photographer. He hated Balon for some reason and really wanted the story to run; some revenge deal, I guess.'

'So how did you get around Jo?'

Deena smirked.

'My boyfriend was moving out of his apartment in the Village. Great place, rent-controlled, and he was tight with the landlord. Jo said she'd have a word with Spencer and make the feature happen if my boyfriend made sure his apartment was turned over to her.'

Helen tried to keep her face neutral, but inside she was punching the air. This was exactly the breakthrough she had been hoping for.

'Why didn't you write the story?'

'Because I didn't know enough about Balon. My boyfriend told Jo to use one of his old friends from London, Ted Francis.'

Francis was a named co-defendant, along with the editor and Steinhoff publishing.

'My boyfriend phoned Ted and said he had got him some work at *Stateside* magazine. Every serious journalist wants to get commissioned by *Stateside*. But the deal was that the story had to expose Balon.'

'Your boyfriend,' Helen said. 'I need his name.'

Deena gave a laugh.

'I know you do, but as I said, this has to be worth my while.'

Helen's lips tightened. Usually she would dispense with little chancers like Deena Washington, but she knew she was running out of time.

'What do you want, Deena?'

'The summer rental on this place isn't cheap,' she said, inclining her head back towards the house.

Helen took a breath of the sharp, salty air. She knew that Deena would be sharing the cost with some of the others hanging out around the barbie.

'Okay, what's your split of the rent? Five thousand dollars?'

Deena shook her head.

'Five thousand bucks for pissing off the most powerful editor in America? *Come on*.'

'But you're in TV now, Deena,' said Helen. 'What do you care about Spencer?'

'Spencer has friends in high places everywhere. I'm pretty sure he can screw me over with one phone call if he chooses. No, I want the whole rental. Forty thousand bucks.'

Helen swallowed. 'I'll give you fifteen,' she said.

Deena shook her head. 'My guess is that you want to win this case a whole heap. Otherwise why else are you out here in the middle of a trial? I want the lot or you get zip.'

'Fine,' said Helen, smarting. 'My colleague will speak to you when we get back to the house.' She always avoided getting involved with deals of this nature; it was simply good practice. Besides, Mark Carrington was an expert in diverting whatever funds were needed through a dozen accounts in as many countries so that should anyone wish to trace the cash, it would never come back to her. She turned her steely gaze on to the girl. 'The name of your boyfriend, Deena.'

She hesitated for a moment, then shrugged.

'Dominic Bradley,' she said. 'Works out of the Eleven Street Studios downtown, fashion stuff mostly, but it's August and everyone in fashion goes on holiday, so my guess is he'll be back in London to visit his folks.'

Helen smiled as they walked back towards the house.

'Out of interest, why did you just tell me all that, when Spencer had told everyone to keep quiet?' asked Helen.

'Spencer's a jerk, that's why,' said Deena with feeling. 'He promotes yes-men and whoever will suck his cock. He pushed Lizzie out and made Jo head of features, and with Spencer to open doors for her, Jo didn't need me any more. The moment that happened, Spencer called me into his office and said he was letting me go.' She turned to Helen, her cheeks pink. 'You screw that prick,' she said. 'He deserves a fall.'

Helen smiled and nodded. The girl clearly was an operator, but in reality she was naive. If *Stateside* lost the case, it would have little or no impact on Spencer Reed personally. So he'd angered Jonathon Balon, but Balon was a big fish in the small pool of London, and Spencer moved in higher circles.

'Don't you worry,' she said, slipping her heels back on. 'We'll screw him all right.'

But first she had to find herself a photographer.

46

Anna smiled as the handsome steward handed her another glass of bubbly.

'Thank you, Martin,' she said, watching him sway back down the narrow gangway of the Cessna jet.

'Oi,' laughed Sam, watching her from his cream leather seat opposite. 'Stop flirting with the crew.'

'I'm not sure I'm his type,' she whispered, as Martin flirted with another handsome male steward at the back of the cabin.

'You could turn him, I'm sure,' Sam teased, popping a handful of fat cashew nuts into his mouth.

Anna sat back in her seat and sipped her champagne, wondering whether to pinch herself. Dull solicitors like her just didn't get to spend the day in a private jet with a Hollywood heart-throb like Sam Charles. But there was more to it than that, wasn't there? The way they had chatted and giggled, flirted and teased; this wasn't a normal lawyer-client relationship, not by a long chalk, especially as no one from Donovan Pierce even knew she was missing. Helen Pierce would have a fit if she knew she was careering off to India with one of the firm's most high-profile clients. But Anna couldn't help it; she was having a fabulous time talking with Sam, hearing his stories of Hollywood, his early life in a working-class part of west London and his struggles to become an actor. Listening to such intimate details in such an enclosed space made her feel as if they were the only two people in the world. She'd tried to tell herself that this was just business, but it wasn't – it *couldn't* be. Not the way he was looking at her. Not the way they were getting on like they'd known each other for years. Or perhaps he was like this with everyone. Wasn't that what celebrities were good at – making you feel like the most important person in the room?

'So is this thing actually yours?' she asked, gesturing around the jet's luxurious cream leather interior with her glass.

'Not really,' he smirked. 'I just say that to impress people like you. I share it on the NetJets owners' programme.'

'Only a share?' She grinned. 'I've been brought here on false pretences. What kind of pauper are you?'

'Don't you start.' He smiled. 'Jess was always trying to convince me that we needed to buy one outright.'

It was irrational, of course, but Anna was starting to really dislike Jessica Carr. Obviously Sam wasn't going to paint her in the most flattering light, but she did sound like a greedy, self-centred ogre. Or perhaps Anna was just getting annoyed at the regularity with which Sam mentioned her name, like some recently divorced man on a date. It's not a date, she reminded herself. But hell, it felt like one.

'So can you fly?'

He took a sip of his vodka tonic. 'Not really. Jess got us his-and-hers lessons. She heard that Angelina had her pilot's licence and she wasn't going to be beaten. She wanted it to be one of those things we did together.'

'And did you?'

'Nah,' he said. 'It just made a nice soundbite for a magazine.'

They laughed.

'What about you?'

Anna shrugged. 'I can't fly and I haven't got a jet. Not even a tiny share in one.'

'So what do you like doing? Other than work.'

'Nothing as interesting as the things you get up to.'

'Why not?'

'Because you're a movie star and I'm a solicitor from Richmond.'

He looked at her, a playful smile on his lips.

'Come on, tell me something interesting about yourself. At least something I don't know. A boyfriend?'

'No,' she said, a touch too quickly. Why was he asking her that? Was he really interested in her private life?

'What happened to that journalist bloke? The one you didn't want to talk to?'

Anna gave a loud cough.

'The less said about him the better, I think.'

'Well what about since then?'

Anna pulled a face. 'Not much, I'm afraid. I really don't have the time.'

'Well I have to say that's a real shame,' said Sam, fixing her with his blue eyes.

Anna felt her mouth go dry. What was he saying?

'A shame?' she said. 'Why?'

'I was thinking of setting you up with Martin.' He grinned.

She threw a cushion at him.

'Right, that's it, I'm going to sleep,' she said, reaching for her sleep mask. 'Wake me up when we're in Paradise.'

Kerala wasn't quite Paradise, but it wasn't far off. The landscape was lush and tropical, dense jungle pressing in on every side as their air-conditioned taxi drove along the snaking roads from Cochin airport towards the resort town of Alappuzha. Refreshed from her nap in the jet, Anna peered out of the car window, fascinated by the countryside. She had expected the dusty, impoverished India she'd read about, but Kerala was as vibrant as the vegetation. The lime green of crops as they passed a tea plantation, the bright canary yellow of a sari or the posies of scarlet blossom. The villages they passed through were small but well kept, the houses neat and painted white, children in pressed school uniforms waving as they passed. It felt like the Garden of Eden, only with added Coca-Cola signs.

Finally they arrived at Alappuzha, a busy tourist town on the south-east coast criss-crossed by miles of backwaters, all leading down to a long strip of yellow beach and a rickety pier that jutted out into the shimmering Arabian Sea.

'Wow, look at the lighthouse,' said Anna, pointing to the red and white striped tower on the headland. 'This place is lovely.'

'Remember why we're here, Judith Chalmers,' said Sam as they paused at a crossing, watching the backpackers in shorts and flip-flops strolling up the main drag. 'Louise Allerton could be any of these. It's a long way to come to look for someone then get distracted by the scenery.'

Anna nodded. 'Sea View Hotel it is, then. Pronto.'

The Sea View Hotel was salmon pink, with crumbling balustrades and flaking paint. It didn't have a sea view, or indeed a view of anything except the back of a warehouse selling agricultural supplies.

'You'd better stay here,' she said, getting out of the cab. After the cool of the taxi, it was an almost physical shock, and she could feel herself beginning to perspire on the spot.

'Why?' said Sam, frowning. 'I want to play detective.'

'Because it's a hotel full of backpackers who will almost certainly recognise you. The last thing we want is a tip-off to the *Sun* that you're in Kerala.'

'So? I could be here for a spa holiday.'

'Not in this part of town,' she said, glancing around. 'And by the looks of it, this is the sort of place that rents beds by the hour.'

'Okay,' he said. 'But if I hear any shooting, I'm not waiting for the cops.'

'My hero,' she laughed.

The guest house had probably seen better days, or perhaps it had always been dirty and cramped, with the faint smell of patchouli permeating the air. There were a few young Europeans lounging around the lobby drinking tea from little glasses, their rucksacks by their feet, but apart from that, the Sea View was quiet. Anna walked up to the reception, where a wizened Indian man in a faded smiley-face T-shirt was sitting. He gazed at her without interest, until she produced a thousand-rupee note and placed it on the desk.

'I help you?' he said, not taking his eyes off the money.

'I'm looking for a white English girl, name of Louise Allerton. She stayed here six months ago.'

The man reached towards the money, but Anna pulled it back an inch. Finally he looked up at her.

'Lots of English come here. I don't remember names.'

'Don't you have a hotel register?'

The man gave a ghost of a smile.

'This is not the London Ritz, lady.'

Anna picked up the note and folded it in two.

'Pity.'

'Okay, okay,' said the manager. 'Go speak to Amber in the apartment at the back. She been here long time. Maybe she know her. Not in right now. Works at ice-cream parlour by the sea.'

'Thanks,' said Anna, handing him the note and walking back to the taxi.

'Louise? Of course I remember her,' said Amber, a boho-looking brunette, clearing up the empty bottles of Mongoose from the tables. She wiped her brow with the back of her wrist, making her rack of bangles jangle. 'We got to Kerala the same week and shared a room for about a fortnight. She moved on. I stayed at the Sea View in the flat they rent in the garden.'

'Do you know where she moved on to?'

Amber wrinkled her nose.

'She in trouble or something?'

'Why do you say that?'

'Just a feeling.' She smiled knowingly and slung her cleaning cloth over her shoulder. 'So what do you want her for?'

'We're worried about her.'

'Who's we?'

'Friends, family,' said Anna vaguely. 'She left her job out of the blue.'

Amber laughed. 'And that's strange? I hear it two, maybe three times a day out here. Kerala's full of people who've skipped the rat race. Doesn't mean to say you have to be worried about them.'

'Even so, how can I contact her?' pressed Anna.

Amber sighed, her shoulders wilting as if they were weary from the heat.

'Apparently Lou was a beauty writer back home. She was into spa therapies, things like that. So last time I heard, she was about to do an Ayurvedic beauty course. Said she'd come back and give me a massage once she'd finished. I'm still waiting.'

'Can you remember where?'

'Green something study centre. Can't remember its exact name.'

Anna was already on her iPhone, locating all the Ayurvedic training centres in a fifty-mile radius.

'Don't forget to tell her I still want my massage,' shouted Amber, as she watched Anna run off towards the waiting taxi.

Raj, their driver, knew the village where the Green Leaves Ayurvedic training school was located, and told them it was better to go there by ferry than by road. He dropped them off at the dock, a worn patchwork of bleached boards crowded with about fifty people all trying to squeeze down the gangplank on to a strange flat boat, shouting to be heard over its chugging engine. The ferry was like an iron shoebox with an engine house stuck at one end and a rusted chimney bellowing oily smoke.

Anna looked out at the wide brown expanse of water between them and the other side.

'You think this thing's really going to make it across?' she said dubiously.

'Come on, where's your spirit of adventure?' laughed Sam, grabbing her hand to help her on board.

Once they had cast off, the teeth-rattling clank of the engine gave way to a rhythmic thrum, and they sat at the side of the boat, feet dangling over the edge, watching the town disappear and give way to jungle and mangrove. Anna was expecting to see crocodiles sunning themselves, but had to make do with a single water buffalo drinking at the water's edge before they came to Kumolrula, a small village on the far banks of the Vembanad lake.

It wasn't hard to find Green Leaves, as apart from a scattering of huts and houses, it was the only building you could see from the jetty: a flat, rather unremarkable construction with a dark blue awning over the entrance.

'Can I help you?' asked an Indian woman the moment they stepped inside, grateful for the air-conditioning. 'Massage or treatment?'

She was about forty, with short red hair and a black linen shirt.

'We're looking for Louise,' said Sam, giving her his best Hollywood smile. 'Is she around?'

The woman shook her head.

'It's only a half-day class today. She'll be back home, or I think she works in a guest house along the lake as well.'

'Could you tell me where she lives?'

Louise Allerton was out front of the house when they pulled up, a tanned blonde woman wearing a simple green shift dress, unpegging washing from a line strung between two wide-boughed trees. She continued with her task as Sam and Anna got out of the car and walked towards her.

'Have you come about the yoga?' she asked, picking up her basket. 'Because I'm not giving lessons today . . . Shit, you're Sam Charles.'

'Yes, I am.' He smiled, evidently pleased to be finally recognised. Anna rolled her eyes.

'Wow. *Blue Blood* is one of my favourite films,' said Louise, stuttering.

'Mine too, actually. To film, that is,' he added. 'I hate watching my own films.'

'Really? Why's that?' asked Louise, before Anna gave a theatrical cough and held out her hand.

'I'm Anna Kennedy.'

'Right,' she said vaguely.

'His lawyer,' added Anna quickly.

Louise began to look nervous.

'And you're here to see me because . . .'

Fat spots of rain began to plop down on to the path. One, then three, then a dozen all at once. Anna squinted up, seeing the heavy dark clouds too late.

'Can we come in for a minute?' asked Sam, shrugging his shoulders as the rain began to soak his shirt.

Louise paused, then gestured towards the house, and they all ran inside. Louise put the washing basket in the corner and closed the shutters.

'Can I get you tea?' she asked, clearly unsure of how to behave with a celebrity in her home.

'Maybe we should get straight to the point,' said Anna kindly. 'It's about Amy. Amy Hart.'

Louise didn't reply, simply turned and began taking the clothes from the washing basket, folding them and putting them away on a shelf. The rain was thrumming down on the shutters and the roof of the house. Slow and steady at first, increasing in pace until it was a roar.

'What's all this about?' she said finally, turning back to them. 'Research for a movie or something?'

'No, we just want to find out what happened to Amy,' said Sam.

'Why do you care?' snapped Louise, her hands on her hips. 'You didn't know her. Neither of you did. So why don't you just keep out of things that don't concern you?'

Anna caught Sam's worried look. She wasn't sure how he'd expected this to go, but Anna had certainly guessed that if Louise was scared enough to leave her career and family and run halfway across the globe, she would be frightened about talking to anyone, let alone a movie star and a lawyer who had literally walked in off the street.

'Look, I know this must be freaking you out a bit,' she said gently. 'But we're here because Amy's sister Ruby got in touch with me after the inquest.'

'Why?' said Louise.

'Ruby wanted a lawyer to challenge the inquest result.'

Louise turned away again, started putting dishes in the sink.

'And what do you want from me?' she said. 'I don't know anything.'

'But you can tell us what you think,' said Sam.

Louise turned on the tap, then snapped it off and swung round to face them again.

'Look, I hardly saw Amy for months before she died.'

'But you were good friends, weren't you?' asked Sam.

'She was my flatmate for a little while; she was lovely then,' said Louise, a smile creeping on to her face. 'But towards the end? We didn't have so much in common. She was a party girl and, well, she had her own agenda.'

'Agenda?' prompted Anna.

'She wanted to marry a rich man,' said Louise. 'Started hanging around with people who could help her towards that goal.'

'She was dating someone wealthy, wasn't she, around the time she died?'

'I don't know,' Louise snapped.

'My life went to shit a while back and all I wanted to do was get away,' ventured Sam kindly. 'I buggered off to an island in the middle of nowhere. And you know what I realised when I was there? That it doesn't matter where you go, you take the problem with you. You just can't escape.'

For a few moments they were all silent. Rain bounced off the roof like a kettle drum. Anna wasn't going to have come all this way to let this girl curl up into a little ball and hide, however scared she was.

'Louise, I think you know something about Amy's death,' she said. 'Why she might have been killed.'

'*I don't know.*'

'Then why did you leave England three days afterwards? Why is your mum lying about where you are? Why are you pretending that none of this matters?'

'Can't you just leave?'

'If that's what you want,' said Anna finally. 'But look, I'm just a solicitor from London and he's some bloke from the movies. We're hardly MI6, and we found you easily enough. If someone with money and influence wanted to track you down, then believe me, they'd find you too. It's obvious you're frightened, but Sam's right: you can't run for ever. And whatever you know, we can help you.'

The light was dim in the cottage, but Anna could see that Louise was crying now. She moved across and the girl fell into her arms, sobbing on her shoulder. Finally she began to talk.

'Amy and I clicked from the minute we met. We had lots in common, liked a drink, a laugh, the London party scene. She moved into my flat, I needed a bit of help with the rent, and we'd go out every night to all the launches and parties we got invited to through my work and her modelling. Amy was focused, though. She wanted to find a rich man and started going to swankier things than I could get us invited to. I went with her a couple of times but it was just a bunch of leery old men who wanted a bit on the side. And then she met someone. I only know his name was Peter. It was Peter this and Peter that. All the places he'd take her, all the stuff he bought her. She never told me his surname – apparently he was married, so she was cagey about the details of who he was – but you could tell he was rich and influential.' She looked up at Anna.

'Was this man one of Gilbert Bryce's friends?'

'I don't think so, but she told me she met him at a country party Gilbert took her to.'

'Was it James Swann's party?'

'I don't know. I'm sorry.'

Anna looked down, disappointed.

'Can you tell me anything else about Peter?'

'She was in love with him, you could tell that much. She told me she'd marry him in a heartbeat.'

'But he was already married.'

'I think she expected more from him, especially after he paid for that posh flat she was in by the Thames. But when he said he wouldn't leave his wife, she got really angry with him. Threatened him.'

'What with?'

'She said she'd tell his wife.'

'And did she?'

Louise nodded.

'I told her not to do it, but she was determined. She knew where he lived and sent the wife a letter saying her husband was having an affair.'

'And that obviously didn't work.'

'Apparently not. But she wasn't going to give up that easily.'

She curled her slim arms around her legs and peered over the top of her knees.

'About a week before Amy died, we went out for drinks. I asked her how it was going with Peter and she smiled this little smile, like she was really happy. I said, "Has he finally decided to leave his wife?" and she said no, but it was only a matter of time before he would.'

'Why? She'd tried telling the wife and that didn't work.'

'She had something else on him. Something about his job.'

'Do you know what it was?' asked Sam.

Louise shook her head.

'Apparently one of Peter's close friends had committed suicide a couple of months earlier. Peter was devastated about it. In fact he broke down in front of Amy. He was sobbing, saying, "it was my fault, it was my fault".'

She took a breath.

'Amy found something out about Peter and she told him she'd go to the press with it. She was blackmailing him. She was desperate for him to leave his wife, and that was the only way left she knew how to do it.'

'She told you that?'

Louise nodded.

'I told her not to be stupid, but she was so headstrong.' She started crying again. 'If only I'd managed to persuade her, she'd still be alive. That drink. That was the last time I spoke to her. A week later, she was dead.'

'Do you think Peter killed her?'

'He paid for the flat so I assume he'd have a key. Even if he didn't, Amy would have let him in. Maybe they just quarrelled. Maybe she slipped. Maybe it wasn't murder but he just walked away without a second look back.'

'What did Amy have on Peter? Do you know?'

'I don't know. If I did, then maybe I'd be dead too.'

'Is that why you're out here?' asked Sam.

She nodded.

'When Amy died I got scared. Maybe I overreacted coming out here, but I just wanted to step back from it all. I guess I'm a coward.'

She stood up stiffly and walked over to the shutters, pulling them open.

'Rain's stopped,' she sniffed. 'It does that. Over before you can blink. Now if you hurry, you can catch the five o'clock ferry.'

47

Sam and Anna didn't speak at all on the boat back to Alappuzha. Raj was waiting for them at the dock, and they got into the taxi, each preoccupied by their thoughts.

'Where to, boss? Ajunta?' asked the driver.

'Is Ajunta the hotel?' asked Anna.

Sam shrugged.

'I guess. I asked Josh to book us somewhere off the tourist trail.'

They were surprised when Raj turned the car out of the town and off the main road, swinging on to a series of dusty tracks where the jungle pressed in so far that palm fronds and creepers were brushing the sides of the taxi.

'Certainly off the beaten track,' said Anna, beginning to wonder where they were being taken. Finally they pulled up next to one of the canal-like waterways. Anna looked out of both sides of the car. She couldn't see anything like a hotel anywhere.

'Raj, where are we?' asked Sam anxiously. The driver just grinned and held the door open.

'Ajunta,' he said, pointing to a boat. 'In Kerala we call them *ketuvallum*. They're the best places to stay when you are in this part of the world.'

Sam didn't look convinced until they stepped on board.

'Wow,' he whistled, looking around at the interior of the sumptuously crafted longboat. It was around one hundred feet in length with a curved roof made of jackwood and thatch. Arched windows were carved out of the beautifully panelled walls and it had an open stern and port. At the bottom of a short gangplank, two smiling women in cream saris were waiting for them with elaborate cocktails festooned with fruit.

Raj brought the bags aboard and went over to talk to an ancient-looking man in a blue and white cap.

'This is Captain Sanjiv, he will look after you tonight. I will meet the boat tomorrow, but if you need anything – anything at all,' he added with a knowing wink, 'just ask the Captain.' He bowed and disappeared up the gangplank.

'Sam, this is amazing,' breathed Anna as they walked the length of the boat. There were two bedrooms; the largest had a dark wooden bed facing the open window, covered by just a thin curtain of voile, which looked out on to the still green waters.

'You have this one,' offered Sam. 'I'll slum it in the servants' quarters,' although the smaller room was no less luxurious, with a claw-foot bath and a walk-in shower room.

They walked back and up on to the main deck, where a table had been set for dinner. Anna noticed that they were already moving down the waterway and they climbed some wooden stairs to the bridge, where the Captain was at the wheel, his eyes fixed ahead as they motored along the white waterlily-strewn waters.

They both went to change before dinner, Anna putting on a turquoise dress she had picked up as they had rushed through the airport. Sam came on to the deck barefoot in a pair of chinos and a pale grey T-shirt. The sun had tanned his face, bringing out the blue of his eyes; it reminded Anna of that first time she had seen him standing at the rail of the yacht in Capri. She wondered how it was possible for one person to be so handsome.

'Well I don't know about you, but I need a drink,' she said, sitting at the table, where chilled wine had been left for them in an ice bucket. They clinked their glasses together and watched the padi fields and coconut groves slip past, ancient temples silhouetted in the growing dusk. Anna felt herself shiver at the magic of it all. There was a platter of fruit on the table – starfruit, lychees, pineapple – and they picked at it in silence as the sun set below the horizon, sending the clouds pink and mauve and turning the ripples in the water a shimmering lavender, while the women lit candles along the length of the boat, spilling warm light across the deck.

A steward brought out sweet-smelling curries in earthenware pots and laid them on the table. Anna tried a vegetable dish made of melting cubes of aubergine flavoured with lemongrass and coconut. She closed her eyes in delight.

'This is just amazing,' she said.

'The food or the setting?' asked Sam.

'Both.'

She looked at him, feeling that shiver again.

'Apparently these things used to transport rice from the padi fields to the port. And not one nail was used to make the entire craft,' she said quickly.

Sam chuckled.

'I like how you gather facts about where you visit.'

'I wanted to be an explorer when I grew up. My dad used to be in the army and had travelled all over the world before he met my mum. The places he'd been stationed – Hong Kong, Cyprus, Brunei – they all sounded so exotic. I had this big globe in my bedroom that lit up at night and I'd dream about all the places I'd go one day. Funny thing is, the furthest I've been on holiday in the last three years is Crete for a week.'

She stopped, knowing that she was babbling. She felt as if she was parachuting into a date situation for which she was woefully unprepared. She wanted the easy banter and jokiness of the aeroplane trip back, but it seemed to have been replaced by something else. Sexual tension? She was both terrified and thrilled by the prospect.

They had finished eating. Sam went to sit on the white cushion at the bow of the boat and beckoned Anna to come and join him.

'So do you think Peter had Amy killed?' she asked, sitting down beside him. She said it both as a way of defusing the tension and because it had been weighing on her mind since they'd left Louise's house.

Sam took a sip of wine and looked thoughtful.

'Possibly. It certainly sounds like Amy was prepared to cause him a lot of trouble to get what she wanted.'

'I found that part of it a bit sad,' said Anna. 'She was in love with this guy and wanted him so much that she couldn't see that blackmailing him to be with her was going to send him the opposite way.'

'Love does the strangest things to you, though,' he said, fixing her with those blue eyes.

'How hard can it be finding a Peter who socialises with James Swann?' she said, thinking out loud.

'There'll be hundreds of Peters in that rich corporate set.'

'How many will have a good friend who committed suicide?' She took a swig of her wine. 'I definitely need to get to James Swann's party.'

'Let's discuss that when we get back to London, because right now I don't want to think about much at all.' Sam picked up the bottle. 'Another?'

Why the hell not? thought Anna, holding up her glass.

'I'm sorry I slept with Katie Grey,' Sam said quietly.

'I bet you are,' said Anna. 'Your girlfriend leaves you, your career implodes, and now your lawyer's dragging you into some murder mystery halfway around the world.'

He shook his head.

'My career will be fine. Jess and I should have finished months ago, and I've been to worse places than this amazing houseboat in the middle of Paradise.'

'Nothing to worry about then.'

'Except I don't want you to think badly of me for being unfaithful to my fiancée and sleeping with a prostitute.'

He looked at her, his confidence gone. He seemed nervous, almost bashful.

'It doesn't matter what I think, does it?'

'It does,' he said. 'Do you think I'm a sleazeball?'

She couldn't help but laugh.

'Maybe. A little bit. Before. But I think I know you a lot better now.'

'Good.' He smiled. 'You know Mike has spent the last month persuading me to downsize and simplify my life. How come it's suddenly got more complicated now that you're in it?'

A bolt of excitement rushed down her spine.

Sam reached over and touched her fingers then stretched forward to brush her lips with his. His kiss was slow and seductive. In the creamy moonlight, Anna felt like a leading lady in some sweeping fifties romance. Her brain felt dizzy. Desperately she tried to recall the solicitor's code of conduct. Was there anything in it that prohibited a sexual relationship between lawyer and client? She wasn't sure, but right now she was certain of nothing except the sensation of his soft lips crashing against hers and the swell of desire that curled between her thighs.

He took her hand and led her up the stairs to her bedroom on the mezzanine platform overlooking the backwaters. They were not even in the room before he had pulled off his T-shirt. *Rule Three, Rule Three*, a little voice told her. Did Rule Three forbid sex between lawyer and client? Not expressly, but it didn't matter. Her resistance had evaporated.

They tugged at each other's clothes, kissing, tasting, fingers through hair, lips against skin. And then they were naked, her nervousness forgotten as they tumbled back on to the huge bed, the river breeze washing over them but doing little to cool their need.

Laid back on the mattress, Anna's eyes fluttered closed. Her thighs parted instinctively and Sam knelt between them, lowering himself to plant soft, tender kisses on her lips and neck. She groaned as his tongue moved south. He traced a circle around her swollen nipple, then took it in his mouth, sucking sweetly until his lips moved lower, over the curve of her belly, through her soft scrub of pubic hair. Gasping, she grabbed his hair to push him deeper. She cried out as his tongue lapped her clitoris; hard, firm strokes that sent an arrow of lust directly to her belly.

Don't climax now, don't, she told herself, wanting this extreme sensation never to stop. His mouth, damp and musky, returned to hers, and as his hand parted her legs wider still, he pressed his weight against her, entering her slowly until he filled her completely, their bodies melded into one. They moved in time, slow at first and then faster, more urgent. 'Don't stop,' she pleaded, as they rolled over and she pushed herself up so she was straddling him. Her hips rocked against his, her muscles squeezing around him, every nerve ending jump-started to life, waves of pleasure building to a sharp, shivering crescendo. For so long she had denied herself, for so long she had convinced herself that sex was overrated, but as her body surrendered to a sweet, potent orgasm, her head tipped back, and crying out in screams of unfettered joy, she knew how glad she was to be back in business.

48

'You looked harassed, so I made you a coffee.'

Matt stood at the door of Anna Kennedy's office, holding two mugs.

She glanced up from her computer, still typing furiously.

'Strong and black, I hope,' she said as he put the cup down next to her keyboard. Now that she mentioned it, he could see that she was tired too: dark rings under her eyes.

'Good weekend, then?'

'Actually, yes.' She smiled playfully, her clever grey eyes not meeting his.

His curiosity was piqued. Anna Kennedy did not seem the type to go crazy at the weekend. She was hands-down the most attractive girl in the office. It was a fact, as her employer, he had tried not to notice, although he hadn't been shocked to hear that her sister was that fit chef off the telly. Anna didn't have that minxy over-sexiness that got Sophie Kennedy on the front covers of the Sunday supplements, but then Matt found those sorts of women quite intimidating. Actually, Anna was if anything prettier than her sister; it was just that she looked more clever and officious and . . . what was it? Sad, he thought suddenly. He'd never noticed it before, but she always seemed a little sad.

'So what did you do?' he asked, suddenly eager to find out more.

'Just went away for the weekend,' she said vaguely.

'Boyfriend?'

'I'm not sure yet,' she said, beginning to blush. He felt bad for embarrassing her and changed the subject, keen to carry on talking.

'What are you working on so feverishly?'

She rattled at the keyboard for a few more seconds, then hit the return button and sat back, letting out a long breath.

'Just a ton of stuff for Helen. The bloody Balon case is still going on, and now I've got to go and babysit Chantal Elliot.'

Matt chuckled. 'What's she done this time?'

'Nothing, actually,' said Anna, getting up to feed paper into the printer. 'She's been quite well behaved and I think that's what's troubling her management; they're expecting an explosion any minute, which could scupper some big deal in America.'

'But she's won a Grammy, hasn't she?'

'Doesn't matter,' explained Anna. 'The record industry is screwed at the moment and they want dull safe bets, not aspiring artists who are going to be trouble.'

She took a long swig of coffee, tapping a press release on her desk.

'Chantal's singing at some all-day charity thing near Richmond today, loads of celebs, and that means . . .'

'Loads of paparazzi.'

'So I've got to go and make sure they keep their distance.'

'Surely that's a job for security, not a solicitor?' said Matthew.

Anna shrugged. 'I'm taking no chances.'

Matthew picked up the press release as she prepared to leave.

'Is this it? The Fallout Festival?' he read. As his eyes scanned the musical line-up, one name jumped out at him. 'Kim Collier's going to be there?'

'One of many.'

Matthew looked at her.

'Can I come with you?'

Anna eyed him cynically.

'Why do I have the feeling it's not to see Chantal sing?' she said.

'Who's the boss around here, Kennedy?' he chided.

'Well don't dare try and bill it to my client.' She smiled, grabbing her sunglasses and slinging her bag over her shoulder. 'And it's going to be full of young people,' she whispered playfully. 'So if you insist on coming, you'd probably better lose the tie.'

*

The festival was being held at Parkstead House, a Palladian mansion on the fringes of Richmond Park, a thirty-minute cab journey from the office. The front of the house reminded Matthew of the White House, with curly Ionic columns and marble steps facing the estate's park, which had been transformed into a music festival enclosure with a stage at one end and a fairground off to the right.

'Bloody hell, it's like a posh Glastonbury,' said Matthew as they left the cab and walked through the gate, eyeing the overgroomed blondes in skinny jeans and flip-flops sitting on the grass smoking and drinking.

'Glastonbury,' said Anna wistfully. 'Those were the days. From what I can remember of them, anyway.'

'*You* went to Glastonbury?' said Matthew with surprise.

She nodded.

'Every year from sixteen to twenty-five. Before I got sensible and tied myself to a respectable career.'

They flashed their wristbands at a security guard and were directed through into a VIP area. The house itself was being used as a production-headquarters-cum-dressing-room for the artists and the backstage area was full of famous faces from television and music, either dashing about or just lolling on the grass enjoying the sun.

'Christ, if someone dropped a bomb in here,' said Matthew, 'the whole of the music industry would grind to a halt.'

They walked past a spiky-haired singer Matthew recognised from one of the TV talent shows Jonas liked watching. Anna pulled a face.

'On the other hand, it might do us all a favour and get some real music on the telly,' she whispered.

'Ooh, Little Miss Rock Chick.'

They stopped at a stall and got a fresh lemonade each, then sat down on the grass. From where they were, they could hear the music blasting out from the stage.

'So is that what attracted you to media law? Drugs, sex and rock and roll?' said Matthew, enjoying the sun, the atmosphere and the company of his associate.

Anna shook her head.

'Actually, it was a substitute career for journalism,' she said, sucking on her straw. 'I studied law to please my parents, but I got the writer's bug in my first year, when I signed up for the uni newspaper. I really wanted to do it, but everyone kept telling me I'd have to start in regional press, covering jumble sales and doorstepping the families of dead people – which didn't sound like the sort of news career I was after. Then I got offered a shiny well-paid job at Davidson's, which I knew had a media law division. It was as if I could combine two careers – law and journalism in one.'

She squinted at him.

'What about you? Just following in daddy's footsteps?'

Matthew snorted.

'Hardly. We barely spoke for twenty-five years.'

'So why follow him into the law? Why not make a statement and do something completely different, like a fireman or an archaeologist or something?'

It was a question Matt had asked himself many times over the years and one he had never properly been able to answer. Graduating from Cambridge with a 2:1 degree and a rowing blue, he could have gone into banking or insurance or any number of other sideways career paths, but he'd stuck with the law.

'Maybe that was my statement.' He shrugged. 'Choosing family law actually pissed my dad off in a big way. He sees it as the poor relation no one talks about. Media, M and A, property, tax, they all have prestige, but Larry sees family law as one step up from those dusty little high-street practices you only visit to make a will or sell your house. Which is funny really, considering the huge amount of time he's spent in the divorce courts himself. Disappointing him seemed the ultimate way to rebel.'

They slurped their plastic cups empty.

'How is your dad anyway?' asked Anna.

'He'll be okay.'

He felt guilty that he hadn't spoken to Larry since their argument in the pub.

'I wish I'd had the chance to work with him.'

370

'Well at least you get to learn at the feet of Helen Pierce. Helen and Larry are cut from the same cloth.'

'Ruthless bastards, you mean.'

They both laughed.

'Helen obviously sees some steeliness in you. She wouldn't have hired you otherwise.'

'I'm not sure she sees anything in me these days except a cock-up.'

'After the Sam Charles thing?'

Anna nodded. 'I thought she was going to fire me.'

He put a reassuring hand on her shoulder.

'We've all screwed up, Anna. Don't you think Helen's had her failures?'

'I thought she was indestructible, like Superwoman,' she laughed.

'That's the secret of high-achieving people: good spin. You never hear about the knock-backs, the disappointments, just the good stuff. History is written by the victors, isn't it?'

Anna nodded. 'Wise words, boss man. But I still don't want Superwoman blasting me with her laser eyes, so I'd better go and have a little word with our friends the paparazzi.' She stood up, brushing the grass off her skirt. 'Are you going to stay here?'

'I've got a little mission of my own,' he said, trying to sound mysterious.

Anna smiled.

'My guess is that she'll be in the production office up at the house. I don't think she's on for a couple of hours.'

Matthew watched her trot over the grass, her ponytail bouncing from side to side. The photographers were stationed at the entrance to the VIP area, waiting to catch any celebrities going in or out. He couldn't hear what she was saying to them, but he could see her face, serious and no-nonsense, as she jabbed her finger at one of the paps, warning him to keep his distance from Chantal or face her wrath. Matthew chuckled to himself as he watched those burly, scary-looking men with their big cameras and their stepladders all looking at the ground and shuffling their feet. You go, girl, he smiled admiringly, then turned and strode towards Parkstead House.

Kim Collier was standing on a balcony at the front of the mansion. The event was being filmed for TV and there were cameras pointing towards the stage. She was watching Chantal Elliot perform on one of the monitors.

'Hello,' she said as she spotted Matt, folding her arms defensively across her chest. 'I'm not sure I should be speaking to you.'

Matt knew he had to play it cool, make it seem like a coincidence.

'Don't worry, I'm actually here for her,' he said, gesturing towards the screen. 'Chantal's a client.'

'Well shouldn't you be down there, then?' said Kim.

'Better vantage point from here.'

'Like a sniper?' she said frostily.

They listened to Chantal's soaring vocals.

'Bloody hell. I wish I had a voice like that,' Kim said more softly. 'You know, if she only got her act together, she could be the new Ella Fitzgerald.'

'We all make mistakes,' said Matt evenly.

'Is that a swipe?' she asked.

He took a breath, knowing it was his moment to speak. He had been mentally rehearsing what he might say to her in the taxi over, but now he was here, the words seemed to have deserted him. He knew he had to speak from the heart rather than the script he had written in his head.

'Do you know how long I've been at Donovan Pierce?' he said finally.

'No idea,' she snapped.

'Six weeks. Three months ago I had my own little practice in Hammersmith. Then one day, a man I barely knew called Larry Donovan came along and gave me his share of this big media firm.'

She frowned. 'I thought Larry Donovan was your dad.'

'He is.' Matt met her gaze directly. 'In twenty-five years I met him maybe a dozen times. He missed my entire childhood and I'll be totally honest with you, I've never really got over that.'

He could see he had Kim's attention.

'Don't get me wrong, I loved my mum and she was a brilliant woman. But when my dad hurt her, she took the decision never to see him again. Which meant she took that decision for me too. The other week, he nearly died. You know what I was thinking about as I sat in that hospital waiting room? All the things we never did together.'

Kim turned away from him.

'I'm divorced too,' continued Matt, determined to finish his piece. 'I have a son, Jonas. Me and his mother hated each other for a long time, but without fail, I see him every weekend, every holiday, every Christmas. I've never missed the big stuff, but it's the little stuff, the everyday things, that binds people together.'

She blinked hard and drew herself up in her red high heels.

'I knew you'd come to work on me.'

'And I make no apologies for it.' He paused. 'Kim, I have no idea what went on inside your marriage, but I know that even if two people can't live together, a child still deserves to have his dad.'

A tear trickled down her cheek, leaving a white rivulet of foundation.

'You've got a bloody nerve, harassing me like this. Using emotional blackmail to get what you want.'

'You're right,' he said. 'I shouldn't be talking to you about the case. And if you choose to, you can indeed use this against me. But I'm not talking about the divorce right now. I'm talking about your son.' He touched her arm and was surprised when she didn't pull away. 'Do the right thing, Kim, please. Not because there's a lawyer breathing down your neck or you're scared what the press might say about you. Moving to Miami, you might as well be moving to the moon for the amount of time Oliver is going to see Rob. Every child wants his dad. I know, because I've been that child.'

Off on the main stage, Chantal was winding up her final song, a big band number complete with horns and gospel choir.

'She's finished,' said Matt. 'I'd better go.'

As he turned and walked away from Kim, he heard a sound

that at first he thought was just the music, until he realised it was a soft and spluttering sob.

49

Once a month, Donovan Pierce's weekly partners' meeting was held off the premises in one of the many restaurants that dotted Soho. Usually it took the form of a long lunch, but with the Balon trial taking up so much of her time, Helen had arranged an early supper at Nobu. There were only five partners at the firm: Helen, Matthew and the three junior partners, Alex Bard, Will Proctor and Edward French, all of whom had been elevated to salaried partners by Larry three years before and consequently worshipped the ground Donovan senior walked upon. In fact, Helen had to suppress a smile when Edward, a balding, rather owlish chap, ordered sake for the table. It was exactly the sort of thing that would have got him a slap of approval from Larry.

'So where's Matt this evening?' asked Edward as they all ordered from the vast menu.

'At some festival in Richmond,' said Helen.

'What's he doing there?'

'Trailing Anna Kennedy around with his tongue out,' smirked Alex. He was the youngest of the partners, but he was smart. Helen could see he had potential; none of the others would have dared make fun of Larry's son, especially with Helen there.

Will Proctor sat forward, perhaps showing himself a little too eager, thought Helen. She had noted with interest how Will always seemed to be leaving the building whenever Anna was, just so they could share the lift down or perhaps a taxi to court, although somehow she doubted that someone as attractive – and as clever – as Anna would go for an overweight vintage car enthusiast still suffering from acne in his mid thirties.

'So what's the gossip?' Will asked. 'Is there something going on between Matt and Anna?'

Helen simply raised an eyebrow.

'One would hope not. But like father, like son,' she said with a thin, knowing smile.

She was pleased when the three men laughed. Predictably, the young partners had been very much Larry's boys; even before their promotion, he had often taken them out on his more risqué outings with clients to lap-dancing clubs and late-night drinking dens. Consequently, whenever the partners had had to vote on internal issues, the three younger men had always followed Larry's lead – and so had Helen, knowing she was outgunned from the start.

But that's all in the past, thought Helen. Things are about to change around here. She waved the waiter over and ordered a bottle of excellent wine without looking at the menu, knowing that that would impress the others. It was all part of her bigger plan; ever since Larry's departure, she had been wooing the impressionable younger partners with glimpses of the high life, tastes of what could be theirs if only they played ball. Alex had been given the use of her Devon house for a long weekend with the new girlfriend he was trying to impress, while Edward had been invited to her South Kensington townhouse for an intimate dinner with his fiancée. Helen had been certain they would be blown away by both the size and the gorgeous interior of her home. Will had been even easier; she had arranged for a client to sell him, at a knock-down price secretly subsidised by herself, a pristine 1967 AC Cobra in British racing green. She knew her favour was paying off every time she heard its thrumming engine pulling into the staff car park.

It had been slow, careful work getting them on side, but now it was time for Helen to call in her markers. Her conversation with Timothy Hartnell at her birthday party had only hammered home how badly she had been left exposed when Larry had retired from the firm. She would not be outmanoeuvred again.

'Actually, I'm glad Matthew's not here,' she said, as they sipped the wine. 'I wanted to raise an issue about the partnership agreement.'

She watched them exchange alarmed glances – that was only to be expected.

'Donovan Pierce is having a bumper year,' she began. 'Every one of us around this table looks set for record fees and I think you'll all agree that that success is only a reflection of our collective dedication and hard work.'

They all murmured their assent.

'But I think we all also agree that this firm cannot support unproductive partners.'

'Meaning Matt,' said Alex. Helen smiled.

'Exactly. Look at what he's bringing in: roughly the same as our best trainee. Not good for a senior partner.'

'Sure, but he's only been here a few weeks,' said Alex. 'Shouldn't we give him a chance?'

Helen nodded.

'Absolutely. I'm not suggesting anything else. I'm merely pointing out the obvious: his area of law is an additional service for this firm, not a core one, and I'm not entirely convinced that a family law solicitor is going to generate the same level of fees that the rest of us do.'

She paused, letting that particular nugget sink in.

'So our hard work will be rewarding the largest stakeholder in the firm,' said Edward with a hint of bitterness. Helen had guessed he would be the easiest to sway with the money argument; she had got the distinct impression that his fiancée Caroline was a woman who responded well to extravagance.

'What are you saying, Helen?' said Will. 'You want to get rid of him? Larry would be furious.'

She had prepared herself for this argument; after all, they were Larry's boys.

'Not at all. We just need to have an agreement that rewards effort equally.'

She looked at each of them individually.

'Look, Larry was an incredible figurehead and leader for this company, but he's gone, and if I'm frank, his insistence on keeping his name on the masthead is really confusing the client base. In the last week alone I've had two major football agents and one FTSE 500 CEO calling up expecting Larry to represent them. When I told them he was no longer on active duty, they turned very sniffy indeed, thinking we were making excuses, that Larry didn't consider them important enough. Is it any wonder that they took their business elsewhere?'

She laid her hands flat on the table.

'I'm not saying that we oust Matt from the company. Simply that we de-equitise him.'

De-equitisation. It had been a buzz word around the big city law firms since the financial downturn. Getting rid of under-performing partners, cutting away the dead wood. They all knew that to survive in a shrinking marketplace, they needed to stay lean and effective. No one could afford to carry passengers any more.

'So he becomes a salaried partner and not an equity one?' said Will.

'That's right,' nodded Helen, although she was quite sure Matt Donovan would leave the firm rather than suffer the humiliation of being demoted. That would force a sale of his equity, and Helen would make damn sure she was in a position to snap it up this time. Pierce's. Helen smiled to herself. It had a much nicer ring.

'Okay,' said Edward. 'Let's say we all agree this is the way forward. I'm not sure there's anything in the partnership agreement that allows us to remove someone.'

'You're right,' said Helen. 'It doesn't, not at the moment any-way. But as you all know, changes to the partnership agreement can be made with a super-majority partner vote, so if all of us around this table think we should do it, then we can make it happen.'

Alex was frowning. 'I still think we should give Matt a chance.'

'We are,' said Helen firmly. 'All we're doing is adding a clause to the partnership agreement that says that if anyone under-performs, we can reconsider their position as a partner. So if Matt performs as well as he should be – as well as *we* are – then he should stay. This is simply a safeguard. Many other big firms are doing it, and I think it's fair and sensible.'

'But the partnership agreement applies to all of us,' said Will nervously. 'Surely that will make our own positions more precarious?'

'The three of you are bringing in ten times the fees Matt Donovan is billing, so I really don't think you have anything to fear. Besides, with Matt out of the equity partnership structure, that leaves more of the profits to be spread around. At the moment, you're each getting what, three, four per cent? I'm sure you'd all prefer a fairer slice for all the work you're bringing in?'

She didn't point out that once she'd bought up Matt Donovan's shareholding, they would still only have a tiny percentage each.

'Umm, Helen?'

Helen turned in her seat to see Sid Travers standing there holding a document case.

'Sid? What are you doing here?' she snapped.

The young trainee almost melted on the spot.

'Sorry, Helen, but I've got an urgent "By Hand" for you to sign,' she said. 'We've got a bike waiting for it and I wasn't sure if you were returning to the office.'

Helen held out her hand.

'Pass it here,' she sighed, hoping the girl hadn't heard anything of their conversation. When Sid had gone, she turned back to the table, her unruffled composure completely returned.

'So, gentlemen,' she coaxed. 'Are you in or are you out?'

She watched as they each wrestled with their own internal debates: Alex wondering about the ethics of blindsiding a colleague, but ambitious enough to see that it helped his own career; Will desperate to please Larry, but enough of a toady to follow the others; and Edward, well, she expected that Edward was already rehearsing telling Caroline that they could start looking at houses near Harrods. It was Alex who spoke first, just as she knew it would be.

'Well I think we should go for it,' he said, glancing up at the others for support. 'Matt won't be pleased, of course, but at the end of the day we're not pushing him out, just levelling the playing field.'

'I'm in if you guys are,' mumbled Will.

Finally Helen turned to Edward.

'Me? Oh, you had me at "more money",' he laughed. 'Count me in.'

Trying hard to hide her joy, Helen signalled to the waiter to fill their glasses, then raised hers in toast.

'To us,' she said with a flourish.

50

'Are you out of your friggin' mind?'

Sam had seen Jim Parker angry before; in fact it was almost his default setting. He'd once seen his agent grab a waiter by the throat for bringing him the wrong brand of bottled water, and with Sam in the car he'd rammed his Porsche into the back of another expensive sports car he believed had taken his parking space. But Sam had never seen him this worked up before.

'This is fucking insane, Sam!' he said, stalking over to his office window and looking down on to the traffic of Wilshire Boulevard. 'Why d'you want to throw away years of hard work? You need to see a shrink, get laid, something, 'cos you sure ain't thinking straight.' He threw a rubber stress ball against the wall. 'Jesus, we're talking fucking millions here.'

Of course, Sam hadn't really expected his agent to do back-flips when he announced he was leaving LA for London to work on a comedy script. On the face of it, it *was* crazy. Even with the current black mark against him, Sam still had a profile, a track record and a certain notoriety, and with an agent of Jim's influence, there was always a good chance of finding someone prepared to put him in a great movie. But Sam simply had no interest in going back to all that.

'Jim, you should have been there,' he said, his eyes wide. 'That gig in Edinburgh was just *incredible*. The intimacy of it all, the connection with the crowd. It was like theatre but better.'

His agent sniffed. 'Well maybe I could have experienced this transcendental happening if you'd thought to mention you were doing it. Imagine how frickin' dumb I felt when the phone is ringing red hot with people wanting to talk about your Edinburgh show and I'm like "What show?"'

Sam placed his hands together.

'I'm sorry about that. But I didn't tell you because I knew you'd talk me out of it. Sometimes I have to make my own decisions, you know.'

'Sure, and what great choices you've been making lately,' Jim sneered. 'Cheating on Jess, battering a photographer. Not to mention like three or four separate disappearing acts.'

'This is what I want, Jim.' Sam's voice was low, controlled, his eyes locking with the agent's. He could have reminded Jim who was in charge, who employed whom, but that would only have riled him further. Sam still needed him on side.

'Okay, if you really want to connect with your audience, I can get you something major on Broadway,' said Jim, exhaling sharply. 'Arthur Miller, Mamet, some shit like that. To be honest, it might not be a bad idea. With the right play, director, you're looking at a Tony, no question.'

Sam placed his hands flat on Jim's desk.

'I don't care about a Tony Award and I don't care about Broadway. I want to write. Those people in Edinburgh thought I was funny, Jim. They were laughing at my words, not just at the way I delivered a line.'

'Of course they found you funny,' snorted his agent. 'They were drunk. They were laughing *at* you. *Schadenfreude*, my friend. The movie star reduced to some dick-end hole in the middle of nowhere.'

Not for the first time, Sam thought about firing Jim. Right then he could have told him where to take his ten per cent and shove it. But Jim Parker was the best – a savvy and ruthless power broker who made millions for himself and his clients. At thirty-five he was already being talked about as the new Mike Ovitz; whispers were he was making a pitch for the CEO job at his agency, MTA, and if the board were fool enough not to give it to him, Sam felt sure he would end up running a studio by forty. Jim Parker was not a man you wanted as your enemy.

'Look, Jim,' said Sam in a more conciliatory tone, 'I'm not saying I don't ever want to make a studio movie again. I just want to take a little time out.'

'And do what?' said Jim. 'Pretend you're twenty-three again? You've made it, kiddo. You make eight million bucks a picture. You've done all the hard work already. No more sucking cock and brown-nosing assholes to get some shitty walk-on. You don't have to do all that crap again, capisce?'

Sam frowned.

'This isn't about money, Jim. It's about re-prioritising. Changing pace. Getting back to grass roots.'

The agent looked at him aghast.

'Grass roots? You really think you can go back? You're not one of them any more, Sammy.'

'But I can be, Jim. I *need* to. None of this' – he gestured around Jim's plush office – 'none of it is real. I want to find myself again.'

Jim threw his hands up in frustration.

'Sam, you want to *get* fucking real. You gonna sell up the place in the Hills and the cars and the jet? You gonna give it all to some orphanage? No? Then you ain't never gonna be "real" like those stiffs down there on the street. You might have this romantic fucking little illusion going on in your head, but you can't go back. You can't become unfamous. Life has changed for you. Permanently.'

Sam shook his head. He knew there was a certain amount of truth in what Jim was saying – he couldn't erase the last ten years and go to work in a butcher's, hoping that no one would ever mention his former life – but he was exaggerating. People stopped being famous all the time, moved on to other things, other places, otherwise Hollywood would be the biggest, most crowded city on earth.

'Anyway, you want to write a script, why d'you have to go to London to do it? We'll get you a place out at the beach, that way you can still take meetings.'

Sam was starting to get aggravated by Jim's refusal to see that something had changed in his life.

'I like it in London,' he said firmly. 'Being here a few days has reminded me of that.'

Jim looked at him shrewdly.

'You fucking some girl there now?'

Sam needed every bit of his acting skill not to betray himself.

'No,' he said, feeling disloyal. 'And anyway, Jim, this is not for ever. I just want to try out a few options.'

Jim's mouth curled in distaste.

'You leave this town, I can't keep you hot.'

'Don't exaggerate,' said Sam. 'Look at Demi Moore. Disappears to her ranch for a few years, comes back, bags Kutch, they're the new King and Queen of Hollywood.'

'With respect, Demi didn't leave town with the baggage you've got.'

Sam took a deep breath.

'Look, remember when we had that council of war at my place in England? You said that we needed the right vehicle for me to get back in the game. A really great rom-com – that was your idea, you even said I should write it. It was a great idea, Jim, and now's my chance to do it.'

Jim pouted, thinking it over.

'You got a plan?' he said, looking at Sam sideways.

'Yes,' he said. 'It's a cracker. I think it's got sleeper hit written all over it.' This was an out-and-out lie, but he couldn't admit to Jim that his Big Idea consisted of a few illegible notes he'd scribbled on the back of the in-flight magazine on his way into LAX.

'Well I guess Sly Stallone wrote *Rocky* in a fortnight,' said Jim, rubbing his chin. 'Take the rest of the summer off and we'll talk again when you've got something.'

Sam stood up eagerly, thrusting his hand out to shake. 'Thanks, Jim, it means a lot to have you on side.'

'Yeah, yeah,' said Jim, waving him away. 'Don't start getting all kissy on me, it's only a fucking script.'

Sam walked towards the door, a spring in his step.

'Hey, Sammy,' said Jim. 'This shit better be funny. Because if it's not, you're not going to be able to get a job scooping poop on Santa Monica Beach.'

No pressure, then, thought Sam. But as he walked out into the sunshine, he felt as if someone had given him wings. No more red carpets, no more schmoozing studio heads, no more bloody Hollywood. He was free.

51

Larry was feeling proud of himself. Even for someone of his legendary guile and underhandedness, his plan to bring Fabio Martelli and his lovely new girlfriend to heel on Matt's behalf had come together nicely. A few hours of research, a few calls to some well-placed sources, and Larry had found out enough about Martelli's business affairs to write his biography. The playboy – Larry scoffed at the term; it was the sort of label they stuck on any Eurotrash with a yacht these days – had made his money in New York nightclubs in the eighties, shifting into the hotel business in the nineties, and now he had a string of boutique bolt-holes around the globe; the Miami Beach Martelli had just opened to great acclaim. But that was just Fabio's bread-and-butter business. Clearly his ambition stretched way beyond fluffy robes and pillow mints. He had spent the last five years planning, financing and doing the groundwork for a vast billion-dollar leisure development in Dubai that would make the Vegas casinos look like seaside arcades. Larry had seen the 3D computer plans of the site, and he could tell immediately that it was a fantastic, ambitious and risky development – but it was a development that was about to hit the skids if Fabio Martelli didn't play ball.

Sitting in the bar at the One Aldwych hotel, Larry looked at his watch. He was early for the meeting, and he certainly didn't expect Fabio to arrive on time. People like that never did; it was all part of their 'so busy and important, had to take a call from the Queen' bullshit image. Glancing around to make sure he wasn't overlooked, Larry picked up the manila envelope in front of him and pulled out the photographs inside. He almost laughed out loud. Fabio's mahogany tan would turn white when he saw these babies. Sheryl Battenburg's photos had been invaluable for Larry's investigation – who Fabio's friends were, what sort of women he invited to his yacht, the sex and the drugs – but on their own, they did very little, and certainly didn't give Larry the leverage he needed. So Larry did what he had always done in such situations: he gave them a little helping hand. He had visited an old drinking buddy called Porno Kev, who just happened to work in the adult film industry. Kev had taken Sheryl's shots and, via the magic of computer manipulation, had overlaid them with hardcore images he had taken with models. Kev truly was an artist, thought Larry, putting the photos back into the envelope. No one would be able to tell; they looked like one set of photos all taken at an orgy on a yacht. Crucially, Larry knew that Fabio wouldn't be able to tell the difference. He would assume someone had leaked real shots from his White Party and would know this spelled disaster for his development in Dubai. All foreign development in the emirate was controlled by Dubai World, a holding company owned by Dubai's strictly Islamic government. They would not react well to the revelation that Fabio Martelli held such parties.

Larry sat back and took a sip of his whisky. He knew he shouldn't be drinking it, but he'd watered it down with ice, so it wasn't a real spirit, was it? More like a cocktail, really.

He realised how much he'd missed this: the drama of meeting powerful men in bars, cutting deals, power-broking, manoeuvring to gain advantage. Wasn't that the definition of politics? The effective use of power?

Well today, he held all the cards. The choice for Fabio would be simple: abort his plan to move Kim and Oliver to Miami or give up on his dream to rake in billions in the Gulf. Larry was confident which way he would jump. He had met countless men like Fabio before, and knew that women like Kim Collier didn't matter half as much to them as their global enterprises.

Just then, his mobile began to chirp and he snatched it up, half expecting it to be Fabio's PA saying he was going to be ten minutes late.

'Hey, Dad,' said a familiar voice.

'Matty?' frowned Larry. They had not spoken for almost a fortnight. Larry was immediately alarmed. 'Is everything okay?'

'Yes, yes,' said Matthew cautiously. 'I just wanted to clear the air since the outburst the other night.'

'Well I was about to call you,' Larry said guiltily.

'I also wanted to say thank you,' added his son.

'Thank you? Whatever for?'

'For telling me to think outside the box.'

'I thought you didn't listen to a word your old man said?'

'Well he's right about some things. Sometimes you don't need to use the law. Kim Collier just called me to say she's not going to take Oliver out to Miami after all.'

'What the hell happened?' asked Larry, stunned. 'What did you have to do?'

'I just appealed to her better judgement. I found her when she was on her own and we had a long talk. I told her about my relationship with you. How a son needs his dad, all that stuff.'

'And that *worked*?' said Larry.

'Apparently so. She loves her son, and I think somewhere deep down she knows that moving across the Atlantic, uprooting her life to be the trophy girlfriend of a well-known philanderer, might not be the best move.'

'Wow,' said Larry quietly. He looked down at the brown envelope in front of him. Suddenly it felt grubby in his hand.

'You sound surprised.'

'No, no. Not at all,' he said, picking up the envelope. 'I always had faith in you.' There was an awkward pause.

'How about we try again? Another night. Another pub supper. No arguments this time.'

Larry felt a wide grin uncurl across his face.

'How about my place? Thursday night. I believe it's the best boozer in town.'

He hung up, then rang Fabio's PA.

'Sorry, my love,' he said. 'Just had a call from the Queen, needs her will changing. Tell Fabio I'll call to reschedule.'

He paid his bar bill and left the hotel, filling his lungs with the London street fumes as if it was mountain air. Spotting a rubbish bin on the Strand, he dropped the envelope in with a satisfying thud, then walked away, a spring in his step. And his supper date with Matt on Thursday made him feel even better. Somehow it was more of a real step forward even than his phone call to offer him the partnership.

It was an occasion that called for a cigar. A trip to see Parnell, the head buyer at Davidoff, would round off this fine morning perfectly. Larry marched down the Strand towards Trafalgar Square, the sunshine warming his neck. It felt like today was the first day of . . . of *what*? Larry had never been the poetic type, but he knew that he was on a new path. To where, he had no idea, but he was sure that his son would be a part of it, and that was a wonderful feeling.

He was snaking around the back streets of St James's debating the full flavour of a Bolivar Corona versus the peppery bite of a Montecristo No. 2 when he saw a familiar figure get out of a grey sports car fifty yards in front of him. For a moment he wasn't sure if it was his wife. The car was certainly unfamiliar, and hadn't she said she was going to visit her friend Jacqui in Esher? But there was no mistaking the theatrical way she swung that blond hair over her shoulder as she stood, no mistaking that knockout body. It was Loralee all right. But what was she doing here? Immediately Larry felt a sense of unease. He switched his attention to the man climbing from the driver's seat. Tall, around forty, but in good shape under that expensive-looking suit. He looked like one of those sports stars who advertise razor blades. The man touched Loralee's back to guide her across the road, disappearing into St James's Palace, a big stucco-fronted hotel popular with well-heeled Middle Eastern tourists. Larry knew that sort of touch. It was intimate, familiar. He could feel his heart beginning to pound as he followed them inside the hotel. Maybe he was overreacting. After all, there was an excellent Moroccan restaurant in the hotel and didn't Loralee like Moroccan food? He couldn't remember.

Larry turned towards the Gulshan restaurant and, peering around a corner, scanned the line of customers waiting to speak to the maître d'. Loralee and her companion were not there – and in that instant, Larry realised his happy morning was over. He knew with bitter certainty what he was going to find when he turned back towards the reception. His wife and the young stranger would be checking into a suite, grinning like newlyweds. He knew this because he himself had been in this situation so many times before with other women, with other men's wives. They would be trying to retain decorum, trying not to giggle in case anyone was watching, yet finding it impossible to hide their glee at the thought of the illicit pleasure that lay ahead. Larry didn't need to see it to know, yet still he followed, watching from behind as Loralee whispered something into the man's ear, watching as he stroked her arm and chuckled. Watching as the receptionist handed them the key to their afternoon playtime den. Larry stayed there watching, his mouth dry, his hands trembling, until the lift doors closed on them.

He'd seen enough anyway. There was a pain in his chest and he struggled for breath. For a second he thought it was another cardiac attack, until he felt a single tear dribbling down his crêpey cheek. At which point he knew he did not need to call for an ambulance, because what he was feeling was just the crushing ache of a broken heart.

52

To a casual observer, Helen Pierce was her normal glacial self. Smart and crisp in a white shirt and claret pencil skirt, she sat in her usual place in court behind Jonathon Balon's barrister Nicholas Collins, a woman completely in control. But inside, she was anxious and insecure as Collins stood to address the judge.

'M'lud, I'd like to call Dominic Bradley as a witness for the plaintiff,' he said.

This was the source of Helen's unease. As far as she was concerned, the whole case hinged on this one witness. Dominic Bradley didn't look much like a star witness as he shuffled to the box. Mid thirties, unshaven and receding, he had obviously tried to dress up for the occasion by adding a tie to a casual checked shirt and tucking it into his jeans. Helen wondered for a moment how someone like Bradley had managed to date someone as connected and pristine as Deena Washington, but years of experience had taught her that when it came to ambitious women, physical attractiveness was way down on their checklist. Dominic Bradley wasn't bad-looking, but he clearly had something else, something Deena wanted. Connections, an entree into the glamorous worlds of fashion and media, who knew? All Helen cared about was the fact that he had made it to court in time. In the forty-eight hours after her meeting with Deena Washington in the Hamptons, she'd had every private investigator on her Rolodex scrambling to locate Bradley and discover the reason why he hated Balon. Thankfully he'd been easy to find. As Deena had guessed, he was at his parents' house in Berkshire. The second part of the equation had proved more difficult. Unsurprisingly, Bradley had been extremely unwilling to help. Why, he had asked her, would he want to assist Balon's legal team and thus anger the powerful Steinhoff publishing house? He was a jobbing photographer; he could lose his entire livelihood. Helen knew Bradley was playing the same game as his ex-girlfriend, angling for a pay-off, but she couldn't risk being accused of trying to influence a witness. Anyway, in this case, the law provided: no more incentive was needed than a witness summons from the court.

'Mr Bradley,' said Nicholas Collins, 'can you tell me about your most recent ex-girlfriend, and what she did for a living?'

Helen watched every move Bradley made. The deep breath before he spoke, the nervous glances at both Jonathon Balon and Spencer Reed, the hands gripping one another, the knuckles white.

'She was called Deena Washington,' said Bradley, his voice wavering. 'We were together for three years before we split up after Christmas. She was a subeditor for *Stateside* magazine.'

'A subeditor? They check and edit copy, don't they?'

'That's right.'

Jasper Jenkins leapt to his feet.

'Relevance to the case, m'lud?'

Judge Lazner raised a hand to say he wanted to hear where this was going.

'But subeditors are not generally involved in the commissioning and writing of features, are they?' said Collins, fixing Bradley with that confident expression that told the court he already knew the answer to the question.

Bradley shook his head.

'Not on *Stateside*, no. It frustrated Deena. She wanted to be a writer, or maybe features editor one day.'

'Hearsay, your honour,' boomed Jasper Jenkins.

'But she told you she wanted to be a writer, isn't that correct?' pressed Collins. 'That she was frustrated that she was simply correcting other people's copy.'

'That's right. I saw her spend a lot of time at home coming up with ideas to submit to the features team in the hope of being commissioned.'

'And was she?'

'No.'

'And how did you assist Miss Washington in her career?' asked Collins.

Bradley exhaled deeply, as if he was hesitant about proceeding.

'I knew that the two biggest, most prestigious story slots in *Stateside* were the true crime and society scandal slots. I gave her a story idea based on something I had heard in London.'

'Which was what?'

'I told her about Jonathon Balon, the billionaire London property developer. He used to be my landlord when I lived in north-east London in 1999.'

Nicholas Collins held up his hands in an exaggerated shrug.

'What was scandalous about that?'

Bradley paused for a moment.

'Some of his tenants thought he was a crook. There were local rumours about where he got his money from too. How he was being bankrolled by the Weston crime family. Their financial backing meant he went from a mid-level landlord to a billionaire developer in little over a decade.'

'They were no more than rumours, though,' stated Collins matter-of-factly.

Helen was glad he had pointed that out. Jonathon, after all, was their client, and the judge's patience appeared to be wearing thin.

Dominic Bradley looked uncomfortable.

'I didn't have any actual proof they were true, no.'

'And what did *Stateside* think of this idea?' said Collins, cutting him off.

'Deena told me she'd submitted it to her friend Joanne Green, the commissioning editor. But she'd turned it down because it was too UK-focused. She also said that Spencer, the editor, wouldn't go for it.'

'And did Deena give up on the idea?'

'No. She knew it was a great story.'

Collins looked at Bradley, tilting his head quizzically.

'You didn't give up on it either, did you, Mr Bradley? You

had an idea that might get Joanne Green to change her mind about the story. A little sweetener, if you like.'

Judge Lazner grumbled, 'Stick to English, if you please, Mr Collins.'

'Apologies, m'lud,' said Nicholas Collins, turning to look at the jury. 'You offered Miss Green a *bribe*, didn't you?'

Helen saw the disapproval cross the faces of the jury.

'Jo and I cut a deal. I told her that if she made the story happen, I'd make sure the rent-controlled apartment I'd been living in would be turned over to her when my tenancy lapsed.'

'But did Miss Green have that sort of power with her editor?' asked Collins innocently.

'Seeing as she was sleeping with him, I'd say so,' replied Bradley.

Jasper Jenkins jumped up, his face pink.

'Hearsay!' he shouted, looking decidedly angry.

Helen glanced at Spencer Reed, who had a similar look on his face. As well he might, she thought. She had met Spencer's wife in New York and she hadn't seemed the sort of woman who would take this revelation lying down.

'I'm sorry, I'm a little confused,' said Collins. 'Weren't you just telling us that you suggested the Jonathon Balon story to Miss Washington as a way of helping your girlfriend get her foot in the door as a writer? And yet the byline at the bottom of this story reads Ted Francis.'

'Joanne agreed to commission the story but wanted a London-based writer to do it. '

'Who suggested Mr Francis, the author of the piece?'

'I did.'

'Why?'

Bradley shifted uncomfortably.

'Because he knew a lot about Jonathon Balon. And he's a good journalist.'

'You and Ted Francis are old friends. You've worked together many times. You told him that in return for getting him a commission at *Stateside*, he had to do a hatchet job on Mr Balon.'

'I wanted him to tell the truth about Balon,' said Bradley angrily.

Nicholas Collins snorted. 'The truth? There were some serious criminal allegations in here: money laundering, favours given to known gangsters, and by extension, the insinuation of illegality to the whole of Mr Balon's operation. And yet, as you acknowledge, as this court has heard again and again over the past weeks, there is not a shred of evidence to support any of these allegations.'

'I just thought it was a great story,' said Bradley defensively. 'Rags to riches, mysterious shady benefactors. All I did was tell them about it. If they choose to spin it to make it sound more glamorous, that's not my problem, is it?'

'Spin it,' repeated Collins. 'Interesting choice of words. You mean spin as in "embellish", spin as in "lies"?'

'No!'

'Let me repeat my question for the benefit of the jury. Did you ask Ted Francis to write about the unsubstantiated stories about Mr Balon's connections to the Weston gangland family?'

'Yes.'

'And did you tell Jo Green when she edited the piece to keep it as incendiary as possible?'

'I don't have that power.'

'Did Miss Green still get rewarded with your apartment for running the story?'

'Yes.'

'Why?'

'A deal was a deal.'

'Rubbish. You dangled that fabulous apartment in front of her again on the understanding that she keep the Balon story as derogatory as possible. Yes or no?'

'Yes.'

'Why was this story, the tone of this story, so important to you, Mr Bradley?'

'Because I want to see crooks exposed,' he said fiercely.

'You have a personal interest in this story, don't you, Mr Bradley? You hate Mr Balon and you bribed Miss Green and Mr Francis to work to your agenda of getting revenge on him.'

Bradley shifted in his seat.

'What happened to you in 1999, Mr Bradley?' asked Nicholas

Collins, still looking down at his notes. 'The weekend of September the twelfth specifically.'

Helen noted the look of alarm crossing Bradley's face. Jasper Jenkins saw it too and jumped to his feet.

'Relevance, m'lud?'

The judge sighed.

'Get to the point, Mr Collins.'

'Certainly, m'lud. Mr Bradley was beaten up in an alleyway close to his flat. Beaten up rather badly, sustaining injuries that necessitated admission to hospital for . . .' he checked his notes, 'three days, I believe. Is that not correct, Mr Bradley?'

'Yes,' Bradley said quietly.

'I understand you still bear a scar on your forehead from the assault.'

'Yes.'

Helen saw the jury crane their necks to look. This was excellent stuff. Libel trials were usually mired in boring detail, and drama like this was all in Balon's favour.

'Was anyone charged with this serious assault?' asked Collins.

'No,' said Bradley, his voice shaking with anger.

'But you called the police about it, didn't you? You told them you knew who was behind it.'

His questions had now hardened into statements of fact. Helen could see the jury sitting forward in their seats, all eyes trained on Dominic Bradley. Slowly he began to speak, as if he had finally decided that it was time to come clean.

'Balon was my landlord. I was a student, I'd got into arrears, so Balon sent round the heavies. I still couldn't pay. I sort of became a squatter. A few days later, I was jumped on and attacked when I was walking back from the pub.'

'And did the police interview Mr Balon?'

'Apparently,' said Bradley. 'But the whole thing went quiet. No evidence, they said.'

'Even so, you were convinced Mr Balon had ordered the attack on you,' prompted Collins.

Bradley's face grew hard.

'Yes, I was. I asked around, I even spoke to the local newspaper. Everyone said Balon was in with these thugs and that this sort of thing had happened before. Apparently everyone was too scared to challenge him, because of his connection with the Weston family.'

'So you were angry.'

'Yes.'

'You wanted revenge.'

Bradley looked at the barrister sharply.

'Wouldn't you?'

Collins didn't reply; he simply looked over at the jury.

'Who wouldn't be angry when something so awful has happened to them?' he asked. 'Especially when the person you believe is responsible has escaped prosecution. And who wouldn't *stay* angry when they still bear the scar of that attack, reminding them on a daily basis? Wouldn't you be incensed if you saw the person you regarded as the culprit rising to become a billionaire?'

He turned back to Bradley.

'They say that revenge is a dish best served cold, and that's exactly what happened, isn't it, Dominic? You moved to New York, met your journalist girlfriend Deena, all by happy coincidence. But when she needed a story, you saw your opportunity to finally get back at Balon for what you thought he had done to you all those years ago. No wonder you were so keen for this story to run, why you were prepared to bribe Joanne Green with your chi-chi apartment and force her to use your friend to write the article. A smear story against Mr Balon was your way of getting revenge, wasn't it, Mr Bradley?'

Dominic Bradley looked from Balon to Spencer Reed, his expression one of fear, of a trapped animal. But Helen could see something else there too: triumph. He had finally got his story out, he had finally been listened to. She was fairly sure Spencer Reed would make sure Dominic Bradley never worked in the mainstream media again, but in that moment, she was equally sure Bradley didn't care.

'Mr Bradley?' prompted the judge. 'Answer the question, please. Did you propose the story to get even with Mr Balon?'

'Yes,' he said.

Helen held her breath as Nicholas Collins turned to Bradley for the death blow.

'And your friend Ted Francis, the man who wrote the feature, did he know about your motivation?'

'Yes,' said Bradley.

'And did you ask him to – my apologies again, m'lud – stick the boot in?'

'This is most irregular, m'lud,' began Jasper Jenkins, but no one was listening.

'Yes, I did,' said Bradley, looking at Jonathon Balon with a satisfied smile. 'I told him what a thug and a gangster Balon was, and that I wanted him to bury the bastard.'

The court was immediately in uproar, with both sides shouting objections and threats and the judge calling for order.

Helen Pierce simply sat where she was, closed her eyes and smiled.

'Gotcha,' she whispered.

53

It was easy to spot who was going to a party. Cath was waiting for Anna outside Sloane Square tube station dressed in a sparkly silver dress, like a space-age flapper girl lost in the sea of drab commuters piling into the station to go home. Anna smoothed down her own emerald-green shift dress, wondering if it was dressy enough. She wasn't entirely sure how this evening was going to go, but she was glad Cath was there to hold her hand.

'This is so exciting,' said Cath, giving Anna a hug. 'Where are we going again?'

'You're excited about something you don't even know about?' laughed Anna, flagging down a taxi.

'Hey, you're the one who sent me this cryptic message saying "drop everything, I'm taking you to the most glamorous party you've ever been to".'

'It's the launch of a big hotel. Very high end,' said Anna as the cab rumbled down Lower Sloane Street towards Chelsea Embankment. 'Think the Plaza in New York, only more modern.'

'Will there be any celebrities there?'

'Wall to wall.'

Cath gripped her arm. 'Why don't you invite me to things like this more often? I've got a dozen Karen Millen party dresses in my closet collecting dust and my best mate has a hotline to the stars.'

That wasn't strictly true. They had Sam Charles to thank for this invitation; using his name had been the only way Anna could think to get inside. And she needed to get inside, because there was someone there she desperately needed to meet.

The traffic was in gridlock as they approached the Chelsea Heights, a stand-alone suite-only hotel catering specifically for high-rollers, people who came to the capital for Bond Street and Canary Wharf, people who thought nothing of spending over two thousand pounds per night, breakfast extra. It also incorporated the Duel, London's first high-concept restaurant, where two Michelin-starred chefs, placed in separate kitchens, would compete nightly to create the best menu possible, no expense spared.

'This place is amazing,' gasped Cath as Anna gave their names at the door and they walked into the cavernous lobby. That was an understatement. It was as if someone had taken a giant apple corer and pulled out the centre of the hotel, replacing it with a golden waterfall that cascaded from the roof, disappearing into a hole in the floor of the lobby. It was a marvel of science or civil engineering or magic, thought Anna, not really sure which. It was certainly impressive, though. As was the gathering for the party. TV stars rubbed shoulders with novelists, artists and sports stars.

'Wow,' said Cath, clasping at Anna's arm. 'Is that David Beckham over there? And Elton *John*? Oh please, please tell me that you come to things like this every week.'

Anna giggled.

'I'm afraid not. Most nights I'm still in the office at this time.'

Live jazz floated through the marble lobby, whilst the canapés were like miniature works of art. A handsome waiter handed them each a deep red cocktail and the two girls clinked their glasses together.

'Well I'd say all that hard work was worthwhile,' said Cath. 'I work stupid hours too, and no bugger has ever invited me to anything more glamorous than All Bar One.'

Anna was happy Cath was so excited, but at the same time she felt bad about having dragged her friend into her deception. She scanned the crowd, but there had to be five hundred people packed into the hotel's lobby, and besides, she only had images from magazines to go on.

'Listen, Cath . . .' she began, pulling an awkward face.

'What is it?' said Cath warily. 'I know that look; you're about to tell me we have to serve the nibbles or something.'

'No, but I do have a confession to make. I'm here to find a man.'

'Aren't we all?' Cath grinned.

'A specific man, by the name of Johnny Maxwell. He's a society fixer and I need to charm him into . . . well, it's something to do with work.'

Cath sighed, putting a hand on her chest. 'Is that all? Honey, you can chat up Jabba the Hutt for all I care, as long as I get to ogle Beckham's bum while drinking free booze.'

Anna pulled her BlackBerry from her clutch bag: one message. Sam. She clicked on it: 'Missing You. S xx'

She looked up to see Cath examining her face suspiciously.

'What are you smiling at, young lady?' she said.

'Just some work thing,' stammered Anna.

'I knew it!' cried Cath. 'It's a bloke, isn't it? You sly little minx. Have you been on Match.com like we told you?'

Anna shook her head, wishing her cheeks didn't feel so hot.

'It's just Sam,' she said, quickly slipping her BlackBerry back into her bag.

'Sam who?'

'Sam Charles.'

Cath looked at her incredulously.

'*Just* Sam Charles. I thought he fired you?'

'He did. But he came round to apologise. We're working on something together.'

'He came round to your *house*? OMG. You've slept with him, haven't you? I don't believe it, you dirty old sod. I knew there was something different about you today. It's that "just been shagged" glow.'

'Keep your voice down,' said Anna, steering Cath to a quieter alcove. 'I don't want to get fired again.'

Cath's mouth was still hanging open.

'My best friend has shagged a Hollywood star. This is historic.'

'It was only one time,' she said. Four times in one night, she thought dreamily, but now was not the time to go into that.

'Only once? I swear if it happened to me I would think my work on earth was done now.'

It felt good to finally tell someone about it. After their time on the longboat, she'd been resigned to the fact that it had been a one-night stand brought on by the romantic setting. The whole experience had had a decidedly holiday romance feel to it. They were drunk, they were in India, they'd been caught up in the drama. It had been wonderful, and he'd been funny and attentive on the flight home, but she wasn't kidding herself that she could expect anything else. He was Sam Charles, for goodness' sake – and anyway, after dropping her home, he'd flown straight back to LA. Who knew what bimbos were waiting for him in his swanky Hollywood Hills shag pad? But Sam had surprised her. He had called her. Part of her had felt happy and hopeful that this was the start of something. The other part felt as if she was about to step on to a rollercoaster, and wasn't sure if she was ready for the ride.

'If you're going to get all soppy over Casanova, I'm going to have a crack at a footballer.'

Anna put her hand on her friend's arm.

'There he is,' she said.

'Who? Sam Charles?'

'No, Johnny Maxwell.'

He was standing in a group of model-type girls. In his mid sixties, wearing a loud purple and green checked three-piece suit, with his shoulder-length white hair swept back, he looked like a rock star gone to seed. Every now and then he would use the silver camera hanging around his neck to snap a shot of one of these beautiful women.

'Is that the guy you need to speak to?'

'I need to chat him up, actually,' said Anna.

'So you and Sam have an *open* relationship, then?' She looked over at Maxwell. 'Anna, he's about eighty.'

'Sixty-four, I believe.' She'd spent an hour Googling him that afternoon. Whilst Johnny Maxwell had a decidedly sleazy reputation as a party animal, his lineage was pure. The son of a wealthy minor aristocrat, he was an Old Etonian who had dropped out of Oxford to join the Carnaby Street scene. Inspired by Bailey and Donovan, he'd become a photographer, primarily as a way to get girls. Since then, he had never really gone away, becoming a fixture on whatever was the most happening scene: Studio 54, eighties LA, Britpop London, finding his niche somewhere between portrait photographer and society party planner.

'What do you want to chat him up for?' asked Cath, wrinkling her nose.

'I need him to invite me to something.'

'What? A Saga holiday?'

'Just run with me on this one, okay?' said Anna seriously. 'Think of it as role play. We're going over to speak to him, and when we do, we're going to have to pretend to be someone else.'

Cath frowned. 'Would it ruin the surprise to ask why?'

Anna took a swallow of her cocktail and prepared to tell her friend a little white lie. 'Johnny Maxwell organises these big parties, networking things, for this society guy. I need to get to one of the parties, but the host hates Donovan Pierce lawyers because we've sued him.'

She hated lying to her friend.

'It's like James Bond,' laughed Cath, and Anna gripped her arm.

'Come on, we're going over. He's looking at us. I think he wants to take our pictures.'

'Pictures? What for? You sure this is kosher, Anna?'

'Absolutely,' she whispered, and stepped forward.

54

The weather had finally turned, the long hot summer slipping suddenly into melancholy autumn in just an afternoon. Light rain spotted the pavement and a brisk wind whipped off the river, making Matt wish he had worn his trench coat rather than this thin summer suit jacket. He looked up at the leaden grey skies, surprised at how jittery he was feeling. He'd had dinner with his father on numerous occasions before; always at some flash restaurant where everyone knew Larry's name and would approach his table to exchange ribald anecdotes while Matthew fixed his gaze on his carrots and wished he was somewhere, anywhere, else. Tonight he was eating at Larry's house; something that to most people would sound everyday and mundane. Yet this felt so much more significant. Matt had not eaten with his father, at his house, since he was four years old and it was the Donovan family home. Tonight didn't feel just like supper. It felt like the start of a new family life. Or perhaps a way of claiming back a lost life that had been snatched away from him.

Larry answered the door in a white apron scarred with something crimson.

'What's all this?' said Matt, smiling.

'You said you wanted supper, so I'm cooking for my son. How hard can it be?'

'I had rather assumed you would be getting some famous chef in to do the hard work.'

Larry waved his hand dismissively as he walked back into the house. 'Chefs? I've seen those telly programmes. They just drizzle olive oil on everything and bang it in the oven. I'm perfectly capable of that.'

Matt handed his father a bottle of wine and followed him into the warm kitchen. Whatever Larry was cooking did smell delicious. It reminded Matthew of the early days of his marriage, when Carla had just given up work and used to keep the house smelling wonderful with expensive candles and Waitrose suppers.

'What's cooking?'

'Coq au vin.'

Larry held the bottle up, casting a critical eye over the label. Grunting, he quickly uncorked it, then pulled the roasting tin from the oven and poured Matt's Merlot over the top of it.

'That should perk her up a bit,' he said.

'Shit, Dad, that cost me forty quid.'

'Good food is made from good ingredients,' Larry quipped, closing the oven door with a clang. 'Anyway, I've already got something waiting for us,' he added, disappearing into the next room.

Matt walked over to the far wall, where dozens of photographs had been hung in smart black frames. There were some of Larry and Loralee's wedding, and their honeymoon too, somewhere hot and beachy with the groom in a Hawaiian shirt and shorts. Then there was a series of pictures of Larry with famous clients, and shaking hands with Muhammad Ali and Nelson Mandela. The biggest photo was of him laughing with Bill Clinton, looking like old friends.

'Now that figures,' murmured Matthew with a bittersweet smile, realising how little he knew about his father's life but excited by the idea of hearing some of the stories behind these pictures.

Larry came back holding a balloon of red wine aloft.

'Here, try this,' he said. 'One of the great bottles of claret of the twentieth century.'

'Sounds expensive,' said Matthew, sniffing the wine.

'It was. I've just been waiting for an occasion to drink it.'

They clinked their glasses together and each took a seat at the oak-topped island in the middle of the kitchen. It was funny: there had been a time, not so long ago, when the thought of having a convivial supper with Larry Donovan would have been impossible. Matthew had been too angry, too resentful. He had grown up embarrassed by his father and ashamed of the failure of his family. It wasn't the missed Christmases and birthdays and graduations that had upset him; it was all the little things. The disapproving whispers at the school gate, the sight of other dads having a kickabout with their kids in the park, the lack of anyone to ask about girls, shaving, even sport. His mother had done her best, trying to be enthusiastic about Lego and Action Man and rugby, stretching herself thin as she tried to juggle her career and Matthew's needs. She was a stoic, independent woman who neither encouraged contact between father and son nor badmouthed Larry to Matt either. It was as if Larry barely existed. But the truth was, Matt had thought about his father a lot, never sure if Larry was some kind of monstrous bogeyman or whether life would be more exciting with this unreliable, but unpredictable man in it. And that was what he wasn't sure he could ever forgive his father for. For abandoning him. For being able to cut him out of his life as if he was a piece of gristle on a prime cut of fillet steak. Since he'd become a father himself, it was something he felt more fiercely.

As if he was reading his thoughts, Larry gave his son a slow smile.

'Who'd have thought we'd be doing this, eh?'

Matthew nodded. He felt bad about their argument in the pub, especially when his father was clearly not recovered from his heart attack. Still, he wasn't sure if he was ready for the Hollywood ending.

'So where's Loralee?' he asked, keen to change the subject.

'She's out,' said Larry quickly.

'Good.'

Larry raised an eyebrow.

'I don't think she likes me coming round.'

His father shrugged. 'She's jealous of you.'

'Of me?'

Larry waved his glass at Matt.

'Well, she's jealous of us, what we could be. I think she liked it as it was before.'

Matt had always wondered about Larry and Loralee's

relationship. Was his father really arrogant enough to think that Loralee had married him for his sparkling wit and virile good looks, or had they struck the classic 'Chelsea bargain' of money and stability in exchange for youth and beauty?

'I bet she hated you giving me the firm,' said Matt quietly.

Larry swilled the wine around the bottom of his glass in wide circles.

'I have enough money. The law's been good to me. I wanted it to be good to my son too. After everything that's happened, I suppose it was the best way of telling you that I loved you.'

Matt felt a spike of emotion so strong he thought it would knock him off his bar stool.

'You could have just said I love you.' He grinned. 'But thank you,' he added slowly.

They sat there and smiled at each other, and Matt knew then that their relationship had mellowed.

'You know Loralee is having an affair?' said Larry, still caught up in their moment of complicity.

Matt looked at him in shock. 'What? You've only been married three months.'

'Like that ever stopped anyone,' he said. 'Me included.'

'What are you going to do?'

'It's more what I was hoping you could do for me.'

Matt felt himself move into professional mode.

'Of course, Dad, anything. Obviously I couldn't actually represent you, but . . .'

Larry put his hand on top of his son's. It looked smaller, weaker than Matt remembered.

'You misunderstand,' he said. 'I was rather hoping you would check on the cats next Friday. Feed them. Loralee insists they have Jersey milk, you see. I'd get the housekeeper to do it, but she's going back to Poland on Friday.'

'The cats?' frowned Matt. 'What about Loralee?'

'I'm taking her away for the week. Somewhere fancy.'

'When you know she's having an affair?' said Matt incredulously.

Larry gave him a sad smile.

'I'm not stupid,' he said quietly. 'Would Loralee be with me if

407

I was thirty and poor?' He shook his head. 'I think we both know the answer to that one. And I know it looks pathetic, a man my age with a woman like her. People see us together, they think she's only after me for my money. Well maybe that's so, but the truth is . . .' Larry's voice caught in his throat. 'The truth is, Matty, I love her. I open my eyes in the morning and I look at her lying next to me, and I think how lucky I am to be with her. I know you think – everyone thinks – she's just a gold-digger, but she's been good to me. Through the illness, I don't suppose it's been easy for her.'

'But you can't just pretend she's not having an affair.'

Larry waved his hand dismissively. 'I tell myself it's just sex. Since the heart attack, I've not exactly been active in that department.'

'Dad . . .' began Matthew, but Larry squeezed his hand.

'It's what I tell myself,' he repeated, and Matthew knew that this particular conversation was finished. They sat in silence as darkness fell outside, sipping their wine, the rich smell of the meal filling the kitchen.

'So how about you?' said Larry finally. 'Seen any more of Carla since her separation?'

Matt rubbed his chin.

'I slept with her,' he said in the spirit of shared secrets.

He felt a wave of relief that he had finally told someone. Granted, it was embarrassing discussing such things with your father, but Larry had more experience with difficult women than any man he knew.

'My, my. It has been all go in the bedroom department.'

Part of Matthew wanted to bury the thought of what had happened between himself and Carla and put it down to the raised emotions of the situation, but he knew he had to talk about it, to try and make sense of what he wanted to happen next, because he was struggling to do it on his own.

'Does she want to get back together with you?' asked Larry.

'I don't know. She's in Ibiza. We're meeting for dinner when she gets back.'

'And how do *you* feel about getting back together?'

This was the difficult part. If you'd asked him two, three

years ago whether he wanted to get back with the beautiful ex-wife whom he had loved and who had hurt him so much, the answer, despite himself, would have been an unequivocal yes. But everything felt much more complicated now. For the first time in a long time he felt happy, secure, confident in his own skin and the life he had built for himself. He had got used to being alone, and in many ways, he enjoyed it.

'She's a beautiful woman.' He meant the sex, of course, but he didn't want to elaborate any further; Larry was still his dad, after all.

'Do you love her, or are you just lonely?' asked Larry.

How were you supposed to tell the difference after so long? thought Matt, opening his mouth to speak.

'The day at the New Forest, Jonas was so happy . . .'

'I didn't ask how Jonas felt about it,' replied Larry.

Matt shifted in his chair. 'But this is everything to do with Jonas. I'm his dad. We're a family. If that's not a bloody good reason to get back together again, I don't know what is.'

'So you think you should get back with Carla because of what Jonas feels?'

Matt sank into a silence, defeated by the question. He dealt with this every single day of his life. He saw first hand why people stayed in relationships and why others left. Whenever clients asked him for advice – 'What do I do now?' – he always gave them the same answer: there was no right thing to do when your relationship faltered. The only thing to do was what felt right to you.

Larry put his empty glass on the table.

'Let me ask you another question. Would you have wanted your mother to stay with me, even if neither of us was happy?'

'But Mum *was* happy. And then you had an affair and left us. Why did you do that? Were you really that unhappy, or was it just a case of the grass is greener?'

Larry stood up.

'Stay there,' he said, and walked out of the kitchen. Matt could hear his slow footsteps going upstairs. He was away for a few minutes, and when he returned, he was holding a small envelope.

'What's that?'

'A letter to me. From your mother,' said Larry, handing it to Matthew.

'Should I read it now?'

'I think so.'

Matt pulled out the single sheet of ageing cream vellum, instantly recognising the small, precise writing of his mother. He began to read.

Dear Larry,

How do you say goodbye to your husband and the father of your son? By letter, I think. I'm not sure I can say the things I want to say without turning back, retreating into a situation that's wrong for both of us. Your affair with that woman was a betrayal, you don't need me to tell you that, but I was surprised you came back. I was even more surprised I took you back. But I did it for our son. I did it to be a family again.

So why does that decision now feel wrong? Because a family is more than three people living in a house together. Because when you come home every day, I know that you would rather be somewhere else, with someone else. Because one day Matthew will be old enough to ask why his parents don't sleep in the same bedroom, and I don't want to tell him that it's because I can't bear to touch you. Not after your affair. But mostly because we both love our son and we always want what's best for him. I want Matthew to be brought up around love, not around two people who have nothing to say to each other any more, who have broken whatever they once had. We don't want him to grow up feeling guilty that he was the only glue binding two unhappy, resentful people together.

Love dies if you don't water it – I think you said that to me once – and that's what happened between you and me, Larry. Love isn't an obligation. It's a life force, a gift of nature; love is about finding that one person who makes you feel so happy your heart could sing. We had it for a while, but it's gone; we both have to face the truth of that.

410

Perhaps we can find it again, somewhere else. I hope so.

Yours truly, Katherine

Matthew folded the letter and slipped it back into the envelope.

'Mum left *you*?' he said. 'You left us. She told me that.'

Larry fetched the decanter and filled Matthew's glass, putting it down again without filling his own.

'For five amazing years we were so happy, me and your mother,' he said. 'I doubt anyone anywhere was ever as in love as we were at the start. But after she'd had you and thrown herself back into her career? Well, things changed. She had papers published, she was being asked to lecture abroad, there were whispers of a professorship one day.' He shrugged. 'I was busy too, of course, and I'd come home from work long after you'd gone to bed. Kathy would be in the study, working. She made time for you and her job, but there was not enough time for me. I'm not making excuses, just trying to give you some context.'

He held up his hands.

'So I had an affair. My first one. They become quite addictive once you cross the line of morality, but that's another story. This first one, her name was Jan, a client's secretary. Twenty-one, pretty, plus she thought I was fabulous and I drank every drop of flattery as if it was good port. I honestly thought I was in love with her. Looking back, I was just in love with how she made me feel.'

He paused, as if he was reluctant to go on. 'Your mother found out – deep down I think I wanted her to – and kicked me out. But a month later I came back. For you,' he said earnestly.

'But if you came back for me, why didn't you stay?'

Larry tapped the letter in front of Matt.

'I think she says it best in there. Love isn't an obligation; you can't love someone out of duty. We'd changed as people, but we hadn't changed together. She resented me, my long hours, my affair, and I suppose she'd replaced me with a new passion: her own work. And you, of course. On my part, perhaps I couldn't cope with a strong, strident woman like Katherine. It was the seventies, remember. Everyone still expected husbands and wives to fall into their prescribed roles.'

'So why did she keep us apart?'

Larry sighed.

'In part I suppose she was angry, resentful, and wanted to prove that you two could get along just fine without me. But I didn't fight for you. I let my pride get the better of me and I walked away. I walked away from you, and for that, I'll forever be sorry.'

Matthew could see tears glossing over the whites of his father's eyes.

'I know you're a better father than me, Matt. I know it's not ideal living apart from Jonas, but you've shown that you don't need to live with him to be a brilliant dad. Get back with Carla because you love her, because she makes your heart beat faster,' he pleaded. 'Not out of duty. We both love Jonas too much to want him to be brought up in an unhappy household.'

Matthew gave a small smile.

'You make it all sound so simple.'

'I've had a lot of experience of getting it wrong.'

They both laughed together.

'Oh, and can you do one more thing for me?' said Larry, getting up.

'Sure, what is it?'

Larry yanked open the oven, sending a cloud of thick grey smoke rolling up towards the ceiling.

'Can you call the pizza place?' he coughed. 'I think dinner's off.'

55

For a Friday afternoon in late summer, the Limelight Productions lot in Burbank was heaving. This time of year, most media executives were on vacation, but there was a hive of activity around the warehouse-like sound stages as Jessica swung her Aston Martin on to the lot. People always assumed Hollywood was Glamour City, but the fans would have been disappointed to visit a working studio. It was like a rather drab industrial estate, with each of the anonymous warehouse buildings housing a set. Inside, you might find a suburban living room, familiar as the setting for a sitcom perhaps, or maybe a realistic operating theatre from one of the many medical dramas Limelight seemed to pump out season after season. But from the outside, that magic factory could just as easily be a storage facility or an auto shop.

Jessica pulled into her named parking space right by the doors of the *All Woman* production offices. The show was due to start filming three weeks ahead of a mid-October premiere, and John Hartnett, the executive producer, had called the senior team in to run through the storylines for the new season. Jessica had already had Harry Monk, her agent, pre-check it all of course; she had her sights set on cracking the movies, but for now, *All Woman* was her meal ticket and there was no way she was going to leave Sally, her character, in the hands of some overexcited junior writer. Two seasons ago, she had been so unhappy with one episode she had jumped on the first plane to Palm Springs and refused to shoot a frame until they axed the storyline.

'Jessie, you're looking so gorgeous!' exclaimed John Hartnett, kissing her on both cheeks. 'Have you been away? You look a million bucks.'

Jessica waved the compliment aside impatiently.

'Where is everyone?' she said. She could see the boardroom through the glass panels of John's office; it should have been full of writers, producers and actors.

'They're on their way. I pushed it back by thirty minutes.'

'You could have told me,' said Jessica, thinking that she could have dropped into the cute little nail bar near the lot. Amazing French polish and ego boost – the Korean technicians loved the show – and only ten bucks, too.

'Actually, you were the reason why I pushed it back,' said John, showing her to a chair. 'I wanted to talk to you in private.'

'John, it's okay, I'm fine,' sighed Jessica. 'All that crap with Sam's in the past. I've moved on.'

'That's great to hear, but I wanted to talk this through with you.'

On his desk was a stack of scripts. He took one and handed it to Jessica.

'Episode One,' he smiled.

'About time,' said Jessica, leafing through, mentally estimating the ratio of lines for Katie and the other characters. It was always important to get the most face-time on screen.

'So we've got a hot new writer this season,' said John. 'Robert Levine. You know his stuff?'

'Of course,' she lied.

'We've been thrashing out the story arc for Season Five, making a few tweaks.'

She looked up. 'I thought we'd discussed where this season was going. You ran through it with my agent.'

'Sure we did, and we took on board everything you said. But, well, we have to keep things fluid, Jess. Adapt, change it to keep it fresh.'

Alarm bells were immediately ringing. Words like 'change' and 'fresh' always made her nervous.

'Okay. So what's the plan?'

'We're ramping up the drama a little. I think we've been playing it too safe.'

Jessica couldn't really disagree with that. After several seasons it was easy for shows to fall into a rut. If she was honest, that had happened with *All Woman*. The characters had been fully fleshed out and their storylines exploited – and consequently the viewing figures had begun to dip.

'What did you have in mind?'

John held up his hands dramatically.

'A love rival for you and Billy.'

Billy was the on-screen love interest for her character Sally. He'd started off as her flatmate, a hunky shoulder to cry on through numerous ill-fated love affairs, including a fling with her dentist and a farcical relationship with a pair of identical twins. But through it all, he and Sally had crackled with sexual chemistry, and their 'will they, won't they?' storyline had been one of the most electric on-screen relationships since *Moonlighting*.

Season Three's finale, where Billy and Sally were trapped in an avalanche and finally consummated their love in a log cabin, had pulled in the highest ratings of any sitcom that season. But Season Four, following Billy's bumbling attempts to propose, just hadn't had the same tension. Hence the love rival angle. But Jessica didn't like the word 'rival', not at all. Sally was the undisputed star of *All Woman*, and Jessica didn't want her to have a rival anything.

'What are you thinking? A one-night stand? Or how about a dream sequence starring the twin sister Sally doesn't even have? I'm thinking good twin, bad twin.'

John shook his head.

'I'm talking a proper knockout love interest, Jess. A real adversary for Sally – and I've found an actress who I think would be perfect.'

He picked up a remote control and zapped on the seventy-inch television at the far end of his office. The screen popped on to a beautiful brunette smouldering through some dialogue.

'Brooke Geller. She's great, isn't she?' gushed John. 'Twenty-four, only done a couple of duds in pilot season before now, so she's fresh.'

Jessica's stomach turned over as she watched the audition tape. Brooke Geller was stunning, a smouldering raven-haired yin to Sally's all-American yang. John was right, she would be perfect. This girl was gorgeous, had a Victoria's Secret body – and looked at least a decade younger than Jessica. Brooke Geller was a star, plain and simple, and there was no way Jessica wanted her on *her* show.

'What do you think?' said John, pressing the pause button.

'Billy wouldn't go for someone like that,' she said tartly.

'Didn't you see that rack? Billy is a man.' John smiled, taking off his glasses to clean them. 'Besides, we need to make Billy more fallible, more rounded. He was too much of a goody-two-shoes before.'

'I didn't notice his two million fans on Twitter complaining.'

'Well they're going to Tweet even more when Billy and Brooke start an affair.'

Jessica's mouth dropped open

'Tell me you're kidding,' she said, her voice quivering with anger. 'Billy cheating on Sally with some tramp? It's a bit insensitive, isn't it, in view of everything that has happened to me this summer?'

'Jess, it's not meant to be about that.'

But the way John's face coloured, she knew that was exactly what it was meant to be about. They were cynically chasing the ratings, pulling back the audience with the promise of art imitating life. No wonder Hartnett and his new writer had kept the script such a secret until now.

'What a low shot,' she hissed. She was so livid she was struggling to breathe. 'And how long do you see this storyline continuing? One episode?'

'Six episodes initially; we'll see how the fans react.'

'You mean the whole season, don't you?' Jessica's heart was thudding. 'Is this about these "Desperate Jess" headlines? Because if it is, don't worry, I'm taking those bastards to court.'

'It's not about that, I promise you.'

She jumped to her feet, grabbing her cell phone.

'I'm getting Len on the phone right now,' she snapped. 'We'll see what he has to say about this.'

Len Morgan was the head of the studio. He was a disgusting lech who had spent years trying to touch her up, and Jessica felt confident she could wrap him around her little finger.

'Stop a minute, Jess,' said John, putting his hand over her phone. 'This was Len's idea. He's a businessman. He's only interested in the bottom line.'

'No,' she whispered, trying to hold it together.

'Jess, look. You are a wonderful, wonderful actress. You are the undisputed star of this show. But you know how important the eighteen to twenty-five demographic is for advertisers. Unless we can convince the studio we can bring that revenue in, there might not even be a Season Six.'

She steeled herself. 'And you think Brooke Geller is the answer to your problems? She might have sucked your cock to get this gig, but it will take more than that to convince the American public. They love *me*.'

'They *did*, Jess,' said John. 'But things change.'

'Screw you, John,' she growled. 'Expect a call from my lawyer.' She grabbed her bag and wrenched the office door open.

'Stop, Jess. Come on,' he called after her. 'We can sort this out.'

But Jessica was already running out of the building, her eyes clouding with tears. How dare they? How dare they use her heartbreak as a way of shoring up the ratings? It was disgusting, immoral.

Scrabbling her keys out, she jumped into her car and flipped down the vanity mirror. *You know how important the eighteen to twenty-five demographic is*. Like she was too old. Like she was becoming irrelevant. She peered into the mirror, pulling her cheeks back. Well, a good cosmetic surgeon would ensure that didn't happen. She'd show them who the public wanted – America's sweetheart or some slut with perky tits. She shoved the key into the ignition and revved the engine in a roar, screeching across the lot. She indicated right to turn the car on to Mulholland, and as she put her foot on the gas, she peered into the mirror again. Maybe a bit of under-eye work wouldn't go amiss either, she thought. Then her whole body jolted sideways, her head slamming into the windscreen, metal squealing and crumpling as another car smashed into hers. And then she felt nothing.

56

'Another round?' said Helen, summoning the waitress with an elegantly raised finger in the heaving wine bar underneath the Embankment arches. 'Or how about shots?' she added with an unsteady smile.

'I think she's pissed,' whispered David Morrow into Anna's ear. There was certainly no question that Helen was cock-a-hoop. Jonathon Balon had been awarded seventy-five thousand pounds in libel damages that afternoon at the High Court. It wasn't a huge amount, but then Balon had never been particularly bothered about the level of compensation. The key thing was that his name had been vindicated; after two long weeks of wrangling, Mr Justice Lazner had declared the *Stateside* allegations to be 'seriously defamatory' and the magazine's Reynolds defence had failed. Helen had taken great delight in giving a long statement on the steps of the High Court to the waiting media, declaring the verdict to be 'a triumph against irresponsible journalism'.

'I never thought I'd see the day when Helen Pierce wasn't one hundred per cent in control,' said Anna. 'She can barely stand.'

'All part of her act,' smirked David. 'You watch: at eight o'clock on the button, she'll leave, go to the gym, do two million sit-ups to work off the booze, then she'll be straight back to the office to call the States, drum up some new business.'

He gave Anna a wicked little smile.

'So then. A little bird tells me you've become very friendly with Sam Charles.'

Anna felt herself blushing furiously. She was glad the light was low.

'Where on earth have you heard that?' she said, as innocently as she could.

'One of the secretaries told me they'd heard you giggling to him on your mobile. "Ooh Sam . . ." you were going, "talk dirty to me . . ."'

She slapped him on the forearm.

'I did not say that. He's a client. Of course I'm not shagging him.'

'You were the one who mentioned shagging,' laughed David. 'I merely suggested that you were friendly.'

She avoided his gaze. Did he know she was lying?

All week, since their trip to Kerala, Sam had been texting and calling her. She had teased herself that she had been playing hard to get by default – she had no idea about the etiquette of dating a celebrity and had let him do all the running purely because she didn't know what else to do. And boy, had it worked – that morning he'd invited her round to his Chelsea Harbour apartment, telling her to pack a bag for the weekend. Anna couldn't pretend she wasn't excited. She felt sure they'd had a connection on that trip, not just between the sheets, but elsewhere, in the laughter and the conversation. Surely he wasn't that good an actor?

'Well I wouldn't get all moralistic about him being a client,' said David, flapping a hand. 'Where else are you supposed to meet your other half but at work these days? I bet half the Donovan Pierce staff are at it with each other. I hear the PAs have a bet on to see who can bed Matt Donovan first.'

'But he's the boss.' Anna frowned. She was surprised to feel a jolt of protectiveness about her colleague.

David laughed, showing his big claret-stained teeth.

'You weren't so full of ethics when you were nuzzling into Sam Charles's ear, were you?'

'I'm going to the bar,' she said, planning her escape route. The conversation was getting a little too close for comfort, and she could do with a soft drink to sober her up, especially with a busy night ahead planned.

'Not joining us in the tequila, Anna?' said Helen, coming up behind her holding a shot glass.

'I'm seeing double as it is.' Anna smiled.

'Fair enough,' said Helen. 'But you won't deny me a toast?' She clinked her glass against her associate's. 'To Balon,' she said, downing her spirit in one. 'Actually I wanted to say thank you for all your help,' she added, meeting Anna's gaze. 'I appreciate everything you've done.'

Anna was taken by surprise at the compliment.

'No problem,' she shrugged. 'What a great way to start at the firm, with a successful libel trial.'

Helen gave a low chuckle. 'Well I know we got off on the wrong foot. But you belong in this firm, Anna, I knew it the moment I met you. Lesser people would have been crushed by that Sam Charles incident, but you came out fighting. I like that.'

Words of praise from Helen Pierce were as rare as hen's teeth, so it was impossible not to feel proud. Seizing the moment, Anna looked Helen in the eye.

'So does this mean you're not going to turf me out after the three-month probationary period?' She said it light-heartedly, but she knew she'd never get a better chance to put her case forward.

Helen smiled.

'On the contrary, Anna. When I recruited you, I thought I would have to decide between you and David Morrow for the partnership. But if business comes flooding in, as I suspect it will after the Balon trial, then perhaps we can take on both of you. So long as there aren't any more cock-ups,' she added pointedly.

Anna stayed at the bar, watching as Helen picked up a tray of tequila shots and took them back to their colleagues. It was seven thirty already and she knew she had to leave. Her colleagues were so wrapped up in their tequilas that no one noticed her slip out of the door, out on to the streets, which had an agreeable buzz of anticipation of the Bank Holiday weekend ahead. She hailed a taxi and instructed the cabby to take her to Docklands. Partner, she thought to herself. Helen's announcement had made her feel nervous, considering where she was now heading to. She had wanted this opportunity her whole working life – and part of her didn't want to do anything to jeopardise it.

But keeping her head down was not her style, and she had come too far with Amy Hart to give up now.

The cab drew up outside the modernist east London headquarters of Media Incorporated: Andy's workplace. Anna had come here to meet him many times when they had been dating, and it felt strange now to be here to ask him another favour. She hated herself for it, of course, but then again, she was running out of options.

She paid the cabby and walked towards the entrance, pushing against the tide of workers flooding out, keen to start their long weekend. Andrew was waiting for her on the eighth floor.

'Haven't you got better things to be doing on a Friday night?' he said, his voice a mixture of amusement and interest.

'I've been doing that since we left court this afternoon,' she replied, following him through the newspaper's offices, an open-plan jumble of desks and bodies, still buzzing even at this time with chatter, ringing phones and the rattle of keys. *News never sleeps*, wasn't that the excuse Andy had always given her on the many occasions he'd stood her up?

'Been celebrating your win on the Balon trial, I'm guessing?' he said, steering her into a small office. 'We're running a story about it in tomorrow's edition.'

'Then I'd send a reporter down to Gordon's wine bar if I were you. Helen Pierce was on her fourth tequila shot when I left, and I think she'll be as loose-lipped as she'll ever be. You might get an exclusive.'

Andrew sat down and folded his hands across his chest, suddenly the businesslike newspaper executive.

'So what's going on, Anna?'

'I've got a story for you,' she said quietly.

'Really?' he said with surprise. 'One of your clients?'

'You wish,' she said. 'It's to do with your pal Gilbert, actually.'

'How did that go? I haven't heard back from him, so I assume you behaved yourself.'

Anna frowned. That was odd; when she had left Gilbert, he had been mightily pissed off. She had actually been expecting an

421

irate call from Andy telling her off for upsetting his contact. Why hadn't Gilbert complained? For some reason, that was unsettling.

'Well, he told me virtually nothing.'

'MPs. They love to talk, but hate to actually say anything.'

'Which is why I've come to see you,' she said. She opened her bag and pulled out the file of newspaper cuttings on Amy Hart, handing them over. Slowly she began to tell him the story: the visit from Ruby, the possible cover-up with Sam Charles and the long trail she had been following that had led her all the way to Kerala. When she had finished, Andy sat for a long moment, staring out of the now-dark window.

'Why are you getting involved in this, Anna?' he asked. His expression had the soft, anxious look of concern.

'Because a girl was possibly murdered and whoever did it has got off scot-free.' She hesitated for a moment. 'But I'm not sure I can do this on my own.'

He smiled.

'Now that's one admission I thought I'd never hear.'

'I mean it, Andy. One girl is dead. Another is in hiding . . .' She didn't want to add that she was scared, but Andrew knew her better than anyone.

'Okay, well let's start by saying that there is no story here.'

Anna began to object, but Andrew held up a hand.

'There is absolutely nothing to suggest that Amy Hart was murdered, or that anyone else was involved in her death. No police investigation and nothing particularly suspicious in the inquest. Then there's Amy's boyfriend. We don't even know who he is, apart from the fact that he's called Peter and he's friends with James Swann – maybe. Let's assume for one minute that Amy was blackmailing this Peter; we still have no idea what she had on him. And even if we do know all these things, how the hell do we connect any of it to Amy's death? Because that's what you're suggesting, isn't it? That mysterious Peter had her killed because of what she knew?'

Anna felt her shoulders slump with disappointment. The sad truth was that Andy was completely right: there *was* no hard evidence of any kind; their information was sketchy and incomplete, nothing they could present to a court, just a trail of crumbs leading to the foot of Amy Hart's stairs.

Andy looked at his watch, then picked up his phone.

'Amir, can you pop over?' he said officiously. Anna could tell that the meeting was finished. She felt panicky.

'Look, Andy. Bear with me,' she pleaded. 'I know this sounds spurious . . .'

'Yes – it is. Which is why I've just called Amir. Maybe he can move things forward.'

'Amir?'

'Our deputy investigations editor.'

'You mean you believe me?'

'There's bugger-all here,' he laughed, tapping Anna's cuttings file. 'But if we only followed up on stories that had everything cut and dried, newspapers would be very dull and very empty. So I'm prepared to let Amir have a look at this. Let's shake the tree and see what drops out, eh?'

Anna sat back, letting out a long sigh.

'Thanks, Andy,' she said with relief.

'If we can prove any of this, which admittedly is going to be extremely difficult, then this is a major society scandal. Swann's set is one of the richest, most powerful circle of men and women in the country. Which is why I am not having you poking around all this on your own.'

'Spoken like you care,' she teased him.

His expression softened.

'I always did. I still do.'

She brushed his comment away.

'I'm not here to discuss that again.'

He shrugged.

'So, is it true about you and Sam Charles?'

Anna fought to keep her expression neutral.

'What do you mean?'

'Oh, just something I heard from a girl on the gossip desk at the *Globe*.'

She could tell the information had needled him.

'Just gossip,' she said innocently. 'And you can tell your friend that if she prints that, I'll have her in court faster than

423

you can say "record damages".'

There was a tap at the door and a slim Asian man stepped in.

'Anna, Amir,' said Andy. 'Amir, Anna. Anna's the top arse-kicking media lawyer in the country, Amir's the best investigative journalist. You are now a team.'

Amir smiled and shook Anna's hand.

'Glad to have you on board,' he said, sitting down.

'Okay, Anna,' said Andy. 'Do you want to tell Amir what you've just been telling me?'

57

Jessica sat on the balcony of her Malibu beach house and stuck her spoon into a gallon tub of Ben and Jerry's. She'd spent the last hour on Google, finding out everything she could about Brooke Geller, and felt she deserved a little pick-me-up. Brooke was like a Girl Scout, she thought miserably. No one had a bad word to say about her. Clever, pretty, a 'beautiful soul', she'd been an all-state athlete and come top of her acting class at the Orba Festen Drama School, which had a reputation for producing serious acting talent and edgy playwrights. She'd done some pretty shitty pilots, sure, but had managed to get good reviews for her characters. Jessica was sure that there would be something hidden away – a secret pregnancy, an early 'artistic' photo shoot, a drugged-up mother – but who was interested in winkling that out at the moment? Right now, Brooke was Shirley Temple. Jessica put the ice cream down on the table. Four mouthfuls in and she was already feeling sick. Maybe it was the meds she was on.

Jessica knew she'd been damn lucky to escape serious injury in the car accident. It had only been the airbag that had stopped her going through the windscreen. Apparently if the other guy had hit her a fraction of a second earlier, her legs would have been crushed like flower stems. As it was, he'd caught her front end which had spun the Aston around a few times, ending up perched on the central reservation. Jessica had been in shock, but she had still had the presence of mind to grab her phone. Her first call had been to Sylvia. Despite the fact that she had fired her in Maui, her publicist was the only person she had wanted to speak to after the crash, pleading with the older woman to help her. And what a marvellous job Sylvia had done too, wiping the car crash from history. Not one hint that anything untoward had happened had appeared in any newspaper or tabloid. Even better, she had somehow managed to come to some agreement with the emergency services and the driver of the other car. According to Sylvia, the poor sap didn't even know who she was and thought it was all his fault, so there was zero chance of him trying to sue her. Of course Sylvia had got her pound of flesh – she was back on Team Jess, and getting an extra three thousand dollars a month in her retainer. Still, she was earning her keep. Maybe Sam should have employed Sylvia, thought Jessica. Then none of us would be in this mess.

She picked up a tumbler and downed the painkillers she was taking for whiplash and bruising. In the background, the intercom was buzzing. She crossed the room to press it.

'Hey, gorgeous, it's Jim. Jim Parker.'

Not exactly the first person she wanted to see after a spell in Cedar Sinai, but she had been intrigued when he had called saying he had a proposition for her.

Jim walked in holding a slim leather briefcase in one hand and a white cardboard box in the other, giving out the delicious aroma of Chinese food.

'What's that?' Jess said, wrinkling her nose.

'Lunch.'

She shook her head.

'I've eaten.'

'Yeah, right,' said Jim, setting the box down on the kitchen counter. 'A handful of shrimps and asparagus?'

'Actually I've just been working my way through a tub of Ben and Jerry's.'

'That's my girl,' said Jim. 'You don't get a body that good without letting go every now and then.'

He looked at her, his face serious.

'How are you, by the way? After the accident, I mean.'

She shouldn't have been surprised. Jim Parker was one of the most connected men in the industry; of course he would know about the crash. Sylvia had probably called him up with the news, to be filed away against some future favour. It was how

Hollywood worked. Jess waved a hand; she wasn't going to bother pretending.

'I was lucky, I guess.'

'Well you look amazing,' said Jim.

Jessica almost laughed out loud. She'd made no effort at all for Jim's arrival; wearing J Brand jeans, a skinny-rib T-shirt and no bra, she looked as if she was off to Whole Foods. What would he have said if she'd dressed up? she wondered.

Jim was unpacking the food: honey soy spare ribs, salt and pepper squid, yellow bean duck. She wanted to eat, it all smelled so good, but now that Jim knew about the ice cream, she couldn't indulge again.

'You go ahead, Jim,' she said, opening the fridge and pulling out some white wine. 'A little something to go with it?' she asked.

'Sure, let's live dangerously.'

Jim perched on a breakfast stool and popped a couple of pork dumplings into his mouth while Jessica poured out two large glasses of the Sancerre. It will probably react with the meds, she thought, but what the hell. If you couldn't mix things up after a near-death experience, when could you?

She sipped her wine and watched Jim eat. He was a handsome man, the sort of bone structure that could have got him a gig on a daytime soap if he'd chosen a different career. He was wearing a sheer black polo shirt and grey slacks, but she could tell he was super-toned under there. Ten years earlier she'd have jumped at a man like Jim: sexy, powerful. In fact she *had* jumped at many men like Jim. She'd worked out early on who could help her and who was just bullshitting, who it was worth giving up a little pussy for. She had never felt any qualms about it. She had never really enjoyed sex, but she was well aware of the power she had in her body and was happy to use whatever leverage was required.

'So have you heard from Sam?' asked Jim, wiping his mouth on a napkin.

Jessica had almost forgotten that the last time Jim had been here was to remove the last of Sam's possessions. That all seemed so long ago.

She shook her head.

'He knows better than that.'

'Don't be so hard on him, honey,' said Jim. 'Sure, he acted like a prick – I mean, who would risk losing someone like you? – but I think he's hurting. You must have seen he's gone a little AWOL?'

She had read about Sam losing the Dreamscape contract and his crazy theatre production in Edinburgh. It did look as if he'd gone off the rails. But she wasn't sure if that was grief or just symptomatic of whatever crisis that had made him jump into bed with that hooker in the first place.

'You know, I think you two should get back together,' said Jim softly.

'Get real! Like that could ever happen.'

'I'm serious,' he said. 'Think about it. Everything that's gone wrong in your career has happened since you split: all that crap in the press about "Tragic Jess", "Loser in Love". You and Sam were happy together.'

Jessica felt a lump in her throat and swallowed hard. It was true, they had been happy, hadn't they? They'd certainly been the golden couple of Hollywood, but since then it had all gone downhill. She shook the thought away.

'Is that what you think of me, Jim?' she said, turning towards him. 'I'm a loser in love?'

'I think you're an incredibly beautiful woman. But I think you deserve better than what's happening right now.'

She glanced away from him, feeling a sob rise inside her.

'Don't blame yourself,' said Jim, stroking his fingers down the curve of her neck. 'None of this is your fault.'

There was a long, electric pause.

She turned back and gazed into his blue eyes, wanting someone to tell her it was all going to be okay, wanting someone to make it all better again. The mood in the room had changed suddenly, the air prickling with a sexual charge she'd not felt in years. Their eyes locked and she knew he was feeling it too. She touched his thigh and he took her fingers. Her mood changed from misery to defiance as she stepped off her stool and moved towards him.

It was instantly clear where this meeting was heading.

'Are you sure?' he said haltingly.

'Absolutely sure,' she whispered, melting towards him.

He pressed his hard, gym-toned body against her and kissed her neck, slipping his hands down from her shoulders to her breasts.

'Not here,' she said, taking his hand. 'The bedroom.'

He practically carried her on to the bed, falling on top of her, his mouth finding hers in a searing kiss. Impatiently she lifted her T-shirt over her head as his nimble fingers unzipped her jeans and pushed them down over her lean hips, taking her tiny thong with them.

'You're beautiful,' he moaned, planting kisses all down her hard stomach, running his thumb up and down her wet labia, then twisting two fingers inside her.

'Yes!' she cried, pushing her hips towards him, groaning as his mouth moved down to pleasure her.

With strong hands he turned her around, bending her over the bed. She heard the clank as he unbuckled his trousers, a fumble as he put on a condom, then pushed his hard cock against the curve of her ass, skin against skin. He gathered up her hair so that he could plant greedy kisses on the nape of her neck, then, losing patience, roughly parted her legs and sank into her with one thrust.

'Yesss . . .' she hissed, stretching out, her hands gripping the sheets as he rocked back and forth inside her. It felt so good, she thought, her breath catching as his cock reached some sweet spot she hadn't even known was there. Sex had always been a commodity for Jessica, a means to an end, but this . . . this was something else.

He grabbed her hips and pushed her up on to her hands and knees as he pumped from behind, deeper, faster now. His hands cupped her buttocks and she smiled, knowing that a full-body micro-dermabrasion the day before meant her ass looked like a peach.

'That's it, please keep going, please,' she gasped. The ripples of pleasure were building, building, contracting into her stomach like a tight coil and then releasing back out around her body in electric waves of pleasure. She let out a deep cry, as much of surprise as desire, then collapsed on to the sheets, relishing his weight, his strong arms around her, two perfect post-coital bodies uniting as one.

Finally catching her breath, Jessica stretched over to her bedside cabinet and pulled out a menthol cigarette. Her battle to quit had been a losing one, and with Jim Parker naked beside her, she needed one more than ever.

'We shouldn't have done that.' She smiled, taking a long drag and blowing a smoke ring towards the ceiling.

'Oh yes we should,' he laughed. 'I've wanted to do it for five years. But then I always knew we would.'

She propped her head on her elbow. 'You arrogant bastard,' she murmured.

He took the cigarette from her and had a drag.

'It's why I'm so good at my job. And it's not arrogance, it's self-belief. There's a difference. You're an amazing woman, Jess,' he said, running a finger along her thigh. 'That's why I hate to see your career going the way it's going.'

The lazy smile faded from her face.

'What are you talking about?'

Jim pushed himself back up on a pillow.

'Jess, I think we both know there have been a few wrong turns this summer.'

'Wrong turns? You'll remember it was your slimeball client who did the dirty on me.'

'Sure, but you haven't exactly made strong moves since then. What about the naked *HQ* shoot?'

'How do you know about that?' she asked, startled. 'It's not out for two months.'

'Jose Silveira isn't the most discreet man in the world.'

She could feel her heart beginning to hammer.

'And why the hell did you let the *All Woman* execs bring in another female lead?' Jim continued. 'If I had been your agent, you can be goddamn sure it would never have happened.'

She stubbed out the cigarette and got off the bed.

'Shit,' she muttered, pacing across to the window. 'Does everyone know every detail of my life?'

'Hey, don't blame yourself, kiddo. You just need better

representation, someone who can actually deliver what's best for you.'

For years Jess had felt a strong loyalty to Harry Monk, the legendary agent who had plucked her from the other starry-eyed hopefuls stepping off the bus in LA and guided her to superstardom. The bond had surprised her ruthless instinct, but deep down she had always been grateful to Harry. Yet Jim's words now struck a chord. Jessica knew she should simply not be in this position, and she could only hold her team to be responsible.

'Better representation? Like who?' she asked cautiously.

'Like me.'

She barked out a laugh.

'You're kidding. What about Sam?'

'What about him? Lots of couples have the same represent-ation. You can build your brand as a couple. Look at the Beckhams; you can barely tell where one starts and the other ends.'

'We're not a couple any more, Jim. Or haven't you noticed?'

Jim paused for a moment.

'And was that the right decision?' he asked.

She turned back towards him, fury on her face.

'He cheated on me! What the hell do you expect me to do?'

'I understand your anger, Jess. Hell, I'd have cut his balls off and made a smoothie. But the split wasn't all bad. Everyone likes drama, and it's made you more normal.' He eyed her carefully. 'Jess, this isn't about how you both feel. It's business, pure and simple. You have to think about it logically. Are you and Sam more powerful as individuals or as a conglomerate?'

'So you think we should go back to being Jess and Sam, the power couple?'

'Think bigger,' said Jim. 'You don't want to be one of the most popular couples in Hollywood. You want to be one of the most powerful couples in the world. You should be getting invitations to the White House, appearances at Davos, being courted by world leaders, like Angelina is. The sky's the limit, baby, believe me. You just got to have the vision.'

He got out of bed and went out of the room, returning a few moments later with the slim leather folder.

'I've prepared a document for you.'

'A document?'

'A business plan. Taking your career to the next level. Taking the Sam and Jess brand to the next level.'

Her anger rose again.

'Is that why you came round? Is that why you fucked me? To get me to sign on some dotted line?'

'No,' said Jim calmly. 'We had sex because we both wanted to.'

He sat on the end of the bed and patted the space next to him. She glared at him for a moment, then shrugged and sat down. Jim reached out and stroked her hair away from her face.

'Just read it, okay?'

She shook her head.

'I don't need to.'

He looked offended, but she smiled. 'I mean I don't need to read it because I know how good it will be. You're the best, Jim. You know it.'

His expression softened.

'Believe me, honey, you and Sam could be great together, and I'm talking Liz Taylor and Richard Burton great. Legendary.'

She picked up the document and started flicking through it. At first she was just humouring him. But as she read, she felt the hairs on her arms stand up. It was fantastic, even better than she had hoped. Lists of impressive brands who would be willing to pay multimillion-dollar endorsements, together with the name and number of each company's CEO – Jim wasn't just talking theoretically; he'd actually spoken to them to talk numbers. There was a list of the *Forbes* top twenty highest-earning couples – David and Victoria were there, Jay-Z and Beyoncé, but despite four hit movies between them, Jess and Sam hadn't made it in. Jim was right: clearly they weren't maximising their potential.

Then she got to the big one: projections for the earnings of Brand Samica. Year one, $110 million. She'd own a Gulfstream outright before she knew it.

Further on in the document were a raft of what Jim had labelled 'options', business ventures or franchises she could pick and choose from, each bringing in serious passive income, money she would have to do little or nothing to earn, each of them solidly 'on brand'. A chain of chic restaurants, complete with branded cooking sauces for the supermarket, a range of swimwear bearing her signature, a movie production company ready-loaded with the rights to a dozen books Jim already knew the studios would kill for. A range of perfumes – Jim had already thought of a name: 'Innocence by Jessica Carr'. Jessica had to admit she'd always found the idea of a personalised scent tacky, but looking now at the amount she could earn, it was phenomenal. A large chunk of Elizabeth Taylor's fortune had come from perfume revenues – and Jessica hadn't even known Liz had a scent!

Half a billion dollars in ten years, that was Jim's estimate, and Jessica could feel the flutter in her chest at the prospect. Money still mattered, it was *all* that mattered. She had never forgotten the humiliation of having to queue for free school meals or wearing unfashionable jeans because they were hand-me-downs. 'Welfare! Welfare!' her school friends had chanted. All because Daddy had fallen off some scaffolding.

'You've not got to the best bit,' said Jim quietly, wrapping a towel around his waist.

She turned to the back of the business plan.

'Internet TV?' she queried, reading the proposal.

'Baby, you're not thinking big enough. *All Woman*, your little movies filmed during hiatus.'

'They're not *little*, Jim,' she objected. She'd worked her butt off to break into movies.

'Jess, ten years ago, every two-bit actor on TV would have sold their grandmother for a big Hollywood career. But things are changing real fast. In five years, there's hardly going to be anyone left going to the movie theatre, and you're going to get left behind.'

She opened her mouth to speak, but Jim was on a roll.

'Think about the brand, Jess. People love Jessica Carr because you're in their living rooms, you're part of their lives. That's what they want from you, so give it to them.'

She frowned.

'Internet TV is small fry.'

'Right now. But by the end of this decade, TV, movies and the Internet will be completely integrated. I want you to own that new medium, Jess, creating, producing and starring in your own show, watched by a global audience. I think you can be the female Seinfeld.'

She didn't need Jim to tell her how wealthy Jerry was.

'What about *All Woman*?'

'They're screwing with you, honey. I've heard about Brooke Geller. Do this season and then ship out.'

'To what?'

'I have a client, a writer who has come up with something that is perfect for you. There's a great role for Sammy in there too. You know how great he is with comedy.'

'You want me to work with Sam?'

'We introduce him season finale. Think of the ratings, baby.'

'He'd never go for it.'

'He would if you were back together.'

Two weeks ago, if Jim had suggested not only getting back with Sam Charles, but also working with him, she would have screamed, but now? Now it seemed like the only thing that made any sense.

'So do you want me to set up a meeting with him?' said Jim, coming up behind her, stroking his hand across her belly. 'Somewhere romantic? Maybe that island in Scotland he vanished to after the story broke?'

'But do you think he'll want to get back together?'

Jim didn't speak for a moment, and she turned around, looking up at him anxiously.

'Tell me he hasn't met someone else?'

Jim shook his head.

'Absolutely not. It's just he's convinced himself he's happy being back in London. You know, there's this little trailer-trash streak in Sam. So I think you might have to do more of the running.'

'I'm not gonna beg, Jim,' she said angrily.

'Sure, baby,' he said soothingly. 'Just go see him in England. Woo him. Once he feels wanted, he'll see the sense of this too.'

'But what if he doesn't bite?'

Jim raised an eyebrow.

'Then we might need a few additional incentives.'

'You mean the document?'

'I meant something even more persuasive than that,' he said, cupping her breast. She moaned with pleasure as his fingers stroked her nipple. She felt hornier than she'd done in years. 'So, we got a deal?' he breathed into her ear.

'Come back to bed and I'll think about it.'

'I can't, sweetheart, I've got to get back to work,' he said, nuzzling into her neck. 'Especially if you want me to start on everything we've just talked about.'

He held her face gently between his hands.

'So what's it to be?'

'Let's do it,' she whispered. 'I want you to represent me.'

He placed a slow, lingering kiss on her lips.

'I won't let you down.'

She lay back on the mattress. Sunshine streamed into the room, over her naked body, making her feel blissfully lazy and happy.

'I'll let myself out,' winked Jim, already dressed.

'Call me,' she smiled, watching his tight ass exit the bedroom. She picked up the business plan and began to read it again, feeling turned on once more as she absorbed and visualised every little detail. She was so engrossed in the document, she didn't notice that it was a few minutes before her front door closed. Enough time for Jim Parker to remove the bugging devices he had planted around her house three weeks earlier.

58

The hire car wound through the hills behind Nice airport, up, up until the blue Mediterranean shrank to a thin silver strip and the smell of the air changed from sea salt to the pine and lavender that characterised this part of Provence. Mougins was one of the most famous foodie destinations in Europe, a medieval village that clung to the hillside just a twenty-minute drive from its bigger, ritzier neighbour, Cannes.

'Sam, this place is just gorgeous,' gasped Anna as they drove towards the sandstone walls of the town. It was like something from a fairy-tale. Honey-coloured townhouses with bloom-filled window boxes and red-tiled roofs crowding into winding streets, a clock tower tolling the hour, cypress trees soaring into the blue sky. Anna listened with excitement as Sam told her stories about the town: how Picasso had lived here, shooting the breeze with Cocteau and Man Ray, how Churchill had holidayed here and Dior came to be inspired. 'It's magical,' she sighed.

Driving past the town itself, they finally pulled up in front of an old watermill set in beautiful grounds.

'*Voilà*,' said Sam, taking Anna's hand to lead her inside to the Michelin-starred Moulin de Mougins. It was chic yet casual, and Anna felt glad she had softened her smart aqua silk dress with bronze gladiator sandals.

'Monsieur Shaarlz!' cried the maître d'. 'So good to see you again.'

He led them to a table on the terrace outside and brought them glasses of crisp white wine, 'especially recommended for you by the sommelier'. Anna wondered if there was a more delightful place to have lunch – and to think she'd wanted to stay in Sam's bed watching old movies. Plenty of time for that later, she smiled to herself. And not so much of the movies, either.

'You like?' said Sam, reaching across the table to touch her fingers.

'Oh yes,' she replied. 'It's wonderful.'

'You know, we should do something like this every weekend,' he said. 'Where do you fancy next week?'

She searched his face, but he didn't appear to be joking. As each day slipped by, she'd convinced herself that Sam would tire of her and that his phone calls would trail off to nothing. But he seemed to be getting more keen, not less. Since Andy, Anna had gone out of her way to protect herself, building up a hard shell that would make her impervious to pain. But now here she was, playing boyfriend-girlfriend with a man who was now as well known for his infidelity as he was for his acting. It was as if she was just begging to have her fragile heart dropped from a great – and very public – height.

'Anywhere except Tuscany,' she said, smiling.

'Hey, Tuscany's one of my favourite places,' Sam protested. 'What have you got against poor Italy?'

'Oh, I love Tuscany too,' she replied. 'It's just that my sister is getting married there next weekend. To Andy – my ex, the love-rat journalist you were jealous of, remember? So you can see why I want to give it a wide berth.'

'But that's silly – you should be there with bells on,' he said seriously. 'There's no better way than showing them you've moved on.'

'I know I should, but . . .'

'But what? What's stopping you? Pride? Well that's a pretty negative emotion,' he said, before stopping and smirking. 'I got that from a shrink. About the only thing of value a psychologist has ever told me, actually.'

Anna took a drink of her wine. She hadn't heard from any of her family since her father's email about the hen party, and the guilt had been gnawing away ever since.

Sam leaned forward. 'And if you need a date for it, I look good in a tux. Or at least, that's what they said in *People* magazine's Fifty Most Beautiful People last year.'

Anna gaped at him.

'Are you serious? You'd really go with me to the wedding?'

'Let's think of it more like a free mini-break. Plus I assume since she's a famous chef the food will be pretty good.'

'But Sophie might think I'm trying to upstage the bride.'

'We'll skulk at the back. I'll even grow a beard. I'm not exactly looking for attention at the moment.'

Anna couldn't believe he was prepared to go to such a public event with her, especially as Sophie had probably sold the photos to *OK!* or *Hello!*.

'Sam—' she began, reaching out for his hand, but she was cut off before she could say anything more.

'Anna Kennedy! I don't believe it!' squealed a familiar exotic voice.

'Ilina!' cried Anna, standing up to air-kiss her glamorous former client. The Russian was looking incredible in a thigh-skimming mini-dress and aviator shades. 'It's so great to see you,' she said. 'What on earth are you doing here?'

'Oh, we're staying on at the Costa Smeralda for a week or two,' Ilina purred, turning to wave at some dark-haired male model type in an open-necked white shirt. 'We popped over for a little light lunch for a change of scenery.'

Popped over from Sardinia. Anna smiled to herself. Ilina certainly hadn't let the newspaper reports on her wanton spending cramp her style.

'And what, pray tell, are *you* doing here?' asked Ilina, peering at Sam over her sunglasses, a smirk on her lips.

'Ilina, this is my friend Sam Charles.'

'Charmed, darhling,' said Ilina, proffering a hand.

'Would you like to join us?' asked Anna.

'No, I won't stay long. I can see you two want to be alone; besides, Juan doesn't speak much English. But then I didn't bring him for his conversation,' laughed Ilina.

'So how are you?' asked Anna, sipping her wine nervously, trying to pretend that she lunched with movie stars and billionaires every day of the week.

'Good, good. And yourself?'

'Keeping busy,' replied Anna. 'Speaking of which, I have you to thank for my new job.'

'Really?'

'Remember that victory party you threw at the start of the summer? Well I met my new boss there, Helen Pierce. She heard the nice things you said about me and offered me a job.'

'Helen Pierce?' Ilina frowned, taking a moment to place her. 'Ah, the blonde lawyer?'

'Don't you know her? She was one of your guests.'

Ilina shook her head. 'Not really. She came with a guy who's one of these corporate publicists. He wants to do work for my company.'

'And who would that be?' asked Anna as casually as she could. It was one of the running jokes in the Donovan Pierce coffee room: no one knew anything about Helen's private life.

'Simon Cooper.'

The name sounded familiar to Anna, but she couldn't immediately place it.

'Simon heads up Auckland Communications. Big city PR firm.' Ilina lowered her voice. 'Actually, someone at that party told me that he and Helen are having an affair, although I hate to repeat it. I don't want to be the target of a slander suit.'

She touched Anna lightly on the arm and stood up.

'Anyway, we must talk back in London. I need a lawyer to work on my team. Contracts, liaising with magazines, issuing a few letters, very easy, part-time really. I know the job is beneath you, but think of all the *fun* we'd have.'

For a second it sounded tempting. Anna had certainly got quite a taste for private aviation and luxury hotels. But she realised there was someone who would appreciate the job a lot more.

'I think I have just the person for you. Sidney Travers, a very smart woman on my team. Just qualified, but very clever and enterprising.'

'Super, fix me up a meeting with her.' Ilina kissed Anna on both cheeks and disappeared back to her dark-eyed friend.

'Sometimes I think you've got a more showbiz life than me,' laughed Sam, brushing his bare foot up her leg towards her thigh.

'As if.'

'I think we should stay here till Monday,' he announced suddenly. 'They've got rooms at the restaurant. And I'm sure Ilina will invite us to her place in Sardinia if you ask nicely. I bet she's got a big fuck-off yacht.'

Anna shook her head.

'I couldn't anyway. I'm going to James Swann's party tomorrow; I can't miss that.'

'Whose party?'

'James Swann. Remember, the big secretive society thing where Gilbert Bryce met Amy?'

He still looked blank.

She lowered her voice. 'Gilbert Bryce, the MP who had an affair with Amy Hart.'

'Oh them,' said Sam, the penny dropping. 'Why are you going there?'

For a second she wondered if Sam had actually listened to anything she had told him over the past week. She found that a lot with celebrities. If something didn't directly relate to them, some part of their brain just edited it out as useless information.

'I need to find out who this Peter is. The only way I can think how is to go to the party and talk to people. I've swung an invite through Johnny Maxwell.'

Sam frowned at her. His disapproval was obvious.

'What is it?' she asked.

'Look, Anna,' he said, sipping his wine. 'It's none of my business, but when are you going to give this up?'

'Give what up?'

'Playing Miss bloody Marple.'

She looked at him with astonishment.

'But it *is* your business! This could be the reason your injunction failed. And anyway, you said you wanted to find out what had happened to Amy. After all, you've been paying for it for the last month.'

He sighed.

'I wanted to spend time with you. I suppose it was just a good excuse.'

She forgot to breathe.

'Hang on, you said you'd help me, just to get into my *knickers*?'

'Stop being dramatic,' he said, lowering his voice. He put his palm on the table. 'Look, I am sorry that this girl is dead, and I feel for her family. But I don't care about that injunction any more. In fact, I'm glad it failed, because if it hadn't, I wouldn't have done the Edinburgh show, I wouldn't have split with Jessica. I wouldn't be sitting here with you now,' he said pointedly.

She couldn't help feeling angry and disappointed. She had genuinely thought they were in this together, a team, but clearly Sam had tired of the mystery.

'Sam, there's more to life than your bloody injunction, you know. A girl died.'

'*My* bloody injunction?' he huffed. 'Nice to know you thought so much of it. Maybe *that's* why it all went tits-up.'

Anna jerked back. It felt as if he had slapped her across the face, and she could see that a French couple on the next table were looking over at them and whispering.

'I'm sorry. Come on, Anna, this is stupid,' said Sam, his voice softer. 'We shouldn't be fighting over this.' He hesitated. 'I just think you've got involved in the case because you want to distract yourself from your sister's wedding. And to be honest, I can't blame you. But you've got me to distract you now. Stop obsessing over Amy Hart. Let your mate at the newspaper sort it out. Let's just get a room, go to bed and have some fun.'

Ruby and Liz Hart popped into Anna's head, and she couldn't shake them away. She was not going to give up on them.

'No, I don't want to go to bed,' she said coldly.

Sam shook his head.

'Shit, Anna. What is the *matter* with you? Get off your high bloody horse and let it go. It's not as if you've been the most principled lawyer in the world before now, is it? Why is this crusade suddenly so important to you?'

'Not principled? What's that supposed to mean?'

'I mean the sort of work you do. You're a media lawyer, Anna. You cover up for rich people. You're a shark.' He gave a small smile. 'Although I admit, I kind of like that about you.'

She closed her eyes, fighting back the tears.

That was exactly why Amy Hart mattered so much to her. It wasn't as simple as wanting to help Ruby find out the truth about her sister's death, although she did want to do that, very much. It was also about trying to make up for all the other stories, all the other uncomfortable truths she had helped bury. Anna couldn't deny that she loved her job and the sense of fulfilment she felt from being very good at it. It was fast-paced and exciting, even though she sometimes had to justify her professional actions. Whenever she won an injunction protecting an adulterous footballer or celebrity from the glare of the media, she convinced herself that by gagging the press they were protecting his wife and family. And yet deep down, she wondered if that argument rang hollow.

She looked at Sam Charles, and suddenly wanted to leave their little pocket of Paradise.

'Amy matters to me,' she said softly.

'Whatever,' he replied, looking unconvinced as he summoned the waiter to fetch the bill.

59

Anna had never been one of those little girls who wanted to go to ballet lessons or tap dance class. That was much more Sophie's thing: amateur productions of *Annie* or solo spots in the school choir. All of which explained why Anna was particularly anxious tonight as she stood outside the Royal Opera House waiting for Johnny Maxwell: acting was not her forte. When she had introduced herself at the Chelsea Heights party, she had haltingly told Johnny that her name was Natasha and that she was a researcher at the Royal Academy, currently writing a paper on Canova. She had felt a wave of relief when Johnny had declared himself a complete dunce who knew nothing whatsoever about sculpture. Anna didn't like to say that clearly he knew more than she did, as she had thought Canova was a painter. Either way, he seemed to buy the cover story, and they had discussed appreciation of the human form, which Johnny had clearly taken to mean that Anna-stroke-Natasha was up for a spot of Spin the Bottle or whatever happened at the Swann parties.

Anna looked anxiously up and down the road. Where *was* he? They had arranged to meet at seven, and it was a quarter past already.

'Natasha, darling!'

Anna turned to see a man with white hair hanging out of a black cab window.

'Over here, darling,' he called, opening the door. 'I've been screaming at you for an aeon.'

'Sorry, Johnny,' she said, stepping inside as elegantly as she

443

could in her sexy academic costume of tight pencil skirt and sheer stockings. 'I was miles away.'

'Thinking about Canova, no doubt. What on earth are you doing working on a Sunday anyway?'

'An academic's life is busy, busy.' She smiled nervously.

'Well you're here now,' he said, taking her in with an appreciative smile. Anna had clearly hit the right note with her five-inch heels and a push-up bra under her crisp white shirt, like a naughty secretary. She'd guessed that subtlety was not required at this stage. Johnny himself was dressed like a country squire in a green and blue checked suit and shiny riding boots and holding a large lit cigar, despite the 'No Smoking' signs.

'Natasha, meet Tanika,' he said breezily, waving a hand towards a lithe blonde perched on the swing-down seat in the corner. Anna hadn't expected any other passengers and was momentarily thrown, until Johnny whispered behind his hand, 'Estonian, doesn't speak any English, so we can say what we like.' Anna nodded politely to the girl, who merely raised her nose and looked out the window. 'Not the friendliest of girls,' sniffed Johnny. 'But I rather think the chaps like the mute model types who don't speak. My idea of hell, though, sugar plum.'

The cab moved off into the network of back streets that only London cabbies seemed to know about, making quick progress westwards.

'So tell me more about yourself, darling,' said Johnny.

'Nothing much to tell, I'm afraid,' said Anna. 'I go around cataloguing paintings and writing papers about them.'

'Darling, you're a female Simon Schama. Gorgeous but brainy, the perfect combination.'

Anna smiled.

'I wish,' she said. 'As you can imagine, it's a rather conservative atmosphere. They would be scandalised if they knew I was in a taxi with a man I hardly knew.'

He looked at her shrewdly.

'And tell me, Natasha, what are you expecting from tonight?'

'Whatever the night brings,' said Anna, doing her best to sound sophisticated.

'Splendid,' smiled Johnny. 'I do so hate it when I bring girls out to the house only to find they're treating it like a posh version of some online dating agency. Most of our gentlemen partygoers are available, if you follow my drift, but back in Civvy Street you may find they have – shall we say – prior arrangements.'

'Married, you mean?' said Anna, shrugging. 'I'm not looking to settle down, Johnny, I'm just here to . . .' she paused and gave a little smile, 'to have a good time.'

He grinned and squeezed her knee. 'I think you and I are going to get along famously.'

Anna had spent the afternoon reading up on the art of the Renaissance in case she was asked about her background, but she need not have bothered. Clearly Johnny's job was simply to provide the Swann set with suitable willing girls – 'companions, not sluts', as he had put it – not to do a thorough security check on them, and anyway, he was far more interested in talking about Johnny Maxwell and his pivotal role at the centre of society.

'So who owns the house?'

'James Swann,' he said distractedly.

'And how do you know him?'

'We went to Eton together. He's a very smart man. The party I'm taking you to, people would kill for an invite.'

'How so?'

'It's where alliances are formed. People come down to mix with like-minded other people. Achievers. And of course they come to have fun.'

'I'm looking forward to it.'

She didn't have to wait long. The house was on the fringes of Buckinghamshire, which was just over an hour out of the city. The taxi swung through a pair of gateposts, each topped with a rampant stag, then into parkland dotted with ancient oak and beech and finally up a long drive leading to a white mansion with long gabled windows.

'It's beautiful,' she said, as the cab pulled up and they clambered out. 'How often do you come here?'

Johnny threw his arm around her and laughed.

'I knew it!' he said triumphantly. 'You've only just got here

445

and already you want to come back. Well, if you fit in here as well as I anticipate, I should think we'll be back before too long. I do hope so; it's not often I meet someone as intelligent as you, darling.'

He offered the girls an arm each and they walked towards the imposing iron-studded door.

'So what's the occasion tonight?'

'Because it's summer, my dear,' said Johnny, gesturing flamboyantly. 'Because the flowers are in bloom and the bees are making honey.' He pulled her closer and chuckled. 'Well, that and the bank holiday, of course.'

There were some serious-looking security guards flanking the house's wide stone doorway, but they barely looked at Anna or her mute European counterpart clinging to Johnny's other arm. The three of them stepped into the entrance, a warm, open hall with stairs to one side and a large fireplace in the centre, tonight filled with an extravagant flower display rather than crackling logs. With the well-heeled, well-dressed people laughing and chatting among uniformed wine waiters carrying trays of champagne, it immediately appeared to be just like any other country house party.

'Come this way, ladies,' said Johnny. 'Time to meet the host.'

James Swann was not at all what Anna had been expecting. In his early sixties, but still handsome, he was tall and regal, with swept-back black hair the colour of liquorice. Anna immediately thought of the old Hammer vampire movies her dad loved, and suppressed a smile.

'James Swann, may I introduce my two newest and loveliest aquaintances, Tanika and Natasha.'

Swann gave a slight bow and bent to kiss their hands, almost sending Anna into a fit of nervous giggles. He'll be turning into a bat next, she thought.

'Please, ladies, make yourselves at home, treat my house as you would your own. Nothing is out of bounds to my friends. Johnny, show them around.'

They walked into the drawing room. Piano, tasteful furniture. A bar at one end. Girls draped over red-faced men.

'Those are my regular girls,' said Johnny. 'They know what

makes a party go with a bang, if you follow, so they get invited back.'

'You say some of these men are married,' said Anna casually.

Johnny nodded. 'A few of the wives even attend.' He grinned. 'I could introduce you to some couples . . .'

She picked up his coded meaning.

'Let's get a drink first, shall we?'

'Very wise. But first, Tanika, why don't you go and say hello to that nice old gentleman over there?' he said, pointing to a rotund man in a double-breasted suit. 'I believe his grandfather had significant business interests in your mother country, so you should have plenty to talk about.' The girl dutifully walked off.

'I just need to freshen up in the bathroom.' Anna smiled.

Johnny nodded his approval. She found a downstairs loo and phoned the local taxi firm. 'Have a car waiting for "Natasha" at the Swann house,' she instructed. 'I've no idea how long I'll be. But be there as soon as you can, and wait. Tell security at the gates that you're picking up a guest of Johnny Maxwell.'

She returned to Johnny.

'Beautiful, darling,' he purred. 'Right then,' he continued, leading Anna to the bar and perching on a high stool that gave him a view of the whole room. 'Let me see if I can give you a run-down.'

He pointed to a sandy-haired man in a blazer.

'Charles Butler-Cash, very well connected in the City, beautiful place out in Barbados, very good skier.'

'And is he single?'

'Course not. It's the old golden handcuffs, you see? If any of these men got un-married, it would cost them tens of millions. That's why they come here. They're not after anything permanent, but like you and me, they want some fun.'

He continued his sweep of the room.

'Over there is Piggy Allsop; he's some big noise in haulage. Deadly dull, but pots of money.' He glanced down at Anna's legs. 'Piggy likes very skinny girls, though, so he's probably out.' He nodded towards a good-looking man in his late fifties. 'And that fellow in the red tie is Peter Rees. He works in oil and engineering.'

Anna's heart skipped a beat. Peter. Could he be Amy's Peter?

'And is he . . . attached? To a girl, I mean?'

Johnny looked at her, a wicked smile on his lips.

'Do you like him?'

'Perhaps. Is *he* single?'

He shrugged. 'Wife back in Gloucestershire of course, horrible old trout, although you didn't hear that from me. But no lady friends, as far as I know. I think he got his fingers burned a little while ago.'

'Oh. What happened to her?'

'I don't know,' he said, looking away from her. 'Sometimes they can get a little clingy. Come on, I'll introduce you.'

Peter was standing on his own, swilling bourbon around a glass as they approached.

'Peter, I'd like you to meet Natasha. Natasha is a fan of the arts.'

'Really?' said Peter, smiling at her. 'That's very interesting.'

Johnny gave Anna's arm a squeeze. 'I'll leave you two to chat,' he said and melted into the crowd.

'Actually, I'm very dull,' said Anna. 'Johnny was just trying to talk me up.'

'Oh, I'm sure that's not true. What branch of the arts are you in?'

'Sculpture, oils, the Renaissance,' she said vaguely, hoping he wouldn't be a collector and call her bluff. 'I want to hear all about you,' she said quickly, touching his arm. 'What do you do?'

'I'm on the board of Dallincourt.'

'Oh really? What's that?'

'We're an engineering firm, largely we build oil rigs, do the casing for mines. Things like that. Rather dull.' He smiled.

'What do you do there?'

'COO,' he said with a hint of pride.

Anna gestured at the room with her wine glass.

'So do you come to these things often?'

'Well, Jamie Swann and I have interests in common, so we're often to be found close by, yes.'

'Business interests?' asked Anna.

'Sometimes,' smiled Peter. 'Tell me, has Johnny given you the grand tour?'

He linked his arm through hers and led her towards the rear of the house, where there was another comfortable lounge full of sofas and alcoves, the lighting somewhat more subdued.

'This is the red room, designed by Kenneth Sway in the nineteenth century, I believe.' Anna looked up towards the roof, which was dominated by a crystal chandelier suspended from an elaborate gold-leafed ceiling rose in the shape of an eagle in flight. 'I thought you might be drawn to that,' laughed Peter. 'It's magnificent, isn't it?'

They walked on through an orangery looking down on to moonlit gardens, then back into the hallway.

'Shall we take a turn upstairs?' asked Peter.

Anna was beginning to feel a little out of her depth and looked around for Johnny, not that he would be much use. He was hardly anyone's idea of a chaperon.

'Are you all right?' said Peter, reaching up and touching her chin. 'I wouldn't want you to feel uncomfortable.'

'I'm fine,' smiled Anna. Don't wimp out now, she told herself. Okay, so this guy was called Peter and he came to Swann's parties, but that didn't make him Amy's Peter, did it? She needed more information, and the only way to get that was to press on.

'I can't wait to see the rest,' she said as he led her up the stairs and on to a corridor. A door to their left was open, and Anna almost gasped as she saw an overweight man, naked from the waist down, thrusting into a woman half-wearing a scarlet cocktail dress. As they passed, the woman looked at Anna and gave her a knowing smile.

'Some people like to be watched,' said Peter, opening a door and steering Anna inside. 'I myself am a much more private person. How about you, Natasha?'

She found herself in a bedroom suite overlooking the gardens dominated by an old oak four-poster bed, the only light coming from a small tasselled bedside lamp. As Peter closed the door behind him, she walked quickly over to the window in a vain attempt to put distance between them.

'The house is so beautiful,' she said, looking out at the grounds, hoping to start a conversation about design.

'Yes, but not as beautiful as you,' he said in a low voice. He touched his hand to her cheek and she flinched. She knew why Johnny brought girls to the party, but she had naively thought that any relationships would be started afterwards. She turned away from him and looked out of the big bay window.

'You are one of Johnny's girls, aren't you?' he said, coming closer behind her.

Her heart was hammering. Amir Khan had volunteered to come out to Buckinghamshire with her; he knew he would not be allowed access to the party, but had offered to wait in a nearby pub until she had finished. Now she wished she had taken him up on his offer.

'Of course,' she replied.

'Good,' he said, pressing himself into her as he kissed her neck softly. 'Take off your clothes,' he whispered.

She swallowed hard.

'Let's take this slowly,' she said quickly.

His fingers began to pull down the zip that ran the length of her spine.

'Fine by me,' he murmured. She felt a cool rush of air on her bare back as the dress parted. Her mouth turned dry. She knew she had to get out of here, but not before she got what she came for.

She turned around to face him. Peter had begun undoing the belt to his trousers.

'On the bed,' he said.

She smiled coquettishly, although she was frightened. 'I heard you were a good lover,' she said, playing for time.

He looked pleased to hear it.

'And who told you that?'

'A friend of mine. Amy Hart.'

Peter's face was only partly lit, but his expression told Anna all she needed to know. Amy's name brought on surprise, quickly followed by fear, then anger. Not sadness, not shame, not even regret. You bastard, she thought.

'Tell me, what did Amy say?' His voice was almost a bark.

Peter Rees *was* Amy's Peter.

'She said that you were very generous,' she replied, trailing her finger down his shirt. 'In every department.'

His expression softened.

'It was sad about her, wasn't it?' added Anna.

'Sad?'

'Her death.'

'Yes, it was very sad.' She saw his eyes narrow a fraction. Enough to register disapproval.

'How well did you know Amy?' he asked.

'Barely. And you?'

'The same.' His eyes were cold.

Anna knew now what sort of people she was dealing with: men who would use young girls until they became inconvenient, until they threatened to undermine their cosy domestic situation – the golden handcuffs, as Johnny had put it – at which point they were disposed of like flat champagne, casually tossed down the sink.

'Are you going to take off that dress?' Peter said finally. He moved up against her and pushed her gently back on the bed.

Not a chance, she thought.

She stood up and stroked his cheek. Her pulse was racing.

'Stay there and close your eyes,' she commanded.

'Where are you going?' said Peter.

'I'm going to get my friend Tanika, that tall blonde I came in with. I can see you're more than one woman can handle.'

'Wait,' he said firmly, taking her arm in a strong grip. 'Just you,' he added quietly.

'No,' she said, trying to wriggle away.

He curled his arm around her waist and pulled her close. His hand pushed against the bare triangle of skin on her back.

'Get back on the bed,' he ordered, breathing strong whisky breath all over her.

'Hang on,' she said, pulling free and tugging her dress back on to her shoulders. 'I'm getting Tanika.'

She raced towards the door, stumbling into the corridor and hurrying downstairs as fast as she could.

'Having fun?'

Anna's heart gave a lurch. Johnny Maxwell was standing at the door of the drawing room, a slight frown on his face. He'd clearly seen her leave with Peter and was wondering why she was back so soon.

'Just stepping outside for a cigarette,' she purred. My goodness, Natasha really is coming to life, she thought.

'And what about Peter?'

'Waiting upstairs.'

She scurried outside, inhaling deeply as if she had just come up for air.

The drive was empty. Shit, where are you, taxi? she thought, stepping from one foot to the other.

'You all right, miss?' asked one of the security guards, stepping forward, his hand on a heavy walkie-talkie strapped to his hip like a Western gunslinger.

She fumbled in her clutch bag for a cigarette and lit it.

'Fag break,' she said as casually as she could.

Come on, she pleaded silently, willing the taxi to arrive. She glanced back at the house, realising how stupid she'd been to come. It was one thing to infiltrate the society swingers' ball posing as a bohemian good-time girl; it was quite another to reveal to Peter Rees that she knew something about his past.

But then, like the cavalry coming over the hill, Anna heard hope driving towards her. The grumble of a taxi's diesel engine. She tossed her cigarette away and ran towards it.

'Taxi for Natasha?' she whispered.

'Hop in, love. Where to?'

'London. Richmond.'

The cabby glanced in the mirror, then pulled the car away. As it built up speed, Anna felt her fast-beating pulse slow.

She took her mobile out of her bag and tapped in a message to Amir Khan, Andy's investigator. Amir had asked her to tell him the moment she knew anything new. 'Amy's Peter is Peter Rees, COO of Dallincourt. Any use?'

She pressed 'Send' and sat back in the seat. The car was surrounded by blackness, only the occasional farm or house revealed by a gap in the trees. She tried to relax, but her body was still tense, her heart thumping with adrenalin. At the same time she felt strangely dejected, wrung out. In truth, she'd been lucky to get out of there in one piece – and for what? She had Peter's name, she knew he had been with Amy, knew that the mention of her name had made him frightened and angry, but where did that really get her? She had to admit to herself that she hadn't thought any of this through properly; she'd just been stumbling from clue to clue, hoping that the next one would reveal how Amy had really died. The reality was that she might well never know.

'Look at this wanker behind us,' said the cabby, shaking her from her thoughts. 'Pissed, I bet you.'

She turned in her seat, but she could only see the too-bright full-beam headlights of a car coming up fast behind, dangerously close.

The cabby sounded his horn, but the car only seemed to get closer, the lights filling the taxi's interior. Then Anna grabbed the door handle as she felt a bump behind her.

'Christ!' shouted the cabby. 'What's he doing?'

The car had pulled out and had drawn up against the side of them. It was a black SUV, but Anna couldn't make out any driver or passenger, as the windows were tinted. She heard metal scrape against metal as it slammed against them.

'Shit!' cried the cabby as the SUV banged into them again, forcing them up on to an embankment, skidding to a halt. They both watched in disbelief as the red lights of the other car disappeared into the distance.

'You all right, miss?' said the driver, turning in his seat. 'Did you get his plates?'

Anna shook her head.

'Me neither,' said the cabby bitterly. 'There goes my bloody no-claims. What the hell was he playing at?'

But Anna knew exactly what the driver had been playing at, and she had no doubt what that little road race had meant. She had been well and truly warned.

60

'You sure this is where you want to go, love? I thought you said Richmond.' The cabby pulled up outside an anonymous-looking block of flats behind the Tate Modern.

'This is just fine,' said Anna, handing him a fistful of tenners.

'Ride is on me, love.'

'You sure?'

He nodded. She could tell he was relieved that she hadn't taken his insurance details and done him for whiplash.

She looked down at Amir Khan's address, which he had sent by text message. She had called him on the taxi ride home, partly because she was so shaken, and partly because she had become even more determined to nail Peter Rees for what he had done. If the car had slammed into her taxi intentionally, then Rees had sent it. Perhaps it had been because he was angry that she had run away from their bedroom tryst. Or perhaps it was because the mention of Amy Hart had rattled him. Why? Anna asked herself. Because he had something to do with Amy's death?

She felt a shiver of worry for her own safety. Thankfully the South Bank was still busy, despite the late hour. Wanting to get off the street, she pressed the intercom of the building in front of her and was buzzed inside.

Inside, it was just as blank-looking as outside. Long cream corridors lit up by fluoro strip lights.

A door at the end of the corridor creaked open and made her jump.

'You looking for me?' Amir asked, smiling.

Relieved, she almost ran into his apartment.

'Don't creep up on me, I'm jumpy enough as it is.'

'I hope you don't mind coming to my flat after dark,' he said politely. 'But this is where I work most of the time.'

Anna nodded. Andy had filled her in on how Amir worked. Apparently he was the master of the long-range sting, which meant adopting new personas for weeks, sometimes months at a time. He couldn't be seen coming in and out of the Media Incorporated offices too often, as it would mean blowing his cover.

He made her a cup of coffee and a piece of toast and she was grateful for the hospitality. She told him what had gone on at James Swann's mansion. Clutching their mugs, they went from the living space into a large office.

'Bloody hell, Amir, it's like MI5 HQ in here,' she said, looking at a large whiteboard covered in words and photographs.

He grinned, his coffee-coloured eyes dancing.

'This is the whole story of Amy Hart,' he said, walking over and tapping a large picture of the dead girl. 'The flow chart takes us from Amy leaving Doncaster to go to uni, then all the way . . .' his finger traced the direction of the arrows, 'to here.' At the far right was a picture of Amy's riverside flat.

Anna walked up to the chart, examining the material. She was impressed with the level of detail Amir had gone into. He had worked out a range of possible scenarios labelled 'Murder', 'Accident', 'Suicide' and so on.

'So where does all this get us?'

'Okay,' said Amir. 'First let's start with what we know, putting aside the most likely explanation.'

She frowned.

'Which is?'

'A tragic accident. Amy was on her own, she got drunk and slipped down the stairs.'

'But given that we know she was blackmailing Peter, I'd say that's looking less and less likely,' said Anna, disappointed that Amir thought a fall was still the most likely option. 'There's also the fact that Rees was so rattled tonight. If he's innocent, we have to ask ourselves why.'

'The other problem is that we have no way of knowing if she was pushed or if she just fell,' said Amir. 'I've had a medical expert look at the findings of the inquest, and the injuries sustained are consistent with a fall down the stairs: broken bones, fractures, bruising and, in this case, a broken neck. But push or fall, who knows. No coroner will ever be able to tell the difference.'

He walked over to the board and studied the photos.

'Have you looked into Peter Rees since I texted you?'

Amir nodded.

'What made you sure that Rees was Amy's Peter?'

'Well he confirmed that he knew her. And he just looked guilty.'

Amir laughed.

'You of all people should know that a guilty look isn't going to hold up as evidence in court.'

Anna wanted to scream in frustration. All that work, all those leads she'd followed; finally she'd found Amy's lover, the person that Amy was blackmailing, and still she could do nothing about it. And at the same time, she had alerted Peter Rees to the fact that she was on his trail, and might have put herself in danger.

'I think Rees is Amy's Peter too,' Amir said more quietly.

'Why?' she asked excitedly.

'When you texted me his name, I checked him out, although he was already on my radar anyway. All of Swann's friends are. I found this . . .'

He went over to the printer, pulled out a news article and stuck it on the whiteboard. Anna speed-read the item. It was headlined 'Oil Chief Found Dead', and detailed how Douglas Faulks, the chief executive of Pogex Oil had been discovered hanging at his Gloucestershire country home, along with the background to the story: how there had been a huge oil spill off the coast of Newfoundland six months earlier and how the executive had taken tremendous flak from the Canadian government. A series of terrible PR gaffes, where Faulks had denied responsibility, then tried to blame the rig's management, had led to him becoming the company fall guy. Anna remembered reading about it and thinking that it seemed unfair that one man should be singled out for all these attacks. She also remembered that Peter Rees worked in oil and gas.

456

'Did Peter know Douglas?' she asked, piecing things together.

Amir nodded. 'I've found dozens of pictures of them together at society and trade events.'

'Bloody hell, Amir. You don't hang about, do you?'

'There's more,' he added. 'Pogex Oil and Dallincourt work closely together. Dallincourt basically build and repair most of Pogex's rigs and refineries.'

'Remember what Louise Allerton told me about Amy? That she'd found Peter sobbing about a friend's death. He told her he thought it was his fault.' Anna looked up at Amir, desperate for answers. 'How can that be?'

Amir shrugged. 'I don't know yet.'

'So what else do we know about Douglas Faulks?'

'We know it was a tragic death. Lots of people in the City thought that Faulks had been set up. You know, let one man take the blame instead of the entire company.'

'He should have got himself a better publicist,' she said sombrely.

'Pogex have a good PR company. Auckland PR. They are usually experts at keeping bad news out of the media, although they had a job on their hands stopping the Pogex Oil share price going into freefall. They act for Dallincourt Engineering Services as well. They are the bigger client actually, as Pogex are a relatively small oil company.'

'Auckland PR?' Anna repeated. She'd heard that name in the last few days. She took a minute to think where. 'Auckland's chairman. What's he called?' she said, remembering.

'Paul Morgan.'

'No, not him.'

'Simon Cooper? He's the CEO.'

'That's him,' she said. 'Apparently he's having an affair with our senior partner Helen Pierce.'

Anna felt her whole body tingle as she connected all the evidence. She began to think out loud while Amir started furiously writing her thought processes down on his whiteboard.

'Simon Cooper acts for Dallincourt. Peter Rees, who works for Dallincourt, thinks he is responsible for Douglas Faulks's death. Amy Hart is blackmailing Rees, possibly about Douglas's death. Amy is found dead but the story goes largely unnoticed because of the Sam Charles affair.'

For a second she hardly dared think where this was all leading, but one glance at Amir told her that he had made the connection too.

'I think we know who leaked your Sam Charles story,' he said quietly.

She closed her eyes and nodded, knowing that she had come here to solve one mystery, and had somehow solved two.

61

Despite the bucolic surroundings of his country estate, Sam Charles was feeling thoroughly miserable. He walked down from the house, kicking listlessly at stones on the winding path through the gardens. It was a perfect summer's day, with a cloudless pebble-blue sky and the smell of cut grass coming from the striped lawns. The gardener had also made a fine job of tidying up the flower beds, and in the soft sunshine, the bright sunflowers and nodding delphiniums looked like a display from the Chelsea Flower Show. Yet Sam couldn't find pleasure in any of it; he was determined to wallow in self-pity, however cheerful the world looked. The source of his dark mood – *as ever*, he thought bitterly – was women. Specifically, one woman: Anna Kennedy. He had assumed that a down-to-earth lawyer might be easier to work out than his previous actress girlfriends. But clearly not. She was neurotic, paranoid and completely baffling. As least you knew where you stood with actresses like Jessica; you just needed to shower them with constant attention, gifts and compliments and agree with everything they said. But Anna was at the opposite end of the spectrum: fiercely independent and apparently impervious to flattery and Sam's not inconsiderable charm.

I mean, what right-minded woman wouldn't want to come and spend the weekend at a luxurious Wiltshire manor with me? thought Sam, pulling the head off a flower as he walked past. After all, he'd thought his fledgling romance with Anna was going so well. He'd certainly been pulling the stops out – calling when he said he would, inviting her to Provence after she had won that libel trial. So when he'd asked her to come to Wiltshire for the weekend after their trip to Mougins, he had assumed that she would jump at the chance of spending the bank holiday in his bed. Instead she had made some vague excuses about having to work.

Of course, Sam did suspect she was still miffed from their argument in the restaurant – and yes, perhaps his suggestion that the only reason he had helped her with the Amy Hart case was because he fancied her hadn't helped much – but he knew the real reason she'd turned him down was to attend James Swann's party.

A cabbage white butterfly flitted across the path and Sam threw the flower head at it. Amy bloody Hart. He just couldn't understand why Anna cared so much about some dead party girl. No, correction: he couldn't understand why she cared more about Amy Hart than about *him*.

He walked over to the grass tennis court, hidden in the shade of a large spreading copper beech. Setting up the ball machine, he took a spot on the opposite baseline and practised his forehand, slamming each ball angrily yet accurately across court. Then, feeling a little better, he sat down on a wooden bench, wiping his face with a cold towel he pulled from the little ice box next to his seat.

Why am I even bothering with a woman at this point in my life? he thought, leaning his head back to look up through the branches and leaves of the tree. Yes, Anna Kennedy was a great girl, smart, very sexy, but she was definitely too uptight for him. And yet . . . and yet he couldn't stop thinking about how lovely she'd looked in that blue dress in Provence. How great she smelled, how enthusiastic she was when he'd told her about his script ideas. He'd never met a woman who was so supportive on the one hand, but so single-minded about what she wanted to do. Sam just couldn't work her out one bit, and that possibly added to her appeal.

Sighing, he reached back into the little fridge and cracked open a bottle of cold lemonade. Just then, his mobile phone began vibrating in his pocket. Tutting, he pulled it out.

'Yes?'

'Hey, Mr Sunshine, how's things in England?'

Sam recognised Jim Parker's voice immediately and softened his tone.

'Sorry, Jim,' he said, taking a long drink. 'Just a bit distracted. Been concentrating on the script since I've been back here.'

'Is that why I haven't been able to get hold of you since last Friday?'

'Yeah, you know how it is when you're in the zone,' he lied.

'And would that zone happen to include the South of France, too?'

Sam swallowed.

'What do you mean?'

'Sam, I read the British papers. You were spotted at Moulin de Mougins on Saturday looking very friendly with a pretty brunette. If you were trying to stay off the radar, it didn't work.'

Sam swore under his breath. He hadn't intentionally taken Anna to such a famous restaurant; he'd just wanted to treat her, make her feel special. But now it was out, he knew he'd made a big mistake. To the gossip mags, it would look as though he was sneaking around, trying to keep his new relationship a secret – and that would only make them more interested. And just when he wasn't sure what he'd got himself into.

'So who is she, Sam?' said Jim.

'Anna Kennedy.'

'The *lawyer*?' gasped his agent. 'The one who dropped you in this shit? What, was it a thank-you for fucking up the injunction? Or just for fucking up your life?'

'Jim, you know it wasn't like that, and besides . . .' he hesitated, 'I like her.'

Jim didn't say anything for a moment.

'And have you heard about Jess?' he asked finally.

Sam frowned.

'What about her?'

'Jessica's been in a car accident, Sam. That's why I've been calling you.'

'You're kidding me!' His heart seemed to skip a beat. 'When was this? How is she? Was it bad?'

'Last week, and she's okay, but that's only because someone up there is watching over her. Some crackhead ploughed into

461

her in a stolen car; she could have been crippled.'

'Jesus,' whispered Sam, feeling a flood of guilt. What if she had been badly hurt, or even killed? And this was last week? Why hadn't he heard about it? He'd been trying so hard to refocus, he hadn't bothered taking anyone's calls – except Anna's.

'Where is she now? Hospital?'

'Back home. Barbara's looking after her.'

'I should call her,' he panicked. 'I mean, if you think she'll even take my call?'

'Buddy, it's always worth a shot.'

He called her the second he got off the phone with Jim. He wasn't exactly sure what he was going to say, but he felt he needed to speak to her. After all, they'd been engaged a long time; you couldn't just turn those feelings off like a tap. Or a faucet, perhaps.

'Hello?'

Sam's heart sank. Jessica's mother.

'Hey, Barbara, it's Sam,' he said as brightly as he could. 'Do you think I could speak to Jess?'

There was a cold silence for a moment.

'I really don't think she wants to speak . . .' said Barbara, then the line became muffled. In the background, Sam could just make out the exchange: 'Lemme speak to him.' 'No, you're not up to it, he's only gonna upset you.' 'Gimme the goddamn phone.'

There was some bumping and hissing, then Jessica came on the line.

'Sam? Is that you?' Her voice sounded shaky and weak. Sam felt dreadful.

'Yeah, it's me. Listen, Jess, I just heard about the accident; how are you?'

'I'm okay, I guess,' she said slowly. 'As well as can be expected, anyway.'

'What the hell happened?'

'I was just driving back from the studio when some guy comes out of nowhere and crash! He slammed into me, flipped the car

462

in the air a couple of times; I almost got hit by a truck coming the other way.'

'My God.'

'Yeah, the fire department had to cut me out of the wreckage. My legs were almost crushed, can you imagine that? There was gasoline everywhere. One spark and I could have . . .' She trailed off with a sob.

Sam felt as if he'd been punched in the gut. He knew it was irrational, but he couldn't help feeling this was all his fault. He and Jessica might not have been right for each other, but ever since his one-night stand with Katie, things seemed to have gone wrong for both of them.

'Oh honey, I'm so sorry.'

Jessica made some snuffling noises, like she was wiping her nose.

'That's sweet, Sam,' she said. 'It means a lot.'

'But you're okay? Physically, I mean?'

'Sam, they're saying I might need surgery,' said Jessica, her voice cracking again.

'On your *legs*?'

'Maybe some work around my eyes. Jim's put me in touch with his guy out here.'

'I should fly out . . .'

'No, no,' said Jessica. 'I'm fine. I'm up and about now, and you have your own life to be getting on with.'

Sam stopped. Had she heard about the picture of him and Anna in Mougins?

'Are you sure? Because I can easily grab the jet.'

She paused.

'What for, Sam?' she said sadly. 'But honestly, I'm okay. And thanks for calling. I do appreciate it.'

She hung up, and Sam sat there looking at his phone for a long minute. Then he stood up and walked over to the far side of the tennis court, using the scoop to pick up the fluffy yellow balls and drop them into the basket.

Jess had sounded so small and fragile on the phone. There had been times early on in their romance when she had been like that, when she'd shown him her softer, more vulnerable side. He *did* love her back then. And there had been other good times, both of them on their way up, both in it together. Sam realised that he missed those days badly.

'But you can't go back, can you?' he said aloud, bending to pick up his racquet and the first ball from the top of the basket. He threw the ball into the air, swishing the racquet around in a perfect serve, watching the ball slam into the netting on the other side of the court. 'No, you can't.'

62

'Balls.'

Matt put his coffee cup down on his desk and picked up his diary, remembering that there was a list of posh recommended restaurants at the front. He was due to meet up with Carla on Wednesday night and he still hadn't booked anywhere.

He looked at his watch: 10 p.m. Most of them would be closing soon; why had he left it so late? It was exactly the sort of thing she used to bollock him for when they were married. Matt could never understand why she got so worked up about it. As far as he was concerned, the perfect date was a long walk by the river, followed by drinks in some cosy old-fashioned boozer, then falling laughing into bed. Dates were about the conversation and the person you were with, weren't they? Not the poached quails' eggs you had for your starter or the bottle of wine you drank with your meal. But Carla didn't think like that; never had. For her, a date was something expensive and showy, being seen at the right restaurant, at the right table, something she could boast to her friends about the next day.

Had she boasted about their night of passion? he wondered. He doubted it somehow. More likely she had woken up cringing at the thought of what had happened that evening he'd been over to babysit. Yes, the sex had been incredible: passionate, sensual, spontaneous, all the things, he had to admit, their lovemaking had ceased to be long before their divorce. But did that mean that the fire of their relationship had been rekindled? He honestly didn't know. Maybe the answer would present itself at their dinner.

He picked up the phone and tried the numbers in his diary,

the swankiest first. He'd known it was a long shot, and he wasn't at all surprised when one by one, they snootily told him they were booked up for weeks if not months in advance.

Tutting, he put down the phone and took a sip of his coffee. 'Cold,' he muttered. Maybe it was time to go home. The Donovan Pierce offices were in darkness except for the sharp spotlight of his desk lamp and the blue-grey glow of his computer screen. For the first time ever, he was the last one in the office. Shame no one's around to see it, he grinned.

Work had started to roll in for Matt since word had got around the wealthier pockets of London that he was handling the Rob Beaumont–Kim Collier divorce; just this week he had been instructed by a merchant banker and the wife of an England rugby star.

It can wait until tomorrow, he decided, shutting his case file with a thud. He stood up, stretching. He'd been working with the office door closed and just his desk lamp on, which made the room so cosy, he felt as if he could curl up on the sofa and fall asleep.

As he entered the corridor, he noticed the glow coming from beneath Helen's door – a light he was sure had not been on half an hour earlier when he had gone to make his coffee. For one gleeful moment he imagined the look of surprise on Helen's face as she saw him leaving the office last, a responsible and diligent partner who was bringing in prestigious clients and fees.

But if it was Helen, she was being awfully quiet: usually she would be on the phone to the States or barking orders into her mobile or dictaphone. The thought occurred to him that it could be an intruder. He gripped the handle, tensing himself, then whipped the door open.

'Jesus, Matt,' gasped Anna, holding a hand to her chest. 'What the hell are you doing?'

'Oh God, sorry,' he said. 'I thought you were an intruder.'

Now that he thought about it, she *did* look like an intruder, standing behind Helen's desk, bent over her computer keyboard. Although it was dark, Matt was certain her face had that guilty blush that suggested she was doing something she shouldn't.

'What are you doing here, Anna?' he asked, glancing around the room.

'Helen asked me to check something out for one of her cases,' she said, looking vulnerable and unsure. It was a side of Anna Kennedy he had never seen before, and that made him deeply suspicious. He hadn't had any personal brushes with corporate espionage, but he knew it existed in every major business around the globe. Just because he liked the girl didn't mean she should be allowed to cause trouble for Donovan Pierce.

'At 10 p.m. on a bank holiday? And I thought Helen was in Devon . . .' He hadn't meant to sound accusatory, but Anna was looking so shifty.

'I needed to check something . . .' replied Anna, her top lip trembling. She's going to cry, thought Matt with alarm. He hadn't imagined Anna Kennedy capable of such a thing.

'Is everything all right?' he asked, taking a step towards her.

'Everything's fine,' she said, darting her gaze away.

Everything was obviously not fine.

'You know you can talk to me, don't you?'

She flinched, her head down.

'Anna, what's wrong?'

She sank down on the leather sofa.

'Can I tell you a story?' she said, looking so ill at ease it reminded him of the time Jonas had come to him wanting to confess to having broken a lamp, but scared of being shouted at.

He nodded and touched her shoulder.

'Do you want to grab a coffee and come into my office?'

He sat in semi-darkness behind his desk, just listening. They had been there over forty minutes, their coffee undrunk and cold. With typical thoroughness, Anna had left nothing out, telling Matt the entire story of Amy Hart, from the first phone call with her sister Ruby, right through her meetings with a soap star and a lingerie model, a politician and a man who built oil rigs and tankers. He could see that she had been badly frightened by what she had discovered, and by the attack on that dark road in Buckinghamshire. As she spoke, he couldn't help but admire her. Most people would have been scared off, but it only seemed to have made her more determined to get to the bottom of it.

'And after all this, you think that *Helen* sabotaged Sam's injunction because she wanted to help her boyfriend cover up the story of Amy's inquest?' he asked when she had finished her tale.

'I'm sure of it. I just can't prove it.'

'Prove what?' exclaimed Matt. 'That Helen's a murderer?'

'I didn't say that. Doing a favour for a friend doesn't make her a killer. But it shows she's involved.'

'Can you prove *any* of it? I assume you've tried finding out from Scandalhound and the *News* who leaked the story.'

'I couldn't get anything from them. That was the first thing I did. Remember I was trying to prove that Blake and Katie were in contempt of court? I thought maybe I could find out from Helen's end. That's why I was snooping around here looking for something, anything. But I can't get into her email system. Not that she'd have sent an email from a Donovan Pierce address . . .'

Matt shook his head with concern.

'Anna, you could get yourself fired for all this.'

'I was rather hoping you'd help me, not fire me.'

As she looked at him in the semi-darkness, he felt something inside him stir.

Stop it, he scolded himself.

His palm rubbed the stubble on his chin as his thoughts turned to Helen Pierce. She was certainly capable of stitching up a client if it served her own ends in the long run. Perhaps her boyfriend – if indeed she was having an affair with the Auckland PR supremo – had simply asked her to leak the story as a smokescreen and she had done it as a favour. But why would they go to all that effort to bury Amy's inquest . . . unless there was something that needed hiding.

He'd only known Helen a couple of months, but it was enough to realise that she was many things: arrogant, ruthless, self-promoting; no doubt she shared Larry's ambiguous regard for professional ethics in general. But to think that she could be involved in a murderous cover-up? That was going too far. And yet he trusted Anna Kennedy's judgement and shrewdness.

There was no way she'd be risking her job like this if she didn't think that Helen was somehow culpable.

'What are you going to do now?' he said quietly.

'I don't know. It's like I've got all the parts of the jigsaw but can't fit them together. Sam Charles is paying for an investigator to help out, but that's gone a bit cold.'

'What? The trail on Helen, or Sam Charles?' He couldn't help but ask. He'd heard the rumours around the office that Anna had become involved with their celebrity client. It seemed as good a time as any to ask.

'So you've heard the gossip,' she muttered.

'Is it true?'

'Sam's not formally a client any more,' she said quickly. 'Besides, I'm not really sure if it's still *on*.'

Matt held up a hand.

'Look, I haven't got a problem with it.'

He looked down, knowing it was untrue; that the thought of Anna and Sam did make him feel uncomfortable, but not for any reason to do with the solicitor's code of conduct.

'I should go,' she said finally.

'Anna, I think you should drop this.'

'Because of Helen?'

'Because you can't prove anything,' he said, exasperated. 'Everything is pure supposition.'

Anna balled her fist and slammed it on her knee.

'This is about finding the truth and getting it out there, Matt. I thought you believed that more than anyone at this firm.'

He thought back to their first lunch, to their fiery, awkward debate about whether people deserved to know the truth. It seemed so very long ago.

'I just think you need to be careful. Accusing Helen on some hunch. Not to mention getting almost run off the road last night. Maybe it was coincidence, but if it wasn't, you have to ask yourself if this is worth it.'

'If it wasn't coincidence, then it means I'm right,' she replied vehemently.

He felt a protective shot of worry for her safety.

'Let me give you a lift home.'

Anna laughed.

'I'm not sure sitting on the back of your mid-life-crisis machine really constitutes being careful.'

He took a spare helmet from the hat rack by the door and handed it to her.

'Put that on, too,' he said, handing her a too-big leather jacket.

They locked up the office and walked around to Matt's bike, which was parked on a side street behind the office. He got astride and fired it up, revving the engine, but Anna just stood there, rather forlorn in her huge jacket and helmet.

'You getting on, then?' shouted Matt over the noise.

'I've never actually done this before.'

'Just hop on the back and put your feet on those pegs.' When she was on, Matt began to move off. 'And grab on to me,' he yelled above the engine noise. She wrapped both arms around his waist, and he felt the back of his neck tingle.

'Don't go too fast,' she shouted above the breeze.

He nodded and eased off the throttle, letting Anna get used to the sensation of weaving in and out of the West End traffic and leaning into bends. He picked up speed as they passed the House of Commons, gloriously lit up against the inky London sky, and the wind whipped at them as they crossed the river. Her arms tightened around his waist and her head rested softly against his back, and Matt felt his heart beat faster.

Finally they drew up outside Anna's cottage and she clambered off.

'Do you want me to come in?' said Matt. 'Just to check everything's okay?' he added quickly.

'I think I'll be all right. If there was a hit man after me, my guess is he'd have gone home the minute he saw me get on a motorbike with you, thinking his job was done.'

'I'm completely in control of this machine,' said Matt, tapping the handlebars.

'Yeah, yeah,' laughed Anna. 'You take care of yourself Evel Knievel.' Her eyes softened in the low moonlight, and he knew her concern was genuine.

'Call me if you need anything. Even if it's company.'

She smiled and went inside. Matt waited for a moment, then revved the engine and turned back on to the main road, which took him through the brightly lit centre of Richmond. Seeing all the couples strolling through the town he was suddenly reminded of something: he still hadn't booked the restaurant for his meeting with Carla. But for some reason, that didn't seem like such a big deal any more.

63

Sam lay on the sunlounger by the pool, staring down at the almost blank page in front of him.

'Writer's bloody block,' he grumbled to himself, snatching up his cigarettes and lighting one. Why couldn't he think of anything to write? He'd got the best Montblanc pen, bought an expensive notebook – the actual sort Hemingway used to use – and turned off his phone to avoid any distractions. He'd been sitting here in the cool shadow for an hour, and yet inspiration had failed to strike beyond the basic plot: a famous film star decides to give up the fame game and life in a goldfish bowl to return to his sleepy home town. He turned back to the first page in his notebook. He was quite pleased with the titles he had come up with: *Unfamous* had a nice ring to it, he thought, imagining his interview for *Time* magazine when *Unfamous* became a world-wide phenomenon. 'How did you come up with such a zeitgeisty title for your brilliant comedy, Sam?' the reporter would ask, to which Sam would tell him that it had spun off an argument with his agent after his Edinburgh comedy smash show with Mike McKenzie.

Sam blew his cheeks out. Of course, it was slightly presumptuous to be planning your Oscar acceptance speech when you hadn't actually written more than three lines. He looked at what he had so far, imagining who he'd cast as his co-stars: Russell Brand, and Vince Vaughn if he could do a British accent, had been his first thoughts.

Interior: Pub in Margate. Two middle-aged men, TOM and

DAVE, are sitting silently drinking at the bar. SAM walks in. He is incredibly handsome and a movie star.

SAM   All right, lads?
TOM   All right? It's okay for you, you've got a helicopter outside.
SAM   I sold the 'copter. It's all about camels now.
TOM   You came on a camel?
DAVE   I think he's being ironic.

A camel walks past the window.

SAM   No, I came on a camel.

Under this Sam had written 'BIG LAUGH', followed by the scrawled note: 'Why on earth does Sam have a bloody camel in Margate?'

It was hopeless. When he'd been sitting in his flat with Mike, the ideas had just poured out of them; funny, original, clever. Or had it all been Mike, after all? People were always going on about what a genius he was; maybe Sam had only *thought* he'd written those sketches. For a brief moment he thought about calling Mike, who had returned to Eigan earlier that week, to persuade him to return to London. But that would be defeatist, he decided quickly, stubbing out his cigarette.

No, the problem was that he was trying to write the scene longhand; perhaps he should be doing it on the computer. He tore out the page, screwed it up, then tried to toss it through the water polo hoop at the end of the pool. It flew about three feet, teetered on the edge, then sank slowly into the water. Sam watched the limp paper disintegrate, the ink blurring and becoming unreadable. He stood up and stalked back to the house. Maybe he needed to brainstorm with someone. Anna Kennedy would be his first choice – she always made the right noises about how good he was – but she hadn't even called him back, despite his numerous messages. All he'd had was one lousy text from her: 'Manic at work. Sorry for not calling. A lot on my mind at mo. Ax'

He'd read and reread that one, analysing it, looking for all the angles until it sent him crazy. Was it an apology? Did she want to forget about the argument and move on? Or was she saying 'let's cool it, I'm too busy'? Was it a woman's version of the old 'it's not you, it's me' get-out? Still, she had put a kiss at the end. Or did she do that with everyone? No wonder he couldn't write, with Anna playing such cryptic mind games. He'd sent her flowers, of course, but what with it being England and the bank holiday, he couldn't be sure that she'd got them. He knew he could try a bigger, more serious gesture. Jewellery always went down well in LA. Not diamonds, and not a ring, obviously, but maybe a tasteful necklace? It certainly used to work with Jessica, but somehow it seemed too flamboyant a gesture for two people who had only been on a couple of dates.

Thinking about Jessica only made him feel worse. He should probably send something to her as well after the crash. Sunflowers? Lilies? Did Tiffany do safety pins, for her sling?

He walked into the kitchen and grabbed a beer from the fridge. When all else fails, drink, he thought.

'Hey, that's not bad,' he murmured, looking around for his notebook to write it down, before remembering he'd left it by the pool.

Sighing, he opened the fridge and pulled out the poached salmon salad his housekeeper Mrs Hudson had left for him. He sat at the granite worktop and picked at the food with his fork, then pushed it away. He wasn't even hungry. He thought back to his visit to Anna's cottage, and her cosy kitchen. He bet she could just whip up some scrambled eggs and bacon and lightly toasted muffins on her little four-burner gas stove . . .

He was shaken out of his thoughts by the sound of the buzzer. He frowned: who was at the gate at this time? Mrs Hudson must have forgotten the code again. He pressed the button to activate the electric gates, then opened the front door. He needed to have words. But it wasn't Mrs Hudson's battered VW Golf turning into the drive; it was a large silver Mercedes with tinted windows.

'Who the hell . . . ?' he muttered, wondering for a second if it was a particularly ambitious doorstepping reporter. The car

474

pulled up and a uniformed chauffeur got out, nodded to Sam and walked around to open the passenger door.

First he saw a foot complete with red high heel, then a long tanned leg, then she stepped out.

'Jessica!' he gasped. 'What on earth are you doing here?'

His ex-fiancée gave him a full-watt Hollywood smile.

'Is that the only greeting you've got for me after all this time?' she laughed.

Her relaxed manner almost floored him.

'Sorry,' he said, striding over and kissing her awkwardly on both cheeks. 'It's just a bit of a shock.'

'I can imagine,' she smirked. 'But you were so sweet on the phone, and you said we needed to talk, so . . .' She held up her hands and gave her hips a little wiggle. 'Here I am.'

Suddenly thinking of her accident, he took her arm. 'Sorry, I wasn't thinking. Are you okay?'

'Oh sure,' said Jessica, leaning on him. 'I'm much better, almost back to normal.'

She certainly looked good, fantastic in fact. She was wearing a short red dress with thin straps that showed off her curves to perfection, with a white Birkin bag hanging off her arm. There didn't seem to be any evidence of her trauma, but then maybe that was clever make-up; Jessica was always quite the expert with that. In fact the bathroom here at Copley's was still full of thousands of dollars' worth of cosmetics.

'Will that be all, madam?' asked the chauffeur, stepping forward holding an overnight bag.

Jessica turned her green eyes towards Sam.

'I think that's up to the master of the house,' she said, looking over his shoulder towards the front door. 'I did try to call, but your phone was off. I didn't know if I'd be interrupting anything . . .'

'No, no,' said Sam quickly, taking the bag from the driver and fumbling a tip into his hand. 'You're very welcome, come on in,' he said, ushering Jessica inside. He led her to the kitchen. 'So how are you?' he said, sitting across from her.

'I'm fine. A little shaken up, but these things happen.'

'I have to say, you're handling it brilliantly.'

'You can't let it get you down,' she said with a smile that held for a moment, then collapsed, her eyes filling with tears.

'Jess, don't . . .' he said, not knowing if he should come around to comfort her. Instead he reached across the table and touched her hand.

'I'm sorry. I told myself I wouldn't, it's just that . . .'

'What?' said Sam softly.

'I know you've moved on, emotionally, professionally. I heard about the Edinburgh show and I'm so happy for you, I really am.'

Her approval somehow mattered to him.

'But lying there in that hospital bed, it gave me time to think about everything, and, well, about us . . .' Her lip quivered.

'Jess, I'm sorry it had to end the way it did.'

'I thought so too,' said Jessica, the tears still dribbling. 'Considering . . .' she added softly.

Sam felt his instincts prickle.

'Considering what?'

The silence seemed to go on for ever.

'Sam, I'm pregnant.'

He stopped dead, unable to draw breath.

'You're . . . ?'

'Pregnant.'

He was in complete shock. His brain seemed to have shut down, his mouth could barely open.

'How?' he said finally.

'I think you know how people make babies,' she said with a small laugh.

'But when did you find out?'

'When they take you into ER, they need to check before they X-ray you because it can hurt the baby, so they did a test and, well, there it was.'

'Is it mine?'

'Is it mine?' she repeated incredulously. 'You're unbelievable! Do I need to remind you that you were the one that went off and had an affair? I have always been one hundred and ten per cent faithful to you.'

His eyes were transfixed on her belly, wondering if you could

476

see anything yet. He reached his hand out; his fingers were trembling.

'But do you want to keep it?' he asked carefully. 'I mean, your career and everything? Is it the right time?'

'Yes, I want to keep it,' she said, her eyes beginning to glisten again. She took his hand and placed it on her completely flat stomach. 'I want to have *our* baby,' she said. 'It's always the right time for him.'

Sam looked up sharply.

'Him?'

'It's twelve weeks old, Sam,' she said proudly. 'I've had a scan, and while they can't tell the sex for sure yet, I think it's a boy.'

Sam really didn't know what to think. His head was spinning. Could he really be the father? Twelve weeks he tried to count back, but so much had happened in the last two or three months, it was hard to get it straight. He knew he'd gone to see Jessica on the *Slayer* set, but he really couldn't remember having sex with her. Then again, he was drinking pretty heavily back then. I can't remember having sex with Katie Grey either, he thought mournfully.

Jessica snapped open her handbag and pulled out a photograph the size of a Polaroid. It was just a grainy still, a swirling black and white mass, but it was still possible to make out a head and a curled body. Sam drew a finger across the tiny person and felt his heart swell. *His son.*

'You are happy?' she said eagerly.

Suddenly he could hear Jim Parker's words at the *Robotics* premiere: You need stability. A wife. A family.

Back then, the very thought of it had terrified him, but somehow, standing here, watching her place her small hand on her pregnant belly, he knew he had to step up to the plate and accept his responsibilities. He had promised himself that he would change. Was this where the real change started happening?

He felt a wave of sadness for a life that had filled him with such excitement an hour earlier and was now sailing swiftly out of reach, like a branch on the rapids.

'Yes, of course,' he said uncertainly. 'It's just . . .' He wanted

477

to say, 'I've met someone else, someone I really like, someone I can see myself having a future with', and he wanted to tell Jessica the truth, that he no longer loved her, that he had spent the last two months breathing a sigh of relief that he was free of her. He looked back at the scan. But here was a baby, a real living thing that they had created together. That had to be worth something, didn't it? Perhaps it was everything.

'It's just what, honey?' said Jessica.

'Nothing.' Nothing worth repeating anyway.

'Good,' she said, stroking his cheek with the back of her finger. 'So I should go upstairs, freshen up and then we can talk about things, okay? Like when you're going to do the sensible thing and get your ass back to LA.'

When Sam had gone back downstairs, Jessica unpacked her bag in the master bedroom, hanging her clothes – all carefully chosen to show off her body perfectly, of course – in the walk-in closet she had designed for herself only two years previously. There were still some of her own dresses and jeans on the shelves – Sam had either been too sentimental or too lazy to clear them out. When that was done, she sat down on the bed and took the scan out of her handbag. She looked at it for a moment.

There's no way I want a baby, she thought, acknowledging that she had no maternal instincts whatsoever. This particular foetus belonged – had belonged – to some dumb starlet Jim represented. She'd been knocked up by one of the big studio heads, and Jim had used the information to get one of his projects green-lit. With that accomplished, he had talked Little Miss Careless into having an abortion, 'for the sake of her career', and had also had the brilliant notion of putting the scan to a second use with Sam. Jessica chuckled; she really admired the way her new agent's mind worked. She just knew that she and Jim Parker were going to have a very long and lucrative friendship.

She put the photo between the pages of a copy of *The Secret* she'd picked up at the airport. It would stay there for a few weeks and then she would get rid of it, probably round about the time she would fake her miscarriage. If she hadn't reeled

Sam in by then with her body, she would definitely land him with her 'distraught mother' act. She knew how his mind worked better than anyone – certainly better than that little tramp lawyer he was supposed to be screwing. If she thought she was going to get her claws into Jessica's gold mine, well, she could think again.

Jessica got up and walked over to the full-length mirror, dropping her dress to the floor. Pretty damn hot for a cripple, she smiled to herself, walking into the closet and choosing a figure-hugging jersey dress in a vivid forest green. She hesitated for a moment, then took off her underwear before she slipped the dress on. Oh yes, she thought, smoothing the material down over her skin, I think that will do it.

She blew a kiss towards the mirror and headed for the door.

64

With Helen out of the office, taking a short break to recuperate from the Balon trial at her house in Devon, Matt had had to step up to the plate as commander in chief. For the past forty-eight hours he'd been harangued on an hourly basis to sign expenses slips, payment authorisations, letters of engagement; he wondered how Helen ever got any proper work done at all.

Diane, his PA, popped her head around the door.

'Get your wallet out, Matt,' she said cheerfully.

'Who do I owe money to this time?' he smiled, draining his mug of coffee.

'It's for Sid Travers's present. It's her last day today. You're the only one who hasn't coughed up yet.'

He pushed his hand into his pocket and pulled out two twenty-pound notes, which he put into the metal cash box that Diane was waving in front of him.

'Have we sorted out a leaving do?' he asked.

Diane frowned.

'I don't think so. I think the trainees were going to go out for a drink after work.'

'Why don't you book the back room at Chablis?' he said. Lunch at the local wine bar was the least they could do for Sid, he thought, and he didn't doubt that the rest of the team would welcome the break too.

By the time he walked over to Chablis an hour later, the place was packed. The Donovan Pierce crowd were in the small back room, which had a back door flung open to let in some fresh air. Matt had never seen so many of them in one place outside the office, and he'd certainly never seen them enjoying themselves so much, enthusiastically emptying bottles of Rioja and Perrier Jouet and wolfing the finger food.

'Speech! Speech!' cried David Morrow, waving a glass of red wine in the air. 'We can't let Sid drink us under the table without making her sing for her supper.'

'Okay, okay,' said Sid, wobbling slightly as she stood on a chair. 'I wasn't going to do this, but seeing as you've all been so kind . . .'

There was some whooping and whistling.

'Well, when I say kind,' she added with a sly smile, 'I mean bastards for firing me.'

There was a roar of laughter and cries of 'Shame!' and 'Recount!'

Matt watched a fifty-something woman come into the room pushing a buggy. She was obviously in the wrong place, but he had no problem with her having a free glass of wine if she wanted to.

'I just want to say thanks to Matt Donovan for organising this do.'

'You wait till Helen hears,' shouted someone to nervous laughter.

'And to Anna Kennedy for being a brilliant mentor. It's been fantastic working with you and hopefully we'll stay in touch. I might not be working full-time, though, because I'll have my work cut out with this little one.'

She gestured to the woman with the buggy, who picked up the little boy and passed him to her.

'Everyone, meet my son Charlie,' she said. 'Some of you may have wondered why I was sneaking off at six o'clock; well, here's why.'

Matt was flummoxed. He looked over at Anna, who was sharing a knowing smile with Sid.

'Three cheers for Sid!' shouted David.

'And three cheers for Charlie!' added Diane. 'Hip, hip . . .'

As the cheers and toasts went on, Edward French took Matt's arm.

'Did you know about this?' asked the partner angrily.

'News to me,' said Matt.

481

'Duplicitous bloody cow,' hissed Edward. 'Hoodwinks us all and then expects us to pay for her leaving drinks? A total cheek, if you ask me.'

'Good for her, I say,' said Matt. 'Keeping all those balls in the air and not spilling the beans about a toddler. She's got the makings of an excellent lawyer, if you ask me.'

Edward looked at him with ill-disguised disdain.

'Well at least this ridiculous charade is over,' he said, before walking off.

Anna came across holding two glasses of fizz.

'I thought you might like to wet the baby's head,' she said.

'I take it you knew about this, then?'

'I only found out a week ago. I didn't think it was my place to say anything, not when she was leaving anyway. Besides, I was pretty sure Helen would go up the wall.'

At the mention of Helen, they exchanged a look. Matt had barely spoken to Anna since the night he had found her snooping around Helen's office and heard the strange tale of her investigation into Amy Hart's murder. He could tell she was embarrassed about the intimacy of that evening, and of course the accusations she had made about Helen. Matt had thought long and hard about what she had told him, but the truth was that without more evidence, there was little anyone could do.

'About the other night . . .' began Anna, but immediately clammed up as Sid came over to join them.

'Here she is.' Matt smiled. 'The international woman of mystery. Maybe you could consider a career at MI6 with your talent for deception.'

Sid flashed a grin. 'No need. Anna has already arranged an interview for me to work for Ilina Miranova.'

Matt looked impressed.

'So it *is* going to be all private jets and beach club business meetings from now on, is it? Very James Bond – very you, actually.'

'Thanks, Matt, you're one of the good guys. And you're good for the firm. Don't let Helen persuade you otherwise.'

'What do you mean?'

Sid looked at Anna nervously.

'Sid? What is it?' asked Anna, glancing at Matt.

Sid looked as if she was regretting her words.

'The other day I had to deliver an urgent by-hand to Helen. She was having dinner with the partners at Nobu – well, all the partners but you, Matt. I overheard some things . . .'

Matt could tell from the look on Sid's face that he wasn't going to like this one bit.

'She wants you out,' said Sid apologetically. 'I heard her say she wanted to amend the partnership agreement to allow them to oust underperforming partners.'

'And by that she means me?'

Sid nodded. 'That was the gist, yes. I'm sorry . . .'

Charlie began crying, and Sid went to see to him.

Matt looked at Anna, who squeezed his arm.

'You can handle her,' she said reassuringly.

Matt was about to reply when Diane tapped him on the shoulder and waggled a mobile phone in his face.

'I've got Jeremy Benson from Blandings and Co. on the line.'

'Who?' mouthed Matt as she handed him the phone. Diane's expression told him that it was serious.

'Is that Donovan?' barked an upper-class voice.

'Yes,' he replied.

'Jeremy Benson,' said the man, as if Matt would know exactly who he was talking to. 'It's been six months since the case concluded, and Mr Taht would like the laptop returned. As I am assuming that no appeals are to be made on either side, we would appreciate getting it back immediately.'

'I don't believe we've spoken before, Mr Benson.'

'Don't be an idiot, Donovan,' the other man snapped. 'I've not got time.'

The penny dropped.

'Sorry, Mr Benson. This isn't Larry, I'm Matthew Donovan, his son.'

There was a disapproving tsk.

'Well where the hell is he?'

'He's on sick leave, I'm afraid.'

Benson didn't waste any time enquiring about Larry's health.

'So who's dealing with his caseload?'

'Helen Pierce is your first port of call, but she's on holiday.'

'Doesn't anyone work at your firm? Listen, Donovan, or whoever you are, we have made numerous requests about retrieving Mr Taht's laptop, yet we are still waiting. This is a very poor show and I want to know what you're going to do about it.'

Matt tried to keep his cool.

'Leave it with me, Mr Benson. I will track down Mr Taht's property personally.'

'See that you do,' said Benson. 'We don't want any unpleasantness.'

The line went dead, and Matt was left standing there wondering what had just happened.

Sighing, he walked away from the crowd to the bar's entrance, where it was quieter, dialling up Larry's number.

'Matty! Wonderful to hear from you,' came the cheerful reply. 'Is that a party I can hear in the background?'

'Listen, Dad. Does a Mr Taht's laptop mean anything to you?'

There was an ominous pause.

'Arse,' grumbled Larry. 'Jerry Benson been on, has he? I did mean to return that before I left.'

'What was it?'

'Evidence in one of the trials last year; or rather, it was deemed inadmissible due to the coppers involved being on the take. Sorry about this, Matty, but I'd recommend you get that sorted PDQ. Taht's a big-shot Chinese businessman – not the sort of man you want to get on the wrong side of.'

'So where is it?'

'The vault,' said Larry.

The vault was the Donovan Pierce safe, which was in Helen's office. Something of a mythical location in the media business, it was supposedly filled with incriminating documents, files and photographs of the great and the good – things that could destroy reputations and ruin careers if they fell into the wrong hands.

'And it's fine to return it to Jeremy Benson?'

'Yes, yes. Make sure you get all the paperwork in order.'

Matt paused.

'And what's the combination for the vault?'

'Helen not given it to you?'

'No.'

Larry sighed, and then told him the confidential location in the office where he could find it written down.

'Dad, Helen is trying to push me out of the firm.'

'*What?*'

'One of the trainees heard her conspiring with the other partners. Something about an amendment to the partnership agreement.'

Larry snorted. 'I'm not bloody having that.'

There was a long pause; Matt could almost hear the devious thoughts going around his father's head.

'Bloody bitch,' muttered Larry. 'Come round tonight and we'll get it sorted.'

Matt left Diane with the company credit card and went to sort out Mr Taht's laptop. The office was empty and strangely forlorn without the usual buzz of conversation and ringing phones. He found the pass code where his father had told him it would be and went straight into Helen's office. It was a beautiful sunny room with windows overlooking the square, but Matt's mood was dark, fuming about what Sid had told him. How dare Helen and the others push him out? It wasn't so much that he felt he had a right to the firm that bore his name; it was the way they were all so nice to his face, then stabbed him in the back at the first opportunity. Then again, what could he expect? Helen and Larry had chosen their workforce for their ambition and ruthlessness. Why should the internal politics be any different?

The vault wasn't a safe behind an oil painting, but a five-by-eight-foot strongroom opened from an illuminated keypad on the wall. Matt punched in the code, smiling grimly. He was intrigued about what he would find inside. *Private Eye* had once run a satirical piece on the vault entitled 'Raiders of the Lost Smut', speculating on what incendiary stuff it contained.

At first all he could see were rows of steel shelves on both sides of the room, all loaded with brown case boxes, each one marked with a white sticker and a case reference.

Matt felt a tingle of excitement as he walked inside. These

innocuous cartons contained the most sensitive material possible: videotapes, boxes of letters, documents and photographs, each file pertaining to a story that had never seen the light of day because of deals brokered or court orders granted to protect them. What dark secrets lay within them? What scandals might he find if only he had time to rummage about?

'Concentrate, Matt,' he said, running his finger across each row, looking for the word 'Taht'. He couldn't see anything under that heading, but then he didn't know anything about the case; it could well be under another name. Sighing, he pulled his phone out of his pocket and called Larry back.

'Dad? I can't see Taht's computer anywhere. Would it be filed under his name?'

'Possibly,' mused Larry. 'Truth is, I wasn't that hot about labelling things. Usually things went into the vault with the explicit intention of staying there for ever, so it didn't seem that important, given that no one except Helen and I had access. Maybe Helen arranged for it to be sent back. Have you spoken to Diane?'

'She's in the pub and Helen's still away,' said Matt, losing patience. 'What colour is it?'

'Silver, black? I don't know. Laptop colour.'

The phone cut out and Matt looked at the screen: no signal.

Great. The room was probably lead-lined or something. He was just turning to leave when he spotted a bulky black laptop bag on the top shelf. He stretched up and grabbed it, carrying it out to Helen's desk. There was no label on the bag, so he unzipped it and fired up the computer inside, hoping there might be a clue as to its ownership on the home screen.

If it was all in Mandarin, that might be a hint, he thought.

Finally the bright blue screen lit up and the white software registration box popped up in the centre of the screen: 'This software is registered to Amy Hart.'

Matt took a sharp breath, recognising the name immediately.

'Surely not,' he whispered to himself. He quickly pulled out his phone and scrolled to Anna's number. 'Pick up, pick up,' he willed her, but it went straight to voicemail. 'Dammit,' he said, turning back to the computer.

Looking up, he noticed people beginning to file back into the office from Chablis. He picked up the laptop and took it to his own room, closing the door behind him. Opening the computer again, he hit the 'Mail' icon on the desktop. He didn't know what he was looking for, but if Amy had been trying to blackmail Peter Rees, that was the most likely place to find something that might confirm it. Immediately he saw that there were dozens of emails to and from Rees. Some were simple discussions relating to a meeting place in a restaurant or bar. Others were love letters, some of a sexual nature. Amy had even sent Peter photographs of herself. Glamour shots, some more candid: naked, laughing, in bed, with white sheets barely covering her body. There were a couple of shots with an older, grey-haired man in them – Peter himself, he assumed. The images were happy and carefree. It was difficult to reconcile this lively, vibrant girl with the Amy Hart who was now dead. Fascinated, Matt began looking at the emails dated within a week of her death. She and Peter had clearly had a falling-out.

I wish you hadn't said so many hurtful things, darling. I'm not twisting your arm, I just love you and I want us to be together – I thought that was what you wanted too?

Peter had responded:

Haven't I always given you everything you ever wanted? Clothes, jewellery, the flat? But I can't do what you ask, you always knew that. I don't respond well to threats, Amy. I've given you things, but I can take them away too.

Then Matt clicked on another email, a message from Amy to Peter, and his heart began beating harder.

Don't play games, Peter. I can do that too. You shouldn't have left your office unlocked on Wednesday. I've read the report. I know about the Atlanticana rig and I know why you felt guilty about Doug's death. I'll tell everyone about it unless you do the right thing. It's not a threat, don't ever call it that. I'm just doing what needs to be done. We belong together, you know that.

'Oh Amy, you silly, silly girl,' he murmured, feeling as if it was all happening in real time.

He clicked on Peter's reply. It was short and pithy.

Call me. Need to discuss.

Matt stared at the computer screen. Two days after that email was sent, Amy was dead. He jumped as the door opened and Anna walked in.

'Did you call me? I was on my way back to the office.'

Matt gestured to the computer in front of him.

'I've found Amy Hart's laptop,' he said quietly.

She gasped, moving around to his side of the desk.

'Where was it?'

'In the vault.'

They glanced at each other, both knowing they did not need to confirm that Helen was definitely involved.

Matt quickly showed her the emails he had just read.

'Poor Amy,' whispered Anna. She looked thoughtful for a moment. 'I wonder . . .' she said, leaning over the keyboard. She closed the Mail application and began opening other files on the desktop.

'What are you looking for?' said Matt.

'Patience,' she muttered, clicking on a PDF file. Matt could immediately see the fancy logo of some company called Cassandra Risk, followed by the heading: 'Report on Atlanticana Platform for Dallincourt Engineering, May 15th. Assessment of structural integrity'.

'This is it,' she said quickly. 'The report on the rig that exploded. Amy copied it. She knew she needed leverage to get Peter to leave his wife – no wonder the laptop disappeared from the flat.'

'But does this prove that Peter knew about the rig being faulty?'

'Look at the date,' said Anna, pointing to the screen. 'That's months before the oil disaster. He *must* have known.'

Matt nodded.

'Doesn't prove that he killed Amy, though, does it?'

'No, but it does tell us one thing,' said Anna. 'It tells us that Helen Pierce is up to her ears in this. Why else was the laptop in the vault?'

She snapped the computer closed.

Matt looked at her uneasily.

'I think it's time to call your friends at *The Chronicle*.'

Anna's expression was defiant.

'Not before I call Helen.'

65

Helen put down the phone and moved towards the big picture window overlooking the Devon coastline. The view had always soothed her: the jigsaw of interlocking green hills that stopped so suddenly, dropping away in sheer grey cliffs; the curve of shingle sand; the blue-green water that stretched away until it was swallowed by clouds. She didn't come down to Seaways, the big seaside house she had bought when she started making serious money, as often as she'd like. It was the perfect place to be alone with her thoughts and yet now, not daring to leave it, it felt like a prison.

She stepped on to the wide veranda that circled the house, feeling the cool breeze coming in off the sea, and listened to the cries of the gulls and the cormorants. She wrapped her arms around her body, for once feeling vulnerable and insignificant. Straining her ears, she could hear the crunch of footsteps at the side of the house; sports shoes against the gravel path that snaked down to the beach. Anxiety dried her mouth as she watched him approach the house.

Simon Cooper was dripping with perspiration. For a fifty-year-old man he was in fantastic shape; long runs around the headland kept him fit and sharp. He came over, snaking his arm around her waist, making her shirt damp with his sweat. Helen stiffened as he kissed her neck, and he caught the gesture.

'I thought we came here to relax,' he murmured into her ear, his breath warm.

'I've had a call,' she said.

Simon gave no reaction; instead he slid his hand under her shirt, circling the bare skin.

490

'Don't,' she said, pulling away from him.

'What's wrong?' He frowned.

'The call. It was from Anna Kennedy, my associate at work.'

'Sod work,' he muttered. 'Even I've had my phone switched off this afternoon.'

Helen closed her eyes, remembering the glorious hours they'd spent in bed together, undisturbed by anything or anyone. She could still almost feel him moving inside her, making her feel like no man had ever made her feel. For a long time, work had been her passion, but the desire she felt for this man was like an addiction. And what if that stopped? What if he was taken away from her? The thought of it was almost a physical pain.

There had always been a connection between Helen and Simon, even when they had first met five years ago, but nothing had happened until his divorce. They had never discussed whether she should do the same and end her sham marriage to Graham. In the early days of her affair with Simon, they had both seemed content with their snatched hours of sex, meeting in hotels near the places they both worked, but soon it just wasn't enough. And soon their relationship was not simply about sex. Helen was too cynical, too world-weary to believe in the concept of soulmates, but even she could see that she and Simon were a perfect match. He was the one person who had ever made her see that there was more to life than work or money. And to her shock, he had given her so much more: desire, understanding, togetherness, love. Helen had never had to – or wanted to – think of anybody but herself; that was why her marriage to Graham was able to limp on, because he asked for little and let her get on with her own independent life. But her feelings for Simon had compromised her natural default setting of self-interest. And that had got her into trouble.

'She knows,' said Helen simply.

Simon wiped his damp forehead with the back of his hand.

'Knows about what?'

'Amy Hart and Peter Rees.'

Simon looked up at her sharply, and time seemed to stand still.

'Can she prove anything?' he asked, a low, considered malevolence about his question that made her feel chill.

'She found Amy's laptop in the vault.'

'What?' he spat. 'You stupid woman! You were supposed to keep it safe.'

'It was safe,' protested Helen. 'There are only two people who have access to that room: myself and Larry Donovan. And even if Larry found it, he was hardly going to know who Amy Hart was.'

'You were careless,' he roared.

How dare he suggest that? Helen felt her hands shaking and tucked them under her arms. She hated the way Simon was looking at her. No one ever made her feel stupid, no one. And yet the thin, disdainful line of her boyfriend's mouth cut her to the core.

'What does she know exactly?'

Everything, she thought. She knows everything.

'She knows about Amy's affair with Peter,' she said. 'She knows she was blackmailing him. She knows that the Dallincourt senior executives, including Peter Rees, were aware that they had botched a repair job at the rig and that it was highly dangerous for it to keep operating.'

'And the rest?' said Simon. 'Does she know about Peter's involvement with Doug Faulks?'

Helen nodded.

'Shit.'

Helen turned away and took a deep breath, fighting to control her emotions, wondering where it had all gone wrong. She knew, of course. When Simon had asked her to bury the story of Amy Hart's inquest, Helen had hesitated. The quickest way of doing it was to use a big, big story to push everything else out of the headlines. And as the final day of the inquest coincided with the Sam Charles injunction return date, she knew she had the perfect opportunity to help Simon. It would mean sacrificing the best interests of a wealthy and high-profile client and breaking every code of professional conduct. But Simon had been persuasive, in the bedroom and out of it – reassuring Helen that he would make it worth her while, that he would send millions of pounds of legal work her way from his roster of powerful international companies. And it was hard to say no to someone you were in love with.

'I can't believe it,' said Simon, pacing up and down the terrace. 'Why didn't you just destroy the bloody computer?'

'You know why,' she said, watching his face. She didn't need to spell it out. She had kept it as insurance. When you were dealing with men who thought nothing of sacrificing lives like pawns in a chess game, sometimes you needed your own leverage.

'Did they kill her, Simon?' she asked suddenly. It was a question she had not dared ask when Simon had pleaded with her to help him.

'I don't know,' he replied, not looking at her. 'It's not my problem.'

She stepped forward and grabbed on to his arm.

'But it *is* our problem, Simon,' she said. 'I need to know everything if I'm going to work out what we can do next.'

He shrugged her off.

'Nothing is ever a problem,' he said, his eyes cold. 'Not if you are prepared to do what it takes to fix it.'

He stomped back into the house and slammed the door. When he was gone, Helen sank to her knees, covering her mouth with her hand. It's all over, everything is gone, she thought desperately. My life is at an end. For a moment she gave into it, letting the fear and the despair wash over her, consume her.

But she was Helen Pierce. Helen Pierce did not give in to anything for long. And so, slowly, she pulled herself to her feet. Simon was right. You had to be prepared to do what was needed to fix things. She walked back into the house and picked up her phone.

'Peter,' she said, trying to keep her voice even. 'It's Helen Pierce.'

A warm breeze fluttered through the trees as Helen descended the stone steps into the sunken garden in Bloomsbury. She had been surprised when Peter Rees had suggested meeting here, because she had thought she was one of the few people in

London who knew about it. Years earlier, when she had lived in a large apartment behind UCL, she had come to this hidden oasis often. It had been her private sanctuary, a place to clear her head. I could do with a little of that today, she thought, walking along the gravel path.

It was not yet 10 a.m. and, as she had expected, the green space was almost deserted. Just a man walking his dog and two young lovers entwined on a bench who looked as if they had been up all night partying and were loath to leave each other even now. She wondered if they felt as tired as she did. She'd left Seaways immediately after her argument with Simon, arriving home at 2 a.m., and had lain awake, turning things over in her mind, until the sunlight cut across the ceiling.

Across the garden, Helen could see a slim, silver-haired man sitting on a bench, one long leg crossed over the other. She had only met Peter Rees once before, introduced by Simon, of course, but even at this distance she could tell it was him.

'So, the cat's out of the bag?' he said with a small smile as she sat down next to him. 'I don't suppose it's in my interests to sue you for professional negligence.' His expression lacked the anger that Simon had displayed the night before. Instead he seemed sad, worn down. He looked up and tapped Helen's knee; almost a paternal, reassuring gesture.

'In a way, I think I'm glad that this has got out.'

'Glad?' said Helen.

'You can keep the headlines out of the newspapers, but you can't hide the truth from yourself,' he said quietly. 'It's not been easy living with what has happened. I loved Amy, you know, in my way. She made me feel young, clever, handsome, and that doesn't happen much these days, let me tell you.'

'But you couldn't commit to her?'

Peter held his hands open.

'I couldn't give her what she wanted from me. My children would never have forgiven me.'

Helen swallowed, then looked at Peter.

'Amy didn't just fall down the stairs, did she?'

He didn't speak for several seconds.

'A few weeks before it happened, we'd gone out dancing.

494

Ridiculous for an old fart like me, but like I say, she made me feel young. I'd had too much brandy and got sentimental. I told her about Doug Faulks's suicide – well, not everything, but I was drunk, unhappy. I told her I blamed myself.' He snorted. '*In vino veritas*, eh? I blamed myself because it *was* my fault.'

'But how did that lead to her death?'

Peter shook his head, remembering.

'I was stupid. Amy used to stay in the Bloomsbury flat I use during the week and I left my computer on. She'd been putting pressure on me to leave my wife and she obviously thought she might find something about Doug on the laptop, something she could use to force my hand. She did. She found the Atlanticana report and copied it.'

Peter looked at Helen, his eyes red.

'She was a clever girl, Amy. People thought she was an airhead, but she had enough intelligence to connect the engineering faults in the rig with Doug's death. So she threatened me, told me she'd blow the whistle on us; she had that do-or-die mentality.'

'What did you do?' asked Helen, already knowing the answer, but needing to hear it.

'What could I do? I told James Swann about her. Everyone goes to James with their problems. I thought he was just going to pay her off, maybe threaten her. But two days later she was dead.'

'You think James had her killed?'

Peter rubbed at his eye with the heel of his hand.

'He said he'd dealt with her. I guess he did.'

Helen looked away from him, watching the man with the dog, wishing she was back at Seaways the afternoon before Anna Kennedy had called. In Simon's arms, their bodies entwined, no worries or fears.

'So are you glad you know now, Miss Pierce?' asked Peter. 'I'm assuming that's why you never asked before. Because your conscience couldn't deal with it.'

Helen didn't answer. She didn't need to.

The first time she had met Peter, he was a steely and vital

man, but now he looked pale, weak, as if the life force had been drained out of him.

'I should confess,' he said quietly. 'Give the newspapers a little bite to their story, eh?'

'Don't be ridiculous,' said Helen, a little too loud.

Peter's expression was one of pure resignation.

'It's what I want,' he said wearily. 'I don't want to live like this.'

'But why?' said Helen passionately. 'Amy's dead – and yes, I know you loved her, but throwing yourself to the wolves won't bring her back.'

'I killed Amy and I killed Doug. Not with my own bare hands, but I might as well have.'

'Doug committed suicide,' said Helen plainly.

Peter sat back on the bench, his head tilted towards the milky sky. 'We knew the rig was unsafe,' he said softly. 'Half the board of Dallincourt knew. We'd completed a repair job but the materials used were compromised.'

'Cost-cutting?'

He nodded.

'We didn't know at the time that they wouldn't be up to the job, but when the senior engineer gave us some projections and said we'd need to go back down and strengthen the work we'd done, well, we took a chance to leave it. It was all about profit, Helen. We wanted to spin off the engineering arm of the company, and a multi-million-pound repair job would have affected the bottom line and our projected sale price.'

A tear ran down his cheek.

'Doug was CEO of Pogex Oil. They owned the Atlanticana rig. He was my friend.' Peter sighed. 'When Atlanticana exploded, we panicked.'

'Who's we?'

'Myself. Malcolm Wainwright, the Dallincourt CEO. James Swann, a major shareholder in both Dallincourt and Pogex. We went to see Simon Cooper at Auckland Communications, who handled corporate publicity for Dallincourt and Pogex. He said the best way to hide Dallincourt's culpability was to blame Pogex Oil. As Pogex was another client of his, he wanted to miminise corporate reputation damage, but he was prepared to sacrifice a senior-level executive. He said we should create a fall guy, and the obvious person was Doug, Pogex's CEO. A brilliant man, but highly strung, maybe even a little bipolar. I knew he would crumble under questioning, especially if Auckland fed him a few soundbites that made it sound like he was trying to wriggle out of it. And it worked. The press crucified him. And Doug . . . We both know what happened next, don't we?'

Peter stood up and brushed down his trousers.

'Now I think I need to be alone,' he said, nodding a goodbye.

Helen jumped up and grabbed his arm.

'Please, Peter, don't do anything rash,' she said, her heart pounding. 'Remember we're all in this together, and if we work together, we can get out of it.'

Peter looked down at her hand and gently lifted it from his arm.

'We all have a way of dealing with our problems,' he said, walking away. 'You go and figure out yours.'

66

The atmosphere in Media Incorporated's boardroom was electric. Amir and Andy stood by a big whiteboard full of red, black and blue scribbles, arrows pointing to circled names and facts boxed off and starred according to their importance.

'Gentlemen, please,' said Andy, addressing the room. 'We all know this is going to be a big story, but we need to be absolutely sure of our facts – particularly what we can and can't say legally. We've got to be tight as a nut on this, especially as we have the enemy in the room.'

There was a ripple of laughter as the journalists all looked over at Anna, Matt and Larry standing to the side. Anna smiled too. She had been watching Andy at work, seeing him running his team, his eyes blazing with passion for the story, yet completely in control, never letting his excitement run away with him.

I'm over him, she smiled to herself. I finally really am.

She respected him, enjoyed his company, but that little spark of whatever it was that drew people together had gone. And she felt glad. It was a weight that had been pulling her down, an unhealed wound that had kept her from moving on and finding someone else. For a moment, she thought of Sam. They hadn't spoken all week; just a few half-apologetic text messages that had left her with very mixed emotions. Their time together in India had been sensational, of course, and he was so good-looking she could feel a little part of her sigh whenever she thought about him. But another part of her wondered if they were really suited. She looked at Andy, realising that they had been a perfect match on paper, everyone had said so; and yet sometimes things just didn't pan out. One thing she had come to understand was that you couldn't deconstruct love and figure out what made two people connect. It just happened. Or didn't. That was the nature of love; its randomness, its unpredictability, and she supposed it was what made it so intoxicating.

Charles Porter, the newspaper's editor, looked over at Anna.

'Andy's right,' he said. 'We need to know what we can print. Are you sure the contents of Amy's laptop would be admissible in court?'

Anna felt flattered that Charles had addressed the question to her, with her boss and the legendary Larry Donovan standing next to her. She had been getting a lot of respect from the journalists since Andy and Amir had brought the story in. She nodded to Charles.

'Yes, Matt found the laptop, which had clearly been taken, stolen from Amy's apartment. But we should be able to argue that ownership still belongs to Amy Hart, and as she is now deceased, it's passed on to her estate. Of course we've got the full cooperation of her family.'

Charles nodded and looked up at Amir.

'What about this Peter Rees character? Can we name him?'

'Absolutely,' said Amir. 'The emails show he was Amy's lover. I've also been able to nail him through the offshore account he set up to pay the rent on Amy's apartment.'

'Okay, so that links Dallincourt to the dead girl,' said Charles. 'But what about linking the girl to the oil spill?'

Matt shook his head.

'Unfortunately the Atlanticana report was essentially stolen by Amy, which compromises its admissibility. And there's still no way of proving Amy's death was foul play. Not without a confession, anyway.'

Anna loved the energy in the room as they put the story together. Media law tended to move much faster than the rest of the legal system – no one else but a media lawyer would be knocking on a judge's door at nine at night – but the speed with which the news was crafted was edge-of-the-seat stuff. The only person who did not look alive with adrenalin was Larry Donovan. At last he stepped forward.

'Charles. Can I have a word?' he said, touching the editor on the shoulder. He motioned to Anna to follow them into an adjoining office. The two lawyers and the newspaper editor stood huddled in the small room. Larry spoke first.

'Listen, I'll be straight with you, Charles, I'm not happy about Helen Pierce's name being on that whiteboard.'

Charles Porter gave a thin smile.

'But it does look like Helen leaked Sam Charles's private life to overturn his injunction, which is nothing short of a cover-up.'

'I know you ink boys love conspiracy,' said Larry tartly. 'But do you need to trouble the reading public with every last detail?' He inclined his head towards Anna. 'And seeing as it was Donovan Pierce who brought you the story . . .'

Charles raised his eyebrows.

'So we should cut Donovan Pierce some slack?'

'Something like that,' said Larry.

Anna couldn't believe her ears. After all her hard work, after all the risks she had taken, Larry was suggesting they let Helen off?

'But Helen is complicit in all this,' said Anna angrily. 'She's broken the law and she deserves to suffer the consequences.'

Larry turned on her.

'Which means the whole of Donovan Pierce suffers, Anna. Good, decent lawyers such as yourself and my son. The firm will be hung out to dry and you'll all be tarred with the same brush. Is that what you want?'

'It's not what I want, Larry,' she protested. 'It's what's right . . .'

They were interrupted by a knock on the door, and Amir Khan popped his head into the room.

'Guys, you'd better come back in,' he said, his eyes shining. 'We've just had a phone call from Peter Rees. He says he's prepared to tell us everything he knows.'

67

The house was dark when Helen pulled up outside. She pushed her key into the lock, expecting to hear the sound of Graham's opera records, but there was silence as she walked into the hallway and threw her keys on to the table. She was glad: the grey stillness of the house suited her mood. She wanted to hide, to stay safe in a cloak of darkness where no one could see her or touch her. The bullish 'let's conquer this thing together' resolve she had tried to show Peter earlier in the day had crumbled the moment she had left the Bloomsbury gardens, and she had driven up to Hampstead, walking across the heath, lost in her turbulent thoughts, trying to see a way out of the fog.

She cursed herself for leaving the laptop in the office. It was true that no one other than herself and Larry had access to the vault. But with the pressure of the Balon trial, she had been uncharacteristically careless. She should have known, of course, that Anna Kennedy would not have taken Sam's overturned injunction lying down. That was why she had hired the girl in the first place: drive, ambition, a nimble mind. But who would have thought she'd have got wind of Amy Hart? Expect the unexpected was the maxim Helen had always drilled into her lawyers, but this time she was the one who had failed to see all the angles.

Walking into the living room, she went straight to the drinks cabinet and poured herself a large brandy, closing her eyes as the liquid slipped down her throat. She almost dropped the glass in fright as a desk lamp flicked on, and she whirled around to see Larry Donovan sitting in her favourite armchair.

'Jesus, Larry,' she gasped. 'You scared me.'

Larry's face remained impassive, increasing Helen's unease. She glanced towards the door.

'Who let you in?'

'Graham,' said Larry. 'He's gone out. I asked him for a few minutes alone with you.'

'Oh really? Why?' she asked, turning back to pour herself another brandy, the decanter rattling against the glass.

She was playing for time, desperately looking for some hole in the net she felt closing in on her, but she knew that Larry knew. Larry always knew. For years he had been her mentor and protector. They had first met when she was a law student scouting around for a job and he was a young, dynamic solicitor about to set up his own practice. In Helen Pierce he had seen something, a kindred spirit. He had recognised her steeliness and taken time to nurture it, encouraging and advising her, favouring her with the best cases, making introductions to all the right people. Unusually for Larry, there had never been any sexual motivation for his help. Not once in their twenty-five-year acquaintance had he tried it on. Instead their relationship was one of mutual respect, and whilst Larry's profligacy and unreliability had annoyed her in recent years, deep down she had nothing but admiration for him. Fitting, then, that it should be Larry who had come to her at the end.

'You know why I'm here, Helen,' he said now. 'Amy Hart. Anna told me everything.'

Helen snorted.

'Anna Kennedy has lost the plot,' she said tartly, throwing the brandy back. 'She's been looking for some excuse to shift the blame for her failure in the Sam Charles case. She should not be taken seriously, Larry. In fact, I was going to suggest she take a holiday to sort herself out.'

Larry's face remained hard.

'It's too late for bullshit, Helen. *The Chronicle* have got hold of the story, and everything Anna has said has checked out.'

'What has checked out? A load of circumstantial evidence and—'

'Peter Rees is talking,' said Larry, stopping her in her tracks. 'Apparently he's happy to swear an affidavit about the faulty rig, Amy's blackmail, his conversation with James Swann to cover it up . . . everything.'

Helen pressed a hand to her chest. Suddenly she couldn't seem to draw breath.

'Why, Helen?' said Larry softly. 'Why did you get involved? You're too smart for all this. I taught you better.'

He taught her? she thought, suddenly furious. How dare he? She had held Donovan Pierce together when he was too hung-over to get off his office couch; she had built up its reputation and brought in the biggest accounts while he was off playing golf and chasing secretaries – and now he had the nerve to suggest it was all him?

'It was just business, Larry,' she said defiantly. 'Isn't that what you taught me? "Business comes first"? Simon Cooper promised us millions of pounds' worth of work if we'd bury the Amy Hart story. It was a simple transaction.'

She couldn't tell him the truth. She couldn't admit to the weakness that had made her say yes to Simon's proposal. She couldn't admit she'd done it for love. As if Larry Donovan would understand that.

'A simple transaction?' said Larry. 'A girl was killed, Helen. Is that the kind of bargain you're prepared to make?'

'I didn't know about that,' she snapped.

'Of course not,' he replied.

She looked at him fiercely.

'Don't get all pious on me, Larry, for turning a blind eye. Don't say that you've never done it. I know you have. You don't get to the top without sometimes dealing with the devil.'

'Maybe, but I never covered for a murderer,' he growled.

Helen thought about pouring herself another drink, but instead banged the glass down on the cabinet. She needed a clear head, needed to think. She could find a way out – why not? She always had before.

'Are *The Chronicle* running the story tomorrow?' she asked.

Larry shook his head.

'I don't know. But now they have Peter's testimony, I can't see why they'd hold back.'

Helen looked at her wristwatch. It was almost eight o'clock.

If the paper was going with the story for its first edition, she was sunk. But if they were holding off until their second edition, she could still find a judge to grant a temporary injunction. That would give her breathing space at least.

Larry was reading her mind.

'You're not named in this, Helen. I've spoken to the editor, asked him to keep you out of it. For now.'

'I'd say thank you, except I'm not convinced you're doing this for my benefit.'

'You're right. This isn't about you, Helen. It's about the firm. I'm not going to let Donovan Pierce suffer because of your idiotic behaviour. Fortunately Media Incorporated want to keep us on side, so far as that's possible. I've also offered them certain other incentives.'

He was a canny bastard, she thought, looking at him with a mixture of loathing and admiration. What had he done to keep the dogs off? It went without saying that he'd have done a deal with Charles Porter. Keep Helen Pierce's name out of the story and he'd feed them a story about one of his other clients. Just the same as she had done with Sam Charles, but somehow this was worse, more grubby. At least with the Sam Charles case, the media had been an unwitting accomplice. This time Charles Porter was entirely complicit – a deal with the devil indeed.

But Helen wasn't naive; she knew the bargaining didn't end there. Larry would want his pound of flesh from her.

'So what's the deal, Larry? What do I have to do for this?'

'I want you to resign from Donovan Pierce,' said Larry.

'Resign?' cried Helen, aghast. 'I *am* Donovan Pierce!'

Larry just looked at her.

'And I want you to sell your equity to me. We may have to do a bit of jiggery-pokery with the partnership agreement to make that happen, but then you're not against that sort of thing, are you, Helen?' he added with a knowing smile.

Helen felt faint, but she was still prepared to fight.

'I know where the bodies are buried too, Larry,' she said in a more threatening tone. 'I could ruin your reputation in the blink of an eye, just as you're trying to destroy me now. Remember that.'

Larry looked unmoved.

'This offer is more than generous.' He shrugged. 'Considering you have broken the law and considering you're trying to screw my son out of his partnership.' He narrowed his eyes. 'This is your Get Out of Jail Free card, Helen – literally. You leaked the details of Sam's case to the media. You did it acting for individuals implicated in the death of a twenty-one-year-old girl. The best-case scenario is that you should be struck off the roll of solicitors permanently. I don't need to tell you the worst-case scenario, do I? A multi-million-dollar damages claim waiting for you the moment you get out of jail.'

'You wouldn't dare do this,' she said. 'You wouldn't dare.'

Larry laughed.

'Don't worry, Helen. I already have.'

68

Ruby Hart ran up to the ice-cream van parked outside Richmond's White Cross riverside pub on the edge of the Thames and bought three enormous Mr Whippy cones.

'A thank-you to the world's greatest lawyer.' She grinned, handing one to Anna and another to her mother, Liz Hart. Anna felt so pleased that the two Hart women had come down to London to catch the first editions of *The Chronicle* hitting the street. And when Liz Hart had wept tears of relief as she had read the story about her daughter, Anna had felt a sense of justice more potent than anything she had experienced in all her time in the law.

'World's greatest lawyer? I don't know about that,' she giggled, secretly feeling very proud of the copy of *The Chronicle* that was poking out of her bag. 'Party Girl in Suspicious Death' read the headline on page three. She'd felt a pang of disappointment that Amir's exposé hadn't made the front-page splash, but a big royal story had pushed it off. Anna knew more than anybody that newspapers were in the business of selling copies and the better story wasn't always the biggest story when the editor came to decide what would drive more sales.

But it was enough. Enough to cause a stir. Enough for the other newspapers to pick the story up. It wasn't enough to bring Amy back to life but it was enough to stop her death being invisible, and in time, with a police investigation to back up the work of the *Chronicle* news team, maybe it was enough for someone to be finally held responsible for her killing.

'Is it true that the paper's going to run a bigger piece at the weekend?' asked Liz, looking visibly less tired and grave than the first time they had met.

Anna nodded. '*The Sunday Chronicle* are going to do a more in-depth piece, yes. *The Chronicle* wanted to break the story, but there's so much to follow up about the Atlanticana rig, and Dallincourt's involvement in the explosion, that the bigger weekend editions can really go to town on it. It's going to be a major international story.'

'I hope Amy's not going to be dragged into all that,' said Liz quietly. 'This is enough. We only wanted justice for Amy. Not celebrity.'

The three women walked along the bank of the Thames in a contented silence as they licked their ice creams.

'Do you think it will be possible to say thank you to Sam Charles too?' asked Ruby hopefully. 'I know he paid for your investigator.'

Anna knew that Ruby was right. On their date in Mougins, Sam had made his motives for helping them sound so flippant, but without him there was a good chance the story would never have seen the light of day.

'I'm sure he'd love to meet you,' she said honestly. 'I can arrange a meeting with him if you'd like.'

'Yes, please,' beamed Ruby. 'When are you seeing him next?'

It was a good question. All week she'd been avoiding Sam's calls demanding that she contact him. Of course, with so much else going on, there hadn't really been time to meet, especially as he was in script-writing lockdown at his Wiltshire country manor. But the real reason, she acknowledged to herself, was that she could not work out how she felt about him; his initial interest in her had been thrilling and the sex had been incredible. But she also knew that dating someone of his celebrity would change her life completely, and she wasn't sure if she was prepared for such a precarious, if exhilarating, ride.

She had thought a few days' distance might give her some clarity on the situation. But the longer she left it, the more Sam Charles seemed to fade back into what he always was to her, a magnificent and yet unobtainable face from the movies.

'I need to see him soon,' she said thoughtfully.

'Today. Go today,' pressed Ruby. 'Me and Mum are in

London until Monday. Maybe Sam can come and meet us tomorrow.'

'Don't let us hold you up,' said Liz Hart with a smile. 'We're happy. We've got tickets to go round Buckingham Palace this afternoon.'

'Are you sure?' said Anna.

'Go,' said Liz knowingly.

Anna slowed the car as she wound through the sleepy streets of Haversham. What a beautiful place, she thought to herself, passing bloom-filled gardens and honey-stone cottages covered in ivy and wisteria; it was like a perfect English village, imagined by Hollywood, created by set directors and then deposited in the most stunning countryside possible. No wonder a British movie star had chosen to live here, she thought, feeling a flutter of nerves as she pulled up at the gates of Copley Manor.

She stopped the car, opened her diary and found the entry code Sam had given her in the south of France. 'Just come by whenever,' he had said on his voice message. 'I'll be waiting.'

The gates swung open and Anna drove in, her heart fluttering. Would Sam be glad to see her? Would he even be in? It would be embarrassing trying to explain herself to a housekeeper. Still, her surprise arrival seemed like just the sort of spontaneous gesture that Sam would approve of – he was always telling her she was too controlled. Picking up her handbag, she got out of the car and walked towards the house, beginning to feel like a deranged groupie rather than a respectable lawyer going to see her client to . . . *to what*?

Make up? Break up? She wasn't exactly sure why she was here, but it had been such a good day so far, she knew things might just work out the way they were supposed to.

She pushed a smooth marble bell and a small oriental man answered the door. She announced herself and he disappeared, and when he returned, Sam was right behind him.

She took a deep breath, ready to say her piece.

'So you were right.' She smiled at him, stepping into the cool interior of the house. 'I work too hard, and to show you I've changed, I'm playing truant from work.'

She stopped, realising he did not look happy to see her. His smile was frozen, his face was pale, while his eyes betrayed his alarm.

'But I should have called ahead,' she added quickly.

'Let's not go inside,' he said. 'The weather's lovely and we should talk.'

Frowning, Anna looked past him towards the staircase; she could hear footsteps coming down.

Sam opened his mouth to speak, but he wasn't quick enough. The figure who had come from upstairs to join them was unmistakable. It was Jessica Carr.

Breathe, Anna told herself. It was perfectly natural for a former girlfriend to be at his house, to collect belongings or discuss a split of assets, but when Jessica slipped her hand around Sam's waist, she knew she had made a dreadful mistake in coming.

'Hey,' cooed the Hollywood blonde. She turned immediately to Sam with a coquettish look Anna had seen a dozen times on *All Woman*. 'Are you going to introduce us?'

'Jessica, this is Anna,' said Sam with forced enthusiasm.

'I'm his lawyer,' added Anna a little too quickly.

'Great, she should join us for lunch, shouldn't she, Sam?' said Jessica, her smile as rigid as Sam's.

'I can't stay,' said Anna, stepping backwards. 'Sorry, I've just got a . . .'

Slipping on the gravel, she turned her ankle over, sending pain shooting up her leg. She squeezed her eyes shut and began limping back towards the car.

'Anna, wait,' called Sam, running after her. 'Jess came yesterday. I was going to call you, but I wasn't sure if you were talking to me anyway.'

She fumbled for her car keys in her bag and put her hand on the copy of *The Chronicle*.

'Yes, I'm sorry I didn't get back to you,' she said, thrusting the newspaper into his hands. 'I was busy. The Amy Hart story – pages three and nine if you're interested. It would never have happened without you, so thank you,' she said, mustering all the dignity she could.

'Anna, stop. Let me explain.'

She avoided his gaze.

'No, it's fine,' she said. 'Nothing should ever have happened between us. It was wrong. Although I hope you got back together with Jessica *after* you whisked me off to Provence and told me you wanted to spend every weekend together having an adventure.' She held up her trembling hand. 'No. On second thoughts, I don't want to know.'

He held her shoulders and looked at her with those blue eyes.

'Anna, I loved every moment I spent with you.'

'Stop it, Sam. Don't patronise me.'

'I'm not,' he said passionately. 'It was just . . .' His voice tailed off. 'I guess it was just bad timing.'

Hot humiliation burned her cheeks.

'Fine,' she croaked. She knew she was too weary to battle with him. And besides, what was the point?

'She's pregnant, Anna. Jess is pregnant.' His voice was barely a whisper. 'She came to see me yesterday and told me. That's why I came out here with you; that's what I had to explain.'

'Congratulations,' Anna said softly. His hand reached out to touch her fingers, but she pulled them back.

'You do understand, don't you?' said Sam. 'It's the right thing to do.'

His eyes met hers, and she knew he was asking her to tell him he was right.

'You'll be a great dad, Sam. I mean that.'

She looked at him with a mixture of sadness and, in some strange way, relief. Her decision had been made for her.

'Really, I must go.'

Through the long arched windows of the house she could see Jessica watching them.

'Sam, go back inside. Do what's best for you and for your baby.'

He nodded sadly, then turned and walked back to the house, closing the door behind him, not even a backwards glance.

Anna squeezed the car keys into her hand. Do not cry, she told herself, knowing Jessica would be watching. She turned and hobbled to the car, got inside and closed the door. One single tear escaped down her cheek. The case was over. It was all over. She turned the ignition to start the engine and motored down the drive.

69

He saw her through the crowd, at a quiet table by the window of Claridge's restaurant, where Matt had managed to wing a last-minute reservation using Larry's name. Carla had always looked beautiful, but tonight Matt knew she had pulled all the stops out. In a cream fitted dress scooped low at the front and her blonde air piled up on her head, she looked sensational. She was holding on to a glass of champagne, her long fingers playing up and down the stem. Was she as nervous as him? No, Carla was always in control, he thought. She always knew what she wanted. But what was that?

'You look great,' he said honestly, bending to kiss her cheek.

'You're not so bad yourself,' she smiled as he took his seat opposite her.

He played with his napkin absently. This was like being on a blind date, that mild apprehension of not knowing how the evening would pan out, or what he would think of the person he was meeting. It seemed ridiculous to feel that way. After all, Carla was someone so familiar to him, whose body he knew intimately, someone he knew inside and out, good points and bad. And yet he had no idea what to expect from the evening and where it might head. Despite the words of wisdom from his father, despite the internal conflict in his own head, he knew that tonight was the time to make up his mind about what to do: try and reunite with his ex-wife, or relegate their media-room passion to one night of madness. But taking a seat opposite her, he was none the wiser about what he wanted. She certainly looked incredible. So much so that he was aware that half the men in the restaurant were looking at her. But instead of feeling pride, he had a vague sense of discomfort. He knew that she had dressed to please him, so why did he feel more guilty than aroused?

'This feels weird, doesn't it?' she said.

'We've been for dinner before.' He glanced at the menu, but his appetite had deserted him.

'Not like this,' said Carla. 'Somehow it feels more grown-up. Like we've finally arrived and we're not just playing catch-up with all these couples who are richer and more successful than we are.' She looked at him approvingly. 'I like the new you, Matt Donovan.'

Her bright blue eyes played with his. Even in the early days of their relationship he had known that she was so beautiful and ambitious, she would one day move up and on, to the next better, brighter opportunity. He'd been right, of course, but now it seemed as if he *was* that brighter opportunity. He couldn't help feeling flattered.

'Well I'm not sure there is a new me,' he joked. 'I have a new job. That's it. I'm still the same underneath this slightly more expensive suit.'

'I suppose,' she said, but her smile told him she didn't believe a word of it. Suddenly Matt felt awkward under her gaze, as if she was seeing something in him that wasn't there.

'So how was Ibiza?' he said, to change the subject.

'Fabulous. Except for the terrible brats that came along with the host's friends, Marc and Lucia Hamilton. Do you know Marc, a hedgie at Solitaire Capital?'

'Not the circles I move in, I'm afraid.'

'I'll introduce you.' She said it as if it was a done deal.

The sommelier came over with the bottle of champagne in an ice bucket.

'I ordered some fizz.'

'Of course.'

Carla leaned forward and touched Matt's hand.

'I can't stop thinking about the other night,' she whispered, a flirtatious smile on her face. 'The night before I went to Ibiza. Was it always that good?'

'I'm sure we had our moments.' Under the table he could feel her touching his leg with her shoe. He imagined her naked in the media room and sat back in his chair.

'Don't be nervous,' she chided. 'Although I am too. I feel like a schoolgirl. Who'd have thought it, me and you, giving it another go?'

She announced it, so typically, as if the decision had already been made, and suddenly it was as if a fog had lifted. He took a breath, knowing that the words he was about to say would change the course of not only his life, but also his son's.

'I'm not sure we should give it another go, Carla.'

As he swallowed hard, he watched her eyes grow larger. It clearly wasn't the response she had been expecting.

'You didn't seem to think that when you were fucking me by the popcorn machine,' she hissed.

'Carla, please,' said Matt, glancing around at the other tables.

'And what about Jonas?' she snapped. 'Have you thought about him? For three years you've been banging on about how Jonas should have a father. I've bent over backwards to make sure you have your weekends together. So how come now, given the opportunity to be a family again, you're running for the hills?'

'Of course I've thought about Jonas,' said Matt angrily. 'I want our son to be brought up around love, not around two people who have nothing to say to each other any more.' He surprised himself that he was quoting his mother's letter.

Carla looked at him with contempt. 'What is this, Matt? Some sort of payback? Just because I hurt you once, you're sticking the knife into me at the first opportunity?'

'Of course it's not like that.'

The waiter came over to take their order, but Carla waved him away.

'You're a jerk, you know that?' she snapped, her mouth puckering to nothing. 'You've had every opportunity in life, and you've thrown them all away. You could have had a job in the City, but you chose your stupid little practice in Hammersmith. You could have me, and yet . . .' She stopped, her eyes widening with the thought that had occurred to her. 'You've met someone else, haven't you? Who is it? A secretary? The office girl? You're the only man I know who chooses to punch *beneath* his weight.'

'Carla, I'm not involved with anyone,' he said firmly. 'But that's really not what this is about.'

'What is it about, then?' she said, her face sour. 'Go on, surprise me.'

'Do you want me, Carla?' he asked quietly. 'Do you love me? And I mean *me*, not the shiny new version of me with a great job and money to afford restaurants like this?' He shook his head. 'Do you like who I am? Even know who I am? That I like blues guitar and Fulham Football Club. That I spend my Friday nights ordering in the world's best dumplings from the takeaway on Chiswick High Street. That I come home from work and want to do nothing but read a Robert Ludlum book and listen to Seventies jazz I collect on vinyl.' He felt a huge wave of relief, knowing he had pinpointed what had always been the problem with his marriage and what he had never wanted to admit. 'I'm not special, Carla. I'm just an ordinary bloke. This is who I am, but I like who I am, and honestly, if you look inside yourself, I think you want something very different to me. Jonas is all we have in common. I've wrestled with it and I'm not sure it's enough.'

Her beautiful face sneered at him.

'So that's what you think?'

He nodded.

'You're right. I suppose we should end this charade and let you get back to your Chinese takeaway,' she said sarcastically.

'Carla, please . . .'

'Have a wonderful life, Matt, thinking about what could have been.'

She threw her napkin on to the table and stalked out.

Watching her go, Matt realised that he would always be a little bit in love with her. *In love*. Wasn't that the thing that everyone aspired to be? But right now, it felt like a shallow, flighty emotion. He desired Carla. He always would. But he didn't love her. Not any more. He wasn't even sure he liked her.

He picked up the champagne bottle and filled his glass to the top, knocking it back in long, greedy gulps. He waved for the bill, apologising that they would not be dining tonight after all, and made his way on to the street. A vendor on the corner handed him an *Evening Standard* and he used it to wave down a black cab.

'Chiswick, please,' he said, slumping back into the seat.

Relaxing in the creaking plastic, he felt an enormous sense of relief. He would never know if he had done the right thing. One day he might even be able to discuss it with his son. But it felt right. It felt honest.

He unfolded the newspaper on his lap. 'Sam and Jessica Reunited!' it announced, above a picture of the celebrity couple. For a minute he forgot about his own dilemma back at the restaurant as he speed-read the short accompanying story.

Poor Anna, he thought, feeling his mouth droop with sadness. She had been out of the office for the last couple of days, but when he had spoken to Liz Hart the previous afternoon – she'd called him to thank him for his contribution to the case – she had told him that Anna had gone to Wiltshire to see Sam Charles.

He looked at the photograph of Sam and Jessica Carr and felt furious. He was glad that Anna wasn't seeing this silly, shallow sod any more, but the thought that Sam had been cheating on her made him feel mad.

She didn't deserve that. Not after the office rumours he'd heard. That her ex-boyfriend, the newspaper guy, was marrying her sister. How could anyone handle two slaps in the face like that?

He pulled out his mobile and stared at it for a moment. It felt strange calling up a colleague to ask her about her love life. But he remembered how lonely it could be in those first hours, days of betrayal. When his relationship with Carla had ended, his friends and colleagues had avoided him. 'We wanted to give you space,' they later said. But all he had wanted to do when she had left him was talk to someone, and right now, all he wanted to do was check that Anna Kennedy was okay.

Thirty minutes later, the taxi grumbled up to her little white-washed cottage in Richmond. Matt didn't need to ask how she was feeling when she answered the door. Dressed in grey marl joggers and a baggy T-shirt with a cartoon pig on the front, she had a sullen 'who cares?' manner about her.

'I hope you like curry,' she said, gesturing towards the silver cartons on the table. 'I'm slobbing out with a takeaway.'

'Perfect,' said Matt, pulling off his tie. 'My meal at Claridge's got aborted.'

'Not because of me?' She smiled.

Matt laughed.

'Now that would be going above and beyond the call of my supervising partner duties.'

'I thought Helen was my supervising partner?'

'I'm not sure she's going to be at the firm much longer,' said Matt. He gave her a knowing look, and she nodded.

'What's going to happen to her?'

'Let Larry sort it,' he said quietly.

'Do you think she'll go to prison?'

'If Larry's got anything to do with it, he'll arrange something much, much worse.'

'I should tell Sam about Helen,' Anna said finally. 'He's got a strong case for damages.'

'That's big of you. I'm not sure he deserves it.'

'Sam didn't deserve to get crucified,' she said, pouring out two glasses of Pinot and handing him one.

'So how are you?' he asked, taking a sip. 'When did you find out?' He wasn't going to let the matter drop.

She spooned out the chicken passanda.

'Before it was all over the *Standard*, thankfully. I drove to his house yesterday and she was there.' She stopped, looking down at the table. 'It seemed a long way home afterwards,' she said quietly.

'Did you like him?'

She nodded.

'Yes. I liked him.'

'Were you in love with him?'

'After two weeks? Don't be daft.' Her cheeks had gone bright red. 'Sam's had a lot of stick, and he brought plenty of it on himself. But I think he's a decent person underneath it all. I'm just not sure he was the person for me. And I certainly wasn't the right woman for him.'

'I'd pick you over Jessica Carr any time.'

He regretted saying it instantly, but it was true.

They clinked glasses and began to drink, sharing stories about their disastrous love lives and other anecdotes from their past, joking at their mistakes and foibles. In the taxi he had felt a bit stupid getting in touch, but now he knew that she welcomed the gesture.

By the time they had finished their curry, Matt realised they were both very drunk. He pointed towards a suitcase that was standing in the corner of the room.

'Going somewhere?' he asked playfully.

She looked doubtful.

'Maybe,' she replied.

He raised his eyebrows.

'Maybe?'

'It's my sister's wedding this weekend. I'm sure you know about Sophie and Andy – the whole office seems to – so you can see my dilemma. It would make my mum and dad so happy if I turned up, but I'm not sure I can face looking like such a loser.'

'You wouldn't look like a loser.'

'Right. The sad, single sister at the back who the groom cheated on. I almost had a solution. Sam said he'd come with me, although that's obviously not happening now. Probably a good thing, mind you. People might have thought I was a right bitch, trying to upstage the bride.'

'Rubbish. If I had the chance to take Cameron Diaz to a traitorous sibling's wedding, I'd be there like a shot. Shame I haven't got any siblings, or Cameron Diaz on my tail, although Erica Sheldon was definitely after me a few weeks ago.'

'Dream on, Casanova,' Anna said, laughing. Her T-shirt slipped off one shoulder. Matt suddenly found himself wanting to kiss her there.

'If you don't fancy an A-list actor on your arm, what about a slightly going-to-seed solicitor?'

'Are we talking about Larry here?'

He smiled. 'Actually, I meant me.'

'You'd come to Tuscany?'

'Well it's Tuscany or watching the cricket with a takeaway.'

'You do look good in a suit,' she mused.

'Glad you think so.'

'According to the secretaries, who have a sweepstake on who's going to sleep with you first, you look snappiest in the navy single-breasted.'

'And I didn't think they cared.'

She paused.

'You wouldn't seriously consider it, would you?'

'Well, my son's at a sleepover this weekend. And I *do* need a tan.' As he looked at her, he could almost feel the adrenalin surging around his body.

Be with the person who makes your heart beat faster. Wasn't that what his father had told him? Twenty-five years of neglect, then Larry Donovan had come out with a happy life's most precious secret.

For a moment he thought about his father, and his efforts to make it work with Loralee. The heart wants what it wants, he smiled to himself.

'I'd love to come with you, Anna.'

'You'll never get a flight,' she said thoughtfully. 'Not at this late notice.'

'I believe the firm has the most efficient travel agent in the business. An old female friend of Larry's.'

'That figures.'

'Right then,' said Matt, taking out his phone. 'Do you think I can get business class on expenses?'

70

Dressed and ready for the day in a pale blue YSL suit, Helen sat in her kitchen looking out of the French windows, her fingers curled around a mug of coffee. She listened to the early morning birdsong, wondering what they were saying to each other. She'd been up since four, watching the night sky fade and turn a muted shade of lavender, rising up over the horizon like a peacock unfolding its tail. The weather was going to be glorious; she didn't need to watch the weather forecast to know that much: warm and balmy, a beautiful late summer's day. How ironic, she thought, checking her watch, knowing it was time to leave for Chelsea.

She turned as she heard footsteps. Graham walked in, yawning and ineffectually smoothing down his bedhead hair.

'Are you going?'

She nodded.

'Soon.'

Her eyes strayed to the documents sitting on the breakfast bar.

'Just sign them,' said Graham quietly.

'I can't,' she replied, closing her eyes, feeling utterly helpless. This was everything she'd ever worked for, and now she was supposed to just sign it all away, surrender her livelihood and her reputation with one sweep of a pen. And yet Larry had made the alternatives very clear indeed. Being struck off the solicitor's roll, perhaps a spell in an open prison somewhere, spending her days reminiscing with all the other unlucky lags who had pushed the boat out too far.

Graham walked over and handed her the pen, then put his

steady hands on her shoulders and waited as she scratched out a signature. First on the letter of resignation from the partnership, then on the transfer of her equity share to Larry.

She dropped the pen on the oak top and turned into his arms, burying her face in his shoulder.

She had told Graham everything, of course. Well, almost everything. Not the real reason why Simon Cooper had been so persuasive in getting Helen to help him bury the Amy Hart story, although she suspected that he had known of their affair all along. He stroked her hair gently.

'Just let it go,' he soothed. 'Everything will be all right. Just the two of us. It's only a setback. You're down, darling, but you're never out. You're a brilliant woman who can turn her hand to anything. And truthfully, you were always bigger than Donovan Pierce anyway.'

For a moment she almost believed him. For years she had been so disparaging of anything that came out of her husband's mouth, and yet now his words of reassurance were the only thing she wanted to hear.

She breathed him in, the soft smell of his pyjamas, and knew she could never leave him.

'You're right,' she said, looking out into the sunshine again. 'It's not over, not by a long chalk. In fact, I've got a feeling this is just the beginning.'

71

Anna had never really realised how wealthy Andy's family were until she went out to Villa Sole for the first time. At the start of their relationship, when Andy had spoken about his family's summer place in Tuscany, she had imagined a rambling farmhouse with delphinium-blue shutters and broken flowerpots. But Villa Sole was truly magnificent, a whitewashed Italianate stately home with tall windows and pillared gables, at once both grand and chic.

'Bloody hell,' said Matt as their stubby Fiat hire car turned on to the arrow-straight drive. 'It's like a palace.' Anna felt her heart give a flutter. Although the summer sun had toasted the surrounding hillsides a deep ochre, the grounds of Villa Sole looked just as luscious as they had when she and Andy had come here to kiss in the poppy fields and swim in the river. It was like seeing an old lover across a room.

'Are you sure this is his family's place, not a five-star hotel?' said Matt as they drew up outside the entrance. 'No wonder he pulled so many birds at college.'

'You knew Andy at Cambridge?' said Anna, her eyes wide. 'How come you haven't mentioned this before?'

'Never really knew him.' Matt shrugged. 'He was the year ahead of me. But he certainly had a reputation as a ladies' man.'

'Well he never used to boast about this place,' said Anna, suddenly feeling protective of Andy. Matt gave her a smirk.

'Not to you, maybe.'

'What does that mean?'

'Well you're not the sort of girl to be impressed by fancy trimmings, are you?'

Anna looked at him sideways.

'Should I take that as a compliment?'

Matt chuckled. 'Yes,' he said. 'Definitely a compliment.'

Anna laughed. She had been surprised at how well she and Matt had got on. She had been nervous about bringing him – in fact she had woken up kicking herself – but away from the office, they had fallen into the sort of flirtatious banter you usually only had with people you'd known for years. They seemed to share a similarly dry sense of humour, and on the two-hour flight over they had giggled constantly, chatting away without mentioning work, Helen or the Amy Hart story once. In fact it had been like a first date: finding out about each other's lives and interests, swapping funny stories. They had quite a lot in common, mutual friends, and had even lived on the same street when they were at Guildford College of Law, albeit four or five years apart.

'Anna!'

She turned to see her father running down the steps, his arms open. He scooped her up and hugged her, squashing her face against his shoulder, and any last doubts she had harboured about coming to the wedding immediately evaporated.

'So you're pleased to see me, then?' she said happily when her dad had finally released his grip.

'When you said you were coming we were thrilled,' he said quietly. 'Thank you. Really.'

Anna was moved by the intensity of his words, and she realised with a flush of shame just how important it had been to him. How could she even have considered letting him down?

'Darling, you're here!' cried her mother, giving Anna an uncharacteristically warm embrace.

'So how are you enjoying Villa Sole?' asked Anna. 'Up to your standards?'

'Oh yes. You should see tonight's menu,' said Sue Kennedy, an excited twinkle in her eye. 'Truffles.'

Anna laughed. It was nice to see her parents both so relaxed, their slightly pink faces shining with pride. Anna had been so wrapped up in her own feelings towards Sophie, it was easy to forget that this must be a huge deal for them, seeing their first daughter tie the knot, and doing it in such grand surroundings too.

'Oh Mum, this is my friend Matt,' said Anna.

'Pleased to meet you,' said Matthew, pulling their cases from the car. 'Where shall I put these?'

'You're in the two rooms at the very top of the house,' said Sue, leading them both inside the house and showing Matt the staircase. 'Fantastic views in the morning; you can see all the way to Siena.' She looked over at Anna meaningfully. 'And if you don't need two rooms, I think the one overlooking the courtyard is the better one.'

Anna glanced at Matt – was he blushing?

'I'll just take these upstairs, then,' he muttered, lugging the bags over his shoulder and disappearing up the stairs.

'I want the room with the view,' shouted Anna after him.

'Yes, boss . . .' came the weary reply, and Anna's mother smiled.

'Good-looking boy,' she said.

'Boy? He's pushing thirty-five.'

'Practically a geriatric,' said her father.

Anna looked back and forth between her parents.

'Now just because we're at a wedding, don't go getting any ideas,' she said firmly. 'He's just a friend, okay?'

'Whatever you say, darling,' said her mother, turning to her husband and giving him a deliberate wink.

The sun was beginning to vanish over the scorched hillside and Anna gazed out at the carpet of wild flowers stretching across the meadow, scenting the evening air like cologne. Her mother was right. The view was spectacular from up here. In the dusky lavender light, the Chianti hills and vineyards folded and disappeared into one another, while just faintly she really could see the dark skyline of the great old town of Siena. Anna had spent many nights at Villa Sole but never in the eaves of the house, which were usually reserved for nannies or children – Sophie and her parents would be in the grand master suites on the lower floors.

Next door, she could hear Matt singing over the rushing sound of the shower at full blast. Was that 'Karma Chameleon'? She giggled; Matthew Donovan really was full of surprises. She walked into her own bathroom and turned on the gold taps of her claw-foot bath, tipping in some lime-scented oil. When it was full, she peeled off her travelling clothes and sank gratefully down into the bath until the foam tickled her nose. Closing her eyes, she let the events of the past week float through her mind. Where was Helen Pierce this evening? she wondered. Matthew had called Larry from the airport, and apparently Helen had formally resigned from the firm that morning. And what would become of Peter Rees and his so-called friends, each of them equally marked and sullied by the affair? Would any of them ever pay for what they did? *The Chronicle* were putting pressure on the police to launch an inquiry into Amy's death, but Anna knew there was no certainty of justice being done. And was there really such a thing as justice when you had money and a team of nimble lawyers at your disposal? She gave a crooked smile, remembering the argument she'd had with Matt that first day at Donovan Pierce, when she had so staunchly defended the legal system and a rich man's right to use the law any way he pleased. She wasn't at all sure she felt the same way now, not after having seen the Swann set hiding behind their millions. So where did that leave her? She knew she still believed in the law – you couldn't give up on it just because the bad guys kept winning, otherwise who would protect people like Amy Hart? There had to be another way; a fair, honest way. Anna just supposed she'd have to find it.

Wrapping herself in a fluffy white towel, she unpacked her bag and laid the meagre contents on the bed. With everything that had happened, she hadn't had time to go shopping for her sister's wedding. She picked up the turquoise silk tunic dress she'd worn in Kerala, remembering the way Sam had smiled at her that night on the longboat.

She felt a knot in her chest just thinking about Sam and Jessica and that horrible scene on the drive outside Copley Manor. She took a deep breath and let it out. That was over now, she had to move on. And anyway, she looked hot in the dress, so why not?

She was just pinning her hair up on top of her head, exposing her long neck, when there was a knock on the door.

'Come in,' she muttered through the grips in her mouth. Matthew appeared at the door, looking relaxed in a pair of cream trousers and a pale blue shirt, open at the neck.

'Look at George Clooney,' she said appreciatively. She had never seen him in anything but a work suit, and casual looked good on him.

'Well I know you like the screen-idol type,' he joked.

'Hey, cheeky,' she scolded.

'You're not looking too bad yourself,' he said as she finished her hair and turned around.

'So why do I feel so nervous?' she asked.

'Nothing a glass of Chianti won't sort out,' he said, offering her his arm. 'What's the betting Villa Sole have their own vineyard?'

'Actually they do.' She smiled, enjoying the feel of him against her hip, enjoying the sense of feeling protected. They descended the staircase and went into the main hall, where Sophie and Andy were greeting guests.

Damn, she looks lovely, thought Anna. Sophie's gown was floor length and the colour of a Bellini, a peach shade so soft it almost made her tanned skin glow.

'She looks incredible, doesn't she?' said Anna, without a trace of envy or bitterness, feelings that had somehow seemed irrelevant once she had got to Villa Sole.

'Beauty is in the eye of the beholder, and from where I'm standing, she comes a poor second.'

'Don't be nice to me just because you feel sorry for me,' she teased.

'You're beautiful and smart,' replied Matt quietly.

'Tell that to Andy,' she said, without any resentment.

Matt hesitated.

'The truth of it is that some men just can't handle women like you, Anna.'

She turned to him with a mock frown.

'Be gentle with me,' she said, her expression softening.

'You know, I spoke to my dad the other night,' Matt continued. 'He told me why he left my mother, a very smart and clever lady if ever there was one. The thing about the other woman, the one he left my mother for, wasn't that he liked her more. He just preferred the way she made him feel.'

'Is that supposed to make *me* feel better about being rejected by the groom? Because it's working.'

Matt touched her arm.

'What I'm trying to say is if the groom couldn't see that he had the prize in his hands, then he doesn't deserve to win it. Now go on, go and speak to her. Tell her you're happy for her, even if it's not true.'

He gave her hand a reassuring squeeze and gently pushed her forward.

'Big sis!' cried Sophie dramatically, stretching her arms out to Anna.

'It's going to be a beautiful wedding, Soph,' said Anna, kissing her on the cheek.

Sophie glanced across at Andy.

'So you give us your blessing?' she said anxiously.

Anna nodded. Over the past year, she had built her sister up into some sort of wicked fairy-tale queen, but standing here, she just looked like an insecure six-year-old again, desperate for her big sister's approval, all her pretensions stripped away.

'I'm happy for you, Soph,' said Anna. 'I really am.'

She wasn't sure she would ever be entirely comfortable with the way it had happened – there had been too many tears, too much history between them – but she could see how much it meant to Sophie, so she was determined to rise above it, to let her little sister have her perfect day. Growing up, the two of them had been as thick as thieves; they had shared secrets, almost spoken a secret language. And maybe in time, they would get that back, maybe the wound could heal completely, who knew? But for today, Anna was happy to put a brave face on it – for her sister.

'Andy loves you,' she said. 'That's all that matters. And you're a far better match than he and I ever were.'

Sophie nodded, her eyes sparkling.

'Thank you,' she mouthed.

Anna squeezed her arm.

'Be happy, okay?'

Sophie produced a handkerchief from her cleavage and dabbed at her eyes.

'Anyway,' she sniffed, 'is it true you were going to bring Sam Charles to the wedding?'

'How did you know?'

Sophie rolled her eyes.

'Mum told me, of course. So where is he?'

'Oh, he's filming,' said Anna vaguely. 'Anyway, he's just a friend.'

'I assumed so,' said Sophie with a touch of bitchiness. 'Especially now that he's back with Jessica.'

Anna was surprised that she could already think of Sam and Jessica with detachment; as if they were characters in a glossy soap opera, which she supposed, now that they were out of her life, they actually were.

'Still, you have brought a rather good-looking date with you,' said Sophie. 'Almost Sam Charles handsome, if you like that Mr Darcy broody thing.'

'Matt? He's just a friend too,' Anna said honestly.

'My, you have been busy, haven't you?' said Sophie, slipping her arm through her sister's and taking her to one side. 'I'm so glad we've put all this behind us,' she said, 'because I want you to be the first person to know my news.'

Anna's hand flew to her mouth.

'You're pregnant?' she gasped.

'God, no,' said Sophie with distaste. 'Much better than that. I spoke to my agent this morning, and *Dorset Kitchen* has been green-lit for a CBS pilot in the States – isn't that brilliant? Obviously they don't want it to be called *Dorset Kitchen*; maybe *Sophie's Choice* or something like that, because I really need to start extending my brand Stateside, don't you think? My agent says I can be the new Martha Stewart.'

'So you'll move to the States?'

Sophie nodded, the little-girl excitement back.

'New York. Isn't it fabulous?'

Sophie took a sip of champagne and pointed her finger in the direction of the crowd, where she could just see Matthew talking animatedly to her father.

'I think you should go out with him,' she said, with the slight slur of someone on her fifth cocktail.

'Matthew?' Anna smiled.

'He's gorgeous. If I wasn't an about-to-be-married woman, I might be interested in him myself.'

Anna felt her back suddenly stiffen.

'I told you he's just a friend.'

'You like him,' purred Sophie theatrically, as if she was licking butterscotch sauce off a spoon.

Matt had moved on from Brian Kennedy and was now sitting on a low stone wall beneath a cypress tree. Anna had to admit her sister was right: he *was* pretty handsome. Bloody handsome, in fact. Perhaps not as beautiful as Sam, of course, more rugged, less perfect. But then maybe that was a good thing; perfection hadn't exactly worked out for her, had it? Somewhere inside her she felt a flutter, which she dismissed as alcohol. Their eyes connected through the crowd, and as he smiled at her, she knew it was too late to turn away. But she didn't want to turn away.

She grabbed a flute of champagne and took a long swig to fortify herself as she weaved through the sea of people towards him.

'And what's so funny?' she asked, perching on the wall next to him.

'Oh, nothing. I was just watching the joyful reconciliation of two sisters. How was it?'

Anna shrugged lightly.

'Sophie is Sophie. She's not going to change.'

They sat silently for a moment, watching the blue-green ripples on the swimming pool opposite them. Anna liked this, just sitting, being together. Some people could make you feel happy and comfortable just being in their company. With Matt, she didn't have to pretend, didn't have to try and impress him. He seemed to like her just as she was.

'So what have you been telling everyone about us?' he asked after a while.

She glanced at him.

'That you're a friend. Why?'

'Because everyone keeps asking when we're going to tie the knot too.'

'Oh, I'm sorry.' She winced. 'I guess it's because it's a wedding; everyone wants to play matchmaker.'

'Don't worry. I've told anyone that asks that we're not dating. It's just sex. It seems to shut them up.'

'You haven't,' she gasped, although the thought secretly thrilled her.

'I told Andrew's mum it's a good job she put us up in the attic, what with all the noise you make when you get excited.'

'Please tell me you're joking . . . ?'

'Okay, I'm joking.'

They were both laughing when Anna felt a tap on her shoulder.

'Hey, guys, I've been looking for you.'

Anna composed herself.

'Andy, how are you? I thought you might still be stuck in the office.'

He smiled. 'I escaped just in time. Sophie wasn't too happy I didn't arrive in Italy until yesterday, though.'

'When duty calls . . .'

'I just wanted to say thank you for the story. I was talking to Charles, my editor, before we came out here, and he thinks his deputy is about to move on to the Sunday paper. He says the job's mine if I want it.'

'That's brilliant news, Andy,' said Anna. 'You deserve it.'

'I know. It's what I've been working my arse off for nearly fifteen years for.'

A jazz band struck up and Andy cocked his head.

'Sounds like my cue. I'd better get back to my bride.' He looked at Anna as he turned away. 'And thanks again,' he said. 'I mean it.'

Anna sat silently as he crossed the courtyard. Matthew touched her on the shoulder.

'Don't let him get to you,' he said.

'What do you mean?'

'Andy. You're too good for him. You always were.'

'Oh, I know that.' She smiled. 'I wasn't thinking about that anyway. I was thinking about what he said, the job on the paper.'

'What about it?'

'Well Sophie just told me she's been offered a job in New York.'

'Ah,' said Matt. 'So she's not going to take it?'

'Of course she is,' laughed Anna. 'Sophie always does what she wants to; you should have grasped that by now.'

Matt frowned.

'But what about that little speech Andy just gave us?'

Anna shook her head.

'He doesn't know.'

Matt let out a laugh.

'Is she going to tell him *before* they get married that she's got his life mapped out on the other side of the Atlantic?'

'Probably not.'

They gave each other a conspiratorial little smile. The courtyard was filling with couples dancing now, surrounded by a happy crowd laughing and clinking glasses in the balmy almond-scented air. Anna could feel Matt's warm leg against hers, her skin tingling at his touch, and suddenly, more than anything, she wanted to kiss him.

'Dance?' he said, seconds before she was about to ask him. He looked at her nervously, as if he thought he'd overstepped the mark, wondering what her reaction would be.

'I thought you'd never ask.'

He pulled her to him, palm against palm, hips moving together, his arm circling her waist. She knew he had come here as a friend, possibly because he felt sorry for her, probably because he had nothing better to do, and yet still, when he pressed his body against her, when his cheek brushed hers, she didn't want to be anywhere else.

'What's your view on professional ethics?' she whispered in his ear.

'Is this about Helen?'

She shook her head. 'I don't even want to think about her,' she said softly.

'So what ethics?' he asked.

She paused for a moment, feeling her throat become dry and her pulse quicken. Just say it, she told herself.

'I mean, as my boss. What would you do if I kissed you?'

He smiled and pulled her towards him.

'Let's find out, shall we?' he said, as his lips brushed softly against hers, tender and soft. He pulled away, then kissed her again, harder. And as she kissed him back, their mouths joined, bodies entwined, she felt every nerve ending shiver with both desire and belonging. Finally the music stopped and she opened her eyes. Her hands were trembling between Matt's big palms.

'Shall we go somewhere a little quieter?' he said as they reluctantly pulled apart.

She nodded, and they walked out of the courtyard hand in hand, following a path down towards the gardens.

'I think I've been wanting to do that since about the first day I saw you,' said Matt.

'The day of the lunch?'

He shook his head, smiling.

'At the lunch I wanted to kill you.'

'I wasn't that impressed with you either.' Anna smiled.

'Well, I hope you've changed your mind.'

'Maybe,' she said. 'Probably.'

They walked away from the party until they found a stone bench hidden in an alcove.

'So why didn't you?' asked Anna. 'Kiss me, I mean.'

He laughed.

'Where should we start? My ex-wife back in the picture, your Hollywood romance, the fact that when I joined Donovan Pierce I was ever-so-slightly aware that the last Mr Donovan at the firm had been a terrible lech.'

Anna pulled a face.

'Good point. Although what are we going to do now? I mean, you're still my boss. Are you going to call me in to sit on your knee?'

Matthew grinned. 'That doesn't sound too bad, actually.'

'You *are* your father's son,' said Anna playfully.

His expression turned tender. He reached out his hand and touched her face.

'Are you ready for this? Working together? Being together?' Anna slipped her arms around his neck and pulled him close. She'd never been more ready for anything in her life. Ever.

Acknowledgements

Continued thanks go to all the team at Headline for their sterling work: Sherise Hobbs (a wonderful editor with great taste in biscuits), Lucy Foley, Jane Morpeth, Jo Liddiard, Vicky Cowell, Emily Furniss, Aslan Byrne and his fantastic sales team, plus Patrick and Yeti in the design department and to the copyeditor and proofreaders.

To the brilliant Eugenie Furniss and Cathryn Summerhayes – it's such a pleasure working with you. And Dorian Karchmar and Matt Hudson in New York make me feel as if I can take on the world! Thanks also to the lovely Claudia Webb.

To everyone else who has helped with the research of *Private Lives* – thank you so much for the nuggets of information you let me take away. The complex area of privacy law is one that takes place behind closed doors so I'm particularly grateful to those who let me have a peep behind the curtain. This book couldn't have been written without you.

It's been a tricky year so my heartfelt gratitude goes to those who have made it easier. To all those at Kingston Hospital and RMH, including Alan Thompson, Mr Khan and Hannah Petty – thank you so much for all the incredible work you do. To my friends, especially Kay for the writers' villa and the hill walks. And much, much love to my wonderful family for all their support, especially my mum, and John, my rock-and-roll rock, my hero, the best husband a girl could ever ask for.